D0266532

SKIN

SKIN

Kerry Andrew

JONATHAN CAPE
LONDON

1 3 5 7 9 10 8 6 4 2

Jonathan Cape, an imprint of Vintage, is part of the Penguin Random House group of
companies whose addresses can be found at global.penguinrandomhouse.com.

First published by Jonathan Cape in 2021

The quotation on p83 is from 'Come Sundown', with lyrics by Kris Kristofferson
The quotation on p163 is from 'Somebody to Love', with lyrics by Freddie Mercury
The quotation on p228 is from 'Barbie Girl', with lyrics by Claus Norreen, Søren
Rasted, Rene Dif and Lene Nystrøm
The quotation on p261 is from 'ALONGWAYTOGO', with lyrics by Christopher
Martin and Keith Elam

penguin.co.uk/vintage

A CIP catalogue record for this book is available from the British Library

ISBN 9781787331648

Typeset in 11.25/14.5 pt Adobe Garamond
by Integra Software Services Pvt. Ltd, Pondicherry

Printed and bound in Great Britain by Clays Ltd, Elcograf S.p.A.

The authorised representative in the EEA is Penguin Random House Ireland, Morrison
Chambers, 32 Nassau Street, Dublin DO2 YH68

Penguin Random House is committed to a sustainable future for
our business, our readers and our planet. This book is made from
Forest Stewardship Council® certified paper.

To Andy, my darling, for everything

The water sustains me without even trying
The water can't drown me
I'm done with my dying
                    Johnny Flynn, 'The Water'

Water, is taught by thirst.
                    Emily Dickinson

PART ONE

1985

Chapter 1

Matty's dad was missing.

He'd gone out in the morning, same as always, on the last ever day of primary school. Half a piece of toast eaten. A hand on Matty's head, Marmitey crumbs getting in the curls, and a peck to Mamma's cheek. Door going. And he hadn't come back.

After school, it had been home to their maisonette above the supermarket for tea, shirt covered in scribbles from the entire class. Mamma turned Matty round like a card carousel, frowning at the scrawled farewells: 'NEVER CROSS THE STREAMS'; 'Call this number if you want sexing'; 'Luv U Matty'. Tea. Telly. Matty had waited up to tell Dad about the football match with the teachers and how they'd played the *Fame* song in assembly and the class had danced around on the stage, but he must have stayed out really late. Bed.

Next morning, still no Dad. Mamma's voice had been carefully stretched. She'd said that maybe he had gone out for a drink with a friend, it had got late, he'd stayed with them. But why would he have to do that when he could catch a bus or two back? You could get anywhere in London, anytime. It was easy.

The next morning. Mamma was angry. Repeating *I don't know*, the pauses between the words getting heavier as she saw to things that didn't need doing, glasses that had already been dried, bread already spread with Vitalite twice over. They didn't go to church. That afternoon, she sat in the hallway, one leg crossed over the other, holding onto the phone very carefully with both hands as if it would come apart otherwise.

Day after, the police were in their living room. Looking ginormous. A man and a woman, black and white checks round their hats like tiny versions of a motor-racing flag. The woman wrote tiny words with a tiny pencil onto a tiny notepad and kept giving Matty soft looks. Mamma had put make-up on, wore her shiny black heels even though she was indoors. The policeman spread his thighs wide, taking deep sniffs, looking around. You could see his willie poking there, just a bit. When he left, the point of his hat almost touched his nose.

Just the woman the second time. Mamma's voice, raised. Her Italian accent always got stronger when she was upset. Matty sat out in the hall, drinking orange squash through a straw, kicking the skirting board, listening. Something about a pond. 'I would have known,' Mamma had said. 'Fine. You have to search. It's your job!'

The policewoman asked Matty questions this time too, shifting her skirt down over her knees. Her tights were thick and deep beige, like her legs had gone on holiday. Lipstick the colour of pink wafers. Mamma had gone to make her a cup of tea. *Thanks, Rosa*, the policewoman had said, as if they were friends.

'Your dad liked swimming, didn't he?'

Did he? 'I don't know.'

'Well, we think he might have gone swimming in the Men's Pond. Someone at his work said as much. You know the one, on the Heath? Did you ever go there with him?'

Head-shake.

'Was he upset about anything? Maybe he and your mum ...' her voice quietened. 'Did they argue much?'

Shrug. Everyone's parents did. Every kid crept out of bed to sit at the top of the stairs, making two dents in their forehead from the banister rails, listening to them shouting, collecting their swearwords like Panini football stickers. Didn't they?

*

4

Just gone, clean gone. He'd been kidnapped by gangsters, whipped off the street, tugged into a car with a handkerchief soaked in chloroform over his nose. The ransom note to them had got lost in the post. Or he was a spy. Top-secret operations, classified. The Soviets had got him because he knew confidential information about cruise missiles, and a sniper had taken him out as he'd been walking to work, which wasn't foreman at Anlow Shopfitters – that had all been just a disguise. He'd been so good at his real job that even his family were none the wiser. All this time, and neither of them had ever known.

Matty daren't ask Mamma whether it was the Mafia or the KGB. But it was clear enough from Mamma's mood that something very bad had happened. She went silent, like she did when she was grumpy, became forgetful. Tins of food were left open, half a can of baked beans in a puddle of orange. Taps running. She spent ages in the bathroom, but when she came out she didn't look any better. Normally, she wore perfectly applied thick make-up, dark-green eyeshadow and deep red lipstick, even if she was just going downstairs to the shop. The phone was left off the hook, gurgling to itself.

Dad. Joe. Who came along to skateboarding, sitting on a bench very far away behind his *Irish Times* so as not to be a gigantic embarrassment, though he might as well have cut holes in it he looked so obvious. Who made really good pancakes, thin and crisped on the outside, with chocolate spread and peanut butter. Who sang loudly to the radio, turning it up when the neighbours banged on the wall, turning himself up. Whose Italian, when he tried to speak to Nonna and Nonno, had a distinctive Irish slur. He always sounded drunk when he spoke Italian.

After the first few days, Matty couldn't stand being at home any longer. Hampstead Ponds, the policewoman had said. Over the other side of the Heath from where they lived in Golders Green. The *A–Z* sat unused underneath the phone book. There were several ponds, chunks of blue along the edges of the green on the map. Three for swimming – the Mixed Pond was near the road, and the separate ones further north. They'd been past them a few times. Highgate Men's Bathing Pond was the second up in a row.

A can of Fanta. The map. Walkman. Matty stood very still in the hallway, like a wolf, hairs raised, ears raised. Upstairs, there was a creak on the floorboards and the dull click of the bathroom door shutting again.

Time to sneak out.

Sitting on the back seat on the lower deck of the bus was like sitting in an oven. The chair material itched. Matty hadn't travelled alone before. School was only up the road, an amble along the pavement if walking with Dad, a quicker one if with Mamma, who always acted like they were late. Three large Indian women got on the bus with shopping bags, talking loudly. An old man holding a bundle of newspapers glanced towards the back. Matty turned to face the window as the bus slowly hauled itself up the hill, headphones on but no tape playing. Just be normal.

Dad wouldn't have gone this way. He got two tubes to work – 'to the Shoplifters', he'd say, with a wink – but maybe he could get a bus to the Heath from there. Swimming. When he came back late, he'd always say that he'd been at the pub or the park, but he'd never mentioned swimming.

He was more of a spectator at sports, generally. Football at the pub or at Barnet, sometimes with Matty, freezing their bums off on the wonky terrace. The odd 'butterfly' on the races, as he called it with a little flutter of his fingers. His winning streaks lasted about as long as a butterfly's lifespan. And he spectated Matty, too. Boxing as well as skateboarding. Matty had been going to the club for six months and Dad was always there, having a quiet word with Freddie, sending a wink and a nod over.

Raised voices at the front, the bus going nowhere. A man with dreadlocks and long, pumpkin-coloured shorts was arguing with the driver about ten pence that he didn't have. Long, loose words and a wet sound through his teeth. The *A–Z* was getting sticky on both knees. They had stopped by Jack Straw's Castle, the big pub. It was near enough. Matty hopped out of the still-open doors.

It was a different world up here. Like going through a magic wardrobe or being spun round to the other side of a secret wall. No shops, just big single houses in neat red brick, and the road signs looked like they had been very carefully painted a hundred years ago. Old-fashioned names – Vale of Health, Squire's Mount, Well Walk. The smell was different, too, not exhausts and baking bagels but heavy, woody.

Matty had been to the Heath plenty of times, going up with Dad to chuck a ball around. It felt different being here alone. Senses on red alert. Traffic still rumbled past, very close, but there was a layer of birdsong underneath the rocking of cars and vans, drawing you in, as if coming from further back in time.

A wide path led into the park with fat, overlapping trees on either side that turned afternoon into evening. Just birds now. Matty still didn't press play on the Walkman. The trees were giants, looking down, wondering what this small, scruffy-haired person was doing. Two women with a dog and a pushchair walked past. *I won't have him do that again, you know?* one was saying. *Gotta have some self-respect,* one said, the other nodding.

As the path climbed higher, the trees fell away. The top of the Heath was where some families from church had picnics on Sunday afternoons, though the three of them hadn't gone for ages. Mamma always said she was busy these days. There was the tall spire on the left and hard glints of the City further over. Kids were everywhere. The sort that would be on the new bus to St George's, kids who weren't really kids any longer. Taller, wider, louder. They sat in circles like Boy Scouts, crisp packets in place of a fire. Smaller children were with their parents. Bikes, pushchairs. And more dogs than people.

The map didn't make much sense anymore. Matty walked straight through the shin-deep grass, eyes down, hoping to hear two syllables called, sounds that would make everything OK again. *Mat-ty.*

He might be here. He'd decided to camp for a bit, live off the land. His Gypsy blood. He often talked about going back to Ireland, where everything was so green. '*Green,*' he'd say, gently shaking Matty by the shoulders. 'Not grey.' But he liked it really, London. He liked the mix of people, and the noise. Flip him like a coin, and he'd say that Ireland was 'quiet as the bloody grave. I'm never going back there. My God.'

Or he might be wandering the Heath. He'd lost his memory and somehow ended up here. Not known his name. 'Joe,' he'd normally say with his hand out to just about everyone he met, people in the international kosher supermarket below their flat, people on the street, cigarette propped in the side of his mouth or between his fingers. They always shook his hand, told him their name.

A quick look at the squashed blue shape on the map. It was just down there. Matty descended the hill and stood by the fence, heart tap-tapping loudly.

Clusters of cow-parsley, like mini-nuclear explosions, sloped down to a wide stretch of water. The Men's Pond. It was the same colour as the clouded sky and had a smaller version of itself drawn by rope-markers, with a square platform in the middle. Inside the ropes, you could see the pink arms of men doing laps. A yellow swimming hat. A red one.

There were a few shouts and a splash. From further along the path, a long wooden platform was visible and behind that a queue of men waiting to dive from the concrete walkway, chatting to each other. Two of them were wearing T-shirts. A man was at the edge of the board, standing very straight, before his knees bent and he made a quick, neat arc into the water. Another two jumped in after him, whooping, and swam together with their heads close. You couldn't quite hear what they were saying. There was a pull, like the birdsong from earlier, something enchanting about the wink of light on the surface of the pond.

The last place that Dad was seen. People might have known him in there. He knew everyone.

The path dipped down and round the corner, where a few men were on a narrow stretch of grass in front of the entrance gate. Sitting, standing, lying down, most just in trunks, though there wasn't much sun. The pool was hidden from here. There was a corrugated iron roof and two Raleigh Burners locked to the fence. Matty stood at the gate, looking at the sign: *NO LADIES ALLOWED TO SWIM.* There didn't seem to be anywhere to pay for entry.

'Going in, are you?'

A deeply tanned man with a white beard that touched his bare belly stood with feet planted apart. He was wearing trunks and fraying leather sandals. Slowly, his eyebrows lifted, eyes twinkling. His belly stuck out like a half-full rubbish bag. He waited a little longer, before walking past the gate with a strange, slow bounce and disappearing round the corner. You could just hear the splashes from here.

No, not going in this time, Matty thought. But the man had asked. So – imagining Arnold Schwarzenegger's wraparound sunglasses and the set jaw – *I'll be back.*

Further up the path, someone was sleeping on a bench, a coat over their head.

Dad might have been attacked. People did that, stabbed other people on the street and took their wallets. Someone had stabbed Dad and taken all his money and that would have been when he'd lost his memory and didn't know that he lived in Golders Green and was from Ireland and sort of supported Barnet, even if they were a bunch of legless eedjits. Matty crept closer to the bench. The smell of pee or beer or both got stronger.

A football sailed over and landed on the person, bouncing off a harder part. There was a sudden sound from underneath the coat like a furious monster woken from hibernation. A flash of grizzled, snot-streaked cheek. White stubble, and an eye black and bright and fixed on Matty.

Run.

Matty let the door slam and waited in the hallway, scuffing toes on the mat. Waiting for Dad to stick his head round from the kitchen, his eyes narrowed in foxish amusement, to say, *what feckin' time d'you call this, crackerjack?*

Nothing. Only the clock, and the traffic outside.

Mamma appeared at the top of the landing. She was still in her dressing gown. 'Where have you been?' Her voice didn't have any colour in it.

'Nowhere. Just out.' Matty kicked the skirting board gently, wanting to ask ten questions back. Where's Dad? *Kick.* Why aren't you talking about him? *Kick.*

'You want to make me think that you are gone too?'

Matty hadn't thought of that. 'What's for tea?'

Mamma's shoulders went straight and her head jerked to the side. 'What's for tea,' she said, in the same flat voice. 'Is this all I do? Sit here and make you tea? If you are old enough to go out on your own and not come back for hours, you are old enough to make your own tea.' She turned and went back into their bedroom.

Madonna was on the telly, the video of one of her songs. She wore loads of wristbands and a cross hung from one ear. Matty had another spoonful of baked beans from the bowl and drank the warm can of Fanta that had remained unopened all afternoon, sitting close to the screen with a sticky orange mouth. In the video, they kept cutting to a man and woman, and the woman looked like Mamma when she'd had that perm. They seemed

10

really in love, and Madonna was holding her microphone as if it was precious. Cyndi Lauper was better. A city princess dancing around with multi-coloured hair and a voice like glacé cherries. Loads of girls wanted to look like her. Sometimes you saw girls like Siouxie Sioux too, even in Golders Green, witchy eyebrows and heads shaved, looking really moody.

Top 40. They never showed hip-hop on *Top of the Pops*, except for Grandmaster Flash and Melle Mel once. That was the best music. Kyle from school sometimes lent his big brother's cassettes, themselves sent from a cousin in America. The Sugarhill Gang, the *Wild Style* original soundtrack. Speaking, not singing, words like little punches. Matty liked the ones about parties and the ones about thieves and problems in the streets. The Eurythmics were on now. The short-haired singer with her white denim jacket and white trousers singing about angels.

There was a new layer of sound in the song. Matty leant over and turned the volume down on the TV. Mamma was on the phone. Her voice was low, but occasionally it got louder.

'*Non lo so. Non lo so, mamma. No, non lo ha fatto.*'

Matty knew some Italian, from the holidays there – as well as from Mamma, who would slip into it as if she was an alien who kept forgetting her disguise. *Sono di Londra. Buonanotte, dormi bene. Cioccolato all'arancia, per favore.* They went most summers, Matty turning red then brown, Nonna tutting and barking in her sandpaper voice at the peeling skin. Nonno walked with a rocking limp on one side and sweets secreted in a palm. His pockets must be full of sugar.

Mamma always complained about London. How Italy was better, hotter, less rough, good values, no Indians, no West Indians. But after a day or two, you could see that she wanted to go back home. 'My mother,' she would say in a dagger-voice to Dad. He was the other way round, itchy and quiet for the first couple of days, and then practically Italian himself, leaning back on the plastic lounge chair in the garden, drinking limoncello and crooning songs at Nonna until she flicked a tea towel at him.

Now, out in the hallway, talking to Nonna, Mamma sounded like she always did. Like she wanted very much to be there, and she wanted very much not to. '*Joe*,' Matty heard. '*Joe. Non lo so. Che cosa ho fatto?*'

***

The next day Matty walked, with a rucksack. It wasn't that far. Up the hill towards the posh houses, until the birds started singing. The sun and the trees' shadows made jigsaw pieces on the path and the top of the Heath was full of people again. The bench where the tramp had been lying was empty, and there was a dull gold sign: *In Loving Memory of Our Mother Mildred Himoff Lewis 1912–1985*.

If Dad had just gone away, he would have left a note. He would have stuck it on the fridge, or under Matty's pillow if it was a secret mission. Some sort of dead drop. He wouldn't have gone without saying anything. 'You've got my back, haven't you?' he'd say sometimes, pointing a finger that was mustard-coloured from nicotine. 'And I've got yours. The Ronans. Family true and true. This version, anyway.' He'd mean 'through and through', but would exaggerate the accent. Both words worked. Matty would nod and imagine the two of them thinly slicing their palms open, and shaking hands to mix the blood together.

Nearing the highest part of the Heath, Matty looked up at the sun, and the day blotted, a split-second of blackness before the sky was nothing but bright blue again.

It was a sign. Dad had been abducted by aliens, aliens who had fireproof skin and could live on the sun, and he was being held in a giant refrigerator which was the only way he could stay alive, and he'd found that he could use his mind to trigger some of the buttons in the control room and he had concentrated and *wham* made the sun go black, just for an eyeblink.

'Matty.' A loud call. Again. 'Matty.'

Dad's voice. He was here. The massed leaves of three trees shifted. Matty stood, ankles stiff. Where was it coming from? Up there, in the sky?

Another call, and a dog the colour of dirty snow hurtled towards someone standing further up the hill. 'Come here, Nancy,' the man shouted, one more time. The syllables cracking like a baseball bat hitting a ball.

It wasn't him.

He never said it right. It sounded more like a girl's name his way – 'Maddy.' Soft, mushy consonants.

'It's "t". *T-t-t-t-t*,' Matty would say, clasping an elbow and making M60 machine-gun noises, the other fingers spraying bullets across his chest.

Dad would put on a sly face. 'Shall I call you by your proper name instead, then?'

Folded arms. '*No.*'

Three different accents bumping against each other in one house. Irish, Italian, and Matty's own London one, harder and clearer. Sometimes Mamma's and Dad's voices didn't sound so far apart, like Ireland had slid off its moorings, sailed right round Portugal and over the top of Africa to Italy, and Matty would feel like an adopted child.

'Oh my God, man, you are such a slag.'

Matty sat on the fallen tree trunk over the hill, halfway to the Men's Pond, watching the dogs and listening to Kurtis Blow and his strutting words. The words of three big girls sauntering past getting mixed in with the rapping.

Strong, like a magnum force. Rough, like a new divorce.

'*You're* the slag. You'd have it off with anyone.'

Two black girls and one white girl, maybe fourteen or fifteen, all with hair tied right on top of their heads. From St George's. Matty remembered them from Open Day, linked together at the gate, their tongues shoved in their cheeks, a single fist pumping in front of their mouths.

'I *got* off with him, I said. So slanderous.'

'*Slag*-erous.'

They threw their bags down nearby and took their T-shirts off. One of them flung out a red checked blanket and the other two collapsed onto it before it was straight, undressing to bikinis. Long legs and lazy actions. They were like lionesses.

'What you looking at?'

One of the black girls had sat up and was staring, dead-eyed. Matty blinked and hopped off the trunk, grabbed the rucksack.

'Nah nah nah, come back here.'

Matty began an Olympic-style walk away, head down.

'Oi! We're talking to you? You deaf?'

There seemed no choice but to turn and go back towards them. *Strong, like a superhero.*

The other black girl sat up on her elbows. Her bikini was luminous blue, ten times stronger than the colour of the sky. Her wide belly was glistening. She squinted at Matty. 'What you listening to, then?' She put her palms out and raised her eyebrows, and did it again with larger, impatient actions. 'Giz.' She took the headphones, the metal band expanding, and the white girl rolled closer to listen. Matty had to hold the Walkman out like the lead of a dog.

Two broad bikinied bottoms in full view, the material disappearing into the centre between their thighs.

'What you doing listening to black music, little white boy?' said the one with the headphones on. The way she said it sounded like *boyeee*.

A small fizz of pride. 'Just like it.'

'Ah, so cute,' said the girl who'd first spoken, in a pretend-soft voice.

'Where you go school?' The white girl stabbed her question. Her bikini was purplish pink, and had a red heart on the bottom.

Matty said.

'Where you going September?'

'St George's.'

'Why you looking at us, then?' The girl in the blue bikini rolled back over and lay her head on the first girl's breasts. 'Wanted some fun time, did you? Thinking about making us girls cry with your killer sex-moves, yeah?' She shut her eyes, tipped her head back and opened her mouth, emitting breathy sighs. A quiet titter from the first girl. 'Go on, show us your knob.'

Matty flushed.

'Yeah, go on, little batty boy.' A little finger, curled in the air.

'Nah, he'll just give us all AIDS up the bum.'

They all shrieked with laughter. Matty tugged on the head-phone lead. The blue-bikinied girl held on fast and did a sharp, definitely negative 'mmm-mmm' in her throat. Another tug. The other two girls stretched out, going for an ankle each.

Matty let go and legged it.

'You better run! We'll get you in school!' From the bottom of the slope, you could see the girl in the blue bikini whipping the white girl with the headphone lead, while she moaned, over and over.

At least at the Men's Pond there were no giant, vicious secondary school girls. Younger and older men were lounging on the green, loads more than last time, reading or chatting. Cigarette smoke drifted slowly above them and there were a few dogs, one barking rapidly. A boombox was playing. Matty stood at the entrance, heart doing salmon-flips, pretending to read the sign about swimming safely and winter swimming and algae levels. And walked through the gate.

The path beyond it was thin and bordered by hedges, and at the end there was a door with dark metal panelling and a notice saying *MEN ONLY*. The door to another dimension. Deep breath.

Inside there were two big spaces of concrete open to the sky. The right-hand side seemed to be a changing area and the left-hand side had weightlifting apparatus in the middle. A few men were seated on the ground on towels, another on the weights bench, cricking his neck and smoking a roll-up, his back matted with ginger hair like an orangutan. A newspaper was spread out in front of one man, who wasn't wearing any clothes, his willie flopped out on his thigh. Matty felt a surge of alarm and looked quickly away, walking over to the changing area, trying to be invisible.

It looked like it had been built a very long time ago, and not touched since. There were old, rotten-looking wooden benches with rusty corrugated-iron walls and awnings over the top, and a noticeboard and big blackboard at the end. A few jackets were hanging off hooks, and some piles of clothes sat above neatly paired shoes.

No willies here. Two old men sat on the benches in swimming trunks, one of them smoking a pipe, staring at the floor as they talked quietly. Damp patches around their feet. The one with the pipe glanced at Matty before going back to his conversation, which wasn't in English and wasn't Italian. In the furthest corner, a younger man was holding onto the green iron rail by the gutter pipe, pulling himself up, his upper arms fattening, going thin again, like a snake eating a rat.

Don't look at anyone. Matty was already wearing football shorts, thin ones with blue piping. They would do. The T-shirt stayed on, like those men the other day. Rucksack bundled into the corner.

*

The Pond seemed much bigger than from the outside. Massive. Like the width of the River Kwai twice over. Straight in front was a slim concrete walkway with a low diving board at the end, and the water stretched wide and far to overhanging trees, a glossy grey-green. A few men queued for the diving board, and the concrete was dark brown and wet underfoot.

'Hang on, mate, not so fast.'

Matty's heart turned to clay, clammy and heavy.

A lifeguard was leaning on an oar in front of a big shed to the right by an older, wooden walkway. He wore wraparound sunglasses and a spray of hay-coloured hair poked out from under his yellow cap. He put his hands on his hips. 'How old are you, then?'

'Eleven.'

He looked at Matty. 'Pull the other one.'

'I am.' Voice too high. Lower. 'I just finished primary school.'

'Can't go in without an adult.' He sounded Australian. 'Where's your dad?'

Heat, rising from stomach to throat. 'There.' A man with a bald patch who was waiting to dive in happened to be turning round and speaking to someone further away. 'Hi,' Matty shouted, putting a hand up.

The man looked towards them, beyond them.

The lifeguard frowned. 'Show us your skills, then.'

Matty gazed at him, not quite daring to believe that it had worked.

He sighed, and waved a finger between the two walkways. 'Swim to there and back again.'

Up close, the pondwater was like army camouflage, splodges of black, green, brown. The lower parts of the metal steps became softer and more mossy. A little breath as cold water reached ankles, calves. The lifeguard was chatting to a swimmer, but still watching.

On holidays in Rimini, Dad would watch from the beach, occasionally looking over his sunglasses as Matty splashed about in the waves next to the Italian kids, even more occasionally putting down his local paper, which he couldn't properly read because it was in Italian, and jogging over to dunk himself in, or chuck Matty over his back. He would demonstrate a bit about breathing, nose in the water, bubbles coming out. The taste of salt.

Now, it was a swallowing-up. Not freezing, but cool enough to make you feel wide awake. Matty did quick breaststroke arms and scissor-feet for the few metres across to the wooden walkway and back to the concrete one and back again, grabbing onto the rail and climbing up to look up carefully at the lifeguard.

He didn't seem that interested. Gave a thumbs-up and waved his hand at the same time and carried on talking to the man. Matty sank back and headed out into the open water, following in the wake of the pretend-Dad, and feeling every cell burst into a little smile.

You couldn't see anything in here. You couldn't see past your hands, let alone the bottom. The bottom could be just under your toes or miles deep. Maybe it was bottomless. There were monsters in here, and pike and piranhas and barracudas. Nuclear submarines.

Dad, swimming here. It was hard to imagine. Moving slowly, like the old man in front with the swimming hat that made him look like a clown. Or slicing up and down like the man at the far end, who took tiny breaths but mostly kept his head in the water. Doing a spinning barrel jump like the teenager on the diving board, which earned him a clap.

White rubber rings were dotted over the Pond. Matty aimed for the nearest one, then another, not straying too far from the platform side and looking for a sandy-coloured head, although if Dad's hair was wet it would be as dark as the water. He wasn't here. But some of these men might know him.

There were specks of white fluff on the water. And tiny weed-sticks, lying crossed over each other to make crucifixes.

Maybe this really was the last place he had come. Someone had pushed him under, like that boy was doing on the far side to his friend, but not for fun. They had held his head down. The Mafia. Or a freak Pond Ness monster had put its mouth round his leg and it had been night-time and the lifeguard was looking the other way, and it had dragged him down. Or he'd had a secret meeting with a double agent from the KGB and it had gone wrong. Or. Or.

Holding onto a tyre with one hand, Matty went under, eyes open. The water was cold black tea, with patches of light that made it green. Full of secrets. What if he was still in here?

Above the water, the world was technicolour, and had the sun's warmth. Another breath, and down again.

It was quiet. Jaws was keeping its fin down, a pale shadow about to loom up from the deep, mouth half-open and crosscut saw-teeth.

There was a slither of movement along one calf, chilled and furry. Matty immediately let go of the tyre, sank, kicked hard and came spluttering back up. Swam, quickly and very badly, to the steps and climbed out.

There had been something in there. Barracuda. Pike. A great white.

Matty sat on a wobbly, rotting bench in the changing area, staring at the scratchy wave of the concrete floor. Trying to get back to normal. It hadn't really been like *Jaws* just then. It was as if Matty's leg had been stroked, just once, by the wet finger of a corpse.

A man came in, small and skinny and dressed entirely in white. White trousers, white Dr Marten boots, white-framed sunglasses, T-shirt, blazer. He seemed to glance at Matty, though it was hard to tell with the sunglasses, before taking a white leather satchel from his shoulder and placing it on a hook.

He looked like Death.

A shiver. It was a proper sign this time, not like the sun flashing, or the man with the dog.

Dad had been here. He had drowned in here.

Chapter 2

Drowning.

Suffocation by immersion in a liquid, usually water.

Matty tried to picture someone drowning in milk or orange squash or cherry Coke.

Water closing over the victim's mouth and nose cuts off the body's supply of oxygen. Deprived of oxygen the victim stops struggling, loses consciousness, and gives up the remaining tidal air in his lungs.

Golders Green Library was an old building only a minute's walk from the flat, on the other side of the road. Matty sat with a dictionary and a large encyclopaedia at one of the desks between two aisles. Edition 8, *DICTA – EMBRY*. There was a strong smell from the carpet, like it had just been cleaned after someone had been sick on it.

Lack of oxygen, anoxia, affects the brain within 30 seconds of the laryngospasms beginning to weaken with imminent brain failure.

New words to learn. *Spasms*, when your muscles went tight in a way you couldn't control. *Larynx* was in the dictionary, with an 'x' not a 'g'. Matty placed two fingers in the little well of the throat and swallowed, to feel the pressure there.

There was dry drowning and wet drowning. Dry meant that the person held their breath or only let in a tiny bit. Wet meant more water in the lungs. At the bottom of one glossy page, there was a diagram of something that looked like a cauliflower wearing a red belt, and a comparison of freshwater and seawater.

Victims immersed for an hour or longer may be totally salvage-able, physically and intellectually, although they lack evidence of life, having no measurable vital signs—heartbeat, pulse, or breathing—at the time of rescue.

Salvageable. The act of saving a ship or its cargo from the peril of the seas, said the dictionary. Dad, as treasure. But it would be too late for that, if he was in there. No one could last eight days.

Over the page under 'Drowning' there was a painting of people in bonnets and wigs, arms outstretched, the sea and the boat swirling around them. Another was of a woman in a long, silver-gold dress on her back in a river, holding flowers. Her eyes and mouth were open and she looked quite peaceful, like she was bored and just thinking about something. There were weeds in her hair.

A pharaoh who drowned in the Nile, probably eaten by croco-diles. Kings and generals and explorers who drowned in the sea. The *Titanic*. Ra-Ra-Rasputin got poisoned with tea and cake, and they got him drunk and shot him and threw him in a hole in the ice on a river. Some say that he didn't die until he drowned.

On a different shelf, down by a dusty window with a spider abseiling from a cobweb, there was a pamphlet. Pink paper. 'Hampstead Heath: a Local History'. The drawings were rubbish, and it was made on a typewriter. There were drownings in there, too. In the Ponds. Four deaths a month in the nineteenth century. A clipping from a newspaper from 1897, William Chitty who slipped and fell. A man at a family picnic. A twenty-year-old doing a somersault, found lying at the bottom with his neck broken. *The bank on one side of the pond, where there were willow trees, was very slippery, and the boatman had on several occasions pulled boys out of the water.*

People did drown in there. They did slip and fall. Dad could have.

***

22

'Um.'

The Australian lifeguard looked down at Matty, frowning, as if no one was allowed to stand on this part of the platform except him. Today, his sunglasses were pushed up on top of his head and you could see the thin lines at the corners of his eyes. Another lifeguard, much older, was sitting on a chair, hands clasped over his stomach, gazing outwards.

No church again. Mamma mostly stayed in bed, like John Lennon and Yoko Ono when they had all the journalists and photographers in there. She had taken the plate of toast that Matty brought in without interest and put it on the bedside table. Maybe it was less like John and Yoko and more like the prisoners who went on hunger strike in Northern Ireland.

'Do you know Joe Ronan?' Matty said to the lifeguard, arms tightly crossed.

'Who's that?'

'Joseph. Ronan.' He hated being called Joseph. Mamma would call him *Joseph Ronan* when they were arguing, and Dad would close his eyes before looking at the ceiling. 'He comes – he came swimming here.'

'Uh-huh,' the lifeguard said. 'Look around you. Quite a lot of fellas swim here. That's the idea.'

'Yeah, but he ...' Drowned in here. You missed him. Lungs letting water in, bit by bit. 'It was the last place he was seen.'

He glanced down. 'Are you talking about the missing guy? Do me a favour. We've already had the police round here. How'd you know about that?'

Matty shrugged. 'Did they search for him?'

'No, they just came and asked questions. Got quite a lot of interest.' He looked down at Matty, quite frankly. 'Uniforms,' he said, as if explaining something.

'They didn't go and look in the water?' Sometimes the police sent divers down on searches, wetsuits and flippers and masks.

'Bodies float, buddy boy.'

Not always. Sometimes they took ages, like Virginia Woolf, the writer in the encyclopaedia. She wasn't found for three weeks. People had not been found for years, another book had said, and their bodies turned to candlewax because of a lack of oxygen. *Adipocere.* 'Sometimes you have to dredge the bottom.'

The lifeguard looked irritable. 'Look, we had a drowning in here. Two years ago. Davy never got over it. Never lifeguarded again. I don't want to be reminded of it, all right?' He narrowed his eyes. 'And *he* bloody floated.' An impatient, slightly suspicious glance. 'What's it all to you?'

Yesterday, Matty had pretended that the man with the balding head and bright purple trunks was Dad. 'Just interested.' Nose-scratch.

The lifeguard folded his arms so that you could see the veins on his biceps. 'All right, Detective Sergeant Pipsqueak. Either get in that water or bugger off. Where's your dad today?'

Matty put a flat hand against both eyebrows and squinted about. 'Around.'

He sighed. 'In you go, then. Don't drown.'

It was earlier in the day than last time, and not busy. The sun was hot when the clouds weren't over it. An old man with a droopy Wild West moustache was doing breaststroke very slowly and a couple of younger men were diving, their stomachs sucked in as their arms stretched up. Two swimmers hugged close to the rope markers, doing front crawl, their mouths opening and closing like goldfish.

Matty swam slowly to the middle of the Pond, heading for the floating platform. Tried to imagine Dad in here, tired after work, having had a pint or two in the pub first and maybe 'gone a bit thin lizzy', like he sometimes said.

No one was on the platform today. You'd be easily missed, here in the water on the far side of it. The lifeguards hardly seemed to watch half the time, chatting to each other, caps pulled down low. Matty turned over and floated face up, arms out flat and eyes closed, the sun beating down.

Lungs like inflatables. Breathe in, and you rose. Out, and you sank, just a little. Like Dad might have done.

Time to stop breathing.

Arms sagged. Legs. A line of cool liquid rose slowly into each ear. The water rocked, a queasy sway, and Matty's body was lolled, 180 degrees round. Face in the pond. Drowning. It would be like dreaming.

Suddenly, a hand was dragging Matty back round and yanking a fist's worth of T-shirt.

Cough. Snot. Cough. Matty fumbled, holding onto someone's bare shoulders, kicking. Blinking madly.

Two dark eyes, right there. 'What in the bleeding hell do you think you're doing? *Dickhead.*' There was a loud whistle blown from the lifeguard's area.

Matty stopped kicking, partly held by the boy, and gazed back. Heart full of water, lungs full of air.

'Are you dead?'

'No.'

The boy prodded Matty in the chest. 'Out. Up.'

His face was very close.

Still coughing, Matty had clambered up onto the central platform and now sat, exhausted, as if having just run the London Marathon. The boy from the water was peering, fiercely, about two inches away.

Slick, dark hair. His eyes, so bog-brown they were almost black. He sat back on his haunches, running a palm over his hair and waggling the water off, droplets that caught the light. His shape seemed liquid, his skin lined in sun. Balancing on his heels, the boy clasped his hands in front of him and let out a breath. A really annoyed breath. 'Seriously. You're a dickhead.'

25

There seemed to be nothing to say. You couldn't thank some-one who had rescued you from drowning when you had been half-trying to drown. Shivers started coming. A head rush. Matty jumped back in and swam very fast toward the walkway. Short, shallow breaths.

'Where're you going?' The boy's voice was flung into the air. But he didn't follow.

A smack-bang crash into the lifeguard at the entrance to the concreted area. He looked furious. 'I said *don't* drown, you little shit. Do that again and you're barred.'

***

Voices. A man's voice. For two seconds in the hallway, Matty's heart was the Black Stallion galloping along a beach, until it became obvious that the voice didn't belong to Dad.

'Well, bloody hell, I don't know what to tell you, Rosa. It's a mystery.'

Matty stood at the living-room door, leaning against the jamb, sliding carefully around.

'It's not like him,' said Sanjit.

Sanjit had always been nice to Matty on the couple of visits to the shopfitters when both he and Mamma had to work on Saturdays. He chucked over a packet of chocolate bourbons and told Matty to get rid of them before they did him an injury, patting his belly. Though Mamma was sometimes mean about Indians, she said that Sanjit's family were nice, polite people. Once, they had all gone for a curry in Islington, though Mamma had ordered fish and chips because she was suspicious of spicy food. Matty had eaten a korma as always, and Dad had ordered something really hot to impress Sanjit and had to drink three mango lassis to get it down.

Today, Sanjit's stomach seemed even fatter than usual, a huge hot-dog roll of it in his lap as he sat, hands on knees, on the sofa. He craned round, the sound of his polyester trousers rubbing on the leather of the sofa. 'Hello, little one, how are you?' he said with a big beam, before he looked confused and tried to look more commiserative. 'Well, of course, what I mean is it is a difficult time, of course, for everyone, oh bloody Nora, mate.' He glanced at Mamma.

Mamma gazed at Matty in a blank, tired way. 'Go and get a drink and wash your face. You look like you have been rolling around in a pigsty.'

Matty slid back into the hallway and did a few loud steps before creeping back to listen.

'I don't know what to tell you,' Sanjit was saying. 'It is a proper bloody mystery. He's a responsible guy, you know? Always has been. Salt of the earth.'

Mamma didn't say anything.

'Well, we'll keep managing for now. Holding the fort. Though he's invaluable, really.' Sanjit seemed to just be filling the silence with words, any words. 'And the police haven't come back with any leads? Any ideas?'

'No. Not a thing.'

'I don't like to say it, Rosa, but – you know how these police people are, they are more interested in missing children, you know? It is a better story. You must keep asking them. Keep phoning them so that they do not forget you. Badger away.'

The card that the policewoman had left was in the hallway by the telephone. Matty picked it up and thumbed the edges.

'I'm very sorry about it all,' said Sanjit, coming out of the living room. 'Bit of a bloody mess, isn't it?' He caught sight of Matty. 'I mean, not a bloody mess, I'm sure it's not that.'

Matty hid the card between two flat hands, as if praying. 'Did Dad go to the Ponds? That day?'

Sanjit blinked. 'He said he was going, yes, mate,' he said, as if it had been quite normal. 'He liked a swim.' Another blink, horrified. '*Likes* a swim.'

The police station was a big red-brick building on Finchley Road, with a hairdresser's and a Chinese herbal medicine shop next door. A Union Jack flag hung down from a pole over two old-fashioned lanterns.

The policewoman who had come to the house was there in her thick black skirt that pointed outwards. 'Hello, love.' She looked across the foyer. 'Your mum not with you?'

Matty was led down a brown-carpeted corridor with plasticky windows and into a room with five desks, all piled high with paper. A man in a beige blazer leant back on his chair legs to glance over, uninterested, before tipping back down and sighing at his typewriter.

The policewoman was shuffling out digestive biscuits from a packet onto a plate. They slid off onto the table and she had to put them back on. 'So is there something you want to tell me about your dad?' she said, breaking off a piece of biscuit. 'Something you couldn't tell me before?'

'Um. No. I just wondered if you could dredge the pond. The Men's Pond on Hampstead Heath.'

She spoke through a mouthful of biscuit. 'That costs money, love. The lifeguards are sure nothing happened there. They would have seen something. It was just one line of inquiry.' She frowned at Matty. 'He definitely didn't take anything from the house that morning? Or say anything to you?'

'Go get 'em, Scout,' he'd said. 'Enjoy your last day.' His fingers in a gun-shape, kissing the top of them, firing gently.

'No.'

She slotted her fingers together. Today her lipstick was the colour of water-wings, and it was straying in tiny paths from her upper lip. 'I'm sorry about your dad, love.' She looked down at her desk, as if she had other things to do. Picked up a pen. 'Sometimes they go. Sometimes they come back. Believe me, I know.' She fiddled with the gold band on her finger and said something under her breath.

Then do something. Find him. 'So …' Matty looked at the floor. 'You don't think he's dead?'

'Well, without – sorry, love – but without a body, no. People go missing. Sometimes it's because they don't want to be found.' She pushed the plate over. 'Have a biscuit.'

***

In warm water the body's need for oxygen increases.

Matty ran a hot bath, too hot, and got in anyway. Slid down until both ears were full, only nose and eyes above water.

Oxygen deprivation caused by immersion is rapidly lethal or permanently damaging to the brain.

Deprivation meant *the lack of material benefits considered to be the basic necessities in a society*, like food and drink and skateboards. Or it meant *the lack or denial of something considered to be a necessity*, like a dad. Dad-deprivation.

Brown bits floated on the surface of the bathwater. The Pond had travelled all the way home with Matty and only come off when in contact with water again.

Such warm water drownings occur frequently in domestic baths.

Matty slid further down. Eyes covered. Nose.

It was different under here. Boiling hot, the surface of the bath underneath trapping you. Maybe it felt like this at the bottom of the Pond, hard mud underneath your back. Matty tried to imagine metres and metres of water pressing down. Filling each lung.

He wouldn't have just gone. He would have wanted to be found.

They were just lazy, the police. They didn't have divers to send out, and didn't want to pay for dredging machines. They didn't care because Dad wasn't like the baby in Australia whose mum said that dingos ate her. He was a grown-up. They didn't know he wasn't in there. They hadn't felt that slithering touch, like Matty had.

You just had to take a breath. One proper breath. Your lungs wouldn't fill up. Just a bit of water would go in and the trachea would shut the trapdoor while your brain slowly began to fail. Until the next breath.

The bathroom door opened and Mamma's voice drifted in, the words soupy and glued together.

Matty shot upwards, water falling away. Bright light and sound.

'What are you doing?' One hand was on her hip. 'You have been in there for too long.'

'Nothing.'

Mamma stood there. A couple of years ago, she would sit on the toilet seat and read out articles from her fashion magazines as the bubbles dissolved. Or dry Matty's hair, the rhythmic rasp of the towel, or clean the inside curves of both ears with a cotton bud. *There. Clean as a little button.* She hadn't done that for a long time.

There were so many questions. Where's Dad? Do you think he's dead? Can we make the police dredge the pond? Can I have some money for tea? Can you make tea? Why haven't you cried?

Mamma leant over and opened the window. 'The walls will get damp.' She turned away. 'Get out and get dry.'

***

There was a different pair of lifeguards on duty today. One was wearing aviator sunglasses, his grey hair pulled back in a ponytail. 'No swimming without supervision,' he said.

Every muscle went stiff. 'The other lifeguard said it was OK.'

'Did he now? Which one?'

'The Australian one.' Spoken at the ground.

'South African. Same difference. Come on.' He made a clicking sound with his mouth like you would to a horse, gesturing to the steps. He seemed satisfied with the same test, the back-forth to the old walkway, as before.

Matty swam to the tyre in the middle. Hung there, one-handed. Last time had been a failure. But if Dad was here, in the water, then he needed to be found.

'Wotcha.' The boy, the slapping, swearing boy, was suddenly there, bobbing, a great grin on his face. Hair pasted down like weeds right in his eyes. Before Matty could answer, he sank down, let water pool into his mouth and spat it out again. 'Going to try and drown again?'

'No.' It came out a bit higher than intended.

'Skill,' said the boy. 'Let's go up there.' He nodded behind Matty's shoulder.

Matty stared at the end of the diving board. Toes two centimetres from the edge.

The boy had already gone in, one high bounce and an almost vertical dive, and was treading water in a strange, manic fashion, looking up. 'Come on, you big wimpy chicken-shit!'

Matty hadn't ever dived before. Had jumped off the little pier north of Rimini plenty of times, but never gone in head-first.

'Are you going in?' A pale man with a soft Yorkshire accent was standing close by, at the head of a lengthening queue. 'You can take the steps, you know.'

'Scaredy-bollocks!' shouted the boy from below.

Matty turned back to the pond. Bent both knees, like some of the men did, and bounced off the diving board, landing hands and knees first.

Whack. Nose like a Soda Stream.

'That was pants,' said the boy, in hysterics. 'That was the shit-stinkiest dive in the history of diving.'

Matty swam back to the platform, not looking back, everything smarting. Hands, knees, cheeks.

*

On the platform, there was a warm arm suddenly around both shoulders. A black man in small trunks with a knobbly mass of hair on his chest. 'Darling. Trust me, the entertainment was lovely, but you need a few tips there.'

'Don't listen to him!' said the boy from the water.

The man's upper arm was a solid weight. 'All right. Next time, tuck your head under.' He waved his index finger at Matty's nose. 'Chin right in. Keep them arms straight all the way, hands too, nice and flat. And again.' He put a hand on Matty's back and gave the most gentle of pushes.

Matty walked to the end of the diving board, wanting nothing more than to go home. The boy was swimming further away.

'Daz, who made you queen of the queues?' A portly man, his stomach hanging over tight orange trunks, a red face. 'People are waiting here if you hadn't noticed.'

The man called Daz put his hands on his hips. He looked very lean and strong. Matty wanted to look as strong as him. 'Oh, I had noticed,' he said. 'Worst bloody chorus line I've ever seen. Police line-up, more like. It's going downhill round here. Better in your day, Ivor, wasn't it?'

The lifeguard with the aviator sunglasses intertwined his fingers on top of his stomach. 'Shut it.'

Daz turned back to Matty. 'On you go, lovie. No panicking now. Do me proud.'

A sheen of expectation on the water. In the air too, it seemed, though in truth most of the men in the queue were chatting to each other. Just Daz, stretching and pretending not to watch.

'You can always try again,' Dad would say, after a bad maths test, or a skateboard crash. 'There's always a second chance. Apart from where Barnet are feckin' concerned.'

Matty stuck both hands up, flat. Took a gulp of air and held it. Dived.

A mouthful of water and a glimpse of the boy and Matty's head was above the surface again. The diving board was still rocking.

Daz was clapping from the platform. 'You were like a bleeding arrow. Beautiful!'

'He's lying his arse off,' said the boy, who was suddenly right there. 'But it was better. Come on.' He headed away, not making a single splash.

'Why do you wear a T-shirt?' the boy said.

Think, quickly. Shoulders turned in. 'Jewish.'

He screwed up his nose, eyes closed and face tipped towards the broad blue sky. 'Weirdo.'

Matty had dived seven more times, each one mostly better than the last, apart from the horrible, fizzy hit up the nose and the stinging eyes. Even the man with the big belly and the orange trunks had given up his place in the line. Now the two of them sat to the side of the walkway on the concrete strip, legs dangling in the pond.

The boy's hair was beginning to turn gold as it dried. His skin was buttery, almost green, like he'd been holidaying in France for a month. He probably had. It's what posh boys did. Though his shorts were old-fashioned and yellowish-brown, Matty was fairly sure that this boy had the sort of family who went skiing and had another house in the countryside where they rode ponies.

'Toffs,' Dad had said, while they were watching a news article about people who had phones that they could carry around with them. 'The flipside to you and me and every other working, ordinary person. Except there's millions of us and about ten of them, owning everything.'

It was hard to tell how old the boy was. About the same age, or maybe a bit older. He sat up on his heels, arms stretched straight out in front of him, balancing. 'Who are you, then?'

Matty didn't answer. Sometimes it was hard to know.

The boy looked impatient. 'Name.'

Matty told him, looking down at both palms, which were covered in a faint dust of pond-stuff.

The boy repeated it slowly, as if trying it out for the first time. It didn't sound right coming from his mouth.

'Who are you?'

'Nicks.' Like Nicholas, maybe? Or it could be his surname, like Nixon, the second Vietnam president. Matty was good on war stuff – sitting up late with Dad on Saturday nights in the dark, the video player hired for the weekend. *The Green Berets* or *The Deer Hunter*. He liked Vietnam films especially, usually borrowed from a friend and really grainy, like watching through a snowstorm. He let Matty snuggle next to him as the screen flared. 'Don't tell Mamma,' he'd say, softly, but his voice all alive. Their secret. 'Now this,' he would say, pointing the top of his beer bottle at Christopher Walken's quiet tears while Robert de Niro shouted opposite him, 'is a performance.'

'Where d'you live?'

'Here,' Nicks said, as if that were a stupid question.

Here. One of the swanky houses close by, even on the little road just outside. The one with the coloured bottles in the window, or the tall fence with the alarms, or the one with the big Dulux dog. So he *was* a rich boy. He looked scruffy, but sometimes posh kids did, their mums and dads letting them run around and grow their hair.

'Is your dad here?'

'Nah.' Nicks flashed over a glance. 'Like yours isn't.' He continued jabbing sticks into the ground.

Matty looked down. He sounded quite knowing.

'Come on,' said Nicks, that conversation snapped shut. 'Let's scram.'

'Where are we going?' A gentle, hopeful warmth, deep down. He didn't really care who Matty was.

He grinned. Bright white teeth. 'You think this is the only pond?'

'We're not allowed in there.'

'Says who?' Nicks was jiggling about in front of the fence, shaking his shoulders and tossing his head from side to side.

Matty pointed to the sign, which said, rather starkly in red paint on white, *NO SWIMMING*.

'*Tss.*' Nicks stuck two fingers up at the sign. 'You the swimming police?'

'No.'

'Come on, then, arse-face.'

Patches of warmer water and cooler water. Matty was a crocodile, nosing along at eye-level. Nicks floated just ahead on his back, doing occasional lazy kicks and humming, not very tunefully.

This pond was smaller, the trees gathering round the water as if wanting it all to themselves. They had climbed the fence, though it went straight into holly bushes and now Matty's arms were covered in criss-crossing scratches, like the trails of just-hit bomber planes.

Could Dad have swum here? Maybe he liked the quieter ponds, not being watched by the lifeguards. The police would never think to look. Matty rolled over to look at the sky, waiting to see if the gravewater feeling came.

A whistle, the sort a shepherd would give, and Matty jerked upright. There was a man standing by the fence with a small fluffy white dog. 'You shouldn't swim in there.'

Matty waited for Nicks to shout something back, but the man just beckoned again. 'It's dangerous.'

A swivel round in the water. Nicks wasn't there. The water was flat and brown, the slightest sway. No ripples.

'Excuse me. Can't you hear me? There's a sign, for goodness' sakes.'

Where had he gone? He couldn't have sunk down. You'd have heard something.

Matty breaststroked to the side and clambered out by the brambles, getting a few more leg-scratches on the way. A quick look back. Still no Nicks. Matty picked up the rucksack and walked to the fence towards the man, because there was no other way out.

The man didn't have a dog on his lead but a long-haired white cat with blue eyes. 'Bloody terror,' he said. 'You know people have drowned in there? Don't tempt fate.'

'OK.' Matty didn't look at him, climbing the fence awkwardly and avoiding his outstretched hand. The cat yowled and delivered the third variation of scratches for the day.

Nicks had just disappeared. Matty changed behind a tree and walked back past the boating lake, putting headphones on. Coins from Mamma's purse had been enough to replace the ones that those big girls had taken, a second-hand pair from the electrical shop on the high street. Mamma never said anything about the money that kept disappearing.

Instead of turning right to climb the hill, Matty wandered back over to the low slope of grass outside the Pond where some men were hanging around, talking. Two of them were dancing, unbuttoned short-sleeved shirts floating by their sides.

There was Daz, wearing dungarees and no shirt, his muscles hard and rounded. The hair on his head was the same texture as the hair on his chest. He was arguing with a man who was lying down next to a boombox wedged in the grass. Daz looked around. 'Oi oi oi, little diving bunny!'

Matty swiped a lock of drying hair to the side and looked over.

Daz was waving, madly.

Me? Matty mimed.

'Yes, *you*, you wally. Get over here.'

Matty stepped onto the grass, rucksack straps clenched in each fist over the chest. You could feel the heat from everyone. Red skin. Brown skin. Freckles the colour of peanut butter sprinkled all over a wide slab of back, and lots of very sporty-looking men, sleek and muscled. What would it be like, to look like that? What would it feel like?

'For the love of all that is good and right,' Daz was putting his hands out, as if explaining something to a two-year-old. 'There's. No. Tune.'

Music was bursting tinnily from the boombox. 'Brother,' said the white man slouched next to it. 'Your ears aren't modern enough.'

As soon as Matty reached them, Daz was gripping a shoulder. 'Right, you. You're young.'

'Puny, you mean,' said the other man. He had scraggy teeth and was seesawing a toothpick in his mouth.

'Youthful. Finger on the pulse. Listen to this.' Daz gestured towards the boombox. 'Tell me what you think.'

Matty stood very still and listened. The music sounded like someone brushing a broom over concrete while robots clapped their hands, over and over. Squelchy, bubbling sounds, too. There was no singing or rapping or anything. 'It's OK.'

Daz leant down. 'What's that?'

'Um. It's OK?' Not far away, there were two men sitting on towels, holding hands.

'It's *rot*,' Daz said, gleefully outraged and as if he was on a stage. 'It's carnage. My ears are bleeding. If you're going to play your music out here, young man, you're going to have to take requests. And mine is The Brothers Johnson.'

'No one else is complaining, you big bender,' said the boombox man with a grin, his toothpick seeming to move of its own accord. He looked like a scarecrow on an afternoon off. Patched shirt and shorts. Tattoos all the way up his arms – girls with big eyes and boobs, 'MOTHER', a faded skull.

'No else has the gumption to talk to such a layabout,' Daz said. 'They think you'll lift their wallet and give them a Chelsea smile or a Glasgow snog or something.' He turned to Matty. 'You're no help,' he said, wagging a finger. 'How's your diving?'

'Good, thanks.'

'What sort of music are you into, geezer?' The scarecrow-man gestured towards his own ears. 'What you got on there?'

'Um.' Matty pulled out the Walkman, clicked open the Kurtis Blow tape, which really needed to be returned to Kyle from school. Handed it to him.

The man looked at it, flipped it over. Took his cocktail stick out of his mouth and nodded in a faintly impressed way. 'All right. Nice. You know this is three years old, though?'

'Yeah.'

He sat up, looked a bit more keen-eyed, like a kestrel. 'You need to listen to some of the UK stuff coming in. On the pirate stations. I mean, they're all doing American accents and that but they're trying, you know?'

Matty nodded, not really knowing.

'Oh God, here we go,' said Daz, to several people around him who weren't really listening. 'Just call Doctor Gegs.'

The boombox man ignored Daz. 'Heard of Newtrament?'

'No.'

He rattled off a few more names. The music had changed to something with a bassline and arcade game gun-sounds. 'Right,' he said. 'I'll see what I can do.' He closed his eyes, face up to the sun, before opening his left eye again. 'Go on, then.' Fingers fluttered up and down. 'Off you toddle.'

***

Matty let the door slam. It had been a long, looping route back home through the park, the sun beginning to turn the grass beige. Then into the woods with their thigh-high nettles. There had been a magpie following from tree to tree, as if Matty was a shiny coin to be nicked and taken back to its nest.

Mamma was in the living room, with the curtains drawn. Silver-blue light from the old film on TV. She liked these ones best, the type with women who stood in the shadows of window-blinds and talked very fast, where everyone smoked, and kissed funny, pressing their mouths together and rolling their faces about.

'You're a bloody romantic,' Dad had said once, to Mamma, having lost an argument about turning over to watch *The Great Escape*. 'You should have been born in the 1910s, I reckon.' He'd say that she was a glamourpuss, that she could be in one of those films, and Matty would imagine her swaying down a foggy black-and-white alley in her fur coat and, by Mamma's dreamy expression, was sure that she was picturing it, too.

Now, though, she was staring at it blankly, a cigarette between her fingers. The ashy part was long, and beginning to curve downwards.

She had still not cried. It had been eleven days and Mamma had not cried once.

Better not to ask what was for tea now. Baked beans and cheese on toast and hot dogs in a tin had been tea all week. Only once had Mamma made anything, boiling eggs and leaving them for Matty to smash with the teaspoon. She'd chucked her own dinner in the kitchen bin.

There was a strange, sharp feeling in the room, like the air had gone radioactive.

'Mamma?'

Mamma didn't turn her head. Shadows from the curtain and the TV on her hair. A tissue, or maybe it was a piece of paper, clenched in her fist.

The ash from the cigarette dropped onto the carpet in grey snowflakes.

'Go to bed,' she said, to the wall.

It was only seven o'clock. But Matty did anyway, stomach growling like a guard dog. Took up two packets of salt and shake crisps. Read *Deadwood City*.

Didn't sleep.

Chapter 3

A jangling, hard sound.

It was another hot morning, everything feeling sticky. Ankles aching. Different parts kept aching at the moment, and if they weren't aching, they were itching. Matty had been dreaming about Dad again, this time diving into a big lake covered in green algae like a rug, looking for treasure. Only his heart and lungs had risen to the surface.

Mamma was in the kitchen, the handle of a mug in her hand, the rest of it cracked into pieces on the lino. She didn't seem surprised.

Matty looked at the floor, imagining the two flowers and the yellow-and-black flag pieced back together. Barnet FC, the mug that Dad had his coffee in every morning. 'Bunch of feckin' losers,' he'd say. 'I could play better on a two-day hangover. Bloody Bungle and his pals could play better.' Yet he still went, every fortnight.

Mamma was in her silk blouse, the one with the high frilly collar and the buttons in the same material.

'Are you going to work?'

'Yes,' she said, and the word felt dangerous. 'I am going to work.' Her voice had begun to rise. 'Someone has to earn a living to pay for this flat, and what is in the fridge, and these bloody bastard mugs,' she almost shouted to the handle, as if it could hear her. '*Pezzo di merda.*'

Matty put some bread in the toaster and listened to Mamma's breath come hard through her nose, like a horse, and how it

40

softened again, almost reluctantly. She got the dustpan and brush from under the sink. The clink of the broken china.

Mamma took out some chocolate spread from the cupboard and put it on the table, before placing her fingers on Matty's arm, over the holly scratches. 'What have you been doing to yourself?'

'Nothing. Just the park.'

One long breath, and her voice was calmer. 'Why do you not play with Johanna? She is a nice girl. Why do you not have her round for tea?'

Because you are not making tea, thought Matty. Because I can only cook baked beans. Although Mamma was spreading margarine on the toast right now, the knife heavy on the bread, as if trying to hurt it.

Dad called her the Queen of the Kitchen, and said there was no point in him bothering. He could mostly do fried things. Bacon sandwiches, pressing the bread down with the slice. Fried eggs and fried bread on Sunday mornings before church, sometimes still in pyjamas, saying, 'God's giving me a lie-in.' Pancakes, scraping the bits off the floor after a failed flip without missing a note of the tune he was whistling. The kitchen seemed so empty without him.

'Go and play with Johanna,' Mamma said, again. 'Stop getting filthy in the park.'

***

Johanna was at the door, giving Matty's shorts and T-shirt a quick glance up and down. 'Wish *I* could wear clothes like that,' she said, a little impishness in with the envy.

She was wearing a crisp white shirt, the arms ironed so that there was a little ridge all the way from shoulder to wrist. A black skirt a bit like the policewoman's. Thick black tights. Jewish people had their own school uniform for the holidays.

41

Johanna and Matty had been in the same class all the way through primary school, often sitting together for art and spelling. She would kick Matty's foot and wrap her thick hair, the colour of a new penny, around her fist.

Her parents ran the Song of Solomon Hotel, ten minutes' walk up the road from the flat. It was a place for only Jewish people to stay – or at least, Matty had never seen any black or Indian or Chinese people there, or even white people who weren't Jewish. There were electric candleholders on the windowsills that were permanently lit, and the carpets were plush and thick. It was always very warm.

Mamma didn't mind Johanna's family, even though they were not Christian. 'They take their religion very seriously,' she'd say. 'Ah, it's all near enough,' Dad would reply. 'Same gaffer managing both teams.'

Johanna turned round in the hallway with thoughtful, narrowed eyes. 'If you're a boy, you have to wear one of these.' Held up a small cupped black circle.

'Do you think that your dad's really dead, then?'

Johanna was sitting cross-legged in her bedroom, the seam of her tights at her crotch on show. She was always asking questions in a cheerful voice that cushioned how frank they were. The teacher in the last but one year had done a double take when Johanna put up her hand and asked whether it was true that male foxes had spikes on their penises and that was why vixens screamed so loudly.

Matty shrugged, reaching up to touch the small cloth cap that Jewish boys and men wore. It was very light, but it was there, and settled. 'Dunno. Yeah.'

'D'you really think he drowned?'

'Yeah. Maybe.'

'There was that one from the Rolling Stones who died in his swimming pool.'

42

Brian Jones. And Dennis Wilson from the Beach Boys, too. Matty was becoming well versed in drowning victims.

Johanna put her lips together and squished them to the side, frowning as a way of saying sorry. Then her eyes brightened. 'I know how we can find out.'

Matty thought that Ouija boards were for witches and demons. And was fairly sure that Johanna's parents thought the same.

'My brother did it once, to see if he could talk to Bob Marley,' Johanna said, looking at it. 'But I think you've got a better chance of talking to someone you actually know. I mean, why's Bob Marley going to talk to some stupid teenage boy with bum fluff on his chin?'

She had brought two proper candles in from her parents' bedroom, already lit. One had blue and white ripples, and the other was tapered and gold. They were for Jewish ceremonies, not for trying to commune with the dead over a piece of stiff cardboard that said CHARMIN: *softer, thicker, more absorbent* on the back.

Johanna's older brother Ron had stencilled the alphabet with biro in two curving rows in the middle, and the numbers zero to nine underneath that. The words *YES* and *NO* were scrawled heavily in bubble-writing at the top. *FUCK OFF* was written at the bottom.

'It's supposed to say goodbye,' said Johanna, shutting the curtains and sitting down opposite, cross-legged. 'But my brother is a gaylord.' She put a guitar plectrum on the board. 'Ready?'

No, thought Matty.

'Fingers.' She put her forefinger on one side of the plectrum.

Matty did the same on the other side.

'You have to be a bit careful or you might end up talking to Satan.'

'I thought your family didn't believe in him.'

43

'He's an angel. Just one who gets in the way a lot.' She grinned. 'If it goes to all four corners of the board, we blow the candles out and burn the guitar pick-thing.' She shifted forward. 'Our knees have to touch.' Her face got serious. The shadows from the candles didn't help. 'Is anyone there?' she said in a new, higher voice.

The cars could be heard on the road outside. A siren, further away.

Johanna had her eyes closed. 'Is anyone there?' she said again.

One of the candles smelt like Mamma's panettone at Christmas.

The plectrum began to move and Matty's breath jerked. It moved up, and to the left. To *YES*.

Matty looked up at Johanna. 'Did … you do that?'

'No.' It was always a bit hard to tell what Johanna was thinking if she wasn't saying it out loud. Her eyes were wide, the candle flickering in them. She pulled in her lip. She was excited. 'Who. Are. You?' she said to the board, slowly, as if talking to an old person in a wheelchair.

Their fingers didn't move, staying up on the left.

'Who are you?' she said, twice as slowly.

Outside, the road had gone quiet. The plectrum moved to the middle of the board. To the letter *J*.

Matty stopped breathing.

Along to the left. *O*.

Their hands stayed pushed together, not moving. Matty was like a freediver, like Hal and Roger in *South Sea Adventure*, lungs full, diving for freshwater to keep them alive. Their hands still didn't move.

I don't spell my name like that, you spanner, Dad would have said.

'You pushed it,' Matty said.

'I didn't!' said Johanna.

It moved again, along a bit. To the *E*.

'Holy mackerel,' said Johanna.

A cold laser, going all the way up Matty's spine.

'What do you want to ask?' Johanna whispered.

'I don't know.'

'Well, go on, ask something.'

Matty was too terrified.

'Are you Joe?' Johanna said, with loads of breath in her voice.

Up, to the left. Johanna's arm seemed too stiff. *YES*

'Are you alive?' she said.

NO

'Did you drown?'

This time, the plectrum went to the middle. The alphabet. Matty sneaked another glance at Johanna. She looked a bit scared. Or was pretending to.

One by one, their fingers shifted over the middle of the board, spelling one long word.

LOOKDEEPER

Matty moved it to *FUCK OFF*, very quickly.

***

Itchy chest. Itchy chest, itchy toes, itchy insides. Matty was lying on top of the duvet, waiting for Mamma to leave for work. An almost sleepless night spent looking up at the glowing plastic stars stuck to the ceiling. Dad was dead and he wasn't dead and you couldn't be dead if there was no body. Missing presumed dead, like they said in wars.

The front door opened, closed again. Matty got up and stood very still. Listening for him.

To their bedroom. The dressing table was full of Mamma's things. Perfume bottles, including really tiny ones, lipsticks. There was a chipped bowl of beaded necklaces like strings of marbles. An ashtray on each side of the bed. It was stuffy in here and you could see the dust on the windows. Mamma normally cleaned them like crazy.

Lookdeeper. Maybe Johanna hadn't been pushing the guitar plectrum. Matty made every muscle slacken, go dead. Toes digging into the carpet. 'Are you there?' Spoken so quietly that the words were all smudged together. 'Are you there? Dad?'

A sudden beep outside, making Matty's stomach do a Karate Kid kick. The sound of a revving engine. Just a car.

In the wardrobe, Mamma's dresses and coats were on one side and Dad's things on the other. His jumpers with diamonds or stripes. Short-sleeved shirts, for work. Not his leather jacket, because he'd been wearing that. Matty put a hand in, pulled out a pair of jeans that weren't folded up. Smelt them. A faint musti-ness, like a farm two fields away in the countryside. He was still here, in his clothes.

Bathroom. After flushing the toilet, Matty turned the tap on and let it run for ages. In the cabinet above the sink, Mamma's and Dad's things were all mixed up together. Cream for cuticles, which were the dried glue-bits at the bottom of your nails. Paco Rabanne aftershave. Toner, the colour of a swimming pool, and Jolen Creme Bleach. Nail clippers, with rust around the screw.

Once, round at Johanna's, they'd watched one of her brother's video nasties where someone closed the bathroom cabinet door and suddenly there was a ghost there, making them both yelp.

One breath. Two breaths. Matty stood straight, skin prickling, and shut the cabinet.

It was just the faded peach shower curtain. Nothing else. He wasn't here.

Matty went to turn the tap off, and stopped. There. Wedged into the grout, as if fossilised, was a single, gently golden hair.

***

'Yes, of course. We can adjust anything.'

Rosa was talking to a customer in the suit shop. You wouldn't know that anything was wrong. Her eyes had flickered over to

Matty for a moment at the sound of the bell, and now were back at the big man by the counter. Mrs Jackson was standing behind the counter too, holding a pair of trousers over her arm.

Outsizes a speciality, Matty thought, wandering past the shelves and rails, touching the odd suit, shiny and pressed flat. Minty green polo shirts were in a neat pile, with braces hanging next to them. Mamma did some tailoring at the back of the shop, where it wasn't tidy like out here, but full of material and tape measures and the loud clatter of the sewing machine.

Mamma would bring something leftover for Dad occasionally and make him stand taller, pulling back the shoulders, tucking up the cuffs, walking round him in a circle while Dad winked at Matty. He wasn't much of a suit guy. 'Weddings and funerals and that's your lot, thank you very much,' he'd say, when Mamma said how much better he looked.

The hair in the bathroom had definitely been his – Mamma's hair was raven-black and Matty's curled and never went gold, only a lighter grey-brown in the sun. Matty had emptied a matchbox and placed Dad's hair in it. Stored it under the bed. A piece of him.

The large man took the slip offered to him and turned, passing Matty. His face was really red, and his shoes were polished to the shine of rainforest beetles. He would definitely need an outsize.

As the bell rang on the door, Mamma's whole face and body sagged.

'You're doing really well,' Mrs Jackson said, and Matty lingered at the rail of pinstripe blazers, pretending not to hear. 'I'm sure it's the right thing to do. Keep your head down and work hard.'

'I want to keep my head held *high*,' said Mamma, and her voice was like a child's.

'No, of course you do, my love.'

Matty tried to picture being grown up and wearing a pinstripe suit. Bowler hat. Tie.

Mamma was blowing her nose. 'Go to the cafe. I will see you there,' she said more loudly, the first acknowledgement that Matty was even present, and disappeared round the back.

'Oh dear,' said Mrs Jackson to the room, in a sort of quiet sigh that really she wanted to be heard, and poked a handwritten slip on a spike. 'Right. Let me have a look at you.'

Mrs Jackson had a big mole at the corner of her mouth, and Matty often imagined tearing it off and putting it on top of a chocolate chip muffin. She stared, very close. Matty gazed past her to the stiff collars behind the counter. You could hear Mamma blowing her nose again.

'Your poor mother,' said Mrs Jackson. 'Look what he has done to her.'

The cafe was on the high street between home and Mamma's work. Dad liked to sit outside and read his paper there. Sometimes Matty would go too.

Today a pair of old Greek men were at one of the tables, playing cards. One of them was smoking a cigar. Matty sat down at the empty table next to them – it had a wobble, the pavement not quite straight – and watched the people walk past. Where did you go when you died? Didn't everyone turn into angels, unless they'd been really bad? Maybe only the best ones became angels and helped people, and the rest turned into ghosts and just hung around, waiting for people to get their Ouija boards out. Did they walk around in the street, in between all the normal people? Matty tried to look harder, *deeper*, into the air, past the two teenage girls blowing Hubba Bubba bubbles, past the man with the briefcase and the lady with the pram, until both eyes hurt.

'Hello, sweetheart.' The waitress with the dirty-blond hair was there. A tiny heart-flutter. 'Where's your dad? Not seen him in a few days.' Her voice was always the same, rough and croaky, as if she had a cold. An accent that was maybe Turkish or Greek.

'Um,' said Matty. 'How long ago? Exactly?'

'Oh,' she said, surprised. She had a thick, low fringe and bright pink eyeshadow all the way up to her eyebrows. 'I dunno. Not for a while, that's all. You just miss me, then?'

Matty looked at the menu, cheeks going hot. 'Just waiting for my mum.'

'*Ahh*,' she said. 'I'll give you two ticks.'

'What have you been doing this morning?'

Something had changed in Mamma. After work yesterday, she'd been nicer, the heel of her hand briefly resting on the back of Matty's head, but later she had been swearing, loudly, in the kitchen, and went all loud and quiet again on the phone to Italy. The broken bits of the Barnet mug were still in the bin. Now she was sitting opposite at the cafe on her continued hunger strike, drinking black coffee and watching Matty devour scrambled eggs and beans on toast.

'Nothing.'

'Perhaps you should be preparing for school. Reading some books.' She touched the side of her mouth with her little finger and looked at it. She had put on more lipstick, the colour of Superman's cape. Some of it was in tiny lines around the edge of her coffee cup.

Inside the cafe, the nice croaky waitress was leaning both elbows on the counter, talking to a man with a red and black leather jacket like Michael Jackson in 'Thriller', and tucking a lock of hair behind her ear. She was so pretty.

Mamma was still watching, with dark, slightly suspicious eyes, as if there was a dangerous mystery to be worked out. She craned round. 'Who do you keep looking at?'

'No one.' Matty sat up. 'I've been to the library.' Once.

'Good.' She sighed and lit another cigarette, and Matty imagined a director with an American accent behind a camera saying, *Get the shadows on her face. OK, Rosa sweetheart, let's do that again. Aaaand ... action!* 'Good,' she said again. 'You should go there.'

49

She smoked differently to Dad, like she hated and loved it at the same time. Dad treated his cigarettes like a friend, protecting them, looking at them fondly, sometimes letting them speak for him.

The waitress came out and put a plate of baklava on their table. One looked like a Shredded Wheat, and one like a torpedo. Both drenched in honey. '*Bak*-lava,' Dad had said once, with emphasis on the first syllable, sniggering, when Matty had said it wrong. He always ordered them. 'You don't cover your face in baklava when you're robbing a bank. And you don't eat a woollen face-mask. Not unless you're starving.' He'd laughed again and popped another one from their shared plate into his mouth.

'We didn't order these,' Mamma said.

'On the house,' the waitress said, and winked at Matty as she turned away.

'What was that all about?' Mamma said, seeming cross. She gestured to the plate of almost-finished beans. 'Finish that first.'

'Mamma?'

'Hmm?'

'Do you believe in angels?'

Mamma's glance was sharp. 'Why do you say that?'

'Just wondered.'

She didn't answer straightaway, gazing across the street. 'Yes, there are angels.' She tapped her cigarette against the edge of the ashtray. 'But he is not one of them.'

***

'The Lord be with you.'

'And also with you.' A little cross, made with the thumb. Forehead, lips, chest.

With its squat turrets, St Edward the Confessor looked more like a castle than a church from the outside, though knights

50

would be able to storm the walls easily enough. St Edward was the son of Aethelred the Unready, which was a rubbish name to have. If you were a king, you should be able to give yourself a good name. Aethelred the Crucial. Aethelred the Wicked.

'Lift up your hearts.'

'We lift them up to the Lord.'

Until the last two weeks, Sunday mornings had always been the same, rain or shine, and even though it had always felt starched and dutiful, it was OK to be back. Everything always happened in the same order and the same words were always said. Nothing was unpredictable. *I confess to Almighty God.*

Jesus was suspended in front of the big stained-glass window. He wore the sort of skirt that girls wrapped around their swim-suits in summer. Yesterday, Matty had gone to the library again as Mamma had said, looked at the photo of Harry Houdini, the legendary escape artist, hanging upside down with his feet in stocks. He was wearing an old-fashioned swimming costume, his head near the top of the tank of water, a padlock on the front. The Chinese Water Torture Cell. Matty imagined Jesus wriggling out from the nails in his hands and feet, sticking two fingers up.

I ask blessed Mary, ever virgin, all the angels and saints, to pray for me to the Lord our God.

It always smelt the same inside. Cigarette smoke and incense and perfume. All sorts of people came here – an African lady in long robes, a Sri Lankan boy in a blazer, Irish, Italian.

'Let us take a moment to reflect on our own sins,' said Father James. It went quiet, apart from the sounds of a baby doing little wolf-howls, and a truck roaring outside.

The day before First Communion two years ago, Matty had sat in the cramped cupboard, Father James on the other side. You couldn't really see him but you could hear his soft Scottish voice. Mamma had said that you had to tell him any bad things you'd

51

done or thought, and Matty had lightly kicked the wooden leg of the chair, totally stumped.

'Just tell him you've eaten too much chocolate,' Dad had said.

'But I haven't.'

'No matter. The man's not to know.'

'But I'd be lying. So then I'd have to confess that.'

'It's just a formality, you smart-arse.'

'When did you last go to confession?'

'I'd have to book the man out for a week,' he'd said, with a darkly amused look.

In the end, Matty had blurted something to Father James about pushing a boy over at football, which was not totally a lie and not totally the truth. 'You are absolved from your sins,' he'd said, from behind the wooden panel.

Matty stared at the thick neck of the man in front. Sins. What were Dad's? Mamma now seemed to think he'd done something bad. Mrs Jackson definitely did. Was it just him dying that had made her angry, or something more? Matty looked up at Jesus again. Imagined Dad strung up there on the cross, except less skinny, not all stretched with his ribs showing like an Ethiopian child off the telly. Joe the Drowned. Matty the Fatherless.

Later, Father James prayed for people. Margaret Devine, who was still ill. John Mark Frost in Australia, somebody's cousin. Sylvia Angelis. Matty waited for Dad's name. *And we pray for Joseph Ronan, one of our regular parishioners, who is missing, presumed dead, after valiantly carrying out black bag operations in brave service to his country, although I am not supposed to say, and for Matty Ronan and Rosa Ronan, who await his safe return.*

'Let us stand,' said Father James. He'd finished without saying Dad's name.

Mamma hadn't asked for him to be prayed for.

Matty didn't move.

'Up,' said Mamma, under her breath.

52

Everybody said the Creed, not quite together, a lazy, bad rap done by the Sugarhill Gang with the backing track turned down. Matty counted the number of times everyone said 'Father'. The Father almighty. Born of the Father. Consubstantial with the Father. The right hand of the Father. From the Father and the Son, who with the Father and the Son. Fatherfatherfather.

Dad was left-handed, anyway. 'Sign of genius,' he'd said to Matty, more than once. 'Sign of the devil in Italian,' Mamma had said.

Time to kneel. The leather whined, and was cool to the touch. Our Father. More fathers. Dad sort of looked all daydreamy when they were in church. 'Tell God I'll buy him a pint later,' he'd say if he wanted his lie-in, and Mamma would tut and pull Matty out of the front door.

Our Father, who art in heaven, which is hopefully Ireland without the crap, hallowed be thy name, Matty imagined Dad saying. *Thy kingdom come, thy will be done, on earth as it is in heaven. Give us this day our daily bread, make it a farmhouse loaf fresh out of the oven, and if you could see fit to have Barnet win a few bloody matches once in a while, that'd be grand. Forgive us our trespasses and all the rest.* Matty finished off with some Run DMC extra quietly, instead. *Amen.*

Bells were rung by the two boys, about Matty's age, who knelt either side and wore long robes over their jeans. Dresses, really. Father James always wore his white and cream dress, though you could see his scuffed, brown leather shoes. Jesus obviously didn't mind anyone wearing a dress.

The communion wafer was always claggy. A caramel wafer biscuit would be better. You didn't have to have the wine, but Matty did because it felt grown-up. Mamma was drinking more wine at home. Daily Communion. The bottles had been filling up the kitchen bin.

'Can I have ten pee?' Matty said, as they went out after the final hymn. 'For a candle?'

Mamma sighed, heavily, and opened her handbag.

Matty stared at the candle, ignoring the others. You were supposed to pray now. *This candle is for Dad. Please make him appear.* If he was dead, then at least his body needed to be found. Even if he floated up with a balloon-belly. If he wasn't going to walk back through the door.

On the steps outside, Mamma was talking to Father James, who held her hand between both of his. She always dressed like she was going to a posh party and not just church. Today she wore one of her black, shiny dresses and her thin caramel-coloured overcoat.

Father James's voice was gentle and furry. 'You know that you can come and chat to me anytime,' he said. 'That's what we're here for.'

'Thank you, Father,' she said.

Father James took her other hand and clasped it with the one he was already holding.

Her calm voice did not last long. Matty could feel the tension in her, winding up like she was a Jack-in-the-box as they walked back along Hoop Lane. 'Why are you so scruffy all the time?' she said, suddenly.

'It's the holidays.' Not more than a mumble.

'What?' She didn't wait for it to be repeated. 'You would not wear this in Italy. You are making me look like a terrible mother.'

You are right now, Matty thought. She used to sit at the kitchen table, helping with homework. Would get Matty to crack the eggs and mix the batter of whatever she was baking – chocolate ring cake, cheesecake – and hand over the wooden spoon to be licked clean. When had this stopped? It hadn't just been in the last few weeks. A year, or more, at least. Since football, and skateboarding and boxing. Hissing to Dad and stopping when Matty entered the room.

Normally there'd be a roast dinner after church. It would take Mamma half the afternoon, and Matty would eat peanuts to fill the hole until she called to have the kitchen table set.

Not today. Mamma let her handbag fall in the hallway and went and sat in the living room. Drew the curtains. TV.

Matty took two pounds from her purse and shut the door quietly on the way out.

Chapter 4

'Half a cunt,' said Nicks, snickering, before wiping a trail of watery snot that dangled from his nose.

Nicks the Weird.

Matty had been explaining about Edward the Confessor and Aethelred and Harthacnut, who was the Viking king before that. Nicks' swearing was strange, off-kilter. Dad would occasionally slip in a *feckin'* or a *bastard* or a *wee shite*, especially when talking about any Barnet opposition. Nicks said *shitwank* and *twat-hell*. *Bastarding blood-fuck*. Now he had a new one. Matty had never heard that word spoken out loud.

He *was* weird. Posh, silver spoon, end of his nose. He'd looked at the skateboard blankly. 'What is that?'

Matty had got on it, wheeled up and down on the changing area's concrete and done one ollie before a man who was doing some stretches said to stop.

'That is the stupidest thing I have ever seen,' said Nicks, and Matty couldn't help feeling disappointed, tucking it away under a bench before they went swimming again.

In the library, Matty had found more drowned people, and now looked for the *shui gui*, the Chinese water ghost from the encyclopaedia that dragged people underwater to steal their bodies. Looked for Ophelia, the painted girl from Shakespeare, who drowned in the stream with her flowers. Looked for Dad. But there was only Nicks, swimming all the way underneath Matty like a blurry beluga whale. There had been no explanation about disappearing last time, and no apology. Matty had just arrived at the Ponds, swum to the central platform, and got a sharp dig in the side.

'Where do you go to school?' Matty said now, sitting next to him at the grass slope end, goosebumps lightly rising. Maybe he'd be going to St George's, too.

'Don't go. Learn at home.'

That sounded *really* posh.

Matty watched the swimmers, imagining Harry Houdini in a straitjacket being lowered into a glass box that was itself then lowered into the middle of the Pond. Imagined Dad in the straitjacket, wriggling like mad. 'How old are you?'

Nicks glanced over. 'How old are *you*?'

'Eleven.'

'Older than you,' he said, and looked smug, putting his hands behind his head, eyes closed up to the sun.

Later, Matty went to the skate spot in the park nearer home. It was a flat stretch of concrete with benches and three steps – you'd get clusters of kids there after school and at weekends, as the nearest proper park was over in Camden. Dad would go with Matty on Sunday afternoons, hand in a packet of Wotsits, glancing over his paper. It was so annoying. Now it felt strange being there alone.

Kyle from class was there, with his older brother who seemed as tall as Giant Haystacks. Kyle wheeled up to Matty. 'Sorry about your dad,' he said, picking up his board and bashing it against his foot.

A pain, right in the chest. Maybe Johanna had told him, though they weren't really friends at school. Or maybe everyone knew. It was like having a handicap, like being in a wheelchair or in an accident. Sorry about your broken leg. Sorry your hand's fallen off. Sorry your dad's dead. Missing presumed dead. Unsalvageable.

'It's OK.' It wasn't OK.

Kyle took the Kurtis Blow cassette, and didn't seem to know what to say next. He dropped his board and ollied down the steps, clattering off, the board going AWOL. His brother headed towards the bench, ollied up and did an effortless rail slide along the edge. Normally Benedict would be here, or maybe Tyrone, and it would be in term time so they could talk about school things or football. But this summer was a bridge between an old world and a new one. Everything had to be reset, like shaking an Etch-A-Sketch.

It had been all right at primary school. Everyone knew Matty. It would be different, come September. Kyle would be going to St George's, too, though not in the same class. But he already had a big brother who would look out for him.

The memory of those big girls, shrieking.

Kyle wheeled back up. 'You going on holiday?' His voice had got a bit lower recently.

Were they? Normally they went out to Italy for two or three weeks in the summer, or sometimes half term, Dad joining them a few days in.

'Dunno,' said Matty, watching Kyle head for the steps again before following him.

***

Once, when Matty had gone into the living room at night, Dad hadn't been watching a war video but a film on the telly in which the actors all spoke like him. Black and white, with a grubby-faced boy and a man who was a tinker.

Dad hadn't said anything for ages, not like he normally did, explaining where the soldiers were attacking or why the bridge was being built. 'My people used to move about like that,' he'd said eventually, in a strange, distant voice.

Matty had looked at him. 'In a cart?'

'Almost. A caravan.' He'd looked over. 'You know the sort?'

58

'Yeah.'

'Well, my dad had one.'

'What for?'

'To live in. Know what travellers are?'

Dad had never said much about his family. He'd left Ireland at sixteen, the age you were when you'd done your O-levels. 'Not for me,' he'd said, finding Matty looking at a map once. 'The whole bloody lot of it.' His sister sent a card every Christmas, and Matty would read the writing and try and imagine what they were like. *Love from Maureen, Kevin, Carly and Michael.* So Matty had Irish cousins as well as the Italian ones. But they'd never come over.

The three of them had once gone on holiday to Ireland when Matty was seven, staying in a caravan, the normal kind. Dad had sighed the whole time and it had rained loads and he and Mamma had argued, more than usual. 'No wonder you left,' she'd said. 'Yep,' he'd said back, though he didn't really sound like he was agreeing with her. 'No bloody wonder.'

Gippos. Pikeys. You could get called that anyway if you looked a bit scruffy, or in the same way as getting called a dickhead or a jerkoff. Matty knew better than to tell anyone, even Johanna, after that night in front of the TV. No one liked a gypsy, even if Dad wasn't one anymore.

Matty had stayed up and watched the rest of the film, imagining Dad as the little boy from the 1950s riding on a horse or at the front of a gypsy caravan. Wearing a stripy waistcoat and a neckerchief. Maybe he hadn't liked being called a tinker.

Now, Matty sat on the floor in the hallway, looking in the address book. Maureen Ronan wasn't there. But then, if Maureen was married to Kevin, she'd have a different surname. Matty didn't find any Maureens at all.

Shouldn't they call someone? Surely they would want to know that he was gone, even if they only sent a Christmas card. Listening to Mamma loudly washing up her tea cups in the kitchen, muttering in Italian, Matty could not imagine asking.

***

It was better to hang around with Nicks. However odd he was, however much he thought that skateboarding was for dorks and didn't go to proper school, he didn't ask about Dad. He wasn't really interested in anything apart from the water.

With the *A–Z* and some trial and error, Matty had worked out the best route from the flat to the Heath. Hoop Lane, past St Edward's and the crematorium and the cemetery. Wild Hatch and the little white cottages with hearts cut into the shutters and iron rectangles on the windows. The overgrown alleyway, where you'd start really hearing the birds, chatting over each other in ten different languages.

Sandy Heath, Rotten Row, Spaniard's Alley, and then into the woods. The smells would become hot and green, dog poo and nettles and perfume, legs getting scratched by brambles.

You could always hear the road, or planes, just. But sometimes they got mixed up with the wind and Matty could pretend that this was not London but the middle of nowhere. *The arse-end of nowhere*, Dad would have said. Even during the weekend it was easy to find places to be on your own. Nestled up under a big beech tree or lying down among the leaves. Good climbing trees too. After some hiding and some thinking, Matty would go the rest of the way – over the top and past the view and the Mildred Himoff Lewis bench to find Nicks.

It had become a routine, though one never agreed out loud. They tended to meet at the Men's Pond – or *in* the Men's Pond, as Nicks would usually be submerged already. They'd swim, do some diving, and then sneak into the Not Allowed Pond. Nicks would only be in his old-looking trunks and never had any bags with him or even shoes – he must just run out of the back door of his house. He would laugh at Matty's goggles, ones that someone had left hanging up in the changing area, and ping the elastic at the back, hard.

The cold was no longer a shock but something to look forward to. Matty was getting stronger, exhaling underwater like you were supposed to, stretching arms out in front crawl. A forward somersault, water rushing in. Nicks swam strangely, like he was an eel, arms by his sides, often going underwater for ages and popping up again in a completely different direction from where you'd expect, or surfacing right behind Matty, bearing gifts. A waterboatman on his palm. Cotton-fluff. A frog once, its pulse beating in its throat. He would get really close to the moorhens and the mallards, almost enough to grab them, and they'd flap away squawking at the very last minute, Nicks squawking back.

Matty would wade through the mud as if there were rice paddies all around and not English trees, the dragonflies now helicopters firing napalm to the sound of loud orchestral music with trumpets blaring. Or would try to beat the world record for holding your breath underwater. The longest time in the *Guinness Book of Records* was 13 minutes and 42.5 seconds. But it was impossible to get past even a minute.

If Nicks wasn't around, Matty would swim in one narrow circle around the Men's Pond and then sit on the floating platform and watch the divers. There were all sorts of swimmers. City workers in their suits, taking their ties off. Orthodox Jews, the ends of their *peyos* going springy. A particular group sat on the weightlifting apparatus in the middle, men with massive arms and massive thighs, either lifting the weights or watching them be lifted.

Matty listened to people in the changing area. A butcher talking about getting a really big cow into the abattoir and his meat-saw being too blunt, and a man who drove a delivery van around London in half the time he was supposed to so that he could come here. But often everyone was quiet, just reading or drying off, simple hellos and comments about how cold the water was, or how it was better than yesterday by a degree. Hardly anyone ever took any notice of the kid in the corner, as if Matty was just as much part of this place as the damp concrete and the moss felting the corrugated iron walls.

Lots of them were naked. You weren't allowed to swim like that, but you could be naked on the enclosed concrete. No one seemed to care about it, and Matty could see their willies, all shapes and sizes. Some were really small, like little moles poking their heads above the soil. Some men's were longer and jiggled around more as they walked. They were different colours depending on whether the man had been for a swim or not yet. Different amounts of hair around them, small tufts or spreading down their thighs and up their stomachs.

Today, in the changing area, two men were talking about a baths in London where you could go and have a warm swim. One had an accent like thick hot chocolate, Greek or Turkish or Russian, and the other man would just murmur and hum occasionally.

The low wood of the gate scraped against the concrete, and there was a tiny gap in the men's conversation, before they carried on.

Matty looked up and froze.

A man was standing in front of an opposite peg, his back turned as he removed his bag. White clothes. The man who looked like Death. White boots, white trousers, and white suit jacket. The arms of his sunglasses were white and sat straight against his head rather than curving around his ear. He turned round, sitting down on the bench, and looked straight at Matty.

***

'You are such a wazzocky wanker. Fine. I'll go again.'

It was OK, Nicks being horrible. He didn't seem to really mean it and was always happy when Matty turned up in the Pond. He was like a whole packet of Fizz-Wizz. Right now, he was climbing back up the ladder to the walkway. He'd already done one backwards roll in the air, smashing down into the water, before clucking repeatedly. But Matty just didn't feel like it today.

'Ready?'

Matty trod water a little way from the board, looking around at the swimmers. Dad was never going to be here, not alive, but it was automatic to look. Just to check. 'Yeah.'

Nicks stood backwards on the diving board, craning round to check that Matty was watching. Flexing his shoulders, rolling his head.

A sudden chill. The Man in White. There he was again, doing breaststroke down the left side of the Pond, his grey-white hair the same colour as the goose down that floated on the surface of the water. He was still wearing his sunglasses. Maybe he had red albino eyes, like lasers. He was an albino and a spy, except you were supposed to not draw attention to yourself if you were a spy, or—

Matty thought of something. A Sunday afternoon film that Dad had insisted they all sat down and watched – one for all of them, he'd said. Mamma had pretended she wasn't crying and Dad had put his arm around her. It was a strange black-and-white one about a pilot in the Second World War whose plane got shot down, except the guide who was meant to take him to heaven couldn't find him. The pilot had to go to heaven to argue why he should be allowed to stay alive, and one of the people there had been a woman, with a white shirt and a crisp white suit. An angel.

A splash. 'Oi, dick-brain. Were you even watching?'

'Yeah.'

63

'Liar. I'm showing you how to do it.'

The man got out, climbing the ladder. His trunks were white. You couldn't see his eyes from here, and whether they were red.

'I have to go,' said Matty.

'What? You only just got here.'

Matty swam to the ladder. There was no time for being scared. Only for following, and asking him if he was an angel.

'Excuse me.' A sunbathing man wearing a gold medallion had his hand up in the air.

Matty had loitered in the changing rooms as The Man in White sat there, chatting to an older man and seemingly in no hurry to leave. After a while, it felt too conspicuous, and Matty wandered out, thinking to sit on the grass for a bit, watch the gate.

'Um, yeah?'

'Someone's trying to get your attention, I think.' He gestured up the slope, to the bushes, where the scarecrow-boombox man from the other day, the one who'd been with Daz, was beckoning.

'Afternoon,' he said as Matty got nearer. He was lying back on his elbows, looking sunburnt. 'You were away with the fairies there.'

Someone nearby laughed.

The man put his cigarette in his mouth and picked up an Our Price carrier bag. 'Right then, mate,' he said, through his cigarette, pulling out a cassette. 'Here you go.'

The tape was a blank one with small handwriting on the cover. A couple of things were crossed out.

'Cool,' said Matty, and handed it back, glancing back over to the gate, not wanting to miss The Man in White's exit.

His laugh was a short, sharp breath. 'No, you pillock, it's for you. Can't have a proper music fan getting behind with the times, can I?' The man sniffed and looked over towards the boating lake. 'Got my mate down at Spin-Offs to copy some stuff for me.'

'Thanks.' Matty gazed at it, unsure what to say next.

The man's look was like a friendly weasel – like the one from *Animals of Farthing Wood*. His cigarette smelt different from the normal kind. Burnt nettles. 'What's your name, then?'

'Matty.'

'Nice to meet you, Matty.' He laid a hand on his chest. 'Gegsy. Let me know how you get on with it.' He sat down and opened a magazine, a man holding a guitar over his shoulder on the cover. It seemed to be a dismissal. Back over towards the gate, The Man in White, now fully dressed, had just come out and turned right towards the boating lake.

'OK, see you,' said Matty, and swiftly descended the slope, after him.

***

The Man in White was walking through the Heath, up Parliament Hill. Matty followed behind, about ten paces away, hands in pockets, shorts still wet and chafing the inside of both thighs. Spying.

He really could be an angel. The other morning in the library, Matty had been reading about ghosts and angels, and came across the angel of death. Michael. An archangel was like the team captain, and he came down at the hour of someone's death, listened to their confession and then took them up to heaven. There was a painting of him, with golden curly hair and armour and wings. The Man in White didn't look anything like that – right now, he was stopping at an ice-cream van – but angels probably moved with the times. After all, the one from the old film had been a WAAF.

The man stood by the bin, peeling open the wrapper. It looked like a Mini Milk. He glanced up and Matty swiftly crouched down, put a hand in the grass, slicing lines into the middle of the blades with a nail. Maybe The Man in White went swimming at the Ponds just in case someone drowned, and then he could scoop their soul up and lob it into heaven. If he *was* the angel of death, then at least he'd be a witness. At least there'd be someone who'd be able to say *yes, your dad is dead.*

Matty looked up again. The man was walking away.

They came out of the Heath past Kenwood House, onto a wide road lined with cars. The man crossed over to the opening of a smaller residential street with a low gate by a green cabin and two signs saying PRIVATE ROAD. He paused there for quite a while, before the gate lifted up and he walked under.

Quick. Matty got to a couple of metres from the gate, scratching an arm, watching him walk away. The gate had lowered again. It would be easy just to duck under it. *Please tell me if you are an archangel.*

'Can I help you?' A security guard was calling over, beginning to stand up.

'No,' said Matty, too quietly to be heard, and walked away very quickly in the other direction.

Useless. Useless, and a chicken, just like Nicks always said, even though the diving had got loads better. Matty took the road homewards around the top of the Heath, thinking of how Nicks would have just distracted the guard, or shrugged and run under the gate anyway. It was easier with Dad around. No chicken-feelings then. Matty knew how to punch a person, at least with gloves on.

'You're going to be my little tough nut,' said Dad once, walking from the bus stop to the boxing club. 'Barry McGuigan of Golders Green. You'll get to the Olympics yet.'

'I'm not going to get in the Olympics,' said Matty. 'And anyway, he's a pro.'

'He fought in Moscow, smart-arse. 1980.' Dad tapped his temple. 'I know my onions. Anyway, you never know.' A wink as he looked over. 'I live in hope.'

66

They went to East Finchley every other Saturday morning in term time. Dad had sweet-talked Freddie, who ran the club, into it. Matty had learnt everything – the soft-kneed stance, guard, cross, hook. Bag work, throwing jabs, ignoring the blank, gum-chewing amusement of the tall teenage boy holding the pads. It was wicked.

Mamma never even knew about the boxing. Dad would just say they were off to the Underhill Stadium, going early to get a good place, though in truth the terraces at Barnet were never that busy. 'A white lie,' he'd say, touching his nose and winking. 'Those ones are allowed.' *White lies*, Matty would think, changing Grandmaster Flash's words. *Blowing through my mind.*

Matty would never get to go now.

***

That evening, Matty stood in the lounge, lifting a tin of baked beans with one hand and a tin of peach slices with the other, imagining the biceps bulging like the muscly men at the Pond. Playing one of Dad's tapes.

Gegsy's tape, though it hissed a lot, was pretty good. Matty had spent the later part of the afternoon sitting cross-legged on the carpet, rewinding it over and over again, scribbling the lyrics down on paper. The second song was best, with a cool bassline and the *swish-swish* of the record being scratched. It had girls behind the rapper on the chorus, shouting like the bikini girls from St George's. Words, rattled out fast. Matty always mumbled, got things stuck, felt shy. Dad was the one who was always talking. Learning more lyrics meant having more words, clever-rhyming sentences that could be stored up, repeated like prayers, like responses. Rapped in secret.

Now though, it was country music. Dad would joke about the singer's name. Matty Mattofferson. He sounded really old in the songs, but although there was grey in his beard, he didn't look that old on the cover. In fact, *he* looked like an angel, in his white unbuttoned shirt, playing his guitar. Or maybe like Jesus. Nice crinkly eyes. His songs were about women leaving him and drinking whisky and robbers and devils.

Mamma was back from work. A collection of sighs and things being taken off. A clunk on the kitchen top. Matty waited to hear the tap turn on. Instead, the fridge opened. The tiny pop of a cork.

The singer's voice was jaded, wrinkly sounding. Matty tried to imagine having a beard like his.

Mamma came into the lounge, glass in hand. White wine today, with condensation on the glass. She looked angry with the heat, even though she was Italian and always complained about England's rain. For a moment she stood there, her glass turned inwards towards her as Matty kept lifting the tins. Then she walked over to the tape player, and turned it off.

'I was listening,' said Matty.

'I do not want to listen to it.'

She liked Kris Kristofferson. That was one thing they'd agreed on. Joe Joseofferson, crooning away to Rosa Rosofferson about sunshine and rain.

Now, Mamma was still standing in the middle of the room, as if pretending to be on a set and waiting for a photographer to tell her where to move.

They did argue a lot. In public, they'd get quieter, not louder, little stabbing sentences while smiling on the outside, until they got home and could yell at each other. Mamma's voice always won, and then she wouldn't talk to him for a day or two. Matty would hide in games and books, put headphones on, and wait for it to be over. Usually, on those days or nights, only one of them would be in the kitchen later, banging plates if it was Mamma, or burning something in the pan if it was Dad.

'Why are you doing that?' She was staring at the tins.

'Exercise.'

'Don't be silly. What are you wearing?'

'Nothing.' It was one of Dad's T-shirts, far too big. The one with the sun and the palm tree on it saying *California*, not that he'd ever been there.

'Take it off.'

'No.'

She came over so quickly that it was almost frightening, and grabbed onto the T-shirt collar. Cold fingers from the wine. 'Take it *off*.'

Up, away from her hand. Matty dropped the tins and pushed past her to the bedroom. Slammed the door.

***

'Did I ever tell you how we got together?' Dad said, years ago, when he played this tape, as Mamma vigorously dusted the shelves.

'Yes,' said Matty. 'Three million times.'

'You monster. I'm going to tell you anyway, like it or lump it,' he said, before giving a happy sigh – typical Dad, easing himself into a story that he'd change a little bit every time. 'Your mamma was this foxy waitress in the cafe near work, looking like a Hollywood actress, and then she turns out to be Italian, which sends me just about over the edge.'

A half-flattered, half-dismissive sound from Mamma, who didn't turn round.

'So I work my magic on her and out we go to a dance, and I'm doing my moves like Elvis Presley, and she can't take her eyes off me—'

'More octopus than Elvis. It was hard to look anywhere else.'

'And we have such a good time that we're the last people out of there, and I belt out this Kris Kristofferson song to her on the street, or should I say *serenade*, and the lights in the houses next to us come on and a couple of windows open, and they applaud me and say I should be on the stage—'

'They said you had had too much to drink. Which was true.'

'Nonsense,' said Dad, standing up and taking Mamma's hand, and though she was reluctant and said that *someone* had to do the housework around here, she gave up and dropped the duster, her hardness falling away into smiles, and Matty watched the pair of them dance around the living room while he sang.

***

Later, in bed, there was the tiny, unmistakeable click of the back door, and three seconds later, another.

Every hair went prickly. It was him. He had come back, in the dead of night, after being away on his spy mission or his stakeout or his alien abduction.

Matty waited for the bottom step to creak. It would be fine if Dad just went to bed. He wouldn't want to wake his sleeping child. He would wait until the morning and be there, as if nothing had happened, toast and the paper and strong tea. *Morning to you, Bright Eyes. What time d'you call this? Trying hibernation on for size?*

There were more sounds, but outside. In the yard. Matty got up.

There were black iron steps going from the back door, ones that used to be scary as you could see right through them. They wound down in a spiral to a thin concrete area with a wall around it. The kosher supermarket underneath them had a larger yard over the wall with big bins. You could sometimes see packets of vegetables dumped in there, unopened.

There was a glow outside. Matty pressed up against the mottled glass. Opened the door a crack.

Outside, in their yard, there were flames, flickering, and next to it was a dark figure. It was the angel of death, come to take Matty's soul up to heaven.

70

No. It was Mamma. And she was burning things.

Matty stayed peeking through the gap in the door. She was throwing stuff into the metal bin and then standing back as the fire went up. The smell wasn't a nice fire-smell like on the Heath at Bonfire Night, but one that made you want to pinch your nostrils together. Rubbery.

In the morning, Matty snuck down early, before Mamma was up. Bare feet marked from the grille of the steps. The bin had gone black inside, and there were tiny bits that hadn't burnt through. Clothes. She'd been burning clothes. And—

Matty leant in carefully and picked up the small, part-melted grey rectangle. The brown tape ribbon had been pulled out and was tangled like hair. Some of the words were still visible on it.

Kris Kristofferson.

***

Rescue operation. If Matty didn't act fast, Mamma would incinerate everything. What if he came back and none of his things were there?

Mamma went to work and Matty got to work. Collected the not-folded jeans. Another of his T-shirts. Cufflinks, before deciding that he never wore them and putting them back. The pack of cards he cut and re-cut occasionally, the corners dead soft. The stubby blue pen from the kitchen drawer, the one without a lid that he did the crosswords with. He'd do the *Mirror* first – 'just revving my brain up' – and then the *Irish Times*. A lighter, though not his favourite yellow one because that would still be with him. Two of his other tapes, Merle Haggard and Johnny Cash. The matchbox with his single hair. Matty put everything in a carrier bag and wrapped it up tight with Sellotape before shoving it at the back of the bottom clothes drawer. Then remembered the bathroom.

There was the bottle of Paco Rabanne, heavy as a brick. Razor, nail clippers. Toothbrush. Matty wet it under the tap, brushed hard. His old, dried saliva, though it had probably all washed off. Dad would brush his teeth for ages. He said he did a lot of his thinking when he brushed his teeth.

Not that long ago, Matty had walked in and found him sitting on top of the closed toilet lid. He'd looked startled. His eyes had been glistening a bit. 'Christ, Matty. Out.'

A dad, *crying*. Matty brushed and brushed.

He'd been crying. Dads weren't supposed to cry. The only time Dad did was when *It's A Wonderful Life* was on TV at Christmas – *that* had an angel in it, too – and the man who wanted to kill himself at the beginning of the film got back to his family. There'd been a shine to Dad's eyes as they had all sung 'Auld Lang Syne'. But that time in the bathroom had been different.

Suicide. People had done that in water – made themselves drown, letting their lungs be filled on purpose. *Anoxia.* In the encyclopaedia, there had been a Chinese poet who held a rock and walked into the river, on purpose, to protest against the government. People beat drums and splashed at the water after he had drowned to keep the evil spirits away, and threw in rice as an offering. Virginia Woolf walked into a river with stones in her skirts. Was that what Dad did? Maybe he had wanted to die. He had taken a last tug on his cigarette, stubbed it out and walked into the Men's Pond with loads of stones weighing down his pockets.

There had been suicides there. Matty had read about them in that pamphlet. The boatman had pulled out a man who had been trying to drown himself.

The sure, slithery feeling along Matty's calf in the water. The *lookdeeper*.

Dad had been crying and there had been suicides in the pond. Maybe it hadn't been an accident.

Chapter 5

Hand on toast, hand in hair. Crumbs. His chair tilting as he ate, turning the page of his paper.

Early evening. Matty did the same now in the kitchen, toast-less, tipping the chair back onto two legs and holding the table to balance, as Mamma read a magazine opposite. Italian *Vogue*, her monthly luxury, delivered with the post. She was staring at each photo for ages, occasionally touching her face, before turning the page. 'You'd fit in there a treat,' Dad might have said once, nodding at it, a long time ago. 'I'd put you on the cover over that daft-looking one.'

Matty thought of the bold suicidal Chinese poet, and thought again over those last moments of Dad, the scraps of detail from the morning before the final day of primary school. Toast, hair, chair. Leather jacket. A kiss on Mamma's cheek when he left.

The chair came back down. That was it. Once, the kiss had been on the lips. When had it changed? Matty couldn't remember. Had Mamma turned her cheek to him first or had he gone for it?

'Can we have a Chinese?'

'What?' Mamma looked up from the page, a woman in a gold wraparound swimming costume holding a stuffed bird. 'You know I don't like Chinese food. It is too salty.'

'Can I get some?' Matty tapped out sub-machine gun sounds on the table, rapped a bit of Gegsy's new song very quietly.

'You don't like it either. Stop that.'

'I changed my mind.'

'Fine. Take some money.' Her eyes went as hard as marbles. 'You think I don't know you have been doing that?'

Matty stared back, defiant, like Han Solo or Princess Leia would look. How else did you feed yourself?

'Haven't seen you for ages,' said Nicks.

'Two days.'

'Yeah, well, seemed ages, dickface.'

They were sitting on the platform in the middle of the pond. The sun was out again, really hot, kaleidoscoping the water.

Matty snuck a hand into one pocket again to feel last night's leftover rice, two cool and sticky little balls wrapped in leaves from the woods at the top of the Heath.

Sometimes in the last year or two Dad would bring some takeaway back, even if Mamma had made dinner, and alternate a forkful of pasta and a forkful of prawn stir-fry. It would make her mad. More arguments. 'I'm a growing lad, Rosa.'

'You are disgusting.'

'I didn't know you were making me anything.'

'You did not ring to ask. You did not ring to tell me you'd be late. Again.'

He would say 'Ah, well,' in a sighing voice and carry on eating, or nudge his foil box over towards Matty, who would steal bits when Mamma wasn't looking. The ends of his hair a little wet, maybe.

Why would he want to die? Did he run out of money, like the man in *It's A Wonderful Life?* They weren't like Nicks, definitely not, but they had always seemed to have enough. Did he just suddenly feel really unhappy?

'I'm bored.' Nicks curled his fingers and put them in his hair, as if he was giving himself some sort of futuristic electric shock. 'Let's go find moorhens to scare.'

'In a sec.'

'It's so hot,' said Nicks. 'Come on, fuckarse.' And he bombed into the pond.

While he was still underwater, Matty rolled the rice balls in, one at a time, for the evil spirits. Just in case.

They walked out of the gate together to a loud whistle. Daz was standing up at the highest part of the grass in his small red trunks with a towel over his shoulders, waving. The grass slope was heaving with men today.

Matty looked at Nicks. 'Do you want to go over?'

Nicks was frowning up at them. 'Nah. Let's go to the other pond.'

Gegsy was leaning up on his elbows, gesturing Matty over, pointing at his boombox.

Nicks's face had gathered into a scratchy scowl. He dug a bare toe into the dust of the path. 'Got to go.'

'But you just said—'

'Got to go,' he said again and turned, stalking away, scuffing his heels so that little puffs of dust followed him.

Matty watched him go before weaving between the groups of men on the grass. Nicks didn't seem to like hanging around with anyone else. It was almost nice, like being kept a secret.

'Here's my little apprentice.' Gegsy was lying just in the shade of the biggest tree with long denim shorts on, the edges frayed. His skin was very white and you could see all of his ribs, and the tattoos on them. 'Got a new one for you.'

'Oh Lord, save me,' said Daz to anyone around him who was listening. 'He thinks he's a god.'

'Not a god. Just a teacher, innit? A guru.'

'The Beatles had gurus and it just meant that they went doo-lally on acid and made longer songs with less catchy tunes.'

Matty felt like the whole thing was a performance for an audience of mostly one. But it was fun, watching them pretend to argue, Gegsy grinning up at Daz with that slightly greasy smile.

Daz tutted. 'Giz us a blast, then.' Gegsy pressed play on his boombox and Daz looked intent for about five seconds before making a face like he'd just eaten a bad egg. 'Oh my stars, no. That is not nice. Make it stop.'

'It's your music,' said Gegsy.

'My music? What does that mean?'

'Black music. Your people.'

'Trust me, you vagrant, these are not my people. My people wear sequins. My people *sing*.' Daz put bunched fingers to his lips and threw them out in a star-shape. He focused on Matty, looking rather solemn. 'This man is giving you a wayward education. Do not trust him as far as you can throw him.'

'Why do you have to be such a bumboy all the time?'

'Because that is me. It is the essence of Darren Reid.' He kicked Gegsy's hip. 'Shove over. We've got company.'

Gegsy rolled over to make a sliver of space on the checked tablecloth that was spread underneath him. Matty sat down, legs crossed.

Daz took out a Pepsi from his cool box. 'Last one. Gone a bit warm.'

'I only have ten pee.'

'Oh, go on then. For the little starveling.' He put his hand out, before sitting down next to Matty with a short glance over. 'Your parents are throwing caution to the wind, letting you run amok.'

Matty never ran here, and didn't know what that last word meant. 'My dad came here.'

'Oh, yeah? He get you into it? Show you the wonder and the marvel?'

'Yeah.' Dad had, in his own way. Without realising it.

'Well, he's right to.' Daz sat up, his long arms around his knees. 'You'll learn a lot from being here. You get all sorts. Every sort of man. Gays, straights and all the colours in between. Old boys who fought in the war, some who talk about it, some who keep quiet about it, some who've been coming since *before* the war, butchers, bakers, candlestick makers, and Gegsy.'

'Cunt,' said Gegsy, his eyes still closed.

Daz made a little buzzy sound with his lips, like he was shooing something.

'He's called Joe. My dad.' There was always hope. Matty had not been doing enough to investigate. Getting distracted by Nicks. 'Do you know him? He's Irish.' Is Irish. Was Irish.

Gegsy shook his head, a small, lazy movement.

'Can't say's I do,' said Daz. 'I don't necessarily know names, just faces. Lots of familiar ones.' His voice became more dramatic. 'Some far too familiar.'

Matty tried to describe him. Not tall. Sandy, brownish hair, going a bit grey at the sides. A round nose, like the puppets in *Button Moon*. Leather jacket.

'Doesn't ring a bell. Have you lost him?'

'Yeah,' said Matty.

Daz sat up again and looked around.

'No, he's not here now.' Matty didn't say anything else for a long time, just listening to Gegsy's robot-music and looking up into the sun. 'Do you know anyone who has killed themselves?'

Daz and Gegsy exchanged a glance.

'Blimey, you know how to murder the mood,' said Daz.

'Why you asking that, mate?' said Gegsy, in a gentle voice.

'No reason,' Matty said, to the blanket.

'Most of us are trying hard to stay very bloody alive,' said Daz, and he sounded more serious than he ever had before.

No one spoke for a while, just watching everyone. The man holding the ball above his yappy dog. The swimmers coming through the gate, their hair wet. Three teenage boys lying very close together, their backs the colour of Super Shrimp sweets.

Two olive-skinned men standing doing bodybuilder stretches, all ripples, and other men pretending not to watch them.

Daz made a *tsk* sound. 'It's like bloody tourist season today. All the waifs and gays.'

'What was his name again?' said Gegsy, sitting up and lighting his roll-up again. 'Your dad?'

'Joe. Ronan.'

He nodded. 'I'll try and find out for you.'

***

It was becoming harder and harder to get up in the morning. Matty was aching again, as bad as being on a medieval rack.

Mamma opened the bedroom door. 'It's almost lunchtime.'

'Why are you home?'

'I forgot something. Why are you being so lazy?'

Matty went under the covers. 'It's the holidays.' Dad's not here. You don't care.

'If it was one hundred years ago, you would be working in a factory.'

'It's not, though,' Matty said with a mouthful of duvet. Wanting to cry and to punch things.

'Get up and eat something.' She shut the door.

In the kitchen, Matty opened one cupboard and then another. Peanut butter on bread again, maybe with crisps inside. Or beans.

They should be in Italy, with Nonna and Nonno, and Matty should be on the beach, looking back to see Dad watching and waving. Eating gelato, with Matty always having *cioccolato all'arancia* and Dad always having *fragola*. Playing arcade games with him in Rimini – Phoenix and D-Day – until Mamma came to tell you both that Nonna and Nonno were waiting and could Dad stop being a twelve-year-old boy.

78

She was mean. She was always mean to him. Had been for ages. When they argued, she would sometimes throw things at him.

Matty looked at the cigarettes on the table. Mamma had forgotten them.

Back steps, just outside the door, looking onto the yard and the bins. No one could really see.

Matty sat down, the concrete pressing coldly on the backs of both thighs, holding the lighter from the bag of things stashed under the bed. Dad smoked roll-ups, plucking the strands of tobacco from the tin, putting the little filter in, working the paper around it, all while holding a conversation, or shopping, or having the phone tucked between his shoulder and his ear. Matty would sniff the Old Holborn tin when no one was looking. It smelt of old ships and wet trees.

Mamma always smoked Silk Cut. She had a blouse in the same deep purple as the wrapping inside. Three left. The box smelt sharp and dry.

It took four goes to get the flame to come, and another two before it made the cigarette burn. Matty pinched the orange end more firmly and sucked.

A hot, bitter taste, like popcorn on fire. The cough came instantly, lungs spitting the taste back out with a *no thanks*. For the first few goes, Matty held the cigarette like Mamma would have, quite far away and seesawing between two straight fingers. Took little breaths in and tried not to cough again – because grown-ups didn't cough – and coughed each time anyway. As the cigarette got shorter, it was held like Dad's, fingers curling so that the lit end was turned inwards. A small, angry face, peeling back as the smoke ate away at it.

You could imagine smoke winding its way down, rubbing the inside of each lung. It hurt. Dizziness too, the line of roofs and the train bridge wobbling. Matty gave up and watched the rest of the cigarette burn, millimetre by millimetre.

'My brother says he's a poof.' Johanna nodded at the screen. Her family owned a Betamax video player, and she had recorded Live Aid so that she could watch it more than once. She and Matty were in her lounge, sitting on the thick carpet, with bowls of salt and vinegar and prawn cocktail crisps.

Freddie Mercury was in front of the piano. He wore a bracelet, a studded metal one, around the top of his arm. Lots of chest hair. You could see his nipples. He looked like a miner and not like a miner. Matty could imagine him in his white vest, hanging around with Daz at the Ponds. Now he was stalking around the stage, holding a microphone on a stand like a posh walking stick. A sea of people, more people than Matty had ever seen in one place, were singing along with him.

Johanna was looking over. 'Don't you care?'

'No.' There were poofs at the Pond. Holding hands. Daz was, wasn't he? It didn't seem to really matter.

'You like him anyway?'

They didn't have any hip-hop on Live Aid. It was all big bands, poodle-hair. 'Yeah. He's all right.'

The three of them had watched it at home with fish and chips on their laps, the week before Dad disappeared. 'What does he bloody look like?' Dad had said, nodding at Adam Ant.

'*You've* got a leather jacket,' Matty had said.

'Not with tassels, I haven't. It's a load of nonsense.' He'd waved a chip at the screen. 'Starving kids in Ethiopia aren't going to see a whisper of that money.'

'I think he is an attractive man,' Mamma had said, quite bluntly.

'Ah, sure. Well, you would.' Neither of them had been looking at each other. 'Not a bloody whisper.' He still got up later, when Duran Duran were on, and called the BBC hotline to make a five-pound donation.

'Have you been smoking?' Johanna said. 'You really smell of it.'

Matty shrugged and Johanna grinned, incredulously. 'You're going to be like one of the greasers from *The Outsiders*. Hold on.' She got up and left the room.

Matty was allowed to stay for tea. There'd be proper vegetables, even if they were always mushy. Kosher food didn't seem to taste any different – they still ate meat and potatoes and chips and things, although Johanna had once got Matty to describe the taste of a bacon sandwich to her, her eyes all sparkling. At least she was easy to talk to, unlike most girls. Matty had told her about the *Titanic*, the string quartet still playing even though facing ultimate death, and how drowning in the sea was different from drowning in freshwater, and that they would have got hypothermia and felt pretend-warm and died happy.

'Close your eyes,' said Johanna, coming back into the room with an aerosol can covered in flowers, and spraying it right at Matty.

'Agh.' A hedgehog-roll, on the carpet. 'What are you doing?'

'My mum will smell it on you. Won't yours go mad?'

Matty coughed, more than with the cigarette, before uncurling.

'I've got hairs on my fanny,' said Johanna, sitting down again. 'Well, one hair. I found it the other day. Have you? Got hairs?'

Matty stared at the screen. Freddie Mercury was playing his microphone stand like a guitar. 'No.' A lie. There were some down there, and a few little crimped ones in each armpit. It was horrible.

'Do you want to see?'

'Um. No, thanks.'

Now Freddie Mercury was beginning to play a real guitar. Doing 'Crazy Little Thing Called Love', another song that Dad liked singing while twirling Mamma around the kitchen, in what seemed like two hundred years ago.

'Do you want to go to your new school?' said Matty before Johanna did something scary like take her tights off.

Johanna was going to a Jewish high school where the boys and girls had totally separate buildings on different streets, and had already shown Matty the maroon blazer in her wardrobe. She shrugged, fiddling with her candy bracelet. 'Dunno.' She glanced over. 'We have to learn how to do spinning and weaving.' Pulled a face.

She didn't seem to mind too much really. Matty had no idea what to expect about St George's, except that it was massive, and further away, and that in PE the girls did netball and the boys did football.

Johanna was rewinding the video. 'I want to watch Duran Duran again,' she said, grinning.

***

It wasn't fair.

Night. Matty lay awake, everything feeling heavy and horrible. A sticky, hot anger. Thoughts were all mixed up together, Freddie Mercury in his vest, Johanna's fanny hairs, Nicks, Dad, the pondwater. Matty rolled over and put a fist between both thighs, pushed against the bed. A gentle bruising throb.

'Fuck.' The word seemed especially loud in the thick air of the bedroom. If Matty was a rapper, there'd be a volley of words, tumbling out easily. 'Fuck fuck fuck.' It wasn't fair. 'It's not fucking fair.' Pyjama bottoms off. T-shirt off.

Less of that, Dad would have said. *Less of that right now, you tyke. Think of your mamma's ears.* He wouldn't have thought much of Nicks and all his swearing.

Pants off.

'Fuck you.' Fuck him. He wasn't here, and Nicks was. Nicks and Johanna and even Daz and Gegsy and all the men who would say hello at the pond. The South African lifeguard, whose name was Alexander.

Dad, singing Kris Kristofferson songs in a twangy American accent. *'Cause this morning, she's just leavin', but come sundown, she'll be gone.'*

'You're gone.' A louder voice, to drown him out. 'You're *gone.* Fuck fuck fuck.' Matty grabbed a handful of the wall walkers that were on the desk by the bed and threw them at the wall. They monkeyed down, one at a time, as if falling down into hell, their hearts too heavy and being missed by St Michael, who was too busy eating Mini Milks in his posh house by the Heath.

Chest pain. Matty let both knees sag and bounced onto the bed, lying down again. It hurt on both sides so it wasn't a heart attack, like you'd get if you were drowning in seawater, going hypertonic.

A pillow, over eyes, nose, mouth.

'Matty.' The door had opened. Mamma's voice.

'Go away.' Spoken through the pillow.

'Go to sleep.'

'Go *away.*'

She sat down at the foot of the bed. A hand on one bare thigh. Stroking a bit. She used to sing a lullaby and brush Matty's hair before bedtime. *Fa la ninna, fa la nanna, nella braccia della mamma.*

Matty moved it. 'You don't care.'

'What?'

'You don't care.'

'Go to sleep, *amore.*' She was sounding calm, and gentle, like old times. *Fa la ninna, bel bambin.*

Matty was becoming more like Mamma, going up and down, a Jack-in-the-box. 'Fuck you.' Mumbled too quietly to be heard.

It was getting hard to breathe. There was a wall walker digging into one ear.

Mamma got up and the door shut. The heat from her hand dissolving. Matty took the pillow off, face oven-baked, and stared back up at the plastic stars.

In the changing area, two old men, both naked, were playing badminton with wooden paddles. One man was really tanned and creased, and one was much whiter. Their willies were the same length as the shuttlecock that was arcing back and forth between them. It made a little pocking sound against the rackets.

Matty couldn't have imagined Dad walking around with no clothes on in here. But maybe he had. He was quite skinny, apart from his belly. 'How did that get there?' he'd say, looking down at it as if it only appeared when Matty prodded it. 'Must've swallowed a football.' And he'd prod Matty back, tickle mercilessly. He used to come out of the bathroom with messy hair and a towel round his waist and put his wet arms around Mamma.

'Hello, hello.' Gegsy came into the changing area, dripping, just as Matty was putting a trainer on. One of the tattoos on his ribs was of a snake twisting round a stick. He pointed, one eye shutting. 'I've got someone for you to meet, if he's still outside. Chop chop.'

'No promises or anything, mate,' Gegsy said as they went out of the Pond gate, a towel round his neck like a scarf. 'I just asked around a bit. There he is.' He nodded up onto the grass.

It was him. The Man in White. Sitting on a large white blanket. Gegsy knew an archangel. Matty's heart beat faster as they walked up to him.

'This is Clive,' said Gesgy. 'This is Matty.'

The Man in White put down the book that he was reading, the pages splayed. There was a picture of a person on all fours, but cut in half, on the front. 'Hello there,' he said. His voice was quite low for someone so small, with an itchy rasp to it.

Gegsy sat down on the grass next to the white blanket. 'This geezer knows everyone.'

Matty stayed standing. The man had a pale grey moustache which you'd only notice close-up. *Everyone.* He'd seemed like a loner.

'So, Joe,' the man said. 'Irish chap?'

Nod.

'So high?' He nodded over to another man who was standing up, smearing suntan lotion over one shoulder.

Nod.

'Liked a cigarette? Barnet?'

'Yeah.'

'I know him. You look like him.' He exchanged a glance with Gegsy, who raised his eyebrows. The man had pronounced high veins in his arms like they were straining to burst through the skin, and a copper bracelet round one wrist, thin lengths of metal plaited together. 'He gone walkabout on you?'

Matty looked over at Gegsy. 'Yeah. I think he might have drowned.'

'Ah, mate,' said Gegsy. 'Jesus, what? In here?'

'Yeah.' Or the Not Allowed Pond. 'Or killed himself anyway.'

'Jesus,' Gegsy said again. 'Where's your mum?'

'At work.'

'She OK?'

Matty shrugged. Mamma didn't care. She was angry and she hated him and she was glad he wasn't there.

The Man in White, Clive, put a hand up. Removed his sunglasses.

His eyes were brown. Really dark brown, like a Galaxy bar. Not red. He put his head to one side and looked at Matty, and his eyes seemed to get deeper. 'He might have gone away,' he said. 'But I reckon you'll see him again.' A smile. 'One day.'

***

'No, jump. Then wait. Jump now.'

Matty and Kyle sat at the kitchen table, hunched over Turtle Bridge. Their friend Benedict, whose dad sold expensive cars, lent his games out at one pound a week, or 50p for the weekend. You had to jump on the backs of turtles across a lake to get a delivery to the man on the other side. It wasn't as good as Benedict's new game, Gauntlet, where you could be the man wearing the loincloth or the girl wearing the leather swimsuit, and you had to move through the different worlds, the Castle and the Lost Caverns, to get the Sacred Orb.

Jump. Wait. Jump. 'Skill,' said Kyle. He'd just had his head shaved, the sides really short. Already, he seemed different this summer, stiffer, trying to be as cool as his brother. Not like Nicks, who didn't care what anyone thought of him.

'You'll see him again,' Clive had said. 'One day.' But had he meant that Dad was alive or was he talking about heaven? If Clive was an archangel, he'd know that Matty would see him again. As long as Dad had been good enough and confessed all of his sins.

The door. Mamma came into the kitchen, putting her handbag down. 'Hello, Kyle.'

'Hello, Mrs Ronan.'

She turned the kettle on, before leaning against the cupboards. No one spoke, and Kyle kept looking between them. Matty continued playing, the game making its little spitty electronic sound, a bit like Gegsy's music.

Kyle stood up. 'OK, I'll go now.'

'You don't have to go,' said Mamma. 'Have you had something to drink?' Why was she suddenly saying normal mum things?

'My dad said to be back for tea. Yeah, I had a Lilt before. Thanks. Bye.' He disappeared, very quickly.

The kettle bubbled, shook, and clicked off. Mamma didn't move. She was probably deciding to have wine instead.

Matty's eyes remained fixed on the turtles. Jump. If she wouldn't say anything about Dad, then there was no point in saying anything at all. Jump. Jump. Wait.

Mamma seemed to watch for ages. 'You are going to get your hair cut.' No more nice normal mum.

All this time, and she'd still never properly said anything about Dad. All this time. 'Don't want to.'

'Why not? You would embarrass your mother?'

'No.' The man on the other side wasn't there to pick the parcel up. Wait. Jump.

'You look ridiculous.'

It wasn't long. Just – a bit unruly, like bramble bushes in your eyes. 'I like it.' Jump.

'You are going to a new school. You are not a child any more.' She took in a long, jagged breath. Matty glanced up. 'Things have to change.' Her eyes steeled, and her voice, too. 'You will get it cut before school starts. You *know* you look—'

'Where is he?'

She took a breath, as if she was going to say something more about hairdressers, but just stood there with her lips apart. A bus roared past outside. 'I don't know.'

'Is he in heaven or hell?'

Mamma leant forward, and her sentence was chopped up. 'I. Don't. Know.'

She left the room, and Matty watched as the boy missed a turtle and sank abruptly to the bottom, bubbles coming out of his mouth.

***

'Want some?'

Nicks looked at the Orangina bottle, half-full. 'What is it?'

They were sitting among the leaves of the tall trees by the Not Allowed Pond, having already been in.

'Not Orangina.'

Over the last three days, Matty had laid low. If Mamma was around, it was a quick dash to the bathroom, or in bed pretending to be asleep, or out, as swiftly as possible. That way she couldn't bring up haircuts, or clothes, or anything else. That morning, Matty had taken the remains of two wine bottles that Mamma had left, one on the floor of the pantry and one in the fridge, and poured them into an empty bottle. She hadn't seemed to notice, because she was always getting a new one.

Nicks took the bottle and smelt it. The liquid was a rosy pink colour and fizzed a little bit. 'Smells like disgusting wank.' He handed it back, and started singing the odd words he'd been singing earlier on, *binoree o binoree*.

Matty had thought Nicks would have smoked and drunk and everything by now but in a lot of ways, he was like a baby. He didn't know anything, even though he was taller and older. He scowled again as Matty tipped the bottle up and drank.

Things have to change, Mamma had said, meaning Matty had to grow up. Well, this was growing up.

It was like communion wine mixed with vinegar. It *was* disgusting wank. But Nicks was watching, so Matty drank again, and again, trying to keep the gaps short.

'Shit for brains,' Nicks said. 'Why are you drinking something you don't like?'

'I do like it.'

He sent over a look that was much older suddenly, his eyebrows coming in sharply towards each other. 'Sing me a song.'

'I don't know any songs.'

'Liar. Massive liar.' Drops of water were drying on Nicks's skin, golden and green.

'Can't sing.'

'*I* can't sing. Who gives a monkey-dick-fuck?'

Matty mumbled something.

'What's that? Can't hear you.'

More mumbling.

'You're just saying the words.'

'They're supposed to be said. They're rap. MC-ing.'

'MC for Mental Case. Go on, do a bit more *rap*.'

Neck going hot, Matty did a few lines learnt from Gegsy's mixtape.

There was a long pause, before Nicks burst out laughing. 'That is hysterics.' His shoulders shook. It didn't even matter that he was laughing. It was nice.

'Do you want to come and watch TV at my house?' The words rushed out.

'What?' Nicks was still laughing, little dying-away ones, as he scraped at the underside of a stone.

'TV. At my house.'

'Nah.'

It was ridiculous to press further, ask him to come to Golders Green, sit in the lounge. Mamma would just stare at him funny, anyway. She'd think he was a weirdo. But it was disappointing, how uninterested he was – maybe it was just a convenience, Matty being around. He was just waiting until someone better came along.

'Ah yeah, that's the shitbomb,' Nicks said, suddenly jumping up and immediately squatting on his heels. 'Wanna do something different?'

'Like what?'

'You'll see. Meet you at midnight.'

'But – I can't come out that late.'

Nicks stuck a finger up his nose and dug something out of it. 'Who has to know?'

He watched as Matty finished the bottle, stomach gurgling. He didn't seem very impressed. It probably wasn't the right time to pull out the last two Silk Cut cigarettes and Dad's lighter from the rucksack.

'Pondwater for me,' he said, and waddled down to the edge on his haunches before falling face-first in the water, his legs staying bent, feet in the air. He was doing it on purpose, trying to be funny. He could tell something wasn't right, even more than normal.

89

'*That* is disgusting.' Matty's stomach was burning.

Nicks rolled over, spitting out water in a plume. It was shallow enough for him to sit up, and he plunged an arm down, bringing it out covered in mud – dark, gloopy stuff that dripped from his palm. In a quick movement, he swiped it all over his face.

Matty burst out laughing. It was the first time in ages. Ages and ages. Since before Dad. It was the funniest thing.

Nicks was standing up, his whole forearm still black with pond mud. He made a garbled monster sound, and waved his hands, fingers clawed.

Matty was laughing as much as Dad used to do at *Spitting Image*. When had Dad last laughed?

Nicks waded out of the pond, growling, and Matty scrambled up. Everything went a bit dizzy, like the trees were falling in on themselves. 'No.' Giggled more.

'*Yes*,' said Nicks, as he advanced, in a dastardly villain-voice. 'There is no escape. I am coming for you.' He wiped his palm right down the side of Matty's cheek.

Wriggling didn't help. Nicks grabbed onto a shoulder and wiped the other cheek. He was really close, but in a different way from in the water. His hand was cool and his eyes were gleaming. He drew his middle finger all the way down from the crown of Matty's head. Nose. Lips. Chin.

Tribespeople. The Tribe of the Not Allowed Pond.

'There,' he said. 'Now you're mine.'

An exclusive tribe of two.

Matty stopped giggling and went still, blood pumping loudly.

Nicks's crooked grin slowly disappeared. 'What are you?' he said, in a different voice. Not accusing, just curious. Careful.

'What?' The word sounded tiny.

His hand was still on Matty's shoulder. 'You know what I mean.'

'No, I don't.'

Somewhere, there was a goose cackling. Nicks slowly turned his middle finger round so that he was swearing. But he still didn't move.

Matty swallowed, and felt the taste of it wind downwards.

Then leant over and was sick on his feet.

***

Dad and Mamma's bedroom again, hand ghosting over the pattern on the bedcover.

Nicks had yelped and dashed into the pond, hopping up and down, splashing his feet loads and using all of his swearwords before helping Matty wash off the mud and climb back over the fence. 'Nutcase. See you tonight,' he'd said, with a grin, before disappearing.

No tea tonight. Not even *thinking* about eating tea. Matty had been sick again into a bin on the way home and a girl had said 'gross' as she'd walked past. It was horrible, and the smell of the bin had made it worse. No communion wine, ever again. How could Mamma could drink so much wine and not be sick? Dad too, his wine in Italy, his beers after the football. Shit-skank piss-breath disgusting wank.

Their bedcover had diamond stitching, like a Pac-Man trail. Everything was neater in here than it had been in the first couple of weeks. It smelt better too, less stuffy. Less like that bin.

Matty opened a drawer. It was half-empty.

Mamma had taken all of his clothes out. Just her things on one side, and the peeling drawer liner with the blue flowers where his underwear and socks normally were. Next drawer down, same thing, a space where T-shirts and polo shirts went. Some of them had been burnt in the bin that time, but not *everything*.

She was rubbing him out. Using Tipp-Ex and not writing him back in over the top.

It made the achy feeling come, along with a loud, fizzing fury.

91

Matty gathered all of Mamma's blouses and shirts in both hands, cotton and silk and polyester, and threw them on the floor. Took out all of her underwear, her pants and bras with the wires in and the silky vest and dumped them on top. Unscrewed a perfume bottle. Emptied it out onto the pile.

Lipsticks. Matty broke one off and clenched a fist around it, watching as the red sludge oozed its way between each finger. Hand open again. It looked like a strange hoofprint, blood-red. Matty looked in the mirror, waterfall sounds rushing in both ears, and put some on.

Bottom lip. Top lip.

'What are you doing?' Mamma was there, hand on the door-frame, mouth open.

Matty went to stone, a lipsticky finger held in the air.

Mamma's mouth shut, slowly, as her eyes moved around the room. 'What are you doing?' she said again.

Cold, real fear. Maybe this was how Dad felt sometimes, when they were arguing. She might throw things.

Mamma sat down on the edge of the bed. 'Come here.'

Matty moved as slowly as possible, as if through pond-mud. Sat next to her. Still feeling sick, wobbly. Head hurting.

She looked at the lipsticked finger and palm. Face. Leaning back, Mamma plucked a lilac tissue from the box by the side of the bed and took Matty's jaw in her hand. But instead of wiping it all off, she went around the mouth in a long line, her face still with concentration. You couldn't tell what she was thinking. Then she dipped a finger into the lipsticky mess in Matty's palm and added more to each lip with a light, precise pressure. The feeling of being a doll, held too tightly. Of wanting to please her, just this once.

'You might as well put it on properly,' she said, her voice cool and faraway. She was as close as Nicks had been earlier, the white of his eye and the white of his teeth. She frowned. 'What is that?'

Matty had got most of the mud off, but there was a still a smudge on one temple. 'Nothing.'

She picked out another tissue, licked it and wiped at the mark, before turning Matty by the shoulders to face the mirror. Red lips to go with red, tear-stained cheeks. Would Nicks like it better like this?

'You will clean this up.' Mamma was looking at Matty through the mirror, the firmness back in her voice. 'All of it.'

'OK.'

'And brush your teeth. Your breath does not smell good.'

Chapter 6

Matty waited until all the sounds of Mamma had stopped. TV. Wine glass down on the kitchen counter. Her slippers on the stairs, the creak on the fourth one from the top. Tap running. A few muttered words in Italian. The bedroom door shutting and the short thud as the headboard hit the wall. The finger-click of the light going off.

11.30 p.m. It was still hot, the room muggy. Matty slipped out from underneath the duvet, already dressed, and moved through the flat like a burglar. Missing out the creaky stair, leaning down to wiggle each trainer on. The front door was closed a millimetre at a time.

It was too dark to go through the woods the normal way. Matty took the main road up towards Hampstead, head down. It seemed better to walk than get the bus, so as not to draw attention. But it was like being a ghost – apart from one lady with a briefcase who had an acute stare as she opened the gate to her house, no one seemed to care that an eleven-year-old was alone at this time of night. You just had to look like you knew what you were doing.

Light slowly dwindled. There were fewer cars here, big houses lining one side of the road, the Heath lurking on the other. Matty veered into the car park, heart beating louder, and took the first path.

There were still people here, shadow-figures walking outwards rather than in, talking in low, sun-loosened voices as they headed for the road or the train station. You could only make them out once they were passing – a big man, two girls carrying picnic blankets, an older man with a walking stick.

Night scrubbed away familiar things and drew new, sharper ones. The black trees had different shapes against the sky. The moon, almost full, was the brightest sight now, not streetlights or cars. It made the algaed water of the first pond seem like a soggy lawn, one you could step out onto.

The second path grew darker as it climbed a shallow hill. It felt like walking into a black hole, leaving light and humanity behind. Each tiny sound flared and made Matty's breath lurch, the crunch of a twig on the path or a dog distantly barking. Further up, there was a fire in a clearing, and a group sitting around it. Matty stopped dead, dropped down onto a knee. Private Ronan, US army, Golders Green division. But there was only the snap of wood and lazy laughter, and someone saying some words in a different language, over and over, a chant. A shriek.

From the top of the Heath, London looked like a distant fairground, the NatWest Tower and the Post Office Tower blinking, the curve of St Paul's. Up here, there were clumps of people who had probably not moved all day, spread out on the grass or the benches. The air was still warm, and no one wanted to go home. Cigarette ends glowed. There was the tinny sound of a boombox playing a loud, sad song. The moon was fat as a new blister.

Almost there. Matty took the path down the hill towards the swimming ponds, back into the shadows. There were layers of darkness in the bushes to the side, dark becoming darker. It was better to be in the swamps in Vietnam, leading a platoon through the sweaty-leafed jungle, rifle attached to a canvas rucksack, wearing a bullet-belt.

A sudden rustle, and a man stepped out from the bushes. 'All right?' he said.

Matty walked on, fast, imagining spraying the man with bullets, not looking back until the corner. He had gone, the outline of the hill a long doodle against the sky.

'Oi, wanker.' A voice, low and stabbing as Matty jerked back, heart heaving. There was a laugh that could only be one person.

Matty pushed Nicks in the shoulder. 'Dickhead.'

His teeth flashed, moon-coloured. 'Where've you been? I've been hanging around for ages.' It was only a bit after midnight, just like they'd agreed. 'Come on,' he said, and walked ahead.

It felt easier, now that Nicks was here. The two of them moved like water. They passed a dog with coloured lights around its collar, and a man jogging, wearing a head torch. The air was humid and smoky.

They walked up to the end of the single-track road and along into the much gloomier lane, high fences on one side and woods on the other. There was the squeaky sound of a goose. Nicks was always a few steps ahead.

A sudden, muted rub of leaves to the side, a branch breaking, and this time Matty wasn't frightened because Nicks made them both invincible. There was a movement behind tree trunks, something pale.

Nicks turned round. 'What?' He peered into the trees. 'It's nothing.'

It could be Dad. Dad's ghost. You'll see him again, The Man in White had said. 'There's someone down there.'

'More than one, I reckon,' Nicks said, with a grin before he sighed and sauntered back, the long stick he'd picked up trailing behind him. 'Come on, then. If you want to see.'

Matty ducked under the railing and followed him down the narrow path of half-trodden leaves. Nicks seemed taller in the dark, his limbs relaxed and moving easily. He stopped suddenly and put a finger to Matty's lips, the quickest touch, and jabbed the same finger over to the right.

An agitated sound, twigs tangling and shifting, as if a large animal was there. A badger, trapped – except you didn't get badgers here – or something bigger. A lion. Tiger.

Matty's eyes adjusted. There was a person lying on the ground a few metres away, made whiter by the moon falling through the tall trees. *Two* people, one lying on top of the other, angled strangely.

Another rustle, and the shapes suddenly made sense.

They were moving, or the one on top was. Two men, one making a strange whimper, again like an animal. They were naked, or mostly naked, trousers rolled down one man's ankles. Neat black shoes.

'Fuck off.' The man had an accent, indefinable. He hadn't turned round.

Nicks grabbed Matty's arm and pulled.

'Or you can stay and watch.' Another voice, higher and muffled, and a tiny laugh.

Nicks dragged Matty back the way they had come. 'Seen enough now?' he said. 'Pervo.'

The Ladies' Pond was a new world. An oyster that Nicks was opening up. They had climbed over the padlocked gate and down a short, winding path to a much wider wooden platform than at the Men's, and two huts. This pond was smaller, surrounded by trees, with a single patch of moonlight in the middle. Enough to see by, as they climbed down the metal ladder into the night's water.

Matty's skin sang. It was no cooler than during these last hot days, but it tasted different. Milky-clean. There was a balmy smell in the air.

White tyres dotted the water and Matty swam from one to the other, trying to keep up with Nicks, who moved with hardly

a ripple and kept disappearing under the surface. In the middle
of the pond, two fat ducks sat on a nest on one tyre, not moving.
They must have been asleep. What did ducks dream about?

Nicks was at the furthest end of the pond, holding up the rope
to show that he was going past it. During the stretch between the
next two tyres, there was a little gassy sound, a sharp puff of air
from somewhere, and Matty turned, a quick panic of arms, heading
for the platform again. Waiting for Nicks to come back.

They'd been doing it, those two men. Sex. Matty had only
ever seen people having sex under the covers on TV – or the
start of it before Dad had glanced over, amused, and put his
hand over Matty's entire face. But that had always been a man
and woman. This was like what Freddie Mercury might want to
do, if he was a poof. Maybe it had been Freddie Mercury. No.
No moustache. Matty wanted to ask Nicks who they were, and
if he knew them. Were they always there? Were they getting
AIDS? He hadn't seemed surprised, but this was his Heath. He
knew it all, and he probably knew everything that went on. All
its day people, and all its night people. He seemed to move
between them seamlessly.

Nicks was suddenly close. 'Turn over.' He was hardly speaking
above a whisper, and yet his voice was loud, burrowing.

Matty rolled in the water and looked upwards. Took a breath.

Stars. An explosion of them, a paintbrush flicked at the sky.
The saucepan outline of the Plough. The Little Bear. Orion's
belt, one, two, three. Matty made a star-shape and floated, a
water-star looking at sky-stars.

Something soft touched the outside of Matty's fingers. A leaf.
Not a corpse. It was just a leaf, sliding along one arm. The only
sounds were of breath, long and slow through closed lips, and a
crinkly sound in both ears. Nicks was floating on his back in
just the same way, the moon on his face like a simple mask.

Maybe he had come here. Dad. Lookdeeper. Maybe he came
here one night, like the two of them, because this pond had an

extra magic. He had swum out to the far rope, and something had happened to make him sink, cough, swallow the water. Or this was the place he had chosen to sink under, rocks in his pockets. Laryngospasms. No one would know.

Matty kicked once, enough to drift closer to Nicks. Two stars almost joined, a tiny constellation. There was the feel of Nick's hand, cool and light, as they were gently moved by the water.

Nicks linked a little finger with Matty's little finger.

A single streak of cloud sat under the moon, like an arrow had just whizzed past it.

Voices began to emerge. Two figures appeared from between the buildings – girls, laughing, accompanied by the clink of bottles in a bag. Nicks turned and became a fish, quickly slipping through the water towards the ladder.

Matty walked down the dark lane, made of water and night. Nicks had gone with his usual abruptness, a quick, muttered 'see you' after climbing back over the padlocked gate. It didn't matter. It was just how he was.

At the single-track road, the streetlights were shocking, a shot between the eyes by the Vietcong.

***

'You look terrible.' In the morning, Mamma put a hand to Matty's jaw, and lifted. Her eyes narrowing. But no suggestion of Calpol, or warm squash, or hot Nesquik, as she used to do.

Matty *felt* pretty terrible, now. Not a wink of sleep, the curtains left open, lying on top of the duvet all night staring at the street-lit slice of sky. Glowing.

Most of the day was spent in bed, moving between a dream world and a real world. Matty had a bird's beak and was reading *Secret of the Ninja* and wearing a straitjacket except it was made of dressing-gown material. Mamma was moving about downstairs. Matty had to jump on the backs of crocodiles and made a chocolate cake with Nicks, who put his hands in and couldn't get them out again. Matty smoked the second-last cigarette from the packet of Silk Cut on the back steps, which was still horrible, but not as bad.

There was a sound like a big gong at the beginning of movies sometimes. Matty woke up again and stared at the ceiling. Murmurs of a voice downstairs, as if underwater. Feet thumping. Was Mamma still here? You always knew when she was at home – all of her sounds were distinctive.

Burglars. It could be real burglars. Mamma had always said that people were bad in London and you never knew who would want to take things from you, on the street or even in your home. Had Matty locked the back door earlier?

Another noise. There was definitely someone there.

Down the stairs, just as silently as last night, holding a Snarl Dinobot Transformer – at least its backplates were sharp. A shuffling sound in the living room.

Tactics. Just take one peek, and then make a break for it out of the back door and run downstairs to the kosher supermarket. Dial 999.

Matty was a fireteam corporal, cheek against the bark of a tree. Carefully rolling round the door frame to scope out the enemy sniper.

It wasn't a burglar.

Mamma was home. And she was with Sanjit.

It was like the moment when the camera stopped at the end of *Butch Cassidy and the Sundance Kid*, except instead of seeing Robert Redford and Paul Newman pointing their guns at everyone, there was Mamma sitting on the sofa next to Sanjit. One of her legs was over his leg, and one of her arms was behind his neck, her hand in the hair on his balding head. Her other hand was on his trousers. On his *lap*.

They both saw Matty at the same time.

'Oh, bloody Nora,' said Sanjit, standing up. 'Bloody hell, Rosa.' His cheeks were red. You could see his willie sticking up in his trousers like a joystick. He put a hand down to cover it and looked at Matty as he stood in the doorway. His eyes were thick with guilt and there was a shine on his forehead. He turned back to her. 'This wasn't why I came. Bloody hell.'

The front door shut, quietly.

Mamma was staring at the wall opposite the sofa, her arms over her chest. You could hear the bus stopping outside. 'Go to your room,' she said, and still didn't look over.

Matty went back upstairs.

***

'What's with you?'

'Nothing.'

'Liar on fire,' Nicks said. 'You're being a knob-end.'

Matty eyed a thumbnail and picked at the skin around it. Sanjit. She had been almost on top of him. If they hadn't been interrupted yesterday, the two of them would have had sex, maybe even right there on the sofa, because you could do it anywhere. His trousers round his ankles, like one of the men in the woods. Mamma, who would complain about the curry smells coming from the restaurant at the main junction.

'Fine. Be a knob-end.'

'What are you doing tonight?' Maybe they could come here later and swim again. Matty never wanted to go back to the flat.

'Busy. Got to go home.'

Can I come, Matty wanted to ask. They would play board games and eat chocolate biscuits. Nicks's dad would be kind, and have big shoulders. His mum would make cakes and not drink and neither of them would ever shout. They would love each other.

Nicks seemed to know that something was wrong. He went less jiggly and sat down with his forearms over his knees, watching. The bone of his ankle was touching the bone of Matty's ankle.

Everything was always better with him. He was safe. 'You're mine now,' he'd said. Streaks of mud on one cheek, then the other. Or his finger on Matty's lips, to say *quiet*.

'Do you want to share a cigarette?' One left. Mamma hadn't even noticed the missing pack.

'Nah.' He was still hunched, looking over. 'All right,' he said, in a different, simple voice.

Even though he didn't want to, he would. Just because.

Matty leant over and kissed him.

It was very quick. Cold, sweet lips, like the feeling of a leaf, just for half a second.

They stared at each other. Time stretched out.

Slowly, Nicks's eyes went cloudy, as if someone had poured pondwater into his ears. 'Shouldn't have done that,' he said, quietly.

Matty didn't dare say anything.

Nicks looked at the ground for a long time. His whole body seemed to change, a subtle loosening.

Then he got up, soundlessly, and walked away.

***

He wasn't there the next day. Matty swam in the Men's Pond until both arms hurt, but he never came. Daz was there, doing some diving and talking to the man who was weightlifting. Throwing his head back and laughing loudly.

Afterwards, Matty climbed the fence and wandered through the woods by the Not Allowed Pond, moving between the trees, watching the water. Apart from the moorhens and their wobbling little cries, there was nothing.

'Did you have sex with him?'

Matty was at the counter of the suit shop, having successfully managed to avoid Mamma for almost two days, only hearing her from under the duvet as she opened the bedroom door to look in at night and in the morning, a long pause before it closed again. She had left out sandwiches, peanut butter or cheese and cucumber squashed under cling film, and there had been Fanta in the fridge. Matty had ignored them.

'Keep your voice down,' said Mamma, in a hiss.

'There's no one in here.' Mrs Jackson had gone next door to get change for the till. 'Did you?'

'What if I—' Mamma seemed to stop herself, and gave a small shake of her head. 'No, I did not.'

'Do you want to have sex with him?'

'You are too young to be asking these sorts of questions.'

'No, I'm not.' You're too married to be doing it with your husband's friends. Sanjit was married too, to a nice lady who wore saris in bright colours and had braces on her teeth. 'You want me to grow up.'

She looked almost panicked for a moment, before her face toughened. 'There's something in your bedroom for you.'

A present wasn't going to make up for the fact that she had been trying to have sex with Sanjit. Sandwiches and Fanta and presents would not help.

Matty stomped out.

***

'Well?' Mamma said, later, in the kitchen. She had a glass of wine in her hand.

It was the opposite of a present. The uniform was still laid out on Matty's bed, exactly where Mamma had put it.

Tomorrow would be the first day of September. Four days until school. The whole summer had gone by.

'I don't want to wear it.' They could wear what they wanted at primary school, up to a point.

'I have bought it.' Her voice was tight, like her belt was done up an extra two holes along. 'So you will wear it.'

Matty needed to be grown up. Not throw a tantrum. 'Do you have a receipt?'

Mamma's gaze was stony, furious, and almost disbelieving.

A freeze-frame moment, the air thick, and then in an eyeblink, she was there, grabbing an ear and pulling, before her hand moved swiftly to hold Matty by the neck. Her other hand was raised, about to swoop down, but instead it hovered for two seconds before coming by her side. 'No. I do not. You are *my* child.' Her face was very close, her voice low and strained and right there. Her jaw trembled. The smell of smoke and perfume. 'He *let* you. He let you be like this. And he left you for *me* to deal with.' She let loose a torrent of Italian, a hail of bullets, her grip remaining fierce.

Stay still. Let the words drift through. As soon as Mamma's hand relaxed, just a little, Matty wriggled free and ran out of the room, down the stairs, and out of the house.

***

Matty sat at the curve of the Pond on the bank, up in the dark of the trees, even though it was cloudy. Long grass tickling both calves.

Still no Nicks. No golden-green back arching like a dolphin's, no dig in the ribs. Hardly anyone was here now, at teatime. Just four people doing laps in the water, each on their own, and a man sitting not far away.

Matty's neck hurt, a whole hour later. The shadow of Mamma's hand. She'd wanted to hit Matty. It had been there, in her eyes for a moment.

Once, maybe in April or May, Dad had got a black eye. Not all the way round, but on one side. It went from dark blue to purple to yellow. He'd said it had been from walking into a street lamp – mimed the action and everything, a Laurel and Hardy move.

The wake of one swimmer ribboned behind him. A crow barked overhead.

That time when Matty had opened the bathroom door and found him there, crying. He'd been holding his arm – as if he was cold, it had seemed. But he might have been hurt.

All their arguments. Mamma throwing things.

Maybe she had hurt him really badly. Maybe more than that.

Perhaps Dad hadn't killed himself. Perhaps someone else had. And not in the Pond at all.

'Hello there.' The man who had been further over in the shade was now standing a few feet away, holding his towel.

Matty looked out at the water. 'Hello.'

The man lay his towel down and sat on it, quite close. 'Not so warm today, is it?' His knees were bulgy and very white.

'No.'

The sun had turned the grass to a crackly, dull gold.

'I know who you are,' the man said, in a sing-song voice. Matty stared straight ahead, stomach suddenly stodgy. Did he mean that he knew Dad? Or—

'You shouldn't be here, you know.'

Matty didn't dare speak. *Say no to strangers* – the slowed-down computer-speak on the video they showed in the gym hall at school two years ago, the girl getting into the man's car.

'But I won't tell if you don't tell.' His hand was at the waistband of his swimming trunks, pulling them down a little. The top of his willie was there, crooked against his belly. He looked over, dipped his head down as if asking a gentle question. 'Hmm?'

Matty ran.

***

105

The phone rang. Mamma wasn't home.

'Hello?'

It would be the police, and they would know what just happened. They had been looking for a man like that. He had been doing it to other kids. Matty tried to remember everything. He'd had brown hair, a bald patch on the top. A thin chain around his neck with a tiny silver cross on it.

'I've called once already.' Johanna. 'Did you hear?'

'Hear what?'

'The news. I thought you would have known.'

How did she know already? Maybe the man had already done that to someone else. 'Known what?'

'They found the *Titanic*.'

The photos didn't come until the next day's *One O'Clock News*. Black and white, shadowy. The date and time at the top of the screen. *Argo*, a deep-sea vehicle, and a robot called Jason had found it. There were more photos of the pointy part of the bow and some boilers, all of which looked the same.

Salvageable. The scientist who had found the wreck said it was like 'meeting an old friend'.

They showed the ship from 1912, its four tall chimneys, all the people waving. An English survivor, an old lady, saying how her mum wouldn't go on it and had stayed at home.

Their bodies would have floated, unless they'd been eaten by sharks. Bits of bodies, jagged like the end of a cigarette, floating in dark seawater.

Sometimes you killed someone accidentally, like the people who didn't put enough lifeboats on the *Titanic* or the man who steered it into the iceberg in the first place.

Matty leant over and picked up the ashtray. Looked at it.

Sometimes you killed someone on purpose.

Matty had hovered outside the police station for ten minutes, looking very earnestly at the gum spots on the pavement every time someone came out. Reading the adverts for hairspray and perm setters in the hairdresser's next door. Bold Hold and Aqua Net.

A man that Matty recognised from before, with a dirty rust-coloured blazer and a nailbrush moustache, came jogging down the steps. He sent over a sharp look.

Now or never.

'I. Um. I want to report a murder.'

The uniformed policeman at reception was young. He had red hair and freckles and was doing a wordsearch in a book. 'Oh, yeah?' He didn't look up. 'You do it?'

'No.'

He drew a loop around a diagonal word. 'Who's been murdered, then?'

'My dad.'

The policeman glanced up and pursed his lips together. 'By who?'

'By my mum.'

He put his pen down. 'That a fact,' he said.

Stomach ache. Matty sat staring at the frayed patch of carpet in the corner of the room. The policewoman from before, when Mamma had first reported Dad being missing, had spent an hour asking lots of questions and writing some of the answers down in a little notebook with her purple biro. She had left a plate of custard creams.

Mamma would have phoned and said he was missing to distract them from the real story. He had gone to the Men's Pond

– because he *had* been seen there, the policewoman had said – and then he had come home and they had argued because she had said that she wanted to have sex with Sanjit, even though he had a fat belly, and she had hit Dad with something hard like the iron or the food mixer, in the head, and he had looked up at her, astonished, but he'd never hit her back and anyway it was too late because he already had brain damage and blood clots and was having a stroke, and he fell to the floor and died and she had got his body out of the apartment, maybe into one of the big supermarket bin bags, and it had been collected by the rubbish collectors, and she had cleaned all the blood off the kitchen floor with bleach and the next day pretended she didn't know anything about it.

Matty only said some of this to the policewoman.

Another biscuit. It had been an hour already.

It meant that Dad had never drowned in the Pond. That the odd feeling of the water on the first visit was nothing. Imaginary.

The door opened. The policewoman was there.

And Mamma.

She was clutching her handbag, the strap stretched diagonally across her body. Strands of hair had come loose from her clips, fraying outwards. 'We are going.' Her voice was rigid.

Matty looked at the policewoman.

'Come on, love,' the policewoman said. 'You've had a tiring day. Well, *I* have, anyway. I'd like to get off home.' She was trying to be funny, *now*.

'Matty.' Mamma's knuckles were white. 'It is time to go.'

'Take the last custard cream with you,' said the policewoman. 'It'll only go to my thighs.'

'Thank you. Say thank you,' Mamma said to Matty.

Matty took it.

*

108

Nuclear fallout. Radioactive particles. Nothing that any hiding under a table or desk would help. The Bomb was coming straight for Flat 123a Golders Green Road and there would be no survivors.

Mamma didn't say anything on the short walk to the flat, or as they went inside. She simply pulled back a kitchen chair for Matty to sit on, and sat opposite. No wine. She didn't even light a cigarette.

The policewoman had taken all those notes, and nodded and said *mmm-hmm*. And she hadn't believed a single word. Now there was real danger.

Matty thought through boxing moves. Jab. Right cross. Left uppercut. Right cross.

'They made me sit in there for almost an hour,' Mamma said, finally. 'An *hour*. Do you know how humiliating that is?'

The iron was in the hallway cupboard. The food mixer was in the cupboard by the sink. Pivot. Left uppercut.

'Why would you do that?' Her voice was beginning to rise. 'Why would you do that to your own mother?' You could practically hear her guts, twisting inside her. Jab to the head, jab to the body. 'You hate me so much?' It was coming.

'I'll hit you if you hit me,' Matty said.

'What?' The word jerked out, astonished.

'If you hit me, I'll hit you back. Dad took me boxing. It was a secret.'

She looked blank for a moment, before letting out an almost-laugh, the sort that hated itself. 'Another secret,' she said. 'You two, always so full of them.'

'No, we weren't.' Only that one. And the late-night movies. And the time that Dad had let Matty try some of his beer and laughed at the foamy moustache. And all the swearing at Barnet.

'No?' She shook her head, not believing. 'And now you're stuck with me.'

Matty's head hurt, thick and clogged up. Stay alert. Stay ready. Defend, counter.

'You hold him up like a saint. Like Jesus on the cross.' She folded her arms and leant forward so that her chest was squashed against the table. 'He is gone. Do you hear me? Gone. He is not coming back.'

'You killed him.' Matty's voice had gone as stiff as Mamma's.

'I did not kill him.' She looked exasperated, tired. 'He deserves to be dead. After what he has done to me. To you.'

'You hit him.'

Her mouth opened. Shut again. 'We would fight. That is what some couples do.'

'He didn't hit you, though.'

She didn't say anything.

He didn't. Of course he didn't. Maybe that's why they went to boxing. So that at least Matty could fight back. 'I want him to be here.' The words were slower. Not grown-up. Nose beginning to run.

'We will not see him again. Do you hear me?'

'He's dead,' Matty said, looking at Mamma. It was almost a question, but not quite.

Mamma stared back, and then over Matty's head for a long time, totally still, and finally released a breath as deep as the sea. She leant over and pulled up her handbag, bringing out her lighter. 'Yes.'

***

'It is time to get up.' Mamma was there, sitting on the side of the bed, the mattress sloping. 'We need to get you a calculator and a pencil case.'

Matty made an effort not to roll towards her. 'I don't feel well.' The stomach ache was worse than ever. Hot forehead.

Mamma put a hand up and Matty drew back, snake-quick. She put it down again. 'All right. I will come back at lunchtime. You are not getting out of your first day tomorrow.'

Matty got up anyway, once Mamma had gone, stomach feeling like it was surrounded by a life-ring that was too small. There was only one day left before everything would change. New school, new teachers, new classmates, big blowjob-miming girls. Big boys.

In the quieter part of the Heath, there were some flowers that you probably weren't supposed to pick, all clustered together. Tall pink ones, little purple-blue ones, and some daisies with long stems. It hurt to bend down, but Matty grabbed a big handful. Some snapped in the middle of their stems, and some came with roots and dry, crumbling soil.

Further down, Matty stood in front of the Mildred Himoff Lewis bench. No tramp on it today. *In loving memory, 1912–1985.* The flowers were put underneath one of the legs, where they would get peed on by the thousands of dogs that came here every day.

Matty walked away, not looking back at it.

In loving memory, 1948–1985.

Daz was stretching in front of the weightlifting machine, the muscles in his thighs bulging. 'Wotcha, sport.'

'Um, have you seen Nicks?' Matty had done one full lap of the pond without needing to stop and rest, and there'd been no sign of him. He hadn't turned up for four days.

Daz straightened. 'Nicks? Who's he when he's at home?' He glanced around, quite theatrically. 'Who have I been missing out on?'

'The boy I'm usually with.'

Daz looked a bit vacant. 'You're always on your own, aren't you, love? Our little musical protégé. Gegsy's got high hopes for you. The next generation, you know.' He put his hands together, as if in prayer, and raised his eyes upwards. 'The saviour of electronic music.'

Matty stared at Daz for a bit, and wandered away.

*

Everyone left. Everyone.

Floating in the pond, tummy hurting like mad. Light grey clouds on a pale white sky. It was getting cold, but Matty had to stay in. One more swim. Just one more, before home time and getting a calculator and a pencil case and a compass and a protractor and going to St George's and being the one without a dad. The quiet one. The weird one.

The last day of the summer. Matty could come after school – though it would be further away now – or at the weekends, but for how long? And how could it be the same, if Nicks didn't come back? A gull with a black eye like a bruise flew over and made a raging cry at the same time as Matty's stomach pulled inwards.

Time to get out. Goosebumps and a headache. Even Daz had disappeared now. Matty climbed up the ladder that was halfway along the concrete walkway, shivering.

A sudden movement ahead. Alexander, the lifeguard, who'd had his feet up on the railing in front of him, put his legs down and stood up, staring straight at Matty. Or rather, Matty's legs. 'Bloody hell, you all right there, Short Round?'

The man walking past to get to the diving board stopped, too. 'Good Lord, are you OK? Did you catch yourself?'

Matty looked down. Blood. There was blood, trickling all the way down the inside of one leg in a thin, diluted trail. Sliding along one heel. A quick glance back, at the gleaming green mirror of the Pond.

Barracuda. Piranhas. Jaws.

Alexander had come onto the walkway. 'Come here, then.' He squatted down. 'What've you done?'

Matty took a step backwards. A couple of men waiting to dive were looking over. 'Nothing. I dunno.'

'You're bleeding, mate.' He put a hand out, and almost touched the shorts' hem.

Another step back, with a sudden, awful rush of fear. 'It's OK.' Lower stomach throbbing, back throbbing. The blood wasn't coming from a cut, but from higher, between both thighs. Higher.

'We've got a first-aid kit. Did you nick it on the platform? Come on, I'll patch you—'

But Matty was already running up the walkway, bleeding, Dad-less, in a body that was dividing, one part already floating back out over the Pond, to where it wanted to be.

PART 2

1999

Chapter 1

There.

From a distance, it looked like the slim drag of a biro over cloth. The tiniest flash of silver-black in the water, a spot at its end. Almost soundless.

The sky was beaten flat. Hardly a wind.

Slowly, the spot continued to move. A line was drawn from north to south, dividing the lough into two wide halves. When the spot reached the bay, it bobbed there, surrounded by towering slabs of hill, a sheer drop of dark rock on one side. For a long moment, it became motionless, before gliding smoothly back out, following the memory of the wake it had already made.

At the northern edge, the water stretched and became tall. A slick creature, moving upright now, towards a large boulder patched with moss that sheltered a bright orange rucksack, a woolly hat, and biker boots.

21/11/99
LOUGH _____, Air 10°C, Water 10°C, 1km

It had taken Matty almost an hour to walk there – the van parked on a lay-by – down a private road and then through scrubland that skirted the base of a hill. Deer were up on the higher part, untroubled by the boggy earth and uneven stones, moving like light on water.

But it had been worth it. It was always worth it. The lough was cold, but the shock never lasted long. Neoprene sorted that. Wetsuit, gloves, socks and hat made it pretty snug, after the initial garrotting. Still not as cold as you'd think, for late November. Maybe the low cloud kept the ice at bay. And this place had a lot of low cloud.

Ireland was bullied by water. If it wasn't swelling into loughs like this one, or pools or puddles, it was running off the hills, stagnant in the bogs, or coming at you, vertical and horizontal. A constant immersion, one way or the other.

A car was purring down the road, an opaque windscreen. Matty stepped to the verge as it slowed.

The driver's window was already wound down. 'This is private property.' There was a challenge in the upturn of the last word. A man in his fifties, beaten-up brown leather waistcoat and tweed flat cap. Some woman singing opera on the radio.

Matty shrugged and looked up the hill. 'Sorry, mate.' No point in feigning ignorance after climbing the fence with the freshly painted sign.

He eyed the drybag, and the hair, all back to its bedspring coil apart from the darker, tapered ends. 'Been swimming, have you, then?'

'Yeah.'

'That's mine, too. The water.'

Matty looked round at it, gave a slight nod. 'Right.' It's *mine*.

'I could sue you. Or shoot you.' His voice was rich, liquidy. There was faint amusement in his expression. Possibly.

Hands, held up. 'Whatever you like.' A half-grin.

He chewed on something. 'Well. Don't darken my door again, you hear me?' There was a sun-spark in his eye now. 'I'll get my gun out next time. Blow you to smithereens.'

Forefinger to outer eyebrow, the quickest salute. 'No worries.'

The man gazed a little longer, eyes flicking down to the boots and up to the hair again, before giving a warm grunt, far back in his throat, and releasing the handbrake.

Matty watched the car roll smoothly down the tarmac and turned back to the hill.

Private your arse. There were loughs everywhere and Matty was going to swim in every last one of them. That was the reason for coming over here.

One of them.

Back in the camper van, Matty watched the windows steam up, holding a cup of tea, proper builder's. The way Joe had always had it. *Flash it the milk. Get done for indecency.* Probably good to have a second. The chill of the lough was still there, under the skin.

It often took two teas to get warm, depending on how much of a walk back there was. Two of everything. Two pairs of socks, two swimming hats, a normal one underneath the thick one. Two hot-water bottles, two blankets as well as the duvet. It got toasty enough, most nights. If not, a proper room. A hot shower.

Chicken and chips for dinner, part of a sticky toffee pudding for dessert, in a long, low-ceilinged pub with diamond leading on the windows and arcade games in the corner. Matty tried to stick to a bodybuilder's diet – meat, eggs, nuts. 'Scrawny sort of bruiser, aren't you?' Heather would say back in London, leaning over the bar, batting her false eyelashes. But swimming, especially in winter, made you crave stodge. The body needing to fortify itself after the rude jolt of the water.

Another half of cider. 'Is it all right to park my camper overnight out the back?'

The landlady looked up. 'No, it's not, I'm afraid. We shut it up.'

No harm in asking. 'OK. Ta.' Back to the moorland roads, then.

Matty got Shifty into the mountains, just, peering through the windscreen, the map sliding off the dashboard. Turned off N.W.A. Best not to think about how high up they were, how sheer the right-hand drop might be past the reach of the head-lights. In the end, the van overshot, and had to roll back on a bend before reversing into the deserted car park.

Matty opened the door and switched the torch on.

The wind was engulfing, predatory. Over there in the black-ness was another lough, already ringed in pencil on the map. Matty skirted the tarmac, kicking at a paint pot and an old car radio, rusted black. Took a piss by three alcopop bottles, listening to the gargle of a burn nearby taking the sound over.

Not much chance of being chucked out of here.

There was a knack to opening Shifty's side door, hip pushing against it, handle up and then shoved along. 'Just you and me, mate,' Matty said, to metal and rubber, closing the door and putting the kettle on the hob.

Shifty came from a Welshman's junk and furniture shop in West London. It had been sitting wheel-less and on bricks next to a stack of mouldy lampshades and a life-size plastic elephant, the mustard paint peeling away from the VW emblem at the front. Matty hadn't bothered to haggle. Love at first sight and all that. Some TLC for a couple of weeks, after asking around for a mechanic at the Men's Pond, got Shifty tarted up enough. You needed a serious muscle to move into third gear – Matty's left arm had been aching since Watford Gap – and there was the constant, heady smell of the engine, but already it felt like family. A cocoon.

There was plenty of money now. Even as spending money with the rest in the bank. Enough to tour the world a few times over, but for now the world was here. Ireland.

Home had been a lot of places. Finchley, after Joe had gone. Rimini, for two years. Wood Green, to finish secondary school. The floors of friends, and the floors of near-strangers, here and there, once Matty had left home properly. Bedsits, slug trails on the carpet. Usually Heather's box room with the skylight above the pub when in London, the rooms at the camps, constantly in youth-hostel mode. Canada and America, for three summers.

Now this funny little mustard-coloured bastard was home, at least for a bit. Home was definitely not where Rosa had been found, dead, six months ago.

***

Matty woke with the light, cheek pressed against one cool hot-water bottle. Shifty was gently rocking in the wind that was still going strong, several draughts filtering in through the cracks. Two guidebooks were stacked in front of the curtain – neither to be returned in a hurry – next to a pack of cards and a notebook.

The empty, sheer feeling that was hunger and loss. Matty pulled the woolly hat back down and curled up under the duvet, staring at the piece of paper serving as a marker in one of the books. Tried to sleep a little more, but knowing the water was out there was more effective than an alarm.

A small, dark line of it was now visible from the window, between hills the colour of dank fox. Matty watched it, drinking half a can of Slim-Fast in bed, knowing it was futile to leave until it had been tackled. 'Yeah, yeah, all right.' A stretch. 'You win.'

It was best to be already wearing the wetsuit, not to tussle with it while the wind or rain was coming at you. It was like Harry Houdini in reverse: a wriggle in, one leg at a time, no panicking, hauling it over each shoulder, zip pulled up by its extension. Sealed.

121

'I know why you wear that,' Rosa had said once, when Matty was still sometimes at home, the wetsuit hung up and dripping into the bath.

'Keeps the cold off.'

'More than that. I know it is more than that. You think I am an idiot? It's disgusting. Where did you swim today? There?'

It had all started at the Ponds. Not daring to go back to the Men's Pond, Matty had gone to the Mixed Pond instead, sitting at the far end with the weed-smokers, becoming one of them for a while after the two years in Italy. And not just in the summer but at the edges of autumn and spring, when the water began to pinch. Inside, too, in Olympic-sized swimming pools where the sound bashed off walls and you were sliced into lanes. But it wasn't the same. The hot, nostril-swamping stink of the chlorine, people clustering at the shallow end, everybody at the wrong speed.

The realisation came aged fifteen that cold water meant wetsuits, and wetsuits meant not having to be seen in a costume. When the Mixed Pond shut in September, Matty clenched everything and went to the Ladies' Pond, changed under a tree on the furthest bit of grass to avoid the heavy waft of bodies under the cold showers, the variedly shaped breasts, the low-swelling stomachs. Matty went even when thin tiles of ice settled, when it was so thick that a metre-wide path had to be broken to make a lane. Sometimes, it felt too much, and other places became haunts, too. Old gravel pits with the nearby drone of the M25 and planes going overhead. The sea-coves at Broadstairs. A recommended river. The echo of Dad in them all. Of Joe.

But it began to have its own call. Water had a song, a near-silent lilt. When you got closer – tarn, pool, river, proper swimming lake – the impatience made you sweat. The need to undress, a frustration that the wetsuit didn't slip on as easily as it should. A lust that you forgot as soon as you were submerged.

122

Water was not just looked at, but assessed. Depth, entry and exit points – exposed tree roots, shelving boulders – weeds, reeds. Flow, undertow, rocks lurking under the surface. Rip tides if it was coastal. And not too many people around. Onlookers weren't ideal.

22/11/99
LOUGH _____, Air 8°C, Water 9°C, 300m

Black and blue. The lough's surface was dark, flecked. Matty had taken the slim path around one hill, long-dead heather stalks on both sides, having to lean against the wind. Sinking into moist peat, sinking further once the trainers were off. There were no rocks here, just hill softening into lough.

It felt harder today. The air was brutal, the water petty and spitting. Matty lowered, let the cold trickle down one spine-bone at a time, and slid into it. Face down straightaway. There were earplugs, a nose plug too, but it was still an absorption. You were with the water. Matty pulled through the lough's width, the rhythm beginning to settle. A breath every three strokes, no matter what. Scooping downwards, arcing out above. Arms lengthening.

Swimming got rid of everything else, usually. Thoughts were detritus left bobbing in your wake. The lack of father. Mother, now. The worry about work, where to live next. The always-feeling of being in between things. There was only this, the metallic feel of the water and the movement through it.

At the other end, the shallows were puttyish. Matty turned and headed straight back, stopping once to watch the mist lower. It was so bleak. Reddish hills and not a single tree. For a moment, the wind hushed, just the whisper of it remaining, and something threaded in it. A trace of a woman's voice, with a familiar hardness.

Head down again. Matty swam, too fast, back to the mud, back to Shifty, before Rosa's words had any chance to form.

***

No one had found her for two and a half weeks. Eventually, the postman had alerted the local council to a bad smell. Cue yellow tape and neighbours loitering with looks that were curious and delightedly horrified. The police had kept the details to a minimum, but it was easy enough to imagine. Matty knew what a decomposing corpse looked like – there'd been enough grisly images over the years to look at alongside drowning victims, for comparison.

It would have been quicker than in water. Rosa might have been lying on the sofa, an arm stretched out towards the carpet. Hair, which had never changed in length, partly squashed underneath her, the rest hanging down. Dried blood-foam on her lips. Bruised, grey skin, the blood cells having pressed out to every edge. A stifling smell, like pondweed in the sun. Underneath her clothes, the points of her pelvis and her ribs beginning to be visible. And next to her, a bottle of Cointreau and an empty tub of pills.

She would have wanted to be glamorous in death. She'd have imagined a big studio light over her, or the light from the half-opened curtains giving her a fixed, waxen pallor. Probably put lipstick on specially, her best knickers and bra, lacy and matching, for the coroner.

It was just like her, really, to kill herself. The ultimate way of saying, *See what you did to me?*

Rosa. She hadn't been Mamma for a long time. It had been two years since they had last stared at each other. The impasse was mutual, something that had grown from the time of Joe's disappearance, and stiffened until it became unbearable to be in a room with her because the same things would always be said. Sometimes there'd be a man there, a new one she was seeing, perched on Joe's old chair. She'd be wearing a blouse that showed a lot of cleavage, dismissing the guy's awkward excuses about leaving them to it, though he usually scarpered anyway. Matty would sit on the sofa with a cup of tea and talk about where the last few jobs had been, and Rosa would nod. She was never really listening, looking at Matty from head to toe and gathering her own words together, words that would eventually pour out, one strained sentence loosening and becoming many. The same questions. *Why do you not get a proper job? Why do you not act as you should? What have you done to your hair? When will you behave like a normal person? You will not get a proper job unless you act properly. You know what people think of you? Of me?* It always ended the same way, the cup of tea left half-drunk, Rosa still shouting as Matty shut the front door, vowing that it would be the last time.

The worst thing had been calling Nonna, and trying to tell her in shit Italian. *Mamma è morto, Nonna. Morta.* The quiet howls emanating from the phone, as if listening to a dog on a far hill.

***

The rest of the Slim-Fast in the van, sat back under the duvet. The wetsuit was draped over the rear doors, though this mist wasn't going to help it dry in a hurry. Shifty's windows fogged further as the kettle heated up.

Matty pulled the notepad over and wrote the details down on a fresh page. Lough. Distance. Temperatures. After a while, you instinctively knew the feel of the water. These were the important things, discussed genially with fellow swimmers.

125

Outside, a crow landed, hopping into a puddle, its look not far off Matty's own – black back, grey hood. It lifted its beak and made a violent, cracking cry, right at the window.

***

The funeral was in her church in Wood Green, an odd, modern building with a cross fifteen metres high on a thin concrete post outside. No gothic frills. Mrs Jackson from the old suit shop was there, and a smattering of neighbours. Nonno had fractured his hip and couldn't move, so they didn't come. Matty stood at the front, hands clasped, the words all coming back easily, like a pop song you hadn't sung since you were a kid. Like a rap.

A closed coffin. Matty imagined the decomposition continuing, bacteria feasting on Rosa from the inside, her changing colours, a mossy black-green against the red of her darkest nail polish. Becoming liquid. Becoming nothing.

Matty had gone back to the Wood Green flat, where they'd moved after returning from Italy, and where Rosa had lived for the last eleven years. Sat in the dark. The council had it cleaned, but there remained a furred smell underneath the bright scrape of chemicals. Even when the smell faded, she was still there, as Joe had been for those few months in Golders Green before the two of them moved further north. The tight-jawed essence of her, the nicotine in the corniced corners of the ceiling. A month there, listening to Rosa whispering from the net curtains and clicking in the light bulb, had been enough. It wasn't home.

So Matty sold the house. Transferred some of the money over to Nonna and Nonno, and opened another bank account. Started to stack Rosa's things into boxes, going through every room and up to the attic, where the world suddenly tilted, and turned itself inside out.

Packing up. Bed folded back into seat. Kettle stacked away in the tiny cupboard next to the plate and bowl. The wetsuit hung opposite the cooker, a towel folded up underneath it.

Matty went outside, did twenty squats. Lifts with the pair of dumbbells that stacked tidily under the back seat. A set of press-ups, the gravel leaving teeth-marks on each palm.

A quick fag, to the satisfying throb of worked muscles. Always good to feel hardy, sculpted. The mountain lough looked unknow-able again, as if it hadn't been touched.

Matty took the Old Military Road once more, a high, feature-less pass through the national park. The widest sky. The moorland colours were like Joe's beard, when he used to grow it during the odd winter – blond-red and the beginnings of grey in with the brown.

The first phone book was on the passenger seat. Burning a hole in it.

Tomorrow. Matty would start tomorrow.

Chapter 2

22/11/99

_____*LOUGH, UPPER LAKE, Air 11°C, Water 10°C, 2.5km*

There was a man crouching down by a motorbike in the car park, a grimy cloth in his hand. Shaved head, long ginger beard, leathers. Matty changed behind Shifty's closed curtains, and he looked up when the side door shuddered shut.

'Nice wheels,' he said.

'Cheers.'

'Going for a swim?'

'Yep.' The wetsuit hadn't quite dried enough since this morning, and had taken ages to get on.

'I applaud you, man.' An American accent. 'That's awesome. Don't get into trouble in there.'

Even an experienced swimmer could get the fear. Dark, ungiving water, a new spot – you never quite knew what was in there. You didn't have to be a child to imagine a mutant beast lumbering up from below. And there was always drowning. Getting a cramp, or having a heart attack, the body struck dumb by the cold. Lungs, filling. Houdini, thrashing and failing. The trick was to breathe, slow and methodical, to focus on the stroke and nothing else. There was nothing else.

The lough tasted of iron. It was far warmer down here in the valley, the tall mountains compact with woodland on the lower edges. Matty stayed close to the shore, near the dark paint of the pine trees' shadows, not going too fast. Heart finding its equilibrium, the slowest of hip-hop beats.

A long swim, just occasionally looking ahead to check the course. Each breath revealing a side-shot of black water and torn hill.

And back. Breaststroke always felt weird in a wetsuit, but it was good to take in the view for a few moments, the ridiculousness of scale, the scalped look of the upper mountains. Clouds moving as fast as the water. Then head down again, face beginning to numb.

The motorbike had gone.

This pub had rooms. In the main bar area, there were red velour seats, worn away in places, and a high-beamed roof. A small harp on a windowsill and some generic Irish folk-rock playing in the background. It was quiet, just a few couples and a family with a kid and balloons tied to her chair.

The motorcyclist was at the bar, chatting to the girl there and pointing at some of the bottles behind her, his gestures expansive. One big motorbike boot on the low rail. He glanced over. Matty ordered a jacket potato with beans and a Coke from the other side of the bar and picked up a local paper to take to a corner table. Flicked through articles about a sailing club, a man falling off a pier, a baby winning the chance to be on the side of yoghurts. The food arrived. Brown sauce. A waiter came out with a cake spiked with sparklers and the kid's face lit up as her parents and brother started singing.

Those sorts of birthdays had stopped aged eleven. 'Happy birthday, tiger.' A ruffle of hand in hair and a large, slim present chucked onto the duvet that could only be one thing. One wheel exposed. 'One from me. Don't tell your mamma. Take you out for a spin on it later, OK?'

The family of the kid finished singing and everyone in the room clapped.

Every February after that, Matty would wake, stare at the ceiling as the realisation of the date came slowly in, hear his voice. *Happy birthday, tiger.*

'Hey.' The motorbike guy was standing a couple of feet from the table, holding a nearly empty pint. A big square silver ring on his index finger.

'All right.'

'How was it?' Spoken like they were old friends.

'Pretty good.'

'You go far?'

'To the end and back.'

He let out a single laugh. 'Geez. I walked half of it and that felt far enough.'

I probably swim faster than you walk, mate, Matty thought.

'I'm impressed.' He had a sure, lazy-sunshine drawl. A lot of freckles. He kept looking, glanced at his drink, looked again. Affable enough, intrigued rather than suspicious. 'You like rum?'

What the hell. 'Yeah. I guess.'

Trevor was from San Diego. Tattoos crawled all over him, and he rolled up his sleeves and pulled down the collar of his jacket to show them off. The Harley sign, the pirate woman, the snake and the apple, the big cross. Every time he mentioned Jesus, Matty took another gulp of rum.

'You got any Irish in there?'

'My dad.'

'Me too. Way back somewhere.' That was it. He was looking proud, emboldened. Looking for that common ground, the green thread of noble Oirishness, however faint. He started talking about his great-grandmother, of family trees and some heirloom. Of California, and how when the rain came it was an event and

130

roofs caved in. 'Bet your roofs are a bit more solid for that sort of thing,' he said, looking up.

Matty stared at the ceiling and didn't say anything.

'So, what do you do?'

Swim Sleep Eat. In that order. Even when Matty was sleeping, the dreams were of water – of coursing through it, fully submerged, gilled.

That wasn't what he meant, of course. He'd already gone on about some dot-com company he was working for, the bright new future.

'Different things. Camps for kids. Activity stuff. Working behind a bar sometimes.' Heather would let Matty pull pints at The Haggerston when there was no money to pay her for rent. 'Whatever's going.'

'Good for you, dude. Awesome.' He would have said that no matter what the answer had been. 'A maverick. We should get you on over to the West Coast. You and that van of yours would fit in a treat.' He smelt peppery, cigar smoke maybe, and there was a bearish quality to him, equal parts placidity and pheromones.

Matty held up the glass, letting the liquid tilt. 'Another?'

'You bet. That's the spirit,' he said, and slammed his hand down on the bar at his own joke.

He definitely had the mouth for his supposed Irish heritage. He didn't shut up. Read all day long, he said. Loved Irish literature, better than anything else, and was going to visit a restaurant with a load of first editions tomorrow. 'You should really read him. I thought all you Irish knew Joyce.'

'Nope.' Matty mostly read Stephen King novels.

Trevor started speaking in a grander voice, a couple of old guys looking up from the corner. '*Till tree from tree, tree among trees, tree over tree become stone to stone, stone between stones, stone under stone forever.*'

It was hard to know how to follow that. 'Nice.'

He grinned. 'I like your vibe.' Large elbows on the table, a little closer. His voice more intimate. 'The thing you got going on.' *Vibe.* Hadn't been called that before. But he got it, Matty thought, and imagined his cock, pushed tight against the leather at his crotch. He was gazing over, amused. 'Quiet type, huh?'

Move it on, then. 'Got a room?' Matty drained the glass, put it down and stared back. Didn't blink.

That changed the mood. Trevor looked startled. 'Yeah. Uh, yeah, sure.' He sat up straighter. 'Great. OK. Awesome.'

The pub's room had a view of the car park. Shifty was out there, getting rained on. At least the mud on the wheel arches would get cleaned off.

'And you've got Swift,' Trevor was saying, taking his leather jacket off, releasing the smell of sweat. 'Telling people to eat their own babies to stop the famine. Talk about black humour.'

Matty nodded from the window.

'The guy was a genius. People thought *Gulliver's Travels* was a book for kids, they didn't see what he was doing, holding the mirror right back at everyone, English society, the works.' He paused, only for the shortest breath. 'I really wanna fuck your mouth.'

A charge of electricity, from stomach downwards. Matty turned round and looked at him. Knelt down.

'The human body, you know? Oh fuck. OK. So he was looking at the ugliness of the human – wow. The human – holy shit, you're good at this.'

Tongue. Mouth. Hand. Hands. Bit of everything.

He was hefty, bigger than he looked, the leather having kept it all in. He stood with his hands on his hips, broad girth matted with ginger hair. 'Because, yeah, Gulliver's miniature in this part, or at least he's among giants, so he can see all the blemishes

132

in – oh, man. All right, come on, let's do this.' A hand came down. 'Hey.'

Matty hummed a no.

'No? Well, if you're cool to – shit that's – OK. Great.'

Fourteen, on a school trip. Having to bunk up with the girls and listen to them crying over how cute Jules and Guillaume were but how they'd gone off with Rachel and Ciara obviously because they were slags.

But the activity stuff was good. Abseiling, rock-climbing, gorge-walking. One lunchtime, Matty wandered away from the group, peeling sweaty Edam slices off a baguette, heading along the path to where a bunch of French boys were hurling themselves off a high rock, five metres up, into the lake. Ditching the sandwich, Matty idled nearer, watching their increasingly ridiculous dare-devil stunts – dives, forward rolls and back flips, punctuated with the odd smack of a belly-flop. The smell of rosemary and pine and dust and boys.

Rosa had moved them back from Italy, Matty joining the new school in the summer term in time to sign up for the week's trip. It had been a relief to come back to London, in some ways. In other ways, it was just the same as over there. Suspicious glances, elbows in ribs and grinning nods. Dyke. Weirdo.

It was easier to be a boy in shrugging, monosyllabic French. Matty loitered long enough to be part of a queue of jumpers, and soon was standing at the serrated edge of the rock, looking at a lake as green as wine-bottle glass. The loose, lazy babble of the boys behind. The first jump was terrifying, exhilarating, a slap in the face. Air and air and air and deep water, a perfect encasing, the place Matty was always supposed to be, and an immediate need to do it again.

The second time the edge of a rock shelf met bone on the way down, the click of a wrist going the wrong way, like a light switch. Searing, sickening pain that made Matty want to chuck up, climbing back over the stones to the top, the arm limp and hotly throbbing. A boy – older, deeply tanned – put a hand around Matty's shoulder and walked back towards the school group. On the way, they went into the cork trees, the dark coolness like a church, and he gently got Matty to kneel and put his dick there, right there, between lips and teeth. He had tasted cold and damp and then hot and damp and shockingly salty, more than the sea. The illicit tang of doing something so adult. 'I know that you are a girl,' he said in a muddy French accent as he took it out, wiped it with the back of his hand. He helped pull a gorse thorn out of Matty's knee and they went to find the teachers.

Matty had nursed the fractured wrist for the rest of the holiday, trying to forget what the boy had said, tongue involuntarily rising to remember the salt there, on the red, curved roof.

'Don't worry about it.'

Trevor was sitting on the bed, his leather trousers around his thighs, hands spread wide. 'Come on. I wanna taste you. I can give as good as I get.'

'No, it's fine, mate.' Hands wiped on jeans. 'No need.'

He gave a big groan and stared up at the ceiling. 'Jesus, I'm pissed. How do you take the hooch, little thing like you?'

Not little. Shorter than a lot of guys, taller than a lot of girls. Just smaller than him. Matty shrugged and turned towards the door. 'See you.'

'Hey, where're you going?'

'Back to my van.' He didn't need to know that a room had already been reserved a couple of doors down.

'Don't be a martyr. Come on, crackerjack, stay here with me. It'll be nice. I'll read to you.'

'You're all right. See you.'

Well, don't look at me. I'm not saying anything.

Matty lay in bed, looking at the soft peach walls, the tiny TV in the corner on mute. The sting still there at the back of the throat,

134

just. They tasted different, every one. Starchy or acidic, like bleach or chlorine or mushrooms. But always, underneath it all, salt.

It didn't matter if the guy was forceful, got into it as Trevor had done. A weird mix of servant and master, the wetness between Matty's legs at the possibility of biting down, hard. It tended to be better on the giving end of things.

None of my business. Bit of a twat, though.

The stippled ceiling paint in the room was the same as in the Finchley flat where they'd moved after Golders Green. Matty would stare up at it, listen to Rosa in the kitchen that was next door now, not downstairs. Imagine the ceiling being the clouds that went into heaven, try and use X-ray specs to see if he was there.

What was all that shite about Swift?

Crackerjack. Joe had used that nickname. *Crackerjack* and *scout* and *tiger* and *little gobshite*, once or twice. Names that didn't stop when he'd gone. He'd been there all this time. A version of him, wry quiet voice curling in an ear, taking the piss, calming Matty down sometimes, commenting on things he'd never have seen.

I'd like to see him go on about all that stuff in the North Dublin estates.

It was impossible to shut him up, even now.

Tomorrow. It had been put off long enough. Matty could picture it, the first handwritten line on the notepaper tucked into the guidebook.

J. RONAN GARAGE AND MECHANICS

***

Matty had said no to offers of help in clearing out the flat. It would be a punishment of sorts, touching all of Rosa's things, packing her life away. The few videos – Films of the Fabulous Forties and the Cary Grant Collection. The clothes bought from Italian markets with their tissue paper covers. The stacks of fashion magazines. Her lipsticks, the scooped ends at different lengths.

Matty kept Rosa's wedding ring and a silver necklace that Joe had given Rosa, a droplet with a waxy pearl in it, and sent the rest of the jewellery to Rimini.

Photo albums had been stored in the attic. There were a few childhood portraits, Rosa as a young teenager in a checked swimsuit and black-framed sunglasses, already posing. Wedding photos in front of the door of the church, Joe with a wide collar and Rosa in stiff silk and a white headband. Nonno with his fat, quiet grin and brown suit. Old cards were loose in the box, soft at the edges. Birthday cards, her twenty-first and thirtieth. Matty's christening. And, falling out of a pink card saying New Baby, was a letter, as crinkled as lace.

Rosa –
I'm sorry I did it this way. It just got too much. I had to get off for a bit, and maybe the space will do you good too. I can't be with you anymore, and you know all the reasons why. I'll not be a victim. Give this to Matty. I'll be in touch soon.
Joe

For two hours, Matty had sat back against the eaves, staring at the yellow insulation foam opposite. Punched into silence.

It was something unimaginable.

The note had clearly been crumpled up before being smoothed out again and placed in the card. It curled in Matty's palms, hardly real. Yet it was his writing – almost as alarming as hearing him speak, to see the right-leaning slant, the big looping '*I*'.

Eventually, Matty had slid down and lain on the floor of the attic, breathing in the dust, coming down hours later to find that it was dawn.

Joe. A note that could only have been written after he went missing.

After he *left*.

*

136

Matty had gone to the Heath, dead early. Walked. On Parliament Hill, the note had come out again, held tightly so it wouldn't blow away. His words – you could hear him saying them. Picture him writing it, his forehead leaning on his hand. Looking up at a window. Smoking.

There was no date, but surely he couldn't have sent it that long after he'd gone. Could he? There'd been no envelope.

Give this to Matty.

Back at Rosa's, Matty had gone up to the attic again and pulled the box over, emptied it out. The rest of the week was spent folding and unfolding cards, looking under the flaps of boxes before they were chucked down into the hallway, and until the attic was bare.

Fourteen years of thinking he was dead. Of swimming in the Ladies' Pond and the Mixed Pond before going further afield, always thinking of him when in the water. Nibbled by fish and his bones turned to pond-mulch.

Fourteen years of stories of what might have happened to him, newly shaped as Matty got older. He'd borrowed money to put on a horse, couldn't pay the guy back when it had lost and things had escalated, a car boot opened, bin bags and masking tape. He'd got into heroin, overdosed while holed up in some skag-head's tenth-floor council flat. He'd always died, because that was the only explanation for him having gone.

Fourteen years of imagining what he'd say about things. The Berlin Wall coming down. Hillsborough. Barnet going up to the Fourth Division. Labour winning. Princess Di. Fourteen years of having his voice right there, saying *About bloody time* or *You bleedin' beauty* or *He's a chancer that one, but I tip my hat to him.*

For a day, Matty skulked about in the almost-empty house, sweated in a sleeping bag all night on the living-room floor, wanting Rosa. Wanting her hand, even just to sit next to her, one arm against the cool of her silk blouse. Because he had left. He had left both of them. He'd never called.

But in the middle of the night, with the streetlight pouring through the window, Matty had sat up.

She'd *said* he was dead. Rosa hadn't blinked, that time in the kitchen in Golders Green, and said he was dead.

Matty slammed a fist into the wall, knuckles first. Drove it in harder, again and again, as if it were a boxing opponent, as if it were Rosa's cheek, her chest. Scraped at the wallpaper until it began to peel away, until a fingernail creased back and revealed skin.

I'll be in touch soon.

There'd been no more letters in the attic. No trace. Had he called? Did she talk to him? Matty tried to remember her leaving the phone ringing, and couldn't, one way or the other.

But they hadn't stayed at Golders Green all that long after the summer holidays. Rosa had moved them to the Finchley flat, before the two years in Italy. Too many memories, she had said.

Nonna. Matty phoned, asked her about him. Had Joe called? Written? The slight hesitation on the line was enough to know that they'd been in on it.

A plane to Bologna. Matty hired a car and drove to the hills outside Rimini. There was a smudge of wariness in Nonna's eyes when she pulled back after their hug. She wouldn't say anything first of all, feigned vagueness, busied herself with dinner. Wept at the details of the funeral. It was hard to bring him up.

Nonno was still laid up in bed, his voice a little weaker. Crossword book on the side and a man singing dolorously on the radio. He didn't know, he'd said. Not very much. Rosa only spoke to Nonna. *Non si chiedono queste cosa.* Better not to ask about these things.

Classic, Joe had said, the quiet inner-ear voice. *Absolute bloody classic.*

138

During the middle of the second night there, Matty rifled through the old dresser in the living room, looking for something. Anything. He must have written. Left an address. The lamp had suddenly come on. *Tesoro mio*, Nonna had said, the light showing the shape of her old, slight body through her nightgown, before she sat down on the arm of the corner chair.

Your mother did not want you to know about your father, she said, her words simple. He called, but I did not tell him where you were. Your mother asked us not to. He was a bad person. It was best for him not to be in your lives. The shame. Your mother never got over it. Nonna had broken down again, picking up the photo of Rosa aged twenty or so, half-sitting on the bonnet of a car with large sunglasses on her head, bright-red lipstick, her shoulder awkwardly thrust forward.

The next morning Matty had tried again, gentle questions over drying the dishes. When did he call? Where had he called from? The answers were always the same. *Non lo so, gioia. È stato così tanto tempo fa.* A long time ago. The stubbornness that her youngest daughter had inherited. It was only when she opened the box of Rosa's jewellery again, the golden chains spooling through her hands, that she'd said, not England. He had not been in England when he called. Where, then? A tired shrug was the only answer.

A kiss to Nonno's cheek, and Matty left, without a goodbye to her. Back to the airport, and London, and a world in which Joe now existed.

Chapter 3

A grey day. Clouds skidding across the sky. Shifty's windscreen wipers scraped lopsidedly alongside the beats of an old Public Enemy tape. Matty sat in the camper, shuffling the pack of cards, mentally rehearsing the lines by Robert De Niro in *Taxi Driver*. Marlon Brando in *The Wild Ones*. Chuck D. Imagining him right *there*.

The garage was over the road, a single-storey building with three vans outside. One of them had its bonnet up.

People came in and out. Each one was him for one heart-lurching moment and then not him. A mechanic in an oil-patched boiler suit, too young. A car's brakes squeaking, the middle-aged couple arguing as they got out, the man blond-haired. He was tall and with a sizeable beer belly, stretching, holding his hip.

Joe hadn't aged in all these years, not for Matty. He'd stayed the same slight, bouncing figure, reduced to simple elements: brown-blond hair, stubble, seventies leather jacket, nod, cigarette. 'God, I'm never getting old,' he'd said once. 'Nothing good up at that end of things. Give me a quick death, in my sleep, before it gets too gruesome.' And he'd clicked his fingers, lolled his head and stuck his tongue out. Opened one eye and winked.

After an hour, Matty got out of the van.

A teenager wearing a Miami Dolphins cap was on reception, singing along quietly to an Oasis song on the radio and turning the page of a magazine.

Matty got to the desk. Mouth dry. 'Is there, uh, a Joseph Ronan here? Or Joe?'

The boy had swiftly closed the magazine, a woman with big tits on the cover. Put his hands over it. 'There's not.' His eyebrows pulled together. 'There's a Jimmy. He runs it. He's not here so much nowadays, but he'll be back around later. Is it him you want, now?' He looked encouraging.

Jimmy. Would he have changed it? 'Um. Probably not.' Matty's throat felt dry. It would be too weird to ask how old he was. 'What time's he back?'

There was a women's swimwear calendar on the wall, the girl's legs impossibly splayed, her costume high above her hips. The reception guy caught Matty's gaze, his grin snagged halfway, and blushed. He scratched behind an ear and quickly put his hand back over the front of the magazine. 'About five, I think. Shall I tell him who's calling?'

'No, it's cool. Thanks.'

Recognise me?

Know who I am?

Yeah. It's me.

You thought you'd seen the back of me, didn't you? Think again.

A few hours of driving around, before returning at 4.30 p.m. Drinking strawberry Slim-Fast and eating the odd Skittle. Rehearsing, with slight variations, depending on how aggressive the imagined scenario became. Sometimes it was conciliatory, immediately forgiving. Sometimes it was purely violent. A red car pulled up, low and sleek, and Matty stilled.

The man went inside, a white polo shirt, keys in his hand. He was about the right height. Grey hair.

Matty stayed put, biting a fingernail. The last Skittle sucked slowly and turning to grains.

He came out again with the receptionist, who was showing him a particular van, pointing above a tyre. For a moment, the man glanced up, over the road, towards the camper.

141

Matty sank down into the seat, stared at the wheel.

It wasn't him.

***

Two months after finding the letter, Matty had gone to the sunbathing area outside the Men's Pond. Sat on a jacket for most of the day, smoking, keeping an eye out.

Weeks of doing nothing, stupefied, after the visit to Italy. He had left. He'd never been dead. He had left.

Clive had come eventually. The Angel of Death, living quietly in his posh house north of the Heath, continuing his day job of taking souls up to heaven. Or not, as it turned out. He was wearing pink trunks.

Matty had gone over. There'd been people who waved or offered a few words over the years, and Clive had always given a nod and a gentle smile before going back to his book. The pink was new, though.

'Do you remember me asking about my dad, ages ago?'

'Blimey,' he'd said, closing his book, his hand as a bookmark. 'You're taking us back a bit there.'

'Yeah, I know. I wondered if – you seemed like you might have known something. You said I'd see him again.' It had meant something different, all those years ago. Heaven, angels, afterlife.

Clive had given a searching look. 'He never came back, then?'

'No. Thought he was dead.'

'The Irish guy? Is that right?'

'Yeah?'

'We'd talked about Ireland a bit, I think. I've family there, in the distant past.'

'Do you remember where? Where you talked about?'

'I don't. Sorry. Memory's taken a battering in recent years.' A benign smile, and he'd opened his book again. Matty had stared

142

at the red and orange decoration on the cover, the Indian man with his pointed gold hat. Clive had looked up again. 'He did talk of it fondly, I think. Ireland. Said he'd probably end up back there one day. Ever been?'

'Once. Long time ago.' Not enough to know it. To know one half of yourself. The two years in Italy had been plenty to see that it wasn't right, women never alone but in pairs, girls only ever in skirts, Jesus looking at you from every street corner and every mantelpiece. Ireland – Ireland didn't mean anything, not really.

You could find some people on the Internet now. That's how it started, Matty in a cafe, slowly typing in letters on a new website, the addition of each letter causing more dread. But he wasn't there, only a couple of other Ronans. His lot were travellers, after all. They probably wouldn't have made it onto a site like this.

The next thing was harder, working up the courage to phone directory enquiries, except that of course you needed the address to get a number.

'Look him up. Proper phone book, innit,' said Heather. 'Narrow it down. Like a hit list.'

Joe was the needle, Ireland was the haystack. When Matty had spread the map out and seen how much blue patchworked the paper, it looked like something else entirely. A land to swim through. If he couldn't be found, at least there would be that.

23/11/99
LOUGH _____, Air 8°C, Water 9°C, 750m

Matty had come over on the ferry with Shifty, eight hours of rocky lurching, land legs not coming back for a few hours afterwards. There'd been a couple of nights in a Dublin hostel, getting bearings, surrounded by voices that all sounded like Joe's. It had taken a while not to look for him in every face. Not to want to stop and ask if they knew him.

Instead, Matty had gone to the city's biggest library, and sat with the directory for every area, a finger sliding down a page or two in each one. The business directories, too. Three J. Ronans. The plan was to start in the Wicklow Mountains, zigzag up through the centre. A child's strange dot-to-dot, and each lough swum would be coloured in with black biro.

Galway looked to be full of water. Fresh water, and the Atlantic fingering into it all over. If Joe wasn't found, Matty could head there.

It was grimmer here, in the belly of the country, with nothing of the moorland colours. Shifty lurched down an uneven, unmarked track. Matty swam towards the mist in between two hills, the wind drawing the water into spines. A pair of swans, pristinely white among the grey, served as a guide for the return. They parted on the approach, gatekeepers to the slipway. The water was very clear.

Heather had said to ring the numbers, of course. 'You'll be done in fifteen minutes. None of this gallivanting around the Emerald Isle like a bloody leprechaun.' Matty couldn't do it. What could you say, if it was him? *Remember me? I'm the kid you abandoned. Mum's dead.* No. Each J. Ronan had to be scoped out from a slight distance, appraised, like water was. The danger areas, the depth. Courage needed time.

Limerick. Houses were being put up everywhere on the outskirts. *PARTY LIKE ITS 1999* posters on the windows in the high street. Leaping reindeer strung up overhead, unlit.

One hour.

A little outside the centre, there was a flat above an animal welfare charity shop. Matty had nosed Shifty down a side street, put on the Beastie Boys and watched the doorway, steadily biting each fingernail down to the skin. Imagined Joe pushing aside those curtains, leaning out of a window to have a fag. If nothing else, he would still smoke.

Two hours.

Yeah, it's me. Yeah, I've grown.

'Proactive, Matty,' Heather had said, her girlfriend Val nodding on sympathetically. 'You gotta be big. Be all up in his face. That man deserves a slap-down.'

'And a conversation,' said Val, more pragmatically. 'Don't assume anything.'

Why did you leave. Where did you go. Where the fuck did you go. You left me. You left me with her.

Matty stopped the tape and got out, crossing the road, fists stuffed in both pockets of the bomber jacket.

The shop had mannequins in the window, their arms at awkward angles, stuffed toys clustered at their feet. *FINAL REDUCTIONS* posters tacked onto the glass. A sudden memory of Rosa, taping up signs in the suit shop's windows, pulling a silly, elastic face at Matty outside on the pavement, before Joe left.

Deep breath. Matty went to the neighbouring door and craned up at the window and those half-closed curtains. The sky's wet brightness on the glass.

'Excuse me.' A woman's voice.

Matty walked into the porch to make way, and the woman who had spoken frowned. She was holding onto a small, tear-stained child and had her other hand in her shoulder bag. A swift look up at the window and back down again as she brought out her keys. 'Can I help you?' She sounded tired, irritated.

There was a door buzzer to the side. Two names, written in different handwriting, one stacked above the other. Barnaby O'Shea. Jessica Ronan.

Jessica.

'No. Sorry. Wrong door.' Matty turned and entered the shop, spending five minutes looking at rails of second-hand clothing, before getting back to Shifty, a parking ticket wedged under the windscreen wiper.

Matty was no good at talking to people. Most people anyway. Never giving too much away, not too much eye contact until there was certainty of not being sneered at, gawked at. Even after that, it took a while to warm up, to work them out, decide whether they were worth getting to know or not.

'You're a right enigma, aren't you?' Heather had said early on, arching one perfectly over-plucked eyebrow. They'd first met at a jungle night five years ago, Matty having lost the couple of acquaintances from earlier in the night and dancing solo, earthed by the basslines, until accidentally colliding with Heather, all six foot one of her. She'd been clad in a massive padded leather coat and black latex bra, and came armed with a massive hearty laugh and a maternal air. 'Always so mysterious.'

Shrug.

'Yeah, exactly. That's what you do. Lift those bloody shoulders up like that'll explain everything. It'll backfire on you, you know. Only so long before strong and silent just becomes mute oddball.'

The opposite of Joe, and of so many people here, who had his expressions, or ones like them. All those extra words. *All right now* and *altogether* and *now then*. Matty's sentences were spare, nothing but bone. They'd shrunk even more, since Rosa.

***

'Where have you been?'

'Out. At a friend's.'

'For three days? You are still at school.'

'I'm not there much.'

'What? What did you say?'

In the bedroom, a pile of clothes had been laid on the bed, neatly folded – skirts, ruby-red tights, jumpers with sequins on them.

'I was cleaning out the wardrobe,' said Rosa in the doorway, with a challenging expression. 'I wanted to check that you did not want anything.'

A long, slow breath. 'Mamma,' Matty had said, in jeans and an oversized hooded top. Trying to sound kind. 'You know I don't.'

There had been a moment in which Rosa had just stared, as if trying to decide whether to accept or fight. Then she began to gather everything up, crumpling them in her arms. 'It is a phase,' she said, as she moved. 'This is what I tell myself.'

'It's not,' said Matty. 'It's just who I am.'

'I don't want you to be *who you are*,' she had said, tearful and vicious at once.

Nor do I, Matty had thought, and opened a drawer, began shoving clothes into a bag.

'What are you doing now? You have just got here.'

'I'm going. Properly.'

'Where? Where are you going?'

Anywhere but here.

Rosa was following Matty around the flat, to the bathroom, the kitchen. 'You want me to be even more ashamed of you? Failing at school, leaving home? Leaving your mother?'

'You left me a long time ago, Mamma,' Matty had said, before shutting the front door.

***

North. Level with Dublin, the clouds lifted to leave a slab of colourless sky. No hills. The towns had blank new estates with prophetic signs in the driveways, and the older houses wore their pastel colours badly, streaked by decades of rain. Matty picked up a postcard and watched crows slot themselves into an ancient monastic tower. Bought bottles of beer to take back from pubs painted grey and darker grey. Mac's. Old Pat's. Lawrence's Bar and Off-Licence. The 'Ulysses bar' had a shrine to James Joyce, tinsel round his neck. Trevor would have given his literature lecture to anyone within earshot, maybe tried to see whose pants he could get his cock into. In one pub, some teenage boys with banjos and electric guitars were singing country and rock 'n' roll covers, never looking at the audience. Matty hovered at the bar, imagining Joe up there, acknowledging the crowd, doing the Johnny Cash snarl, trying and failing to get the low notes.

Nonsense. I'd have brought the bloody house down.

A night in a B & B in a smaller town, a proper breakfast to save having lunch later, without the carbs. Black pudding and white pudding. The woman who owned the place was constantly in and out, looking over. The other diners looking over.

Matty stared at the framed needlepoint on the wall, upper arms still throbbing from the morning round of press-ups. God was the main guest in this place, a wooden crucifix above the bed in the room, a large-print Bible in the drawer. The stitching in the picture was purple on cream, the letters jerky. *FAITH IS THE SUBSTANCE OF THINGS HOPED FOR – THE EVIDENCE OF THINGS NOT SEEN.* One of the threads had come loose in the corner.

'Is that all right for you, there?' The landlady was by the table, picking up the butter, a gold crucifix necklace swinging away from her chest. Jesus was trying to make a break for it.

'Yeah. Thanks.'

She hovered. 'So what brings you out here, then? Not so much of a tourist area, this.'

The two couples on the other tables quietened a bit, the chatter on the radio in the kitchen spiking through. 'Just family stuff.'

The landlady wasn't going anywhere. 'Oh, is that right? Round here, is it?'

'Yeah.' It might not be a lie. Matty would find out later.

She let out a sigh, bright with false interest. 'And are you an auntie, then, or ... ?' There it was. Having to confirm.

Matty didn't bother using the napkin, standing up, the cup rattling loudly on its saucer. 'Only child.' Voice a little higher, just in case. 'Do I pay you now?'

It was stupid, coming here. Matty sat in traffic in this sour, puny town, glancing over to see a kid with a lollipop looking back, their tongue blue. At least in London you got looked at less. Sometimes. There was Soho with the gays, old and young, on Old Compton Street, though it had felt different down there since the nail bomb. And Camden, hanging out among the freaks – pierced, tattooed, metallers and old punks, dread-locked white boys and girls in leather kilts and biker boots. For a while Matty had kipped with Al at a commune at the grubbiest end of the high street, four storeys of damp Georgian terrace, light filtering through the wooden pallets that boarded the windows. Al, his slim frame in a sarong, his waist-length chestnut hair and veganism, stroking Matty into shivers with a manicured nail. One of his fellow squatters, Bee, was the first person to ever trigger any recognition, a green-haired bisexual who lent indigestible books by Judith Butler and Jacques Derrida, and talked obsessively about getting surgery with a conviction that felt painful.

She'd been like Rosa, that landlady, for a moment. Disapproving, uncomprehending. God whispering to her that Matty was not OK.

'What has happened?' Rosa had said once, years before, the school having telephoned her.

'Fight.' Matty had bruises already coming up. Right cheekbone, upper arm.

'With who?'

'Fifth-form boys.'

Fucking tranny-fag. Suck me. No, don't bruv, she's got AIDS-breath.

'You disgust me. Fighting. Like a boy.'

Joe would have said, *I hope you gave those beggars a shiner. Knocked out their bloody teeth.* He would have marched up to the head's door, given him an earful, become friendly. Got the boys suspended, not Matty.

It was always Matty's fault. The fighting worked, though, just about. One of the boys fractured a finger, and after that the insults kept coming, but no one got too close.

It did nothing but rain all day. A constant white noise on Shifty's roof. 'Dear God, the rain,' Joe had said once, holding Matty's shoulders as if in desperation. 'It never bloody stops. You know how humans are eighty per cent water? Well, the Irish are ninety-five per cent water. We cry rain.' He'd leant down, his voice lowering, a time when he could still delight Matty with his very occasional swearing. 'We *piss* rain.' A wink.

Leg stretch. A car park next to a graveyard with a massive soaked Jesus. One thing for the real crucifixion – however shit it had been, at least it probably wouldn't have been raining on him as well. Matty had a quick fag, hood up, wandering underneath the dark clot of the yew trees, reading the inscriptions. There was a man in navy overalls, kneeling in front of a headstone, scraping at it. A cigarette hanging from his mouth, too, straight. He nodded at Matty. The letters were splodged with black so that you couldn't read the name.

There had been a lot of loitering in graveyards back in North London. The only two half-decent friends from school weren't bothered that Matty didn't have black-painted nails and steel-capped platform boots. Goths were very tolerant. They would sit in Wood Green Cemetery, or even make pilgrimages to Abney

150

Park, Kensal Green or Mile End, the nice ones, like taking a death-themed school trip. Matty would listen to Michelle and Martin – 'the three "M"s', one of the dickheads at school would say, 'mong, mong and mong' – crooning along to Sisters of Mercy on their shared Walkman headphones. Would kick the nearest headstone, imagine it carved with 'JOSEPH RONAN: DROWNED TRAGICALLY' or 'JOSEPH RONAN: BELOVED FATHER AND BARNET SUPPORTER' or whatever felt right that night.

It was impossible to not think of it, even now, even after finding the letter. Impossible not to have an eye on each stone, just in case. Not to come out of every bit of wild water thinking *he's not in there*, having made sure. Another lake, river, the sea even. The Ponds had wound into Matty's blood, and the ghost-feelings in with it.

24/11/99
LOUGH _____, Air 8°C, Water 9°C, 1km

There were public toilets here, deserted. Into the Men's. A starling shot up to the roof, the panic loud in its wings, before it found its way out, Matty's heart settling again.

The plain urinal was more like a sheep trough. Brown leaves clogged up in its base. The smell of urine, surely as old as the summer.

This never happened, no one being here. Sometimes you could risk it, depending on the place. Head down, into a cubicle. It always felt dangerous. Disabled ones were best. Matty needed an individual sign – a thin stick figure with neither skirt nor legs wide apart, and horizontal, not vertical. Swimming.

A long boardwalk, stretching into clay-coloured water, with low hills further off. Forearm-length reeds banked up against the dark gravel. The yellow of the life-buoy casing was the only brightness in the view, though there was no red ring inside.

151

You weren't supposed to swim alone, not long distance. You should always have a buddy, or boat cover. Let people know where you were. But loughs were good, once you got past the bank. No sharks to worry about, or seals. The fish stayed deep, well away. It was just you and the water.

Halfway back, Matty went vertical, bicycle-kicked as sluggishly as possible, listening to the sound of sheep blurring with a hedge-strimmer somewhere. This singular view, the lough spanning outwards at eye level. The world looked different from here, and it always felt better – easier to breathe, the ache of having to hold this body up floating clean away. Water didn't judge.

Post-swim cigarette, held with the end tucked inwards, shoulders feeling broadened and tough. The hedge-strimmer grew louder, and turned into a motorbike, appearing on the roadside and curling round this way, slowing as it passed. It wasn't Trevor, thank God. Matty had taken off first thing on that morning, not used the shared bathroom, gone light-footed past the door from which a stoutly rasping snore emanated.

Rain came in again, the green-grey of everything. Matty-colours. The wardrobe had stayed the same since the age of fourteen, as soon as they'd come back from Italy. Dark, wan, neutral. Grey-brown hair, usually under a cap or a woolly hat, a few curls poking out at the front.

'You could dye your hair,' Heather once said.

'Not really my thing.'

'It's just a bit … flavourless, you know?' Her false nails ruffling it up.

'Mate. Get off.'

'Ooh, touchy.'

'*You* don't even have any.' Heather went to a barber's every other week for a grade zero.

She'd sucked her top lip into her teeth, a loud sound, mock-desultory. 'I've got divine Nubian princess looks on my side, haven't I?'

Matty had shaved it all off one autumn, just to see the look on Heather's face, but it had been too cold in the water. Everything became about that.

Matty put a towel under the hanging wetsuit, and opened the guidebook. It was mostly castles, monasteries, ornate crosses, but it was still nice to read. To learn.

There'd been no university, or even college. Exams had been a write-off, apart from PE and geography. Rosa had found the results slips crumpled in the kitchen bin, and over another dinner that neither of them finished, the conversation had quickly degenerated into the usual – she railing that she had done everything she could, and Matty biting back before giving up.

But, over the years, Matty had still gone to a library and opened encyclopaedias, starting somewhere and following a trail, hefting a different one over to the corner table. Whales to echolocation to the harmonic series. Coral to asexual reproduction to DNA. It was still easy to feel stupid, though, even if Matty could coil a climbing rope, coil and tail, and could do a C-to-C roll in a kayak.

In the guidebook, there was an insert on the Sheila-na-Gigs, crudely carved stone figures of females with legs outspread, prising open their own black, gaping vulvas.

Matty closed the book.

The last J. Ronan on the list was further north. But it was exhausting, even to think about it. Both times, the garage and the flat next to the charity shop, there had been relief mixed in with the disappointment. More relief than anything else, in truth. This last one – it could really be him.

The middle of Ireland was veined with water. A blue spine of it on the map, a different sort of route. Matty turned left instead of right at the next junction, down a lesser road, tinsel hanging from fir trees. Black fields either side, the peat laid in stacks under plastic.

Still cold – water lingered under the skin. Hungry, too, after no lunch. Sometimes Slim-Fast didn't do the trick. Here was a small town, with a sunbed shop and a takeaway advertising Mekong Asian food. The girl behind the counter was neither, pale olive skin, brown hair with blond streaks in it, and a single dangling earring, rhombus-shaped.

Matty's voice stayed low. 'All right?'

'I might be,' she said. Listless.

'Yeah?'

'When my shift finishes.' Not an Irish accent. Lilting, but not quite the same as the Greeks and Turks back in Golders Green. She took the order, soullessly ringing up the price on the cash register.

'When do you get off, then?' A little warmer, the protective side coming out.

'Four hours.' An eye-roll.

A twangy, Chinese-sounding electric guitar was playing through a boxy speaker high up in the corner. Matty waited underneath it, the sole of one foot resting on the wall behind, listening to the sound of two men, a younger and an older voice, shouting in what was probably Vietnamese behind the beaded curtain.

The cashier was leaning her elbows on the counter, reading a Harry Potter book – or at least holding it up, her eyes repeatedly lifting to the clock above a laminated photo of goo-covered chicken legs.

'Where're you from?' Maybe Matty was starting to pick up the Irish thing. Everyone always asked that over here.

She sighed. 'Portugal.' She turned the cover of the book round. 'I am improving my English. Although it is not maybe so helpful, as the Irish way of speaking is like another language.'

'Yeah. I get that.'

A slanted smile. Matty snuck a glance when she'd gone back to her book. Her hair was scraped back messily, the sides uneven. The strip light above them picked out a single spot on her chin. Long lashes. She was cute.

A man in a filthy apron and thin plastic gloves made the beads rattle as he came out. 'How are you doing, now?' he said, slapping two boxes down on the raised glass top.

The girl handed over the tin casings with a sullen smile. 'Enjoy your meal.'

***

24/11/99
LOUGH____, Air 8°C, Water 10°C, 200m

Four hours later, Matty was slouched in the front seat in a car park next to some public toilets, absent-mindedly cutting and re-cutting the pack of cards. Not watching for Joe, or the possibility of Joe, but watching the Vietnamese takeaway.

Earlier, Matty had coaxed Shifty down a bumpy, sodden track that ended abruptly at another lough. Dark purple leaves and foamy scum massed at the shoreline and the leftovers of a jetty, vertical logs with tyres hanging off. A broken disposable coffee cup. The second swim of the day had been short, listless, preceded by a round of sixty press-ups and stomach crunches with feet hooked under the bumper.

Afterwards, half of the reheated takeaway – cashew nut chicken and rice, as Joe always had. Oily steam filling the van. Matty had put the Merle Haggard tape on, songs of whisky and melancholy to go with the food. Tried not to think about the old days, of Joe playing air acoustic guitar, the side of his mouth curling up.

Ah, cheer up. No one's died.

There was a shout from outside in the car park. Two youngish men, one carrying a fishing rod in a case. He slapped the other on the back and said something else, miming boobs with a cupped hand and pursing his lips. The other man shook his head, laughing, and waved goodbye.

It was seamy, wrong, being back here. But there'd been something in the girl's look behind the counter, behind the tired sarcasm. She was bored out of her mind. Company might be welcome. Maybe she hadn't been over here long, might be up for a few beers and whatever came next. It was always good not to expect anything more, to let it come from them if they fancied it. There could be a few home comforts, even if it was in a tiny flat above a shop. Crisps in a bowl and some Portuguese music playing, whatever that sounded like. Speaking rusty Italian, and maybe being understood. Really understood.

The door to the takeaway opened and the girl slipped out.

Here we are. Look lively. Go get 'em, tiger.

Matty sat up, tugged some hair out from under the beanie hat, fingers going through the curls. Turned the tape off.

There was a beep from a car three parking spaces away, and as the girl walked quickly across the road, the gentle bump in her stomach became visible, and how her hand came protectively across it. When she sat down in the passenger seat, she leant over to kiss the driver, the light illuminating their briefly joined silhouettes.

Ah, well. You win some, you lose some. Plenty more fish in the sea and all that.

A few minutes, to let the car disappear. Matty shunted Shifty into gear, and drove off to find a place to park up for the night.

***

Matty had run into Johanna three years ago, coming the other way on Golders Green Road, having gone past the old flat just

156

to have a look. Johanna had been pushing a buggy with a fat, dark-haired child in it, already one year old. She pretended to be embarrassed about it, saying something about the redemption of the firstborn and being lorded around on a silver tray, but she'd leant down and mopped the kid's snotty cheek, her voice softening. She'd not bothered to take a phone number, or to say that they should stay in touch.

Friends. All the moving around had made it hard to keep them. Italy had disrupted things a bit, and Martin and Michelle had gone to Berlin at eighteen and were never seen again.

Matty drifted after school, out at sixteen, doing odd jobs for a while in North London, never more than a bus or a cycle ride away from the Ponds, before getting involved in a new climbing wall built in an old water-pumping station. The talent for limbering up things, jumping off things, diving into things, had remained. Eventually, an application to a massive kids' camp had taken Matty to America, doing abseiling and gorge-walking alongside all the shit stuff like breakfasts and laundry. More camps followed, not just in the summer. Canada, America, back in the UK sometimes. Matty was never one of the warm ones, the staff members who put an arm round a kid who got The Fear while facing down a sheer rock face and – you were never too far away from the Jesus crowd at these places – little talks about how pleased God would be if they could just put one foot over the ledge. Matty would just sit and wait, tapping fingers on rivets until they'd decided, one way or the other. The fat kids, the tearful kids, the kids with double train-track braces and a nervous laugh, those were the ones Matty landed. And that was fine.

You'd bond with the work-camp staff. Six weeks of living in each other's pockets meant laughing hysterically over in-jokes, declarations of platonic love and promises to see each other, but it never stuck. There was the old-man crowd at the Underhill Stadium, where Matty still went occasionally to watch Barnet hoof the ball around – though in a different spot to the old days. A couple of locals at Bar Italia in Soho, Matty having once been roped into a card game and winning first time. And plenty of familiar faces at the Ladies' Pond, though none were ever past acquaintances, and the conversation rarely strayed past swimming.

Mostly, there was Heather, though it hadn't started out well, following the first meeting.

'Seriously, man, what the fuck is this?' Heather had looked up and down with heavy disdain from behind the bar after a few visits. Matty had started jogging along the canal, coming in to down two pints of tap water before drinking a half of cider more slowly. 'What's this, like, gayboy pretend-lezzer thing?'

'I dunno.' A wary look. There'd once almost been a fight at a lesbian bar in King's Cross, a trio of girls getting aggressive. 'Just – is.'

'Twisted as fuck.' Disgusted delight in each word. 'Fucking decide and be done with it. You're giving us a bad name.' But she couldn't keep it up. 'Can't resist you in the end though, can we?' she'd said, many months later, pouring blackcurrant cordial into Matty's Guinness. 'Big puppy-dog eyes saying "be my mum".'

The box room in the flat above the pub had a skylight window spotted with bird shit, posters of poetry slam nights and Pam Grier films, most of Heather's clothes on two packed rails and a mannequin sporting a large black strap-on. She let Matty pay rent when there was money, and didn't press when there wasn't. It was never permanent, and occasionally there'd be someone else staying there, but it was *somewhere*.

There was Heather, and whichever butch woman Heather was going out with, which for the last couple of years had been Val, a Scottish poet in her late forties with a love of tattoos and tall black women.

It had been Val who'd encouraged this trip. 'You've got to go, lovie,' she'd said, arm round Heather on their brown leather sofa, pointing a finger. 'Scratch at those roots of yours. Even if you

158

don't find him, you'll find something of yourself there. We go deep.'

'Matty definitely does,' said Heather. Stuck her tongue out.

Not much good at relationships, either. For various reasons. They might be drawn in by the aquamarine eyes, the boyishness and generosity – Matty would always buy the drinks, down to the last penny. But it never lasted, partly due to all the moving around, sofa to sofa, bedsit to bedsit, the holiday work. And what would have been the point, when they might take off on you? There'd only really been Al, soft-eyed and dreamy, announcing three years ago that he was off to Australia for a bit, and never returning.

The car park was at the end of a stone-walled road, with an out-of-season campsite and a toilet. No one else here. It was dark, and hard to tell how far the water stretched. Matty got the generator going outside and fiddled with the TV aerial, moving it from worktop to bed and back to the worktop, the sound and screen ashy. *Raging Bull* was on, Jake LaMotta in his peak. A proper Italian, a proper boxer. His lines weren't quite as good as on *Taxi Driver*, but they were usable. *I'm gonna make him suffer.*

One more J. Ronan. Further into the wet heart of Ireland.

The TV screen seemed to be consuming itself. Matty rolled up under the blankets, falling asleep before it had finished, Jake LaMotta's words getting mixed up with others.

Faith is the suffering of things hoped for. Faith. Not seen.

Chapter 4

25/11/99
LOUGH ____, Air 11°C, Water 10°C, 3.5km

Matty woke up scratching. The patch of eczema on the right side of the ribs came and went – the skin flaring red or shimmering like fish-scales – depending on how tight everything was. You weren't supposed to restrict yourself for too many hours at a time, but needs must. It had been trial and error, this. The experiment with cling film and masking tape as a teenager hadn't lasted long. Bee, whose own tits were much bigger, had seen the discarded bandages on Al's mattress in the squat and brought back two sports bras from town, one to be worn backwards and on top of the other, with shoulders turned inwards in a way that would probably cause old-man's-walk at some point. Talcum power to soak up the sweat. Occasionally, Matty would look in the mirror after a bath and feel OK, and just put one on.

The wetsuit sorted everything. Smoothing everything down but not too restrictive, making you neither one nor the other. Simply a swimmer. After a set of bicep curls and lifts with the dumbbells, Matty hefted it on, and walked down to the water.

The lough had revealed itself this morning, a vast expanse dotted with islands, some bearing churches according to the faded visitor's information. The large granite steps of the quayside were obviously there for boats, but the place was deserted. Matty headed for the island with the sixth-century monastery, though it was too boggy to get onto it, the mud sucking dangerously. A glimpse of two ruined buildings, dappled and roofless. The shortest pause for breath, to stop the muscles thickening with the cold, and then back to the quayside, Shifty's mustard colour a motivating flag. A handful of water scooped up before stepping out. It tasted cool, peaty, granular.

The wet things were hung on a pale broken branch. Matty clutched the plastic cup of tea like a votive, the heater on, and spread the map across the steering wheel. The electricity of the lough coursing through each vein.

This would be it. Faith. Substance.

***

'Fuck's sake.'

The sign stuck out of the grass, a few kilometres north-west of Athlone.

JOHN EDWARD RONAN, Landscape Gardener.

'Fuck.' Matty squatted, pushing a fist into the damp pavement.

'Can I help you?' A lady with a mane of grey hair and an ankle-length raincoat was coming along the road with a carrier bag in each hand, turning into the driveway where Matty stood. She sounded open, concerned.

'No.' Matty stood, jammed a thumbnail between two front teeth, and out again. Remembered how to be courteous. 'Sorry. I was looking for Joe Ronan.' It sounded stupid, even to say it.

'Girl or boy?'

'What?' Too tired to fight it.

'As in, is that a girl or boy?' she said, the lines drawn in her face, though she didn't look unkind. 'With an "e" or without?'

'Oh. Boy,' Matty said, the word dry and cracked. Boy, man, father, absent. Why hast thou forsaken me.

161

'Ah, what am I saying now,' the lady said. 'I don't know any girl-Jos or boy-Joes. Is it Seán you're after?' White strands of her hair rose up on her shoulders.

'Just Joseph. Or – Maureen?' It was daft to ask. They were travellers. They didn't set down anywhere. They didn't have addresses. Did they?

The woman let out a long, melodious sigh, as if she'd been set a delicious riddle. 'Not if it's Ronan as the surname, no. I know plenty of Maureens.'

'It's all right. Cheers.'

Matty went back to the van, the lady's rising, falling *hall-oh* cut off sharply as the front door shut behind her. Sat in silence, before administering one swift punch with the side of a fist into the driver's door.

Forget it. Forget *him*. He'd forgotten his child, after all.

***

Despite the pub being up an unlit single-track road, it was busy, and humid with smoke and sweat. There was a *HAPPY 40TH BIRTHDAY* banner slung lopsidedly on one wall, and much of the room was taken up with men in shirts and blazers and women with heavy make-up. Bryan Adams was blaring out from a jukebox. 'Summer of '69'.

Winter of '99. Matty needed warmth. There was a cold coming, a scratchiness in the throat that wasn't solved by drink, as two beers had testified. None of the beers had made any of the anger subside. Nor the steak and kidney pie, which combined with the beers and the Vietnamese takeaway would add half a pound, maybe more. Probably would have to skip breakfast to make up for it, and lunch, and have Slim-Fast for dinner. Twice as many press-ups and squat-lunges.

Fuck him. Fuck him fuck him fuck him.

Matty had driven in circles. Driven to more loughs, only to stare at them before reversing back up the track. Thought of London, wanted to be there, except that the box room was occupied at the moment. Wanted to be in the Canadian camp where there'd be a cute pony-trekking instructor who liked Matty to go down on her when she had her period, who used climbing ropes unexpectedly, causing them both to be in fits of giggles as they came. Wanted to – there was nowhere else. Nowhere was home.

Should have just phoned. None of this grand quest bollocks. Should have had the guts to ring the numbers and hear strangers' voices, like Heather had said.

He could be anywhere.

Queen were on the jukebox now, a couple of girls holding centre stage, singing *Find. Me. Somebody to love* with some stop-start actions. The guys watching them were grinning, one dropping his wrist as he mouthed the words and pouted grotesquely.

Matty remembered the tabloid headlines when Freddie Mercury died. *AIDS KILLED THE KING OF ROCK.* Remembered the adverts on TV before that, the weird clanging music and the violent engraving of the word into stone. Remembered the grass bank outside the Men's Pond, the sadness just under the surface.

Daz had been there, on and off, each summer. At the turn of the last decade, Matty had gone over to buy a can of Pepsi.

'Wotcha sport, long time no see,' Daz had said. Paint-spattered jeans and no top. He looked thinner. 'Been hanging round with the ladies, have you?'

'Mixed, mostly.'

'Very sensible, very sensible. That's fifty pee.'

'Gone up?'

'Moving with the times, mate. Going to be a proper yuppie, me. Loadsamoney.'

'How is everyone? Been ages.'

'Oh, you know, dropping like flies.' A weak grin, just an old hint of the devil in him, before he looked up the hill. 'Gegsy's gone.'

Gegsy. With his *bumboys* and his *shirtlifters* and all the rest. Gegsy, who'd made a couple more mixtapes and advised on pirate radio stations, rattled off the names of clubs that Matty was then far too young to go into.

It had been hard to know what to say after that. Matty had drunk the Pepsi while Daz talked about his plan to move to Ibiza, and when he'd waved to a group of guys, quietly wandered away.

The music had got louder. More rock. Maybe it would go on all night, and Matty would have to listen to it coming up through the ceiling in the room upstairs.

It was damp outside, a mist coming down. There was an incongruous Blues Brothers statue at the entrance to the pub, large and plastic, the two of them gurning in their pork pie hats. Matty walked to the fence line at the end of the car park, and looked up at the blackness. The lack of stars.

'All right now?' A low, musical voice, coming from a deep shadow by the wall of the pub.

Matty didn't feel like talking. Made busy with cigarette and lighter.

'That your van there?'

A plume of smoke, blown out into the fine drizzle. 'Yeah.'

'Lovely. You've got the right idea, so you have.' He stepped out, a large man, not tall. Belly protruding from his long coat, which itself seemed to be bulging, lumpen. 'Those bloody tinkers up Longford way. They park their caravans and turn a field into a rubbish site. Let their children run around with hardly a stitch on. You'll not be one of them.'

No. And yes. 'No.'

'Very good.' The man shuffled back to his spot, a low wall by a drain under the awning. 'You'll have a drink with me.' It wasn't a question.

Matty sat down on the wall out of the rain and watched him pull out a small bottle of Bushmills, half-filling a mug. 'That's not from the pub?'

'God in heaven, no. *This* is from the pub, though.' He leant worryingly far over and pulled out a can of Sprite from one of his pockets, topping it up, the froth just stopping short of overflowing. 'That'll put hairs on your chest,' he said. 'You look like you need a few.' The dull, settled sort of feeling, adding to the headache. Better than being seen as a girl, but still not right.

They sat in silence for a minute. Matty's fist still hurt from earlier. Two knuckles were a dull red.

'I'm using my powers of divination to work out that you're not a local.' He gave a rheumy cough.

'No.'

'But you've Irish in there.'

'Yeah.' Matty had never felt the slightest bit Irish as a kid in London. The reports on TV hadn't meant much, though Joe would sit up straighter on the sofa. But at secondary school, as well as the other stuff, there'd been *IRA = In Ronan's Arse* and *Irish jippo he-bitch* written on the wall of the loo after Matty had won the right to wear trousers. Irish, whether you liked it or not.

'And you're on your way to something?'

Matty glanced over. The man was looking upwards, rocking on his heels. 'I was.'

'Good enough. You'll get there.' Spoken as if he was in on it, knew the whole thing. The attic, the letter, the crippling fear of finding him, the emptiness now. 'Keep on. Keep at it. Right enough, so.'

He muttered those words again, a strange, understated rap. Matty drank from the mug, the fierceness of the whiskey and

165

the fizz of the lemonade. Sheep moved like low clouds through the field in front of them.

Halfway through his own drink, the guy started to show his true colours, his voice riding the morphed sound of the music inside. He'd gone on about his older siblings – he'd been the youngest of ten – and how they'd not had electricity in the farmhouse because his parents had called it 'witchcraft'. He didn't seem to entirely disagree, though he did seem to tip his hat to progress. 'All these young people like yourself having a bit of money to spend,' he'd said.

Matty saw Rosa again, one arm drooping downwards from the sofa, already blueish.

But he'd just been warming up. He'd already gone on about all of the East Europeans who were going to be coming in soon enough and now he'd moved onto God. 'All this feckology the Big Men put out. People turning away from the Church. When I was a snapper it was the priests who said what was what.' He let out a small, clicking burp. 'Anyway, it'll all be coming to a head soon. He'll be getting his own back.' He turned suddenly. 'You know all about it, I'm sure.'

'Know all about what?'

'The Day of Reckoning,' he said, a little more grandly, sniffing and wiping his nose on the elbow of his coat before standing up. A guttural sigh. 'On December thirty-first of this good year, there'll be a raging in the sky, and blood pouring here on earth. Oh, everyone will be told, right enough.'

Matty looked out at the line of hills beyond the dark field. 'Yeah?'

'This century will be the last like it,' the guy said. 'All this technology whatnot will be obliterated. Flattened. There'll be only a few of us left, starting from scratch again, if we're not chosen to join him just yet.'

Lovely. An apocalypse plus a rapture, just for good measure.

166

He was some sort of survivalist, giving himself a backup in case God didn't scoop him out. 'You must repent all of your sins,' he was saying, taking a step forward, moving back again. 'Give up all of your worldly goods.'

'I don't really go in for all that, mate.'

His look was acidic. There was the smell of piss in there with the drink. 'Only those who truly believe will be lifted up to join him.' He nodded faintly upwards. 'Even the dead will rise up.'

I've got no chance, then, Matty thought, and flicked the cigarette stub into a puddle. 'Gotcha.'

'No, no, no, just listen.' He held a hand up, filthy nails in fingerless gloves. 'Listen to me, lad. You've got to put your house in order, before it all turns to hellfire. And –' he leant up, ready to impart his last bit of profound, age-long wisdom. 'Make sure you get a tin-opener.'

Matty had stopped going to church aged fourteen – there'd been no avoiding God during the two years in Italy. But back in London, it felt easier. Wood Green was more mixed than Golders Green – Jamaicans, Brazilians, Somalis, Bangladeshis. There were more Muslims, a few Hindus, way fewer Orthodox Jews.

'I'm not going,' Matty had said one morning from under the duvet.

Rosa had shut the bedroom door over-loudly and leant her back on it. She'd come back with a man the night before, hustled him out first thing. As if Matty hadn't heard the muffled groans coming down the corridor during the night. 'Why not?'

'Don't believe in God.'

'What is this? Since when did you not believe in God?'

'Since Dad.'

It stopped her saying anything, for a while. That seemed to be the trick, to mention Joe. As good as a wheel clamp on her jaw. Rosa left Matty to lie in on Sunday mornings and would stay out most of the afternoon with friends she'd made at the new church. It had been a long time since the lavish Sunday roasts.

God had turned into a wide, silent nothing. A space where something had once been. Water filled it, mostly.

***

Keep on. Keep at it. Faith. Things Unseen.

Matty lay in the pub room's slightly damp bed, trying to work up the energy to go and get the hot-water bottles from Shifty. Might as well have slept in the van after all. It was freezing in here.

Oh, this is a bloody classic.

A Bridge Too Far was on the room's TV, though it was far away in the corner, hard to see from under the covers.

Matty would hang out at the Prince Charles Cinema in the centre of town, where the tickets were dirt cheap and the seats sloped up to the screen. War or action films, old Westerns, a bucket of salted popcorn and an arm round the sweet Welsh skateboarding girl who'd been in London on holiday. 'Your eyes are minty,' she'd said, before the lights went down. 'I could eat them.'

Now, the sound of gunfire mixed with the throb of the music downstairs. No eleven o'clock closing time here. They were actually playing the Blues Brothers now, the party group belting out 'Sweet Home Chicago' in seven different keys at once.

On the TV, the German Panzers rolling across the bridge were on fire, their soldiers still shooting. A British sniper getting a bullet in his arm. Joe used to repeat Sean Connery's lines exaggeratedly, like a drunk, contrast it with the clipped posh-cockney of Michael Caine, and say that Matty could do a far more convincing Polish accent than Gene Hackman.

A bridge and a bridge and a bridge, the film lumbering on, the British generals doggedly moving forwards, keeping on.

Keep on. But there were no more J. Ronans. Ireland, blank of them.

No Joes, the raincoated old woman had said. Plenty of Maureens.

She'd always sent cards at Christmas, Joe's sister. Auntie Maureen, though Matty had never had a chance to call her that, having never met her. Joe seemed to want to leave his family behind even then. Maybe she could tell Matty something. If nothing else, she'd be family.

Matty got up, put the hoodie back on, and went downstairs to the corner of the pub with some coins. Phoned Heather and put a finger in the other ear, not making eye contact with any of the drinkers.

'Hello? Who's this?' Heather sounded suspicious.

'Mate. It's Matty. Sorry it's late.'

'S'all right. Just locked up. Where are you? That sounds like fucking hell on earth.'

'Yeah, basically.'

'Still alive, then?'

'You not getting my postcards?'

'Yeah, I got them. Stuck them up on the fridge, innit. If you had a bleedin' mobile phone I'd know where you were.' The sound of Heather sucking at her top lip. 'Found him yet?'

'Not yet. Listen, I've not got much change. Could you do me a favour?'

A martyred sigh, and the blurred sound of Val in the background. 'Go on, then. Anything for you, angel.'

Chapter 5

'Morning. Message for you. The lady said you'd know what it meant.'

Matty had woken to blood, too much of it, bubbling between both thighs. Scrubbed the pants in the sink, the water icy, a wad of tissues stuffed down there for now. Downstairs, the guy behind the bar had nodded at the local paper. At the top of the sport section was a name, written in capital letters: *MAUREEN MAUGHAN*. Followed by the words *No Address*.

Matty had a coffee, the milk separating into scraggy flecks, staring at the surname. A scratchy throat, itchy ribs, lower stomach throbbing. No squats today. No weights.

Good old Heather. Most of Rosa's things had been sold, given away. But Matty had kept the box of cards and photos, stashed in a plastic tub underneath Heather's sofa. Turned out Auntie Maureen was one of those who liked to put their name on the back of the envelope, even if she had no fixed address.

Matty turned the paper over, flicked through. An Irish football school tournament. One of the guys from Westlife coming back to turn on the Christmas lights in his hometown.

And travellers, trespassing on a farmer's land.

Sanitary towels next to the popcorn and Skittles on the conveyer belt, not looking at the cashier. They might be for someone else. For three days every month it was a wound that needed to be dealt with, as cursorily as possible.

It would still be all right to swim, just about. Keep things quick, hope for the blood to only come when upright and on land again. The wetsuit kept the towel in place.

Matty never put anything up there. That wasn't happening.

It had arisen with Heather one night, a confession after too much cider. 'You've never even used a tampon?' Eyes widening. 'Bloody hell.' She'd poured more red wine into her medieval-style goblets with a baffled silence. 'Look, you tyke,' she said eventually, sitting back. There's plenty of room.' She'd crooked her little finger. 'Start small. Get a box of minis. You won't feel a thing.'

The drizzle was tangible and fast-moving. Matty had left Shifty up at the top of the lane by a new estate, the flats compact and unimaginatively built, and followed a bumpy path until the site came into view.

There wasn't much rubbish, despite what the old survivalist had said. It was a broad expanse of yellowish scrubland, the curved ridges of a corrugated barn roof visible in the next field. Six modern caravans formed a broadly hexagonal shape with a firepit in the centre, the wood black and sodden. One of the caravans had cardboard in place of glass in most of the windows. There were two cars parked close together, and a much older one, rusting and wheel-less, on bricks. No one seemed to be around.

Matty hovered at the gate to the field. Didn't seem right to go in. It felt strange, and sacred. The wind was quieter down here, the mist hanging in fine patches.

Joe was brought up in a place like this. Joe, who loved his home comforts. Who'd stand with his back to the window, warming his calves on the radiator, saying it was heaven. Always ages in the bath, reading the paper, and talking about painting the ceiling again, getting a new kitchen put in. Whose job had been making interiors for other people's houses. He'd spent most of the time on the caravan holiday in Dorset outside, smoking and scowling at it.

A dog suddenly came barrelling out of nowhere, black and white, its bark startling. Matty took a step backwards, but it was already alarmingly close, jumping up with a wide, maroon mouth. Paws scrabbling.

'Get lost?' A man in filthy overalls was walking over, wiping his hands on a rag. He abruptly called the dog, a word that sounded like *feelin'*. It ran to him and back over again, still barking.

'Sorry. Just looking for someone.'

'Not a journalist, then?' An abrasive voice.

'No.'

The man didn't say anything, pressing one finger to a nostril, ejecting a quick globule of snot onto the ground. 'All right. Who's that you're after?'

'Maureen Maughan. Or Kevin Maughan.'

He spat out the dog's name again, clicking his fingers by his knee. The dog stopped barking immediately and limped to the man's feet. 'Friends of yours?'

'Relatives.' It sounded alien to say it. 'There's Michael and Carly too.'

He raised his eyebrows as if far too much information was coming his way. 'That right.' He screwed up his face, a grin to himself, and looked over the field. 'There a reason you'd think they'd be here?'

Matty swallowed. 'Just – it's ... they're travellers.' Was that the right word? What would they call themselves?

The man had dark brown hair, gathered in a roll of curls above his forehead. A dark smudge of oil on his cheek above his goatee. He gazed at Matty, as behind him one of the caravan doors opened and a long-haired child, five or six, swung out, still holding onto the handle. 'You're a Maughan, are you?'

'No. A Ronan. But from London.'

The child let the door swing back, disappearing, before it opened again, this time without her hanging onto it. Instead she peeked out, holding a small cat that might have been a soft toy.

'Well,' he said. 'We don't know everyone. Try up at Cavan. The ____ Pub. Or at the boxing club.' He turned, calling the dog away with him.

26/11/99
LOUGH _____, Air 9°C, Water 9°C, 400m

There was a lough on the way, metal flashes of it once or twice on bends in the road. Matty turned off, parked up by the toilets. A guy with a rod was further up, far enough not to complain about the fish being disturbed.

Windy here. A bellowing wind, plucking the water up into peaks. Not exactly inviting, but you always had to go in. No point in wimping out once you'd come to have a look. You couldn't let it beat you. An old white rowboat bashed itself against the stones, saying *go in, go in.*

Out in the lough, Matty stopped and turned around in a slow circle. A hazy sky. The fisherman was packing up, a faint slam of the car door making crows break out of the trees. The wind ululated against the swim cap, finding its way in past the gap in the neoprene. All you would have to do was stop moving. Let it take over. A strange, unobtrusive death. You'd never be found out here. Only Heather had a faint idea of Matty's location, and even if drowning was suspected, there was so much water to search. Water would steal, conceal, own.

There had been a fair few casualties over the years at the Ladies' Pond, women who had not understood the savagery of the winter water enough, left light-headed and juddery, wordless, as the lifeguards called ambulances. But if you were used to it,

173

the body stood firm a little longer. Just a few months ago, a Swedish woman had been trapped under ice for eighty minutes, a body temperature of thirteen degrees when she was rescued, the lowest ever recorded for a survivor. The doctor on the initial examination had described her as ashen, flaxen-white, and looking absolutely dead. The ice pocket and the extreme slowing of her metabolism had saved her.

Right, daydreamer. You going to be here all day?

Matty lay back, let the small, harrying waves buoy each limb, muscles beginning to thicken with the cold. Headed to shore.

The boxing club was up a side road in Cavan, a town of dark-grey buildings.

What a shithole.

But was it *your* shithole? Matty thought. There was a single light at the corner of the building, a cold tangerine glow over the door.

There'd been no more boxing, once Joe had gone. Matty had returned to the club in East Finchley aged fifteen, after Italy. No Freddie. The old man had snuffed it, the new coach had said. Heart attack. It felt hard asking to join without Joe there. The coach's look hadn't exactly been friendly.

You could have, though. No harm in asking. Got to be a man about these things.

They were coming out now, youngish guys mostly, rucksacks or gym bags slung over one shoulder. Two of them spoke in especially unintelligible accents to each other before it became clear that the rapidly swishing words must be Irish. Another man stopped underneath the light, sparking up a cigarette, doing a loose-limbed shiver.

Matty went over. 'Excuse me, mate. Don't suppose there are any Maughans that come here?'

The guy glanced over, blinking. 'Maughans? Got a first name?' His ears stuck out, and there was a tiny cross tattoo on his neck. Middleweight, or light heavyweight.

'Um, yeah. Kevin, or Michael.'

He laughed through his nose and rolled his shoulders back. He didn't seem to want to stand still. 'Michael Maughan. There's one of them, to be sure.' He cricked his neck, grinning. 'What a pikey cunt.' He held up his cigarette hand. 'Sorry.'

'Do you know where their site is?'

'Site?'

'Um, yeah. Their halting site.' There'd been another article in the local papers, enough to learn the term.

He took a drag on his cigarette and looked over more sharply, before giving a jerking nod. 'Your man's gone indoors these days. Sold out.' He mentioned an estate on the outskirts of the town. 'Still makes him a pikey cunt,' he called after Matty. 'Tell that fecker he owes me money.'

Coophill Estate. A cul-de-sac of terraced council houses painted a dull peach, and several motorhomes parked outside them. In front of one, an old-style gypsy caravan seemed freshly painted, with an Irish flag poked into the hinge of the door. They'd been in the phone book after all, K. and M. Maughan.

The night had been spent in the Forest Park, half a tin of baked beans for dinner, trying to get any reception on the TV, and listening to the wind push at Shifty. There'd been a heaviness in Matty's chest, the feeling of something coming. The same headache all morning, which a quick dip hadn't cured.

Number 14 had a tired bed of tulips and a plastic cat on its side.

Matty knocked, turning immediately round to look at the yard opposite, a wide expanse of gravel and worn-away grass.

There was a muffled bump inside, someone calling and a higher voice calling back, before a shadow came towards the glass. The door opened.

It was a woman of fifty or so, brown and grey hair pulled up in a high, severe ponytail. A tanned, blotchy face. She had a baby on her hip. 'Yes?' She sounded harassed.

A breath, but no words came out. She'd sent a photo or two with the cards, years before, but Matty could hardly remember. 'Is it – are you Maureen?' The words lurched out.

She craned her head, looking at the street and the van. 'Depends who's asking.' Her eyes fixed on Matty's again, and something passed over her face, a fleeting light. Her mouth came open. 'It's not—' She stepped down onto the concrete and peered, as if into a dark cave. 'It's not Matty, is it?'

The baby started crying.

Matty sat at the end of one sofa in the living room, fists bunched. There was a black-and-white TV on in the corner with a kids' quiz show on, the presenter's voice loud and garish. Carly, Matty's cousin, was sitting at the edge of a small, ornate sofa opposite, her posture formal. A little girl was on the floor, teasing a small, short-haired terrier with a woollen rat.

'I knew it almost as soon as I saw you,' said Maureen, coming in. 'You're the spit of him.' Her voice was matter-of-fact, almost robotic. 'I thought you were a boy.' She put the baby unceremoniously down onto the blankets at the other end of the sofa and stood, one hand on a hip. Scrutinising. 'What age will you be now?'

'Twenty-five.'

'Well, that says it all. Sweet Mary, but it speeds by.' There was the sound of the kettle and she disappeared back into the kitchen.

Carly was still staring, making the strange gratification of resembling Joe evaporate. She had on a knitted jumper with the word HERO on the front in large letters, her jeans tight and ripped in perfect symmetry. She was heavily made-up and her hair was piled dramatically on top of her head, as if she was from the nineteenth century.

'How old is ... ?' A gesture to the baby, who was in an old-fashioned white dress and had a bright pink bow clipped in the little hair she had. Cream woollen tights and tiny stud earrings.

'Eleven months.'

The little girl on the floor suddenly stood up and the dog growled.

'And Jessie's three in a month, aren't you?' The way Carly said it made it obvious they were hers. She couldn't have been more than twenty.

The girl shouted 'Yes!' and then ran out of the room. The dog followed.

It was quieter without them. The baby, propped up by cushions, sighed and put a fist in her mouth, sucking rhythmically.

The room was cluttered. Two display cabinets held crockery, and there was a faux-marble table crammed with religious baubles – two glass candleholders with a haloed Jesus on them, and a statue of a saint, his neck laden with rosaries.

'Can't believe I've never met you,' Carly said, brightly and with a faint hint of aggression. 'I've got more cousins than I can count on the other side.'

Maureen came back in with a tray. The cups had four-leaved clovers on them. 'Well, now.' She had large circular earrings, black artificial feathers hanging from them, dreamcatcher-style. A shiny padded jacket with emerald shoulders and fur-lined slippers. She looked at Matty, as if trying to decide what to say first. 'How's your mother?'

On another table next to her, leaning on a sequinned vase of fake flowers, there was a painting of the Virgin Mary, head tilted downwards, crying. 'She's, uh ... she's dead.'

'Ah, no.' Maureen crossed herself. 'Long gone?'

'Not really.' The words came out huskily. Matty should have been there, even though Rosa had become more brittle, cold, drunk. Should have known what was coming, been there to see any signs.

'And how's your father taken it?'

It was like being stunned, hearing him called that. A brief, white light. 'I don't know. He left.'

The baby had started whining. Carly sat her on a knee and bounced her up and down, pointing at the TV.

Maureen was staring. 'Well, isn't that just it.' Her voice hardened. 'He never changed, did he?' The question didn't seem to be aimed at anyone.

'I didn't know if you'd – seen him.' It was already obvious what the answer was.

'You've not?'

'Not since I was eleven.'

'Jesus, Mary and Joseph,' she said, a rushed, exasperated sigh. As if a small child was irritating her.

Matty watched her as she drank from her mug. The nearest to Joe in all this time. There was some of him in her eyes, set a little close together, and the skin colouring, though her face was much longer.

'Well, I don't know what to say,' Maureen said. 'My brother. Not a family man.'

It's not true, Matty thought. He was once.

'And you're looking for him, are you?'

'Yeah. I didn't know he'd left. I mean—' Carly was pretending not to look over, a face that was part puzzled, part incredulous. 'I thought he'd maybe died. My mum had said he had.' It sounded idiotic.

'Is that right?' Maureen said.

The tea was stewed, tiny brown islands floating on the surface. 'I don't know where he is.'

'Well, he's not been in, if that's what you were hoping. I haven't seen him since he was twenty years old. He came back twice after he took off to England. Our mother never recovered. The shame of it. She had a broken heart for years.'

'Where's she now?' Matty remembered being on the phone to her, aged six or so. Standing in the hallway, Joe's hand resting on a shoulder, saying *Hello? Hello?* into the phone and Granna, in a tangled, faraway voice, as if calling from the moon, shouting *Hello? Hello?* back.

Maureen shook her head. 'Gone, God rest her. We don't last as long as you lot.' A dark, wry look that was startlingly like Joe, before she stood up. 'You'll stay for some dinner.'

Kevin came home, a large man in a polo shirt with a rash of black-grey stubble. He seemed unperturbed by the new arrival, putting his hand out to be shaken before sitting on the sofa and gazing at the TV.

In the kitchen, Maureen didn't stop talking. 'We've been renting for a while now,' she said, lifting a pot lid and chucking the potatoes that Matty was peeling into it. 'Since Carly was ten or so. It's not the same, but it's easier. Most of the time. Less hassle off of people, you know.'

A nod, not knowing at all.

'Your father had such notions. Thought he was better than all of us. Born into the wrong family. Our Kevin's a community man now, working on getting kids in education and all that.' She sounded haughtily indignant. 'What was he doing for work? I know it was a while ago.'

'Interiors. Putting in kitchens and that.'

A forceful hum through her nose. 'Not exactly the prime-bloody-minister, then.'

Dinner was chicken nuggets, mash and peas, crowded around the kitchen table. The baby was in a plastic high chair, banging her spoon on the tray and massaging the potatoes with explora-tory fingers.

'Well, I always knew something was up,' Maureen said. 'My Christmas cards started getting returned to the post office. I gave up after three years. Thought you'd all done a runner. Wanted nothing more to do with us all.'

'It's not true,' Matty said, so quietly that it got lost as the front door slammed.

179

''Lo,' called an angular man's voice.

Maureen leant back on her chair. 'You're bloody late. There's none left for you.'

A brown-haired young man stuck his head round the kitchen door. 'Working,' he said, eyes on Matty.

Maureen made a scoffing sound. 'Working my arse. This is your cousin. Joe's daughter.'

Matty tried not to flinch. Gave the slightest nod.

He let out a laugh. 'Is that right?' A keen stare, something doggish in him, before he glanced at his sister, the slightest derogatory amusement between them both. 'How're you going,' he said, before disappearing.

'I want more potato!' the little girl shouted, delighted at the sound of her own voice. The baby screeched a reply and clapped her hands.

'Do you indeed,' Maureen said, giving her a scoop of her own. She looked at Kevin, who was feeding a chicken nugget to the dog. 'Working, he says.' She shook her head.

Michael came back downstairs, bare-chested, his tracksuit trousers low-slung.

'For the love of the Holy Mother, put some bloody clothes on,' Maureen said.

'It's hot,' he said. He must have been twenty-two. There was a swagger, heat coming off him. A cockerel mixed with a pit bull.

He took the chair vacated by Kevin, who'd gone back to the sofa and the TV, and leant rangy shoulders over his plate. He had a ruby-red rosary on, the wooden cross hanging between hard-raised pectorals. Welterweight. 'That your van, then?' A glance up from under heavy eyebrows, scanning Matty as he had done when he first came in.

'Yeah.'

'You live in it?'

'Just travelling around for now.'

He gave a high, sharp hum, looked sidelong at his mother and shovelled potato into his mouth.

Another cup of tea. Kevin was watching the news as the others cleared the plates, his finger in the mouth of the little dog, who worried it lightly. Matty rose to find the loo, and caught the cousins' low voices among the radio.

'What's going on there, then?' Carly was saying. 'She's a bit blokey, isn't she?'

'Lesbian,' said Michael. 'Total lesbo. Would have got that knocked right out of her if she'd been round here.'

'All right now, that's enough.' Maureen's voice, not overly harsh.

Matty knocked on the open kitchen door. Tried to look less boyish. 'Just looking for the toilet.'

Michael turned. 'Down to the end, on your left,' he said, voice artificial, with a dangerous smile.

Carly brought the baby's cheek down to Maureen and Kevin for goodnight kisses before she disappeared with her. Michael was slouched almost horizontally on the sofa, his arms crossed, biceps bulbous.

'We've not the room for you,' Maureen said, briskly. 'There's the sofa there if you'd like it for the night at least.'

Michael's jaw remained slack, but his eyes slid over. Impenetrable, almost.

'It's cool,' Matty said. 'I've got the van.'

'You'll stay tonight.' Maureen already sounded relieved.

'It's all good. No worries.' Up. 'Thanks for dinner.'

Maureen stood in the hallway, holding her ashtray, as Matty put each boot on. A sense of her carefully studying every move, every gesture, struggling a little not to blurt out what everyone always wanted to blurt out.

'When your father was round here, as a kid, you know,' she said, 'he always wanted to go further west. Over the water. He'd sing that song, "Home on the Range".'

A flare of rib-pain, the memory of Joe singing with his arms outstretched, doing a little cowboy hop with imaginary spurs.

'Face off America, he said.' Maureen shook her head and flicked her cigarette into the ashtray. 'He was so bloody self-important, that boy.'

Matty stood up.

'There was a place,' she said, frowning a little. 'Ah God, it's too long ago.'

'Yeah?'

'Up at Donegal. He was always on at us to head up there, just because he'd been with a friend. Ross-something, it might have been. Bet that narrows it down.' A wry look.

'Can you give me a sec?' Matty didn't wait for the answer, going out to Shifty and coming back with the map. Finding Donegal, and gazing at it. Pointing. 'Here?' On the north coast, a lumpy headland butting out into a bay. The Ross.

Maureen glanced at the page, non-committally. 'I think it was on the west side.'

Matty pointed to another village, further south, beginning with *Ros*.

'Maybe. I'm not saying he's there. Your guess is as good as mine. On the west side, though. I'm sure of that. Small place.'

The road map closed. 'OK. Thanks.'

She came out onto the step. 'If you ask me, you're more traveller than he was.' She nodded at Shifty. 'It's good to see you keeping the tradition alive. Don't be a stranger, now.' There was no hug.

'It was nice to meet you.' It was, of a sort. At least her.

'Well, if you see him,' Maureen said. 'Give him a bloody mouthful from me.'

***

182

His raft of songs. Country songs, Irish ones, disco songs off the radio. He'd do naff Bee Gees moves, the Moonwalk, anything to get the laugh. He'd watch *Top of the Pops* with Matty, half an eye to the paper, throwing out comments about their 'daft get-up', as he'd call it. Pointing out that the guitars weren't plugged in.

There'd been no more J. Ronans in the phone book, but maybe the phone book wasn't everything. Maybe he wasn't in it. Maybe he'd changed his name.

He'd sing 'Home on the Range' when he'd had a drink, put his arm around Rosa, eyes all misty.

Where seldom is heard a discouraging word, and the skies are not cloudy all day.

Matty drove back towards the Forest Park for the evening, into a late afternoon sky full of grey clouds.

Chapter 6

A proper cough this morning, a bruised, spreading pain in the chest each time. It always felt damp first thing, throat clogged, but this was worse. Bones heavy, too. Hip hurting from the thin mattress. Matty boiled the kettle again, spat up a few green globules of phlegm into the sink. Ireland was finally working its way in. Back to bed for the morning, listening to rain as hard as hail on Shifty's roof, too tired to get the generator going, the gas rings left on instead for warmth.

It made Matty want to go home. Whatever home was. There was money now, money to buy a place, but it still felt unreal, like it might disappear from the bank, vanish to zero.

Maureen and everyone. They were family and yet – they had nothing in common apart from the dark hair. It made Matty want to go to Italy again, to the house with the lopsided staircase and the constant smell of cooking. Except that Nonna had lied, all this time. So that wasn't home either.

Matty stared at the beads of condensation on the back window. Reached up, wrote *J.O.E.* The letters immediately spilled, growing a single long leg, as if each letter was a struggle and needed holding up. The colourless sky could be seen in the drawn curves.

Another look at the map in bed, a finger working up into Donegal. *Ross*-something. There were several towns or villages on the north coast, and also a large area called The Rosses, but Maureen had said west, and a small place. That left three other black dots at the ends of roads, all on the coast and beginning with *Ros*.

The Northern Irish border was close to here, bulging round to the west. Matty could do the Wild Atlantic Way, skirt round all the green fingers on the map. Look for him in the *Ros*-pubs. If he was living there, he was bound to be in one of them. He'd look up from his pint, face opening in surprise, shock, before his head got kicked in.

Matty headed north and west, following the water.

***

Bleak out here. Signs for BARLEY, OATEN AND WHEATEN, ridges of raised peat in the fields covered in taut black plastic. There were horses in high-vis jackets and abandoned houses everywhere – not just old croft houses, but more recent ones, net curtains fluttering through broken windows. And as many new ones being built, bare concrete walls, the tarpaulin loose against scaffolding. Ghost-country. The rain inked the road.

A glut of water. You couldn't tell what was field and what was pond, and loughs ran alongside everything.

It never rains, but it does cause biblical levels of flooding every bleeding day.

On another single road, Matty realised from the village name and the road markings that this was Northern Ireland. There'd been no sign, no grand welcome to the UK. The sheep continued to graze. The rain fell.

Irish politics wasn't a specialist subject. It never had been much on the radar, apart from Joe explaining about the hunger strikes and why blowing people up was always a bad thing, no matter what you believed. The news had been on at Heather's over Easter last year, the usual programmes dropped. Tony Blair's wide goblin smile, the comical tie, and hail tumbling down on David Trimble's head. The odd simplicity of it. There'd been Mo Mowlam in her

185

suit in the run-up, the cancer obvious from her thinning hair, bullishly going into the Maze.

And the bombs over the years. Phone calls and tip-offs. The new Docklands turned inside out, the piles of glass like snowdrifts. Shoppers unwittingly sent towards the high street in Omagh on carnival day last year, into the mouth of it. Bombs under cars. Policemen. On the other side, British soldiers, firing at people to make one day of the week never sound the same again.

A garage in a small town, further in. Matty topped up the water, filled up the gas canister – it was definitely cheaper here – and fished around for pound coins. It felt odd, a hinterland, and yet no different from any of the garages on the way through England. There were memories of barricades on the TV news, criss-crossing oblongs of metal and soldiers in camouflage.

On the map, spread over the steering wheel, the border wended its way through water and crossed roads. As if the loughs, streams and rivers could accommodate it, absorb it.

And back. Over into Ireland again on another small road, without quite realising. There'd been a rust-streaked sign saying 'Unapproved Road'. The tarmac fresh. Rain. Sheep. A border, and no border at all.

27/11/99
LOUGH _____, Air 10°C, Water 10°C, 200m

Matty had warmed up enough in the van, though still felt head-achey, and the cough was getting a grainy, animal edge to it. At least the voice was sinking further. Fingers crossed that it'd be at Q-Tip levels soon enough.

Illness was a rare thing – the water usually saw that off. One of the hardy white-haired swimmers at the Ladies' Pond had sworn by it, coming every morning, rain or shine. Said she hadn't been ill since 1964. It was only when there'd been a swim-less stint that the germs might creep up. If you did feel ill, going in the water was usually the best thing – the germs took one whiff of the cold and scarpered.

A brown tourist sign for Lough _____ Drive, a scenic route. 'Yeah, all right, mate, you got me,' Matty said to Shifty, braking on the main road and clunking into reverse.

The wind stirred the lough into small, crowded waves. Matty swam out and then along away from the town, before bobbing to have a look around. There was a low island further off, with purpling trees. A long, unnatural-looking ridge of mountain beyond it. It felt harder to breathe today. The cold gripped, and the wetsuit itched. A short one, then. Maybe a B & B tonight, judgemental looks or not.

Back on land, there was a flash of pink. A kid was on a bike by Shifty, looking in at the windows. By the time Matty neared the sloped ramp, the girl was standing at the top facing the lough. She wore a shiny pink coat that matched the glitter on her bike, hood up, elfish. She backed off as Matty got out, but hovered, watching Shifty's door slide open. It seemed a bit much to slam it in her face.

'What were you doing?' she said, holding onto her bike. The handles had green and pink ribbons tied on each end.

'What did it look like?'

A short pause. 'Why?'

'I like it.' A gritty cough.

'We've got a swimming pool not so far away. In the next town. It's got a wave machine.'

'Got my own wave machine.' Nodding towards the water.

'But it's freezing in there.' She took a step closer as Matty's head went under the towel. 'Are you a mermaid?'

Matty came out from underneath the towel and kept rubbing. Curls coming back into focus. 'Yeah.'

'Are you a boy or a girl?' She was eight, maybe nine. Her accent had the softness of the Irish, the surprising lilt of the

187

Northern Irish and a twang of American. Like an out-of-tune banjo.

'Which do you want me to be?' Matty had said that before, to a girl in a furry white coat at a dive bar in Camden. But neither answer ever suited. How to explain that this body was partly a curse, Houdini's straitjacket. How not one or the other would be quite right.

The girl looked out at the lough and made a sucking noise with her teeth on her bottom lip. *F-f-f.* 'A boy.'

'Oh yeah? Why's that?'

'Boys are nicer.' She rang the bell of her bike absent-mindedly, a dull tinkling. 'So you're a boy mermaid? There's not so many of them. I don't know what they look like.' *Ting.*

'They look like me, don't they?' Matty tried to sound matter-of-fact.

'Girls have their tops off except Ariel doesn't, Ariel wears shells tied together.' *Ting.* 'Do you ever wear shells?'

'Modern mermaids wear wetsuits.'

Ting ting. 'I guess shells might be a bit uncomfortable. They might cut you a bit.' She cupped a hand over one side of her chest and looked down at it. 'I've got a book on mermaids. There are stories and facts and tons of pictures. No boys, though.'

'OK,' said Matty, starting to get really cold. The wetsuit needed to come off.

The girl seemed to sense it. 'I'd better go home. I'm not really allowed to be this far down. Don't tell.' She launched herself onto her bike and bounced over the tarmac, the ribbons flying in the wind.

***

Matty sat in the corner, hood up, trying to eat fish and chips, savouring the warmth of the pub. Still trying to weigh up whether to camp or find a proper bed. English football on the telly, high up.

188

The pub was up past Donegal, a quiet road with bogland either side. Almost no one in it, though it was Saturday night. Two families were having dinner over on the other side.

Matty felt weak. It hurt to swallow now, and the afternoon had been spent on the bed until the sky had darkened.

There were a couple of big guys having pints pulled for them. One was especially large, a neck like a joint of gammon, muscles straining against his T-shirt, holding a mobile phone prominently. The other was slimmer though still filled out at the front, reddish pale skin and blond hair. He had his back to the bar and kept glancing over. Why did they always want to talk?

Outside, nothing but darkness, and the knowledge of mountains and moorland again. Frontier-like. It had already been dark on the drive, a vast ridge of mountains taking up much of the deep sky on the right. Definitely more dramatic than the central lowlands, almost Canadian. It made more sense, why you'd want to come back, if it was to this.

Matty got up to pay, buying another bottle of beer for the road or for whatever shit B & B lay ahead. It was probably getting late. Should have got a move on, driven around by now to find one.

'All right, now?' The one who'd been looking over had edged closer. His friend had gone outside.

Nod.

'Thought they were having a winning streak, these lot,' he said, holding his bottle roughly towards the TV in the corner.

'They lost the last one.'

'That right? You keep up with it all, do you?'

'Yeah, sometimes.'

'The thing about football,' Joe had said once, walking up to Dartford's ground for an away match, 'is it's a global language. You could land yourself in bleeding Guinea-Bissau or the middle of the Pacific, utter the two magical words "Kevin Keegan" and everyone would be your friend.'

The guy was called Dale and was quite sweet, in a shy sort of way. Matty talked the talk, nil–nil draws and away form, the goalie nearing retirement. There was a hay-like tint to his close-cropped hair, ruddy cheeks. A gold chain visible underneath the polo shirt, but least there wasn't a cross on the end of it. Every time he laughed, he blinked three times.

Matty got the bartender to open the beer bottle.

'Where yous from, then?' Dale said.

Matty wasn't sure if the new edge to the question had been imagined or not. The closeness to the border, the risk of getting the answer wrong. You could only be one or the other.

'London.'

'Oh, yeah? Nice. My cousin moved to London.' He made it sound as important as if they'd moved to the Far East, or the Arctic.

Outside, there was the distinctive sound of someone speaking loudly into their mobile phone.

'Are you Arsenal, then? Or Chelsea?'

'Barnet, mostly.'

'They any good?' There was a small cut on his bottom lip that he kept thumbing. 'I don't follow the lower-end stuff.'

'Yeah, well, you're not missing much.'

Watch it, you. That's my team you're talking about.

Dale laughed again. Blinked again. It was always a bit of a relief, to be liked. 'Get you another one of those?' He gestured towards the bottle.

'No, I've got to drive. Thanks.'

'Park it here, Bobby won't mind.' He grinned and thumbed at his lip again. 'Maybe.'

Or I could come back to yours, Matty thought, trying to judge it. A mug of tea. Maybe he'd know how to make a hot toddy. Would like turning his radiators up high, wearing only T-shirts indoors.

The door opened, Dale's friend coming back in, shouting, 'Good fucking luck to you and all, pal' into his phone, before

190

stabbing at it with his forefinger, and putting it back to his ear. 'Hello? You there? Hello?'

'Is it nice, like?' Dale said. 'In London? '

'It's … yeah. It can be.'

The friend had suddenly quietened, putting his palm over his phone, watching them.

'Looks a bit mad,' said Dale. 'Isn't everyone a rude fucker?'

'No, just in a hurry. That's all.'

'I should go on over some time. Check it all—'

His friend was jabbing him on the shoulder. You could smell the stout and fags on his breath from here, combined with something more rancid. 'Can I have a word with you?' It came out as *wid ya*.

Dale left his bottle on the bar and followed him to a pillar at the end of the room, fists going into his pockets. The older man was clearly in charge. Matty didn't turn round, but it was easy enough to hear the jagged half-whispers, enough to make every muscle go still.

'What are you doing?'

'What?'

'What are you doing?' The friend lowered his voice, the words pushed through a very small space. 'He's fucking *gay*.'

Time to leave. Matty hooked forefinger and thumb around the beer bottle and quickly slid off the barstool. No eye contact.

There was a pause, filled only by the commentator's voice on the TV rising as a free kick went over. Dale's voice was small. 'What do you mean, he?'

The sound of the away crowd, a chant falling into another chant, the claps eventually coming together to form a pattern. The two of them were glancing over, the back of Dale's neck reddening.

Matty was already halfway out of the door.

*

Light on. Two hot-water bottles. Gas ring. De La Soul on the CD Walkman. Music that wasn't aggressive, posturing, as Matty often liked. This was gentle, lullaby hip-hop.

Shifty had been turned around, retracing the route they'd come in on. It was dark, and Matty couldn't face trying to get a room this late, couldn't face talking to anyone. There'd been a wide parking bay by woodland and water, ten kilometres back, not stopped at before, and the relief at getting there brought shivers. It was a quiet road, quieter even than most, not a single car going past in the hour since arriving.

After a while, a feverish, night-time hunger kicked in. The bread had started to go stale. Matty fried two slices and the last remaining rashers of bacon, and ate it, fingers greasy and burning, under the blankets. Too much eating. Fiddled with the reception on the radio and got mostly white noise. Turned it off again and finished the beer, put the bottle outside by the wheel so it wouldn't stink the van out. Too much drinking.

A piss before bed. The temperature had dropped, a wash of icy air hitting the back of the throat, a new harshness as Matty squatted in the soggy grass.

The small lough was over the road, sopping up to rocks covered in moss that was lurid green in the torchlight. A gathering of bone-pale reeds, each one defiantly separate from the next. The line of the hill on the other side of the lough was shallow, curved.

There was the sound of an engine, a low rub of it, the car's lights appearing intermittently as the road bent.

In the morning, the lough would reveal itself, navy or silver, still or restless. The cough would be gone, the swim easy, and everything else would fall away.

It felt safer here. The water was safer, a rhythmic loll against the stones.

A rasp of gravel. The car was turning into the parking bay. Matty turned the torch off – company was exactly the opposite of desired. Perhaps they were stopping for a piss, too. Or to shout into their new mobile phone.

The car door shut loudly. Matty stayed looking at the water, sensing the driver somewhere at the edge of the bay, several metres behind – maybe checking out Shifty, tucked in under the trees, the light left on. The sound of rubber grips on the tarmac came closer, until they were standing a few feet away on the roadside.

It was Dale. Easy to tell, even in the gloom. He had a jacket on, hands in his pockets as he'd had before. He stood watching the black water. The air was clean and scentless.

'All right?' he said. The word was slight, unreadable.

'All right.' A careful sense of relief. It was OK. He was up for something. Shifty's first time.

He took a breath in, but didn't speak.

Think. Think what to say first. Why else would he be out here? He was tentative, nothing like Trevor, nothing like most people Matty tended to go with.

'Where do you—'

'What's your game, then?' he said.

Wrong. 'What?'

'I said, what's your game?' Almost theatrical. He was drunk.

Matty's blood went cold. 'Dunno what you mean.' The assessing of how far away Shifty was, of getting round to the driver's seat. Having to get past him first. The location of the keys.

He let out a strange, gull-like laugh.

A careful voice. 'I think—'

No. Already too much time had been lost. 'Your *game*, you little … you little bitch,' Dale said. 'Or a – what's with you, playing a bloke? I thought you were—' He moved, fast, clutching at a shoulder. 'What have yous got down there, anyway? Are you a fannyballs or what?' He made a grabbing movement, lower, and Matty wrenched free just in time, able only to get closer to the water, the wrong direction.

193

He lurched forward.

'You just plastic down there? Like a proper little doll?' There was a shade of something vulnerable in his voice. 'Ken mixed with fucking Barbie?'

Matty sidestepped. 'Just go home, mate, all right?' Keep it calm, smooth, neutral. Not too much boy. Not too much girl. A person, barely there. 'It's all fine.'

There was a moment in which Dale seemed to consider it. A moment in which the reeds quivered, the water lifted itself. A moment like a prayer. Then he lunged, gave a forceful push to Matty's chest.

Stumble. One foot slipped on the moss, a knee meeting rock, the sudden pain of a jarred wrist on stone, and something popping. A noisy splash into water, before Matty was hauled up. They were staggering forwards, further into the lough. Calves soaked. Shins.

'You made a fool of me,' he was saying, holding tight onto the shoulder of the hoodie, Matty half-bent, the water too close. 'Do you hear me?'

His knee thundered into Matty's ribs. And again.

An inward howl of pain. His grip was inescapable – shoulder, neck, the skin chafing – and then Matty's head was in the water.

The sudden sub-bass of everything. You are going to die. Laryngospasm. Hypoxia. You are going to die here. You can hold your breath for longer underwater. *The Guinness Book of Records.*

Into the air, and down again, not enough time to inhale properly. The force of his whole body behind his arm. Matty coughed underwater, took in a mouthful.

Up. Matty pushed blindly with the heel of a throbbing hand against his chest, choking, dizzy. Everything swayed.

'A *fool of me*,' he was saying. 'In front of my friend.' He let go, his arm dripping.

It was over. Maybe it was over. He'd had enough, was seeing sense, the cold water sloughing off some of the alcohol.

Matty carefully waded backwards out of the water. Ears hissing and ringing. 'Just go home. Sleep it off.' A hand out, looking for something to balance on, finding nothing. Wrist not working properly.

'Sleep it off.' He grinned, following, large strides. 'Yeah, maybe I should.'

Quick. Matty slipped, slid over the stones and ran towards Shifty, but the shock had slowed the bones, clothes weighed down. The frantic sound of him coming closer.

'Where are you going?' A glancing palm on the shoulder, with force. 'You little cunt.'

Matty spun, fell back into the side of the van. A *crunk* of metal.

He almost tripped, too, before coming back fast. 'I didn't say you could go.' His fist, meeting an eyebrow. A blotting, dumbing pain and then Matty's face was against the glass of the window.

Away, a gap of air, a tug on the back of the hoodie. Face smashing against the window again. Cheekbone.

You don't have to be big.

A black-blue, white-blue light and heat on Matty's forehead.

It's about guile. Know that word? It means wily and quick and clever.

His mouth, close. The stench of alcohol on his breath. 'Bet you like a proper horsing, don't you? Is that what you're after?'

Joe, smashing the air as if he was Barry McGuigan, as if the air was a superheavyweight.

You are going to die.

'Let's see what set-up you got in here, then.' He hauled Matty by the collar of the hoodie, tried to shove open the side door, cursed and tried again. A screech of metal. 'Oh, very nice. Very cosy.'

The sweet copper tang of blood, on lip, on tongue. One eye wasn't opening.

Joe, giving a wink before putting his fag back in the side of his mouth. *Go on, tiger. Now or never.*

Dale began to step up into the van, still holding onto the hoodie. At the same time, Matty leant down, half-strangled by the T-shirt collar, stretched and splayed fingers, fumbling by Shifty's wheel. There. The beer bottle.

'Nope, we're going this way,' said Dale, pulling harder, and Matty followed the momentum of his upwards hoist, and brought the beer bottle up, smashing it into his face.

It didn't break. He gave a weird cry, small and outraged, went to grab it. Matty wriggled from his grasp and pushed him hard in the ribs, further into the van. Bashed the bottle against the edge of the side-door, a spray of sound and shards. Glass in his face, getting stuck, coming out. Glass in his face. Blood. His hands were in front of his head now, trying to get the bottle, bending, too tall for the van.

Matty jammed the glass into his side. Little shark-stabs into soft flesh. Into his arm.

He fell back against the front seats, holding his side, looking at his arm, which was beginning to spill. Gave a cough, surprised, and tried to say something. His eyes were child's eyes. He staggered out of the side-door, slumped forward onto his knees, a hand on the ground. All of him on the ground.

Matty stumbled up, dragged the side-door shut and crammed into the far corner of the back seat, still holding the bottle, only able to see out of one eye. Beyond the window, Dale lay on his back, ribs moving up and down very slowly, before getting up again, standing at the window. The heel of his hand on the window. 'You're ...' he said.

The oblong night. He began backing away slowly, turned, kept walking.

Matty stayed hunched on the seat, fingers clamped around the neck of the broken bottle.

There was the sound of the car door opening and shutting. A long silence. The motor sputtered, stopped. Silence. The engine finally started, the wheels slowly crunching on the gravel, a sweep of lights.

The engine fading. Lights fading.

Then the only sound was Matty breathing, breaths that got higher and louder, breaths that made the dizziness come, and the night air and the empty parking bay, the wideness of the road, and the tarmac, flying up like a great, studded fist.

Music. Distant, otherworldly.

'Hello? God. Hello?'

A fuzziness and a furred mouth and blurred words. Astonishing pain – cheek, face, ribs.

'Is it your van there? Can you hear me?'

Matty blinked, slowly. Sat up.

'Oh, thank God. We need to get you some help.' A woman, hair hanging down, her face very close. A hand, midway up Matty's spine. 'You've had an accident, I think. Can I get you in my car? Get you to a hospital? It's a way away, but I'll drive you there. There's no phone box for ages. I've not got a mobile phone.'

The taste of blood. A lurching stomach, and then Matty was crouched over and there was vomit on the road. One wrist wasn't working.

'Oh God. All right. Let's see if – do you think you can get up?'

Gruel-like saliva, spat out. 'No hospital.'

'What's that you're saying?'

Matty made the words louder, forced them out of an acrid, scratchy throat. 'No hospital.'

'But you're—'

The van. The blood in the van. Matty rose, limped to the open side-door. A small sob.

197

'It's your van, is it?' A pause. She was looking in. 'I'll … OK, then.' Her voice had changed direction. Become more grave. 'I'll drive you to the Garda station, OK? It's not close, but – someone will be on night duty, I think.'

'No police.' Matty had stabbed him. He'd bled so much.

'You've been hurt.'

'Please. No police.' Turning round, wild. 'No police.'

'I'll – all right. I'll get you back to mine. I'm no doctor, but – maybe I can see to you a little. We'll call the guards from there. Will you do that? I'm not sure you can drive.'

The music was coming from the woman's car radio. A violin, florid and winding around a piano. She turned it down, then turned it off. The night had swallowed up Shifty somewhere behind them.

'Can't leave the van.'

'I'll make sure it's picked up. I locked it up for you. Do you not remember?'

Matty said no to the seatbelt, which hurt too much. A wave of nausea again. 'I need to sleep.'

'I think you should try and stay awake. Just for a bit. Shall I put the music back on?'

Chapter 7

A staggeringly sharp rib-pain.

The room was gently undulating. Matty inched a hand round a rib, tentatively testing the area, and then there it was – the memory of it all in one compressed second, of the black lough and Dale, of being smashed against Shifty, of his fist.

There was a side-light on. A thick duvet, and a lighter floral quilt on top. The walls were pale grey.

Each breath, no matter how shallow, hurt in an unnameable way. Matty stayed laid out flat, sensing each bruise, the throb against the skin. Right knee. Left rib. *Ribs.* One wrist was alarmingly loose. Bottom lip split, cheekbone on fire. Eyebrow.

There was a clock, some of sort of antique, on the wall, its tick lopsided. A string of small animals made of cloth – elephants maybe – hung down at the edge of the curtain, a bell at the end of it. A mug of something on the bedside table next to a neatly placed sanitary towel in its packaging. Jeans in a pile on the floor. The room smelt of lemon, and of Christmas.

There was a soft knock. The door opened.

Matty tried to sit up, a whimper coming.

'It's only me.' The woman's voice was gentle, honeyed. 'There's no one else living here. Is it all right to come in?' She did anyway, pulling up a wooden chair from the corner. A moment, while she looked over. 'How are you doing, there?'

Still dark outside. 'What time is it?' The words were broken.

'It's two.' She was in her late thirties perhaps, thick black hair to her shoulders, a fringe. Wearing a peacock-green wool cardigan and a cotton shirt with small, mirrored decorations around the neckline.

Matty swallowed. The feeling of thin blades, crossing over each other. 'I've got to go.'

'You don't need to go. Just rest.'

Limbs, sluggish. Chest, like a block of concrete was on it. And the breathing. 'No,' said Matty, to the injuries as much as to this woman.

'I need to tend to you a little. You didn't let me help you clean up or anything so I just got you into bed. Maybe that's good if – so we can show what's happened to you to the guards?'

The panic rose. 'I have to leave.' A hacking, liquid cough. Matty tried to curl up, failed.

'You're in no fit state. You're badly hurt, and on top of that, you're unwell. That chest sounds terrible. It's maybe an infection there.'

Exhaustion kicked in again, a wave of it. Dale might still be out there. Calling his friend, roaming the roads for a mustard-yellow van. How much had he bled? There'd been so much blood.

'I'll not call anyone if you don't want me to.'

A shuddering, huge breath, and the rib-pain shot through again.

She left the room, for what might have been minutes, or might have been much more. A small white box was placed on the bedside table. 'Painkillers.' She held up a large packet. 'And peas. Put them wherever it hurts most.'

Matty closed both eyes, and saw Dale behind them.

'Sleep for now, then.'

The door closed quietly.

A knock. There was a gauzy light at the edges of the window.

The woman came in with a differently coloured mug and put it on the bedside table. The other one had disappeared. 'A fresh one for you. Hot lemon and honey.' She caught Matty's tentative look. 'I'm not trying to poison you. It'll not do you harm, at the very least.' She sat on the chair and glanced at the unopened packet of aspirin. There was a reddish, slapped look to her cheeks, as if she'd been outside.

The world felt weightless. Unknowable. 'My van.' Words hurt. 'In the garage.'

Matty stared at the ceiling. 'The garage?'

'My garage. I hitched a lift, walked the rest. Took your keys – I hope you don't mind.'

'In the night?'

'First light. Not that long ago.'

Matty's mind flitted. She'd gone to get the van. She must have properly seen the mess inside, the blood, if she hadn't before. And brought it here anyway. 'Did anyone pass you?'

'Not a soul.' It was hard to know what she was thinking. 'Well, one old boy on his buggy, but apart from that.'

'Who did you hitch with?'

'A lad in a truck. He'd come from Belfast.'

Matty put the heel of the hand that worked on the mattress, tried to push upwards. Everything throbbed. 'I've got to go now.'

'You're not well.'

'Thanks for getting my van.' Each rib stabbed with pain. Matty's face felt huge, ogre-ish.

'Honestly. You've – my expertise stretches to cold remedies and tending cuts, but you've hurt your ribs. Who knows if anything's cracked. Internal bruising, maybe internal bleeding. It's not out of the question. And that wrist. I really think we should get a doctor.'

The memory of Dale, lurching away. The black, unspeakable thought that something very bad had happened to him. That Matty had done it. 'No doctor.'

'All right, then.' She drew in a deep, warm-sounding breath. A total lack of panic. 'Will you let me help you clean up a little?' She nodded downwards. 'You're caked in blood.'

Matty looked at the dark crust of red on the pillow. 'Sorry.'

'No, I didn't mean that. Move gently, now.'

Matty sat on the toilet seat as the woman got out a jar of cotton balls and ran the hot tap. She didn't say anything about the boy-pants. She poured a dash of salt into the sink, and something from a small bottle. 'Tea tree,' she said.

There were glasses of stones on the windowsill. The tropical shimmer of an abalone shell.

The woman sat on the side of the bath. 'You don't want photos taken, or . . . ?' She looked carefully at Matty. Each of her eyebrows looked like the silhouette of a far-off bird. Strong, simply sketched. 'I've a digital camera.'

'No.'

'As long as you're sure.' She waited a moment longer, and when there was no response, began to dab at the cheekbone.

A faint sting. The soft, spreading heat made Matty want to cry.

Slowly, the cotton ball was moved up. Eyebrow, lip. The memory of being five or six after a fall, and of Rosa. *No more chasing, Maddy. My silly angelo.* Matty carefully turned a palm over, flexed fingers. Dried blood under two nails. His blood. The fingers on the other hand didn't flex at all.

The woman put her hand under it, examining the skin. 'You've got a bit of glass in there.' She twisted round to a cupboard, turning back with tweezers.

She didn't look up as she spoke, carefully dropping the splinter into the bin. 'I know what happened to you. It's obvious enough. You were attacked.' Hearing the words was like parts of it happening again, in sharp, flashbulb images. 'You'll need a doctor to look at you, if you were—'

'I wasn't. I wasn't—' Matty fumbled for the mug on the side of the sink, hand trembling. The sweetness of honey and sharp-ness of lemon. 'He would've, but—' It couldn't be articulated.

'People like that should be stopped,' the woman said, glancing up.

Did she know? She'd seen the inside of the van. 'No police.' A held breath. 'I think I really hurt him.'

'You were defending yourself.' She carried on dabbing, before reaching for a brown bottle of TCP. Beer-brown. The colour of the glass that went into him. 'I've got someone I could call.'

'No. Please don't tell anyone.' The fierce sting of the antiseptic made Matty hiss.

She held the cotton ball in the air. 'OK?'

'Yeah.' No.

She carried on, holding Matty's hand lightly, swiping the grazes on the palm. 'Anywhere else, do you think?'

A shake of the head.

The woman unrolled a coil of fine gauze and snipped at it with nail scissors. She put it to Matty's cheekbone, and secured it with plasters. Another plaster on the eyebrow.

'I don't think you'll need stitches.' Her eyes were light blue. 'I'm Brigid, by the way.'

'Matty.' Spoken to the floor, instinctively, the comfort of her touch letting all guard drop. Should have made something up.

'Would you like me to run the bath?'

Washing it off meant getting rid of everything. Of him. Of evidence. Tears almost came again.

Brigid helped take the T-shirt off, the pain too much to do it alone. She didn't say anything as she unhooked the first sports bra from the front. Didn't say anything as she undid the one underneath, from the back.

There were marks all along one side, like a landmass, stopping before the stomach. Reddish brown, almost muddy.

'That'll be a sight,' Brigid said, very softly. 'I'll leave you to it, shall I? Unless you want me to stay?' She sounded unfussy, not fazed.

203

Part of Matty wanted to be bathed. Dabbed gently, everywhere else. 'It's OK.'

Back in the bedroom, there was a T-shirt laid out, large and peach-coloured. The bed had been remade, the pillowcases warm.

While the water had run down the plughole, Matty had stood, not fully upright, in front of the bathroom mirror. Around the plasters, the left eye was still half-sealed, the skin around it puffed up. A dark red blotch spreading from the cheekbone dressing. Split lip. The face of boxing heroes from years ago.

The door opened. Brigid handed over a towel wrapped around something. 'Sweetcorn this time.' She looked at the packet of aspirin on the bedside table. 'I've got nothing stronger in the house. I should think you can take more than two at a time.'

Matty moved the sweetcorn down, under the duvet.

'I did a bit of reading,' Brigid said. 'Did you hear a crack? Or feel one?'

'Don't know. Don't think so.'

She nodded. 'They'll take a while to heal, even if they're just bruised. But it's true that a hospital can't do anything. I think maybe we'd know by now if you were truly damaged in there.' She came right over, sat Matty up and began moving the pillows more vertically. 'You need to sleep more upright for a few days. Try and keep your wrist up high. You've to keep it all regularly iced.'

A few days. Matty thought of Shifty, in the garage. Of Dale driving away. Of him going to the police. Would he go to the police? Was he alive?

'And it's best not to wear anything too restrictive around them,' Brigid said, with the swiftest of glances at the sports bras, tangled together on the floor. Matty looked just as swiftly at the wall. 'You'll need to take some deep breaths, even if they hurt.'

'OK.' Inhale. It hurt.

She smiled. 'Call me if you need anything. I might put my head down for a bit, but don't worry about waking me.' It was only then that Matty realised that Brigid must have been up all night.

Matty couldn't sleep any more, listening instead to the wind's odd, shepherd-like whistle as it caught somewhere underneath the roof. The cough kept coming, rough and doggish, more phlegm spat into the mug. Infinitely painful each time, as if things inside there were jarring out of position.

He'd driven away. He'd limped to the car holding his side, his face gashed, arm bleeding profusely, and driven away. It wasn't as bad as it had looked.

Maybe the police were already out there. He could have said anything, that it had been a hook-up and the crazy whore had turned on him. Or he and his friend were turning down every road, and Matty had no idea where this house was.

Up. Each movement took intense willpower. Legs, swivelling. Feet on the floor. It was almost too much to stand.

The view from the window was of a side garden, a long washing line strung from the wall of the house to a low-leaning wooden post, the pegs rattling. You could just see the white front gate and flower beds, colourful for this time of year, and that the outside of the house was painted a deep teal colour. The road was quiet, roofs of bungalows further off. You couldn't see any garage from here.

There were no stairs. Another bungalow. Matty walked carefully down the hall, legs not fully stable, good arm wrapped around the aching ribs. The carpet was soft underneath bare feet. There were framed pictures on the walls, some pencil sketches of nude figures, a primitive painting of duck-like creatures, something else that might have been Indian. Family photos, too – an older couple and a tall, dark-haired man.

205

The living room was empty. The kitchen, too. She must still be asleep.

A large book was open on the kitchen counter – a diagram of a ribcage, finely jagged cracks in the bones on one side. The bile rose. Matty turned the page. *Don't smoke. Ten slow breaths every hour. Broken or bruised ribs heal within 3–6 weeks.*

You could see outside a bit better from here. Matty carefully leant over the sink, not using either hand, and looked out, but it was just a road, an Irish road. Maybe it was a Northern Irish road. How would you know the difference?

'You're up.' Brigid had come in, wearing a long pink dressing gown with blood-red flowers on it. Her black hair was loose and unkempt. She nodded at the book. 'It says it's good to move around.'

The T-shirt that Matty was wearing went halfway down the thighs – Brigid was tall. Matty pulled it down anyway. 'Where am I?'

'My house,' she said, smiling before understanding properly. 'Oh.' She said a name and Matty tried to remember seeing it on the map.

Brigid opened a kitchen drawer. 'I didn't think you could be much of a local.' She turned the pages of the road map and passed it over, pointing.

They were back south of the lay-by, perhaps twenty miles or so. A small village. Not far from the last lough, with the little girl and her bicycle. Just inside the Irish border.

'I'd been to see a friend last night,' Brigid said.

The long bend in the road. The edge of the water where it had happened.

'You must be starving. Do you think you can eat?'

'I don't know.'

'I'll make us something. I'm vegetarian, is that all right for you?'

'Yeah. I need to get something from the van.'

Brigid looked up. 'Not without a coat, you won't.'

*

Blood. There was a fine spray of it along the edge of the sink. A handprint on the counter and another on the side window. A dark patch on the floor.

Matty stood between Shifty's front seats, wearing Brigid's long mac and wellies, swaying a little. The garage was large and damp-smelling, with shelves packed full of old radios and coils of electrical wire.

Two pieces of the beer bottle lay like shards of glazed toffee, the rest sprinkled more finely. The neck of the bottle was on its side in the corner. A strong smell of beer. Matty crouched down, gripped by pain, and picked a piece up. The blood had hardened, lacquered the glass. Everything went woozy.

He'd been in here. He'd almost—

The garage began to spin. Matty clutched onto the edge of a shelf until it faded, and stumbled back to the house.

Brigid was a teacher. Primary school. No kids herself, or no evidence of any at least. On the chair in the bedroom, she talked about her job, and of travelling – six months spent away, Oman, Goa, Malaysia. Matty half-listened, thinking of the flecks of blood on the aluminium of the sink, thinking of Dale falling against the front seats, the baffled expression.

'Is it horrible?' Brigid suddenly said. Matty had hardly eaten.

The opposite. It was the first proper home-cooked meal in – who knew how long. Years. Matty looked down at the bowl of vegetable stew and rice. Like the cafe in Covent Garden that Heather liked, everyone crammed into the basement, sitting on cushions. This house was a bit like it, pot plants everywhere, rugs and sculptures that looked both Eastern and medieval. 'It's really nice.' A gesture towards the throat. 'Just hurts.'

'You poor thing.' She took the dish away. 'I should have made soup.'

The rest of the day was spent in bed, shivering, coughing and listening to Brigid move around the house. The faraway sounds of the radio, which moved between long passages of speech and orchestral music.

Every time Matty tried to sleep, he was there, his breath close. If not that, then the sound of every passing car, no matter how far off, was enough.

In the middle of the night, after going to the kitchen to get some more ice, Matty opened the front door and looked out at the garage and the foggy night.

Shifty had to be cleaned. Tomorrow. Tomorrow Matty would leave, one way or the other.

***

In the morning, Matty couldn't speak.

'How are you?' Brigid was packing a satchel bag with some papers on the kitchen table. The TV was on behind them in the living room, the news just starting.

A cracked whisper.

Brigid looked over again, her hand in her bag. She was wearing a long peasant skirt and purple woollen tights that matched her jumper. 'Blimey. That's not sounding good.'

Cough. Another go. A scraping croak.

'Don't. Don't try.' She took in a brisk, assessing breath. 'Well, I'm not surprised. You were sounding terrible enough already.' She put her satchel on her shoulder. 'I've got to get off for school. You'll make—' she suddenly stilled, looking towards the TV.

Matty turned to see an image of police tape on a country road. A woman standing with a large microphone, the wind slapping her hair against her face. A small red car, its bonnet crumpled into a tree. The driver's door open. The words formed into recognisable shapes slowly. Roadside. Bog. Dead.

Brigid went and stood behind the sofa, watching the screen intently.

208

There were police, gardaí, in high-vis jackets, one holding the lead of a sooty Alsatian. A woman in a white boiler suit and blue gloves carried a large yellow case. The road was just a track with grass growing in the centre.

A man in his twenties. Died in suspicious circumstances. The local Gardaí will not say more at this time. Inquiries are ongoing.

Dale's expression in the van. Almost hurt, as if insulted by someone dear to him. His hand, touching his side, brought up to his eyes.

The reporter kept tugging a lock of hair out of her mouth. Died.

Matty leant over, stomach and throat spasming, the pain monumental. Nothing came out.

'You're OK,' Brigid said, there with a hand on one shoulder.

'It wasn't my fault.' The words emerged in a whisper.

'I know.'

Matty waited for her to say she had to pick up the phone now. That she was sorry it had to be like this, but it was the right thing to do.

'Do you want a drink of something?' she said.

'What?'

'A hot drink.' She looked resolute, and almost ethereal.

Forehead, filled with blank space. 'Why are you helping me?'

'Because you were attacked. Weren't you?'

'Yeah. I didn't mean to. I thought he was going to—' The words were whittled to tiny points.

'I know,' she said again. 'You might have died. Don't try and talk if it hurts.'

'I have to go.' Another grotesque half-whisper.

Brigid put her hands between her knees. 'You said yourself, the van's distinctive. I'm not saying it was spotted. It was pretty tucked away. But just to be safe.'

'You could take me. Take me to a station. Or an airport.' The last place he was seen was the pub. Visions of being recognised at a desk, descriptions put out, an official holding a finger up and talking quietly into a phone as the police rushed up.

She nodded slowly. 'I could. Though you'll be leaving the van in that case. You could, of course you could, but then I'd have to deal with it.' She sniffed, a detached sound. 'Stay here for a few days, lie low, give those ribs half a chance. It's quiet round here.'

Exactly, Matty thought. It's quiet. 'I'm noticeable.'

'Not so much.' She managed to say it in a way that sounded like a compliment. 'Did anyone see you? Anyone who might blame you?'

Dale's friend, in the pub. The barman. Others in the pub, though they'd seemed absorbed in their meals. 'I don't know.' A hand, up in the curls. 'I don't know.' An uncontrollable shiver.

'You're safe here, Matty.' Her look was frank, and comforting. 'Keep your head down for a couple of days. You need to rest.'

***

Lie low. Matty lay in bed, lungs and throat on fire. Dale, found in the bogland by a dog-walker or a farmer, or police dogs after the report of the car. He'd driven away, grown dizzy, crashed. Drifted onto the bogland. Bleeding from his arm and side onto leaves and mud. Eyes open. Eyes shut.

Matty got up and found the road map. The place where he'd been found was three or so miles from the lay-by where everything had happened. The same long road.

It had gone past retching. The feeling, the *knowing*, had sunk into something tight and small, a fist deep in the stomach. A feeling that could never go away. The dead man.

He'd only been in jeans and a T-shirt – he'd have been cold. Had it taken long? Had it taken until dawn?

Matty rose, walked gingerly around the house, wrist held uselessly. Found bin bags under the sink in the kitchen and put the blood-encrusted clothes in them. Perhaps they should be incinerated, but someone might see the smoke.

There was a black bag in the outside bin already, tied only loosely. Inside were wads of kitchen towel and two cloths, all a mottled, pale pink. Fine shards of brown beer bottle glass. Brigid had already cleaned the van. Matty carefully tied the bag up again and put the new one on top. Shut the lid.

From the living room you could see the dark end of the lough, the one with the little girl, and mountains opposite. Rain dragging over the tops.

Standing up hurt. Sitting hurt. On carefully moving to the sofa, one of the cushions suddenly moved with record-scratch yowl. A sharp pain. An imperious-looking cat, huge and rust-coloured, gave a flash of glassy green eyes before it jumped off and stalked away.

Three small, raised lines along a forearm to add to the other injuries. Matty turned the TV on, stared at bland daytime shows from under an itchy woollen blanket covered with ginger fur, one finger repeatedly coming up to touch the dressings on the cheekbone and eyebrow. The raw lip. Tried to take those deep breaths, pushing through the charge of pain and the liquid rattle. Desperately wanted a fag.

The next morning, Matty listened to Brigid's car rumble into life, the engine fade. She had returned in the early evening with co-codamol, left them by the bed. Matty had stayed hidden in the single room, pretended to be asleep, not dared to face her. All night there had been thoughts of stealing the car, driving to

211

Dublin or Belfast or Derry, but with the sprained wrist – ligament damage, Brigid had said, pointing to a page in her book – changing gears would be impossible. She might have reported the theft even if it had been possible, hurt that the help had been thrown back at her. She might have reported everything.

There was a bike in the garage. Probably not much more doable. Matty stared at the road map again, looking for train stations. None for thirty miles. It hurt just walking around the house. It hurt to breathe. A finger trailed up to the *Ros*-villages, known almost by heart now. They were so close. To have come all this way over not to know if Joe might be there.

Maybe it was safest here, for now.

Chapter 8

For the next few days, still utterly caged by pain, by stupefying guilt, Matty watched the news and fiddled with the radio, a large, leather-bound oddity with gold-coloured knobs. Brigid didn't buy a newspaper. There'd only been one more report of it, a local TV bulletin, saying the same things as the first time. Nothing since.

Brigid would make them food, tried to get Matty to talk as the voice returned, about anything, about family. It had been shrugged off as not much to tell. If it wasn't for Joe, none of this would have happened. Instead Brigid talked about herself. How she'd grown up in this house, how she'd painted it and filled it with her own things to put something of herself in there. Their mother – she had a brother – now had early dementia and lived with an aunt down in Cork who had more time to care for her. Their father had died young. She was divorced, having lived further south where the work was, the husband spoken of cursorily just once. She talked about being in charge of the upper half of the local primary school, some of the more idiosyncratic pupils.

She talked about what it had been like to live so close to the border – they were Catholic, though Brigid didn't seem very religious – of her mother being an expert in smuggling sugar and butter back home. Of a boy she knew as a child who'd been part of larger racket taking turkey and tobacco over the river further up. A few years ago, there had been parties when particular roads were re-opened. It still felt transgressive to cross over.

Brigid was kind. She seemed to have a total lack of judgement, an absence of curiosity about Matty. The thought of having to go back out into the world again, to not know where the next suspicious glances, the cruel questions might come from – and of worse, of much worse – was pushed further away. Brigid bought emollient cream for the eczema, even though Matty had never mentioned it. Made hearty meals, cottage pie with lentils instead of beef, vegetable lasagne. She said not to bother washing the dishes. To rest.

So Matty rested. Waited for the wrist to improve, making hot-water bottles for it now instead of ice. Watched TV, lay in bed, avoided the sour, rheumy-eyed cat – its name was Athena – and watched the weather. The mountains changed their face every day – every fifteen minutes. A few days in, the light hit them and they were revealed not to be just blackly sheer but mottled, variously forested, even a couple of houses high up that had looked like rocks. The bungalow was always warm, slightly moist, the feel of a greenhouse.

You killed a man. It kept returning, a sudden thought that became a flood. He would have killed you. He might have crashed anyway, drunk driving. No. You killed him. The spreading queasiness and near-panic, instantly drying lips into ridges. It made eating insurmountable until the evening, when Brigid's chatter would help force it down. Matty imagined telling Rosa. I killed a man. Phoning Heather. I killed a man. Telling Joe.

Distraction. Matty lay in bed staring at hardbacks as heavy as paving slabs, lavish photographic guides to faraway countries, or artist books – Pablo Picasso, Frida Kahlo, Paul Gauguin. Unreal images. Shuffled Brigid's pack of cards over and over, half the deck in each hand, the rhythmic whirr of the edges. Did the breathing, the rib-pain lessening marginally, and drank hot water and lemon, made sharper with the cider vinegar that Brigid insisted was better than medicine. You killed a man.

Matty kept thinking of the bike. Of driving Shifty in the night, the wrist magically working. And of encountering someone new who might do the same thing. Someone stronger than Dale. You killed him.

The news had talk of a fireball passing over a town in County Carlow. A man and a young boy posing with parts of a stone meteorite, black-grey fragments in their hands. Maybe that mad old bastard was onto something after all. Thirty-four days until the end of the world, in that case. That would be OK.

The bruises changed colour, deepening to violet, plum, and almost black.

Imagined scenarios: going to the Garda station, handcuffs. A faint memory of the blandness of the station in Golders Green. Confessing to an initially uninterested officer at reception, being led to an interview room and read rights. It would look indefensible, the wounds cleaned, reporting it so much later, and only after he was found. Only Matty's word for it. Brigid charged with something, too.

A women's prison. Years.

The sky was dusky with rain, the light beginning to go. Matty imagined drawing a pencil line along the low mountain ridge, trying to stay as close as possible to it, no gaps. From the window you could just see the lough, a long swipe over two distant roofs.

'No one can see you from here,' said Brigid as she came in. 'Don't worry.'

Matty half-turned, bunching fists into both pockets of the hoodie. The hills behind that glimpse of lough had almost completely disappeared into mist now. 'It's not that.' Two nights ago, shutting the bedroom door, Matty almost had a heart attack – a black figure, suspended. Brigid had said later that she had thought the wetsuit might moulder out in the garage. Had put it on a hanger.

She was standing quite close. 'Are you all right?'

'No.' A need to be held by her, to disappear into the softness of her cardigan, her neck, her hair. Unable to ask.

'It's OK. It'll be OK.'

It would never be OK.

Mamma. Matty lay in bed, the rain soft against the window, wanting her so badly. Or wanting a memory of her, from so long ago, before she hardened. The old lullabies learnt from Nonna, the heart drawn with spooling honey on toast. Walking along the road hand in hand, she naming everything in Italian, correcting Matty's pronunciation. The words like little songs.

'Why did you do it?' Spoken so quietly, barely there. A question that had, until finding Joe's note, been only for him. 'Why did you die?' Matty turned, curled into a ball even though it hurt. Whispered *I'm sorry*, over and over, the sibilance getting lost among the sound of the rain.

On the news, they were showing the clip of Tony Blair talking about the hand of history. Footage of the new cabinets meeting at Stormont, close-ups of pens on paper. There was an interview with someone who lived yards from the partition in Belfast, sanguinely optimistic.

'Well,' said Brigid, after the report had gone on to something about motorway development. Earlier, she'd talked about being a teenager and going out with a boy who lived in a remote farmhouse just over the border. They'd been stopped once, at night, and feared for their lives. 'We'll see.'

An occasional look at the map. *Ros ros ros* repeated like a gentle tide in Matty's head. It was too far to cycle there. It seemed impossible to leave without knowing, without checking.

Joe had been silent since the attack. Replaced instead by Dale, his words coming back again and again. *What's your game? In front of my friend.* The feeling of his fingers, gripping onto Matty's neck. The look on his face as he stumbled backwards. How he drove away. How he died.

Halfway through the week, Brigid looked at the two twenty-pound notes stacked under the butter dish as she set plates down. 'What's this?'

'I could get more.' If Matty could only get out of the house.

'What for?'

'To pay you back.'

'Ah, don't be talking about that, now.'

'It's OK. I can pay. For anything I'm having.'

Brigid looked amused, and faintly offended. 'Well, if I need your money, I'll ask for it. All right?'

When they'd finished eating, Brigid leant down and pulled a newspaper out of her bag. 'Brought you something. Page six.'

Matty stared at it with a hollowing feeling. Turned to it.

The report covered a third of a page. No photos.

'Do you see what it says there?'

Bogland. Suspicious circumstances. Several lines of enquiry.

'I don't think you're suspected,' Brigid was saying, stacking the plates.

Dale Walsh, who had known criminal dealings.

'Matty?'

A nod.

'OK. I thought you'd want to see it.'

It took a day for it to sink in. A day reading and rereading the report. He'd had previous convictions, though it didn't say what. But there was the suggestion between the lines that police might think he'd been killed because of them and weren't looking for an English camper-van driver. The weight pressing down on Matty's chest lessened slightly, something floating to the surface.

217

That day, a small garbage truck came, and emptied the outside bin.

One morning, the light fell on the lough in a new way, made it gleam. Matty's heart hurt.

Hours were spent listlessly in the house, feeling the water almost as a presence. It was watchful, and calling. Matty read, turned on the TV, steered clear of the cat, skipped between three lunchtime news programmes. Slept. Watched the lough again from the window. Tapped fingers in hip-hop beats on the sill.

It wasn't far away.

On the map, it looked like you could take single-track roads, with probably very few houses.

In front of the bathroom mirror, Matty peeled the dressings off, turned from side to side. The face was still drastically conspicuous. Puffy and indigo-coloured around the eye, as if something was brooding under the skin. The cuts were beginning to scab, but still looked lustrous. New plasters.

The roads were quiet, the air rushing and clean after the stuffiness of the house. Down one hill, and then along the scenic road taken once before, feeling like Elliot in *E.T.* – except that Brigid's bike was a large shopper, not a BMX. Alien and escapee mixed together. Riding one-handed, carefully and constantly engaging the right-hand brake. The ascent on the way back would be tougher, and even more painful.

Sporadic houses were set far back from the road. There were two deserted cottages, one thatched, and one much newer, a sash window ajar. Further down, coaches and minivans were parked in rows, a tourist vehicle company, and a sheepdog came haring out, its bark outraged. Matty veered around it, heart high and loud. The dog kept barking even when out of sight. No cars.

Once the decision had been made to go to the lough, there was a thirst, an unnameable need to get there. Matty had gone into Brigid's bedroom for the first time, dabbed some of her foundation over the bruises. Grabbed sunglasses from Shifty's glove compartment, packed optimistically last month, and nicked one of Brigid's coats.

Fields and a mass of trees kept the water at bay, before the road finally curved alongside it. A small parking area. Matty let the bike fall into the grass, ribs taut from the ride. A long, slim jetty protruded directly outwards, matching the concrete colour of the lough. There were small oblongs carved out of it, mossed at the edges. It was a perfect get-in.

Too soon to swim. It would hurt. And no wetsuit.

Matty walked to the end of the jetty, sat down, pulled out a cigarette. Didn't light it. The water was perhaps hip height here, though probably deeper further out. Easy enough to disappear into, be swallowed up forever. There was a small, uninhabited island 400 metres away, clustered with pastel-coloured trees. Beyond it, the same mountains you could see from Brigid's living room, black and stoic.

A STOLEN LIFE RING IS A STOLEN LIFE. The yellow buoy was here this time, set in a box on top of a rusting iron pole. Matty leant against it, put a hand down into the water.

His face. The engulfing shock of the cold as he pushed Matty's head down into the water, and the muffled, warped sound of him shouting.

Fingers out again, as if bitten. Matty got up, walked quickly back down the jetty to the car park and sat on the top of the black picnic table, shaking.

This life had been stolen. Not just his. It had been replaced by a new one. A killer. Even if you'd done it to protect yourself, it was still called killing.

The fine-grained sound of bicycle spokes. 'Aren't you going in today?' The little girl from the other day was there, a purple scarf tucked into her candy-pink coat, braking. She got off and edged her bike stand outwards with her foot.

'No.' An attempt to look normal. Not like a killer. So much for not being seen.

She twirled around. 'But you're a mermaid.'

Matty stared back towards the opaque water. 'Not today I'm not.'

The girl was staring at the plasters. Too late to hide them. 'Did you fall over?'

'Yeah.'

She sniffed. 'I do that all the time.' She walked over to the shopper. 'One of our teachers at school has got a bike like that. Ms Kilduff.' She pronounced 'Ms' with lots of 'zzz's. *Brigid Kilduff*, the name on the envelopes and *National Geographic* magazine that had dropped through the door this morning. 'Did you steal it?'

'No.'

She crouched down, pulling a blade of grass up and putting it between her fingers. She blew, ineffectually. 'I know quite a lot about mermaids. They don't all have tails. Some have human legs.' She threw a squinting frown towards Matty's lower half. 'Why do they call the boys mermen but girls mermaids and not mergirls or merwomen?'

'I don't know.'

'Maybe it meant that they were the mermen's servants and had to do all their hoovering and chores and everything. I bet mermen are really lazy.' She slid her eyes over, waiting for Matty to smile.

A numb feeling, toes and fingers. The feeling of being in water for too long. 'Shouldn't you be at school or something?'

'I had to go to the dentist.' She drew her lips back and curled her tongue. 'I've got too many teeth.'

'Right.'

'My name's Sheanna. It's like Sheena but better. No one is called it but me. What's your name? Then I'll know. About whether you're a merboy or a mergirl.'

A different name. A new name. 'Scout.'

'Scout? Like Boy Scout?'

'Yep.'

'That's a weird name.'

'Not any weirder than yours.' Matty tried to smile, a small one.

Sheanna scrunched her face up and eyed Matty for a few seconds, her nose smoothing out again. 'You're mean. And that doesn't help, anyway. I have to go now.' She kicked her bike stand away and began pushing it up the short slope. 'Bye!'

Matty looked back at the water, a petrol shimmer on it. Wanted to swim forever and never wanted to swim again.

***

Back to safety, at Brigid's, pushing the bike most of the way up the hill with the working hand. She'd been home, hadn't minded the bike being taken, seemed pleased. Matty had stumbled down the hallway, shut the bathroom door quickly and run the bath.

That crazy kid, turning up out of nowhere. It wasn't quite the same spot where she'd last been, and yet there she was. She was probably imaginary.

Nicks hadn't been real. Had he? He'd haunted Matty, though not in the same way as Joe. Just occasionally, on a sunny day in Hampstead, there'd be a sliver of him, in a flash of green light, the splash of a fish, someone diving.

Brigid's olive-coloured bath turned the water into a pond, the thin film of dirt and tiny specks floating in it like water boatmen. Sage-green skin.

This body. No amount of exercise could turn it into the right shape – it was often hard to know what even was. Matty ran a finger over one rib, then another, tracing the yellowing bruises. Lower. Stomach. Lower. The bath had been the best place for wanking, traditionally. No one else's mouth, no one else's fingers. Imagining drowning. Trying to time it right, listening to the

221

blood moving, submerging again just as the dark, fierce shudders came.

But today, there was Dale. Breathing, trying to go blank, was futile. He wasn't here, and he was everywhere. Matty went under, jamming a fist up in the crotch to find the feeling, and to stop it ever coming. To protect it.

A tiny clicking sound. There was a shape out there, tall and filmy.

From warmth and near-silence to a loud slosh of sound. Matty jolted up, ready to fight, water hefting over the side of the bath.

'Jesus,' the man said. 'Sorry.'

Black hair. Not Dale. The back of him as he swiftly left the bathroom.

The man was still there, in the kitchen. Matty had waited ages, sitting on the bed underneath a towel, and yet there was the exchange of voices again, Brigid's and the lower one in an occasional tag-team, and the sounds of cupboards opening and shutting. Plates.

He had seen everything. One leg hooked over the bath handle, eyes shut under the water. All the bruises.

The smell of food came inching along the corridor. Matty, who hadn't eaten all day, let the towel fall around both shoulders and rubbed a hand through the half-dry curls. Stood up.

Brigid was leaning down, her head practically in the oven, which was humming. She was speaking loudly to be heard over the radio. 'It's always the same. No one can keep anything to them-selves. Matty.' Her voice had suddenly changed direction, a touch higher, brighter. She straightened. 'This is my brother, Cormac.'

The man was standing in the corner of the kitchen holding a glass of juice. The one from the family photos. Taller and thinner than Brigid, with the same thick eyebrows, black hair and bone-blue eyes. More freckles. 'Hello,' he said in a warily

222

neutral voice, the word tipping up just a little at the end. A voice that gave no indication that he had walked in on Matty with a fist shoved between both thighs.

'Hello.' The word croaked more than intended.

'I was wondering if you two would meet,' Brigid folded her arms. 'He's always round,' she said. 'You'd think that by thirty, he might have learnt to cook a meal or two.' Her tone was darkly teasing.

Cormac shifted and drank from his glass, before eyeing it. 'Not much time for recipes, Bridge.'

'I know, I know,' she said, drawing a tea towel out from its holder. 'Always the martyr. Well, sit down, then,' she said, with mock exasperation. 'If you want anything to eat.'

It didn't get any less awkward. Brigid filled the room with words for all three of them, while Cormac gave the odd reply and seemed mostly engrossed in his food, apart from an occasional careful look at Matty, not quite a frown. He had a patch of white hair behind one ear, as if he'd had a freak electric shock or been the victim of a lightning strike. His elbows stuck out either side of his plate, hard protrusions against his jumper. Stubble that suggested he usually shaved but hadn't got round to it. A CD of exotic-sounding jazz was playing in the living room, a man wailing as if the world was ending.

Cormac scraped up a last forkful of ratatouille and sat back in his seat, using Brigid's tea towel to wipe the side of his mouth. 'So,' he said, making eye contact for the first time since the bathroom. 'You're a friend of Bridge's, then?'

Matty swallowed a mouthful of aubergine.

'A friend of Laura's,' Brigid said, putting his plate under hers, her voice just as light as before. 'So near enough.'

There was an Indian man singing now, a tune like swirls in water. Cormac was eyeing Matty's cheek. 'What happened to your face, there?'

'You took a tumble, didn't you?' Brigid said, standing up with the salad bowl. 'Up at Glenveagh. I got wind of it and seeing as you're away from home, I said I'd take you in.'

'You're a climber?' His eyes were a slightly lighter blue than Brigid's. Wintry.

'Yeah.' It wasn't a total lie.

'You got pretty beaten up,' he said, with the same careful, inscrutable tone.

Brigid turned from the sink, looking between them with the slightest confusion as Matty thought of what he'd seen, pale skin and sallow bruises in bathwater. 'Yeah.' A cough. 'Rocks had it in for me.'

He gazed at Matty, one eyebrow a tiny bit lower than the other. The CD had stopped. 'Well, they can get you. Not that I'd know. You'd never find me scrambling up rock faces. What do you call it, when you do it on your own?'

'There are different ways. Solo top-roping.' Easy enough to answer. A couple of the staff at one of the camps in Canada had talked of ascents up teetering cliff-faces.

He nodded, still wary. 'Well, you're in good hands. My sister can patch up anyone.' He stood up. 'Back to work for me.'

'To work?' said Brigid. 'You're on a night shift?'

'Overtime,' he said. 'I'm on that case.'

Matty's throat thickened.

'Which case?' Brigid said.

'Your one up at _____, ' he said, his correction harsh. 'You did hear?'

'Oh, yes,' said his sister, unfussily. 'Horrible. I just didn't know you'd come out this far.'

'The locals need help on this one,' he said. 'Bunch of layabouts.'

***

224

There was another half an hour waiting for him to go, making excuses and disappearing to the back bedroom, listening for the car door, the engine. Watching the lights sweep away before returning to the kitchen.

Brigid seemed ready, her hands in the deep pockets of her cardigan.

'You told him.' A choked breath.

'No, I didn't. I haven't.'

Matty felt wild, untethered. 'You – you must have.' The words were desperate. 'You kept me here.'

'No, I haven't. I promise.' Her eyes were wide, guileless. 'You heard what he said. He doesn't know. He's not looking for you, or anyone like you.' She put her lips together, a sympathetic look. 'I wouldn't do that.'

'But you know what I did.'

'And I know why you did it. I promise, Matty. I'm looking out for you.'

'I'm going now.'

Brigid didn't move. 'Just – take a moment. It's OK.'

'It's really not OK.' Every rib hurt with panic. 'Your brother is a copper. Why didn't you tell me about him? What he did for a fucking job?'

She gave the slightest flinch at the swear word. 'I wanted to call him straightaway. But when you said no police, and I realised what might have happened—'

'What do you care? Why didn't you turn me in?'

'These things don't always go the victim's way.' She shrugged a shoulder. 'I didn't know he'd be on the case. I'm sorry.' Spoken as if she was talking about something on the telly, not what was happening here, *now*. 'But please. Calm down. You'll only make yourself ill again.'

'I have to go right now.'

'Matty.' Her eyes were large, maddeningly docile. 'It's all right.'

'How often does he come here?'

'Not that often. Once a week. Sometimes more.'

'Jesus. You *helped* me, knowing he could find me.'

'No, that's not it, of course not. I promise it's OK.' She laid a palm on her breastbone. 'I'm his sister. He'd never suspect.'

'My bloody camper van is in your garage.'

'He won't see it.'

'It's right there.'

'He won't see it.' She looked strangely calm. Serene. 'Our dad was always in there, tinkering with his radios and whatnot. It reminds Cormac of him too much. He hasn't set foot inside for years. And anyway, there's not even been talk of the van on the television. It's a quiet road, that one. I doubt anyone saw it.'

'You've just incriminated yourself.'

'It's hiding in plain sight. You're not fit to go, and I'm happy to have you here. Until you've healed up a bit more.'

Matty lay awake half the night. Wanting to punch her. Wanting to break her every rib. Wanting Rosa.

Wanting Joe.

***

They hadn't really talked for over a day. And Matty hadn't left.

The fear of staying, and the fear of going. The same questions spun endlessly round. What if Shifty is recognised. What if a description has been put out. What if Cormac knows. What if he doesn't. What if Joe is there. Just *there*.

Another day of volatile weather. Hail clattering on the roof, followed by a tawny light and then a mist, sitting above the lough, as if the water was too powerful for it. The water, always finding its way through the skin. The water of the body answering the water out there.

*

Today, the wetsuit was rolled into the rucksack with the travel towel on top. Brigid looked up from her book in the living room. Matty didn't look back. Rode with the sunglasses on, even with the clouds knotting thickly together overhead, weaving out of range of the mad sheepdog. Tried to imagine cycling thirty miles to a train station with this wrist pain, these ribs. Knew it wasn't possible.

The wetsuit had been too ambitious. Idiotically so. Even bending was difficult. Matty stood at the end of the jetty, jeans shoved up a bit, toes flexing. Just a dip. Not a real swim. Just to feel it. The mist had risen and the water now looked bitter, hard, impenetrable.

He'd come up fast, from behind.

You never regret going in, one of the old women at the Ladies' Pond had said once, standing at the top of the steps, eyeing the thin, isolated diamonds of ice on the black water. It was true. You never did.

His grip had pinched, fingers digging in.

A step down, onto one of the chopped-out slabs of the concrete. The lough was goading, slapping against the rock.

The sluice of the cold water. Dale shouting *You little cunt.* Much longer and Matty would have had to gasp, take more breaths, lough water funnelling into the lungs. Fuck.

It was no good. There could be no getting in. *He* was in there, the memory of him. Matty stepped back up onto the jetty. Turned and walked fast to the bike, tucked in by the wall, shielded from the road. Stared at the tarmac. Kicked it.

Ting ting.

Great.

The little girl wheeled into the car park. 'Hello.' She wheeled around again, braked hard at the loughside and looked out at it for a moment, before pedalling back up.

'Are you following me around or something?' The world's smallest garda.

She looked defensive. 'No. I always come down here. I'm allowed to ride on the road because hardly any cars ever come and I always have to be back in fifteen minutes. I'm not really supposed to come past this line.' She pointed to the final parking space outline. 'Don't tell. Aren't you going to swim?'

A quick glance back at the water. It was hard to imagine ever going in again. 'No.'

She made a small, oddly wise sound, a one-two shake of her shoulders. 'Mermaids can go on land, too. If they grow legs, anyway.'

'Yep.'

Sheanna got off her bike. 'I'd like to be a mermaid. I can sing. You know, that's something they do.' The sound of her speaking morphed into the sound of her singing without Matty even realising it. '*I'm a Barbie girl, in a Barbie wor-or-orld.*'

Dale had said something about dolls. Barbie and Ken.

The girl had her hand on her hip, was waggling back and forth, as she continued singing, miming brushing her hair and taking dress straps off her shoulders.

Matty sat on top of the picnic table, feeling the familiar dynamic from the activity camps, though this kid was younger. Sometimes they got quite besotted with the staff, doing anything to get attention, leaving them hand-drawn cards with adoring messages and lots of kisses. *THANK YOU MATTY YOU ARE AWESOME! I'm never going to be afraid again!* It was always pretty sweet. 'I don't think mermaids sing that sort of stuff.'

'What do you think they sing, then? Do you think it's something like ... Mariah Carey? I bet they can't sing as high as her.' She let out a pearling mouse-squeak.

'Nope.'

'Modern mermaids might, though,' she said, pertly pleased with herself.

'Yeah, yeah. Hadn't you better be off now?'

'Why?'

'Didn't your folks tell you not to talk to strangers?' They'd do workshops about it in the camps, the kids all sat round in pyjamas, sleepy after a day outdoors, being told about the nasty, oblique things that might happen if they didn't follow the rules or pray to Jesus.

'My daddy talks to everyone.'

Maybe there was a different rule in Ireland.

'Do you think the world is going to end?' she said, her hands still on her hips.

'No.' I want it to.

'Because of New Year's Eve, I mean. With the—' Sheanna stopped suddenly and frowned, her next words coming carefully and slowly. 'Minnellium Bug and everything. All the computers are going to blow up. Are you real?' She had a bright, sparrowish look.

Her rapid changes of subject were a little dizzying. 'Are you?'

'Course I'm real. Look.' Sheanna pushed up the sleeve of her coat and plucked at her bare skin, hard, between two fingers. 'Ow.' It was patched, pale brown and a much paler pinkish-white.

'Don't do that.'

'Look,' she said, keeping her sleeve bunched up to her elbow, forearm shoved very close. 'It's called *vitiligo*. Girls at school call me giraffe.'

'They're little shits, then.'

Sheanna looked over with scandalised delight. 'You have to give me twenty pee.'

'What?'

'Twenty pee. For swearing. For my biscuit tin.'

'Your biscuit tin?'

'My swearing biscuit tin. When my daddy swears, he has to give me money. It's the rule. I'd better go. I live just up there.' She pointed vaguely, the houses placed far apart along the single track road, all facing the lough. 'We're having fish finger sandwiches.' She got back on her bike.

Matty rode home with *Come on Barbie let's go party* on mental repeat, the bright, plasticky words getting tangled up with Dale's voice.

Brigid was in the kitchen, her hair wet. She straightened as Matty came in. 'Did you have a nice ride somewhere?'

The kitchen smelt malted, sugary. The oven fan buzzed.

'Down to the lough.'

'Ah, there are some good spots. That's a big bag,' she said.

'Wetsuit.'

Brigid gazed over, as if just realising something. 'You're a swimmer,' she said. 'I thought you might have been a surfer, but – I suppose no board.'

'Not much swimming right now.' I've never not gone in, Matty wanted to say, wanting to tell her everything. Not ever. It's all I am. If I'm not that, then—

'Give it time.' She turned the oven down. 'I'm baking soda bread. A sweet version.' She looked over, one of her dark eyebrows elegantly raised. 'You want some?'

I want to die. I want my dad. Matty sat down at the table and took a deep breath. 'OK.'

Chapter 9

'Ten or twenty?'

This morning, Matty had turned in the opposite direction to the lake, hood up and curls scraped back underneath it. The shop was a mile's walk away, houses dotted along the small road. Brigid offered to go after school but Matty insisted. Might as well brave the world before it ended.

The cashier had already turned to the shelf. It was a newish shop – Brigid had said more had been springing up since the lifting of the customs barrier. They didn't sell Slim-Fast.

'Ten's fine.' Matty had started back on half of one a day, hardly breathing any in.

'Cutting down?' She gave a quick-flicked grin. She resembled someone familiar, maybe the girl from the cafe in Golders Green years ago, blond, green eyes. There was a raised mole in the middle of her cheek.

'Something like that.' Matty added a postcard of the lough, trying not to wince with the pain.

'Oh, are you on holiday?' She gave the faintest glance to the fading cuts and bruises.

'No, just – staying with a friend.' A smile.

She smiled back. 'Enjoy yourself, then.'

Matty thought of the smile on the slow walk back, the significant gap in her teeth, and of what to write to Heather. *Unexpected stop off. Can't swim. Can't leave until I've swum. Might be close to Joe. Might not. Mate. I killed someone.*

There'd been no more news. Not on TV and not in the papers Brigid had started bringing back. Matty needed to run, to London, to anywhere. But the thought of Joe and the closeness of the *Ros-places* kept returning. Brigid said Cormac didn't know anything, that she'd ask about the case, and Matty had said not to. It would only seem more suspicious.

A car was parked on the bank outside Brigid's house. It had a long scratch all along one side and an uneven dent over part of the front and passenger doors. An image of Dale's crashed car, blinked away. The back door to the house was unlocked.

In the kitchen, bending at the knees to minimise the pain, Matty silently unlaced both boots and stepped out. Tiger-feet, cat-feet, just in case. There was a tiny snapping sound from further inside the house, or in the wall.

The back door burst open and Matty darted backwards, almost falling over.

Cormac came into the kitchen, out of breath. He'd been running. His eyes were dark with shock.

Another step back. Spine hitting table. 'You – you don't know why.'

He cast a surprised glance over, but seemed far too preoccupied with breathing to do or say anything else, standing with his hands on his hips, elbows out, torso bent over slightly. His cheeks and neck were blotched red, and he had a reflective coat on and shorts. White, skinny calves. Running trainers. 'Know why what now?' he said, dragging a breath in and heaving it straight back out, loudly.

'Nothing,' Matty said, in not much more than a whisper.

His breath was slowing a little. He tipped his chin up to the ceiling, hands on his back, and stretched his side a little. 'You're still here, then?' Another sideways glance.

'Yeah.' He couldn't suspect. He'd have arrested Matty by now. Why would he be asking? 'Recovering. You know.'

He put a hand out on the counter, holding his side. 'Tell me about it.' He turned on the cold tap. The water slammed against the sink, and he opened a cupboard and filled a glass to the brim, drinking it in one go. Wiped his mouth. 'So what's your deal?' he said, quite suddenly, turning.

'What d'you mean?'

'What brings you over here?'

Lie. Lie well. 'Friends,' said Matty, remembering Brigid's breezy excuse. 'Just visiting a few friends.'

'And climbing,' he said. Another shrewd look, the sort that people often gave. Wondering. Except he'd seen everything, in the bath. So he thought he knew.

'Yeah.'

'How's all that feeling?' Everything. He'd seen the bruises.

'OK. Hurts.'

'Not surprised. How far did you fall?' He wasn't being friendly, exactly. There was something examinatory about it.

'Don't know,' Matty said to the wall. 'It wasn't a straight fall. Caught a ledge. Blacked out for a bit.' Change the subject. 'You're a runner.'

His gaze was steady, before he filled his glass up again. 'That's a very generous way of putting it.' A hint of a dry grin. 'It's nicer here than in town. And my sister is better at making cakes than me.' He leant down to the fridge and opened the door. 'I'm allowed it if I've been out for a run. Isn't that what girls say?'

A smarting irritation, even though now wasn't the time. 'I wouldn't know.'

His smile levelled out. 'Right.' He cut a slice of Brigid's carrot cake. Looked over.

'I'm good. Thanks.'

He sat at the table to eat it. There was an itch to bolt, hide in the bedroom, but maybe that looked more dubious. Matty leant against the wall instead. 'Is that your car, then?'

'Yeah,' he said, through a mouthful of cake.

'Were you in an accident?'

He glanced up, guiltily. 'I'm not the world's greatest driver.' He rubbed his hand over his face. 'A new one's coming.' He'd eaten the cake in about five bites. 'Need the bathroom?' He stood. The blotches on his face had started to fade.

'No.'

'Sure?' It was really hard to tell whether there was the slightest joke in there or not.

'Yep.'

His nod was slight, before he moved past.

He was still there when Brigid came home. On his third piece of cake, taking the piss out of her for chopping vegetables. 'My sister, Ireland's only vegetarian,' he said, half to Matty.

'Oh, shut it,' Brigid said. 'Honestly. You'd think we were still in the bloody seventies.'

'She has to order pineapples from abroad,' he said, sliding the cake plate over towards him. Matty attempted a smile.

'You're the one coming over so you can be fed properly. All you ever eat is chips.'

'What did you think of it up there, then?' he said, suddenly looking over.

Matty swallowed. 'Up where?'

His expression was flinty, deadpan. 'Donegal. Glenveagh and all that.'

'Pretty nice.'

'You been to Slive League?'

'No.' Blinking, trying to remember the map. 'Didn't make it that far.'

'Ah well, you should. Pretty impressive, if you like that sort of thing. Maybe hold off on climbing them, though, if you want to keep all your bones in the right place.'

'Do you know Rosbeg?' Matty said, not quite to either of them. 'On the west coast.'

'Don't think so,' Cormac said. 'Bridge?'

'I'm not sure I've been quite to there. It's a lovely area, though. Done?' She reached for his plate.

'Cheers, Bridge. You're a wonder.'

'How's the investigation going?' she said, turning to the sink. Matty stared at the table.

'Ah, you know. All right. Nothing I haven't seen before.'

'He was a bad fella, was he?' Her brother looked at her. 'That's what the paper said.'

'He'd got plenty of form,' Cormac said. 'The whole family's rotten to the core. Continuity stuff, weapons, you know, always fighting among themselves. There was talk of a lad in a van, but I reckon it's one of the Sligo boys that did for him. And you didn't hear any of that from me.'

A numb, crushing weight. Sternum, collarbone, throat.

Brigid didn't look at Matty. 'God, it's appalling. You'd think this might have died down a bit more now. Wishful thinking.'

'You know full well that some of them don't give a monkey's. They'll just crack on with it, no matter what all the big men cook up between them. Anyways, he bashed his own head in driving into a tree.' He gave them a sardonic look. 'Always wear a seatbelt.' He stood up.

'Are you not staying to eat?'

'No. Got to get off. See you later.'

After he'd left, Brigid looked at Matty. 'He died from the crash. You're safe.'

It still didn't feel that way. 'Is he good at his job?'

'He was arresting people at the age of five.' When Matty didn't smile back, Brigid softened her voice. 'He is, but you heard him. It sounds like that man had a lot of enemies. It can happen around here.'

And none of them helped kill him. 'The van.' Matty scratched at the tabletop.

Brigid took a breath. Nodded. 'I think it's best to stay where it is. For a bit longer.' She put her hand on top of Matty's.

Matty stopped scratching the table. 'Sorry.'

Brigid didn't remove her hand. 'No need.' She didn't look away. She smelt heavily of cherry blossom, of coconut.

They sat still, the vegetables simmering in the pot.

***

Sheanna was squatting down at the near end of the jetty, throwing stones into the lough. She looked round as Matty parked up, shouted, 'Are you following me or something?' Sounding pleased with herself.

'No.' I just have to come, Matty thought, wandering up and staring at the water that called all the way up to Brigid's windows. That called even in bed. To the side of the jetty was a curved beach, trees hanging down with hard, blood-clot berries. It looked sandy, not too yielding. You could wade in, and then – in an instant, Matty's chest and throat stiffened, locked themselves up. And then Dale would be there again, with his words and fists.

Deep breath, or the deepest breath possible with the pain. Back to the present. 'All right, mate?'

Sheanna threw a stone and held up another, grape-sized. 'I'm trying to hit that.' There was a solitary leaf, bright green, a few metres out. 'My coordination is not very good.' She sounded self-deprecating and strangely adult again.

Matty crouched down, lobbed the stone. It landed a few feet away.

'Your coordination is not very good either, Scout,' she said.

It was startling to hear the false name in anything other than Joe's voice. *Tiger, crackerjack, scout.* 'Practice makes perfect.'

They spent a few minutes on their target practice, Sheanna getting up once to gather another handful of gravel.

'Did you bring your wetsuit today?' she said as she dropped them all on the concrete with a spatter.

'Nope.'

'Don't you want to swim in it anymore, then?'

Yes. No. Yes. It's all I want and I'm too fucking scared.

'Are you frightened of the dog?' Sheanna said, throwing another stone in.

The sand was beer bottle-coloured. 'What?'

'Because that's not in there. It's in Lough _____.'

Matty thought blankly of the sheepdog up the road, its mindless, hysterical barking as it ran alongside the bike. 'What dog?'

'It's called the Dob—' She gave a pensive, assessing little hum, before shrugging. 'The Dob-something. It lived in the water and it was really, really big, like a giant killer dog, and then it killed a girl, and then her husband got it back by killing it but when it died, it made a massive cry and its brother came. But the husband still killed it.'

Matty had pulled out a cigarette, lit it. A careful, shallow intake. 'You read too many books.'

'I don't. You can't read enough books. Books tell you *facts.*' She said the last word with heavy relish. 'Could you kill one?'

'Maybe.'

'I bet you could. Mermaids are dangerous. You know how everyone likes swans but actually they can break your arm?'

Matty drew on the cigarette. Just one more puff. 'OK.' It was a myth, that – they'd actually just hiss and flap their wings, but Sheanna didn't need more facts.

'So mermaids sit on rocks and comb their hair – because normally they have long hair – but only if they're bored. They sing songs to sailors and the sailors can't help themselves and they get sucked towards them and they're all in love and then the mermaids eat them all up.' She tipped her head up at the sudden sound coming from above them, to the right.

There was a growl, getting louder. A serrated sound in the sky, and an insect-like shape becoming larger. A helicopter, coming this way. Lowering.

Matty stood, quickly. Shit.

The lough became choppy. It was close enough to see the individual blades, and how they slowed as it landed by the shore, further down on the north side of the water, opposite them.

The helicopter door opened, and a soldier came out, followed by another, and another. They were holding guns, big ones.

They knew. Cormac had worked it out, and had radioed for back-up. They'd already been to the house. They were searching for Matty.

Sheanna had risen too, standing stock still as more soldiers got out, though she didn't seem perturbed.

Ten soldiers, a small gap between each one, moved slowly along the road on the other side of the lough. They didn't even look over.

'They're from the British Army,' said Sheanna. 'They come sometimes and walk down the road. Daddy says it's best not to make a fuss.' She sat down again.

Matty's heart was throbbing, an insistent kick drum.

'He says they'll be gone soon. Did you hear about the dead man?'

Still frozen. 'No.'

The helicopter rose, shunting backwards, the blades beginning to blur.

'I bet it was a *murder.*' A delicious curl in the centre of the word.

'I didn't hear about it.' Fumbling for a cigarette.

'Not here, but further up at _____.'

'Right.'

'If I was a detective, I could find out who did it.'

'Who d'you think did it?'

'A bad man.' The soldiers had disappeared behind a line of trees. 'Do you think I'm right? That a bad man did it?'

A long inhale, too long. 'Yeah.'

'You shouldn't smoke them.' Sheanna was looking sidelong at the cigarette.

'Says who?'

238

'My daddy. He says smoking is for very silly people who only have half a brain. For eedjits.'

Matty gave the slightest of nods. Stubbed it out.

Sheanna grinned and then looked seriously at the lough. 'I wish I was a mermaid. Then I could be dangerous.'

'Why would you want to be dangerous?'

'Bullies,' she said. She looked out at the lough, and then at her knuckles, which were red. 'It's cold. I'm going indoors.'

***

The warmth of the house was nullifying. Matty moved sluggishly round the house. Watered the plants, watching the soil darken and bubble. Took even longer baths. Went back to aspirin instead of co-codamol. Started reading the novels on the shelves, at least the slimmer ones, which seemed to please Brigid. Called Heather once, though she'd sounded harassed and distracted. Thought about calling Nonna. Didn't.

The mornings were dark, the afternoons too. Matty had begun to memorise the mountains opposite, each groove made by water and trees, and charted from day to day the tiny dot of an adventurous sheep straying too high. Began to know how long it would take for rain to come by the pace and heaviness of clouds, that the grassy sunlight was only going to last minutes.

Something in Matty had stagnated. The tiredness kept coming in waves, not just the impact of the injuries, and the guilt, but an exhaustion from long ago. Always moving – camp to camp, room to room, sofa to sofa. It was warm in Brigid's house, a reassuring tick of the radiators, and there was homecooked food. It felt good to sit, and be still. It felt safe.

Nice to be attractive, accepted, too. Matty had started wearing less. It was hot enough. Just oversized vests and tracksuit bottoms, no sports bra – keeping those ribs alive. The eczema patch was shrinking, more than it did normally. Brigid would look, eyes wide for a moment before she blinked and returned to her chores. Some people liked the small swagger, the boyish thing. The girl at the shop maybe did.

'You don't half remind me of someone,' Brigid said on the sofa, some historical show on. 'I've been trying to work it out.'

'Who?'

'Someone off the telly or something. Some matinée idol.' She cast a sly, flirtatious look over.

An almost-blush. 'Hardly.' Folded arms to emphasise the biceps, looking at the screen.

'I don't know,' she said, and smiled.

By the car park, Matty watched the water, white foam on it today. Thought of Dale in the form of a dog, spittle at the corners of his mouth.

Out towards the island, a mallard bobbed, untroubled by the waves. The bar on the side of its wing was the same colour as Brigid's house.

No Sheanna. It was almost a disappointment. It was good to talk to someone different, even if she was a mad little thing. She made Matty think of the best kids in the camps, who weren't always the tanned, sporty ones, but the quirky underdogs, a penchant for wisecracks or dancing their nerves out before being strapped into abseiling ropes. She'd made a change from Brigid, if nothing else.

It started sleeting.

'Did you manage to get in today?' Brigid said, later, coming in with a stack of box files.

Head-shake. The bitterness of it. The defeat. Matty took the boxes off her, though it still hurt to carry things.

'Not a bother. I'm sure it will come back to you once you're yourself again.'

How could you be yourself again when you'd half-killed someone?

240

'You can help me with something if you like,' she said, taking her handbag off her shoulder.

'Yeah?'

'Stuff for class tomorrow. How are you with scissors and glue?' A warm, droll smile.

'Yeah.' A sigh, and an attempt at animation. 'I'm great.'

The kids' work was spread out on the table, some music put on. Poems to be mounted on red and green card. Brigid taught the top year, the age Matty was when Joe left. The poems were bright-eyed and Christmas-themed, the odd solemn attempt at winter darkness.

Brigid had put on a CD, sun-drenched Cuban stuff, all smoky back rooms, pianos and guitars and singing. Heather had the same album. 'When you coming back?' she'd said on the phone. 'When I've found him,' had been the answer.

Matty looked at Brigid, perfectly content with her large kitchen scissors, her apple-curve cheekbones prominently shadowed, moving her shoulders to the music. Not caring about her fortnight-long houseguest.

'Do you want me to go?' The words quiet.

She was absorbed in lining up a poem. 'Where?'

'Go. You know.' Back to cutting the card. 'I feel like I'm taking the piss now.'

'No. You're still recovering. And I like having you here.' She glanced over. Spoke more softly. 'You know I do.'

Skin, rashing into goosebumps in the gentlest way. Brigid had seen everything, in the bathroom that first awful night. Had allowed Matty to just *be*.

The track changed, more joyful, a sashaying trumpet. They cut up the final poems in silence.

When it was finished, Matty stood up. 'Shall I make a cup of tea?'

Brigid smiled. 'That'd be lovely.'

Houseboy, then.

'I'll come with you.'

'It's cool. I can go.' Matty had been to the shop a couple more times, for Skittles and an extra shot of self-esteem. The blond girl had been there just the once. She'd been wearing a T-shirt that slid off one shoulder, coral-coloured bra strap on show. She made Matty feel better, made the angular gestures and the hint of rebel come, River Phoenix in *My Own Private Idaho*, but some sweetness, too.

'No, I'll come with you,' Brigid said, picking up her handbag. 'I need a few things.'

The blond cashier was there and wearing a Santa hat.

'Nice look,' Matty said.

She glanced upwards, eyebrows meeting the white-furred rim, as if she'd forgotten it was there. 'Oh.' An eye-roll. 'You know, Merry Christmas and all that.' There was that gap in her teeth.

'Suits you. You should wear it all the time.' Matty pointed past her shoulder.

'I remember,' she said, turning round. 'Ten Marlboro Lights.'

Brigid had come up, putting a bag of potatoes and shampoo on the counter. Gave Matty a strange look. 'Have you been smoking?'

'Just the odd one.'

'It's not good for your – you know.'

'I know.' Matty took the carrier bag from the girl, who'd been pretending not to listen. 'I can do that.'

They packed the bag together, alternating, the girl biting her lip, trying not to smile as Brigid paid.

Matty crushed up a grin. 'See you.' The slightest wink.

'See you later,' the girl said, before adjusting her hat. 'Be good for Santa.'

Night fell quickly. The air in the house felt muggy, close. Brigid made more noise than usual after dinner, the sounds of the cupboards and pans harsh. The feeling of a thunderstorm, brewing somewhere.

'Is something wrong?' Matty knew, really.

'No. Nothing.' Unfussy, shorn of feeling.

Nothing. What girls – and some boys – said when they meant plenty.

Matty stood in the doorway to the living room. A little wedge of stubbornness. 'Do you want me to go now?'

'What? *No.* I don't want you to go.' Three plates made a bright clatter. 'I want you to – I—' She turned, and there was the tiniest, measured breath from her nose, as if much more was hurling itself about behind her lungs, waiting to be siphoned out. 'I thought you liked me.' There was an equal emphasis on both of the last words, a slight cracking. Self-hate. Embarrassment.

'I do like you.'

'Not like that. I thought ...' Brigid clutched both of her elbows and looked at her spice rack as if she wanted to upend it. 'I thought that was why you were staying. Partly.' She shook her head, her own internal tussle.

It felt like it had been coming to this. There was almost relief mixed in with exasperation, and a sense of obligation. At least she admitted it. And there was something that could be done about it.

Matty got up from the table and stood in front of Brigid, very close. Close enough to smell the trace of sweat under her arms and that musky perfume of hers. Brigid was still looking with fierce concentration at the bright-coloured spines of her cookery books, but she had gone very still. You could practically sense her melting between her inner thighs, and it brought a simple flush of desire in return. Desire, and the desire to give back. To forget everything. Matty tilted up and kissed her jaw.

A slight melting. A kiss to her cheek. Her knee shifted. A kiss on her bottom lip.

Brigid's eyes were on Matty now. Thunderstorms, flashes, very far off. 'You don't have to – don't just do this because you feel guilty.'

'Come on,' Matty said, and led Brigid to the sofa.

*

Matty's first girl. Tara, also sixteen, walking three dogs on Wanstead Flats. Saying 'good morning', a glittering smile full of braces, startling Matty into muttering 'all right,' and turning round to look. A compact body, glowing. Buttocks filling high shorts and dark-blond, frizzy hair down her back like a fountain. She'd turned round again, too.

They had passed each other again going the other way, and Tara had cadged a cigarette. The dogs were a part-time job for a family at the posh end of the flats, and were all named after ballet dancers. She had a proper Essex accent, her voice melodic and airy, and a bright, assessing look.

'I totally had you down as a boy,' she'd said, but didn't get up to go.

They'd gone back to the big house, no one home. Tara had locked the dogs in the conservatory.

'Have you ever kissed anyone?' she had said.

'No.' Kissing made people disappear. Nicks had never come back.

Except that she had stayed right there. Tasted of raspberry lip gloss. 'You can kiss me somewhere else if you like,' she'd said.

From kissing to everything, in about five minutes. She'd been like Bird's Eye custard, and Matty had listened to the sweet, sleepy noises she'd made, while the dogs bumped themselves against the glass.

It hadn't lasted. Tara had said she couldn't introduce Matty to her parents, even though the two of them had held hands in the

244

street. But the sighs she'd made on the three times Matty had gone down on her were kept. Imprinted. Aimed for again.

Brigid's noises were different. Everyone was different, after all. Brigid was like a storm wind battering a window.

Most of Matty's clothes stayed on. Brigid's body was pliant, a walnut tinge to her skin. One breast bigger than the other. She'd moved about as if having a bad dream, but Matty knew how to play it. Not thinking of him. Not thinking. Fingers, thumbs, tongue. In the end, all of Brigid had curled, toes to throat.

Matty started to move off the sofa.

'Where are you going?' said Brigid, her voice wisped.

'Going to – get ready for bed.' It was far too early.

'Will you not stay here a bit longer?'

Matty lay carefully back down and pressed a knee up to Brigid's crotch in a way that made her whimper.

***

'Morning.'

Matty had gone to the back bedroom in the end, saying it was better for the ribs. Came into the kitchen to the smell of coffee, which Brigid didn't normally drink. Obviously a special occasion. 'Morning.'

'You OK?' Her voice was very soft. 'Is anything wrong?' She was different, like she'd been unpinned. The storm clouds had vanished.

'No, nothing.' Meaning plenty.

'Have a nice day. Go gentle, still.'

She hadn't said that last night.

***

'My husband never did that.'

245

The next night. Brigid's pungent, doughy smell was mixed in with the cinnamon of the candle.

'Did what?' Matty gave a rangy stretch and put an arm under her neck, trying to concentrate on the pleasure of being so close to her. Trying to blink away the muted doubt that it wasn't right.

'What you just did.' She rolled her head away and looked at the ceiling. 'Made the wrong choice there.'

'Yeah, you did.'

'Yeah, I did. You're very good at that.' Her hand was on Matty's cheekbone. It was a pale yellow now, the cuts thinned to small slits. 'Did you ever go with a man?'

'Depends what you mean.' Brigid didn't say anything. 'Yeah.'

'You're a tiger, aren't you, Matty?'

Tiger. Crackerjack. Scout.

'I'd ask you to teach me to return the favour but I'm guessing you'd rather not right now?'

'Yeah. Not right now.'

The shadows oozed on the wall, the candle almost out. 'I'm so sorry about what happened to you, Matty. It shouldn't happen to anyone.'

'What about him? Are you sorry about him?'

'He shouldn't have done it. Sounds like someone was probably coming for him anyway, down the road. It doesn't make it better, I know. But I'd sooner some criminal was in prison than you.' Brigid's fingers were at the back of Matty's neck, moving upwards. 'You seem lonely.'

The words hung there. They felt like something that would bruise internally, over days.

'It's OK,' she said. 'I've been lonely, too.'

Being here doesn't make me any less lonely, Matty realised suddenly, watching the shadows on the wall.

Tiger. Aged seven, bouncing like Tigger, then trying to do the rich voice of Shere Khan, flexing huge paws. Joe sniggering, saying, 'Tony from Frosties, more like.'

246

He might be so close.

'Can I borrow your car?' Maybe it would be possible now. The left wrist was starting to have some life in it.

She shifted her head down, gave a surprised hum.

'I've got a couple of places I need to go.' Get up there, look for Joe, leave.

'You could, but it's in the garage from tomorrow. Sorry. It's been playing up.' A hand in Matty's hair. 'I'm borrowing Jerry's, my neighbour two doors down, for a few days to get to school. You can borrow it once it's back on Saturday if you like.'

Four days. 'OK. Thanks.' Matty lay there, letting Brigid twist the curls, feeling them tangle. Looked up. 'Will you cut my hair tomorrow?'

She smiled.

Chapter 10

Matty sat on a chair in the kitchen, bare feet propped on its lowest rung. Grey-brown hair like wood shavings scattered around the floor, and Brigid frowning as she leant close.

'Well, it's not a salon,' she said, holding the clippers. 'But I think I've sorted you out.' She walked round, scrutinising.

A quick feel of the back, the soft stubble. It was always a bit hard, doing it yourself. 'Cheers.'

'My pleasure,' she said from behind, the back of one finger on Matty's newly smooth neck, leaning down to kiss it.

A shadow at the back door became Cormac, the door opening noisily.

Brigid straightened. He stood on the mat, taking in the scene, Matty's bare legs, Brigid's hand curled. The pause a little too long. 'How're you going?' he said, moving to the sink, an upturned glass picked up from the side, getting the bottle of squash that Brigid always bought for him.

'Not so bad,' said his sister, her hand moving to Matty's upper arm, almost protective.

It didn't seem right to move yet.

'I'll give yours a whirl if you like,' Brigid said. 'You're beginning to look like a thatched roof.'

Cormac didn't turn from the sink. 'No, thanks. I'll stick with the barber's, if it's all the same to you. You might scalp me.'

'No skin off my nose,' she said.

'And none off my skull,' he said, straight back, as he turned round. Like a comedy duo, except neither of them was smiling. The quickest glance over, before he drained his glass.

Matty was having a cigarette and watching the magpies do their tag team when Cormac came out.

He put his hands in his pockets, standing a few feet away. 'I don't know what's going on, but—' his shoulders were up around his ears. 'Whatever you're doing with Bridge, you've got the wrong idea.'

'About what?' Matty turned away, towards the garden. Praying he didn't look in the direction of the garage.

'My sister. She's not … she was married. She's not—'

A half-turn back. 'Not what?'

'She's not *gay*,' he said, leaning down, the last word a wide-eyed whisper. Scandalised or impressed, it was hard to say.

'I'm not gay,' said Matty.

Cormac straightened, his eyebrows reaching towards each other, and attempted to start several sentences, none of them getting past the first word. 'Don't take the piss out of her,' he said, finally. 'She's had a shite time. She's been bloody generous.'

'I know,' said Matty. 'I'm going soon.'

'Right,' he said, casting over another perplexed look. 'Good.' He didn't seem especially pleased.

It got colder. Darker. Closer to Saturday, and the use of the car. Three days. Matty kept returning to the map, burning a hole in the coastline, imagining Joe *there*, where those cliffs were, or that small town. Brigid drifted round the house with a self-satisfied smile, her fingers trailing on things. Two days.

They were sitting on the sofa, Matty having cooked sausage and mash, the only dish in the repertoire. Vegetarian sausages burnt more quickly, as it turned out. Brigid was looking over at

Matty, who was turning the pages of a book on Gaudí, the buildings dripping. 'You make me weak at the knees. I feel like a teenager.'

A smile at the book. An untruthful one. Tough, fierce girls were better. Girls who went on top as well as underneath, bashed the bed against the wall, yelled. Sarcastic, sharp.

It wasn't that it was horrible. It was comforting to have skin to touch, hair on the next pillow. To feel wanted, and safe about feeling wanted. Dale was not the end of everything.

Matty reached over and ran fingers underneath Brigid's chin, to the dark, fine hairs tipped blonde with bleach.

'Don't,' she said, suddenly awkward, moving her head away. Looking back, self-conscious. 'I hate them.'

'It's nice.'

'You're welcome to them.'

Plenty of times Matty had rubbed a hand over the pale, clean jawline in the mirror, imagining the stubble. Had drawn it on once with eyeliner, aged fifteen and drunk on cider. Scribbled in a moustache. Scrubbed it off, a faint smudge remaining the next day.

Matty cycled to the lough mid-afternoon, timed to coincide with the end of school, the light just starting to deepen. Getting on for the shortest day.

The birch trees were bleached grey, the hard red berries not quite reachable from the jetty. Matty walked down to the beach, tugged a few off. Stood at the end of the jetty, throwing them in one at a time, the resolve to get in, even for a dip, fading. The water still reeked of Dale. Of being held down. The berries floated, gathered together again.

Happiness at the sound of the bicycle wheels. Matty didn't turn round. Sheanna was already bouncing up, chattering about school stuff.

The pull of her, like there'd been with Nicks. But she seemed real enough. She gave a swift, breathless lowdown on the narrative of the Christmas musical, singing part of a song before rattling into something about snowflakes and geometry. She seemed to know how the world worked, unlike Nicks, who'd been elusive, old-fashioned.

'When's your birthday?' she was saying now.

'February.'

'Mine's in sixteen days. On New Year's Eve. So I'm turning nine on the biggest day of the world, ever. Well, since ten – no, nine ninety-nine, but I bet they didn't have parties then. I'm getting a pink mermaid cake. Do you think mermaids like cake?'

'They love it.'

'No, they don't. That was a trick question. You can't eat cake under the sea, it would go too soggy. How do mermaids make babies?'

'Are you telling me a joke?'

'No. I'm asking.'

Definitely not going there. 'Beats me.'

She screwed up her nose. 'Because, you know, they're all fishy on their bottom half. How do fish make babies?'

Not going there, either. 'Better go and find out.'

She gave a little hum and started wandering back towards the car park.

Matty walked just behind her. 'So who are these bullies, then?'

Sheanna stopped and looked at her nails, a pretence at an adult action. 'Just these two girls.'

'What girls?'

'In my class.'

'OK. What are they doing? Are they hurting you?'

She shook her head. 'Yesterday they rolled my sleeve up and said they were going to cut away the dark bits with craft scissors, and if that didn't work, with a big knife. The other week they coloured a bit of me in with board pen.'

Matty looked outwards. 'Who's your teacher?'

'Miss Leonard.' Not Brigid, then. That made sense. Sheanna was too young to be in her class.

251

'Have you told her about it?'

'No.'

'You told your parents?'

'No. They're busy.' Her voice had shrunk, lacked shine.

'OK. Do you want someone to do something about it?'

Sheanna slid over a look. Nodded.

***

Cormac did his running circuit from the house again, coming back panting into the living room, where Matty had music on. It was colder than last time and his cheeks and knees looked slapped.

'Is she not back?' he said.

Wouldn't he have known that? 'Got Christmas stuff. Concert or something.'

He nodded. Tapped his fingers on his thighs. 'D'you want a cup of tea?'

Hard to say no. 'OK.' Matty could see him wander down the corridor after putting the kettle on, taking the briefest look into the single room. Yes, I am fucking sleeping with her, Matty felt like saying. No, I don't really want to be.

He came back in with two mugs, and stood drinking his in the doorway. Neither of them spoke. The sound of Public Enemy utterly incongruous between them. 'How are your ribs there, now?' Cormac said, eventually.

'Getting better.'

'You took a right bloody tumble.'

'Yeah.' Matty looked at him. 'I thought I was going to die.'

He seemed surprised at the honesty. 'Did someone find you?'

'Yeah.'

He pursed his lips and made a noise that was swallowed up by a slurp of tea. More Public Enemy. 'So, you're not a lesbian, then?' He spoke in a wry, careful way.

252

'What does it matter?'

He raised his eyebrows before giving a chastened nod. 'Fair enough.' Was still looking over. 'That's not one of Brigid's.' He nodded at the CD player.

'No.' Matty got up to turn it off.

'Don't mind me. You carry on with your gangsta raps. I don't really get that stuff. That's the guard in me. More of a Westlife fan, myself.' He glanced over. 'Joke.' He was still completely straight-faced, the minutest ice-spark in his eyes. 'Or is it.'

Matty wasn't sure whether to smile or not.

He gave a sudden, energetic breath in, and drained his mug. 'I'll get off, then.' Rolled his shoulders back. 'It was an early start, so.'

Questioning people from the pub. Re-examining the scene, crouched over the grass, the police tape around it. Though he might not have been working on that today – maybe Sligo Town kept him busy. He hadn't mentioned the investigation again, and Brigid hadn't asked. She'd said that this was good and Matty wanted to believe her.

The more normal, the better. Just ask. 'Do you get a lot of – serious crime?'

'More than you'd think for round here,' he said. 'Bad karaoke versions of "Flying Without Wings" being one of them.' He grinned, and the grin disappeared just as quickly as it had come. 'Be seeing you,' he said, and shouted it again as he banged the door shut.

***

The primary school was a mile up the hill, the opposite direction to the lough. The playground had a wire fence around it and there was a yellow school sign for drivers – the boy was bigger than the girl, dragging her along.

It was the last Friday of the winter term, and the kids were coming out into the playground in twos and threes, adorned in tinsel. It was a long driveway, parents scattered along the pavement and chatting by cars, teachers sending the kids over. Matty passed them all and hovered. Didn't want to look dodgy.

There was no hiding from Brigid, anyway. She was already coming over, her hands in the pockets of her thick cardigan, which had woollen petalled flowers on the bottom. Probably best.

'Hello. Have you come to meet me?'

A gentle grin. 'Yeah.'

'Aren't you a surprise,' she said, pleased. 'Give me a moment. I've just got to get all my lot off. Clear up the carnage they made.' She trotted quickly back to the building.

Sheanna came out in her pink coat with two girls close behind, whispering to each other. One of them kept poking Sheanna in the back, and her head came down, trying to ignore them.

There were methods for dealing with bullies. There'd always be a training day before camp started, learning how to deal with kids who were homesick or ill, or at the darker end of things, cutting themselves or fighting or abuse at home. Excruciating role-plays and some bad diagrams projected on an OHP.

Time to ignore all the advice. Matty followed them out of the gate, caught up with them before they got too close to the cars. 'Oi.'

The girls turned round. One had reindeer antlers on a headband, and the other fluffy cream-coloured earmuffs.

Matty crouched down, elbows on knees. 'Sheanna's my mate.'

They looked at each other. The reindeer girl had a little bubble of pale green snot in one nostril.

'Did you hear me?' Best quiet-assassin voice.

They both nodded. Not such bullies now.

'You two say anything to her again, or try anything, I'll pull your fingernails out. One by one. Then maybe your fingers.'

The reindeer girl curled her lip. 'You can't say that.' Her friend nudged her.

'Yeah, well, I just did. You see me talking to Ms Kilduff?' They both nodded.

'Well, she's my friend, too. I'm going to tell her all about what you've been doing.'

The mouth of the reindeer girl was open.

'Go on, piss off, both of you.'

They walked past, and then ran.

Sheanna was standing a few metres back, watching. Her eyes big.

***

'Well, you're unexpected, that's for sure.'

They were in the bath, opposite each other, Matty with elbows on drawn-up knees, Brigid with one leg resting on the side, gazing over. Essential oils curled on the surface of the water, and the classical music station was on in the next room.

Matty lowered a cheek down, looked away. Same old. Brigid wasn't that different from anyone else after all.

'Not like that,' Brigid said. 'For me, I mean. Not in and of yourself.' She swilled water over her sternum. Her black pubic hair had the slightest seaweed-float. 'Did you always ...?'

They always had to ask. 'Pretty much.'

'Is it different in London? I remember being on the London Underground, and there was a guy all dressed up as a tin man, and no one batted an eyelid.'

A tin man. That was about right. 'I don't know. Sometimes.' And sometimes, it didn't matter where you went, because you might still get the double-takes, the change in tone of their voice. Matty drew both knees up more tightly.

Brigid's fingers lolled in the water. 'Well, I think you're special. Unique.'

There it was. 'I don't want to be unique. I just want to ... get on with it.' A hand, sweeping over the slicked-back hair into a 1950s greaser's. 'Be nothing to anyone.'

There'd been a friend of Bee's, a towering Scouse nightclub dancer, who'd told the doctor about wanting to be a woman

255

in order to get the hormones. Matty couldn't face doing the same, and didn't know if it would be right anyway. The thought of going to a doctor to even ask about hormones, or surgery, caused a nauseating dread.

'Nothing?'

'Just not a – *thing*.'

'I understand.'

Matty laid one arm on top of the other, looked straight at her. 'I don't want to be a she, most of the time, and I don't want to be a he, not all the time. It's no one's business.'

'No. It's not.' Her words disappeared into the steam.

Cheek, chewed. Matty felt bunched up, darkly coiled. Dale had thought it his business. Made it his business. 'Is it still all right to borrow the car tomorrow?'

'Sure. But can I take you somewhere? It'd be better. Seeing as you're not on the insurance. And for your wrist and all.'

'I'll drive safe. I think it's healed now.' Healed enough, anyway. She was looking over, waiting for more. 'I'm just looking in on an old friend.' Matty still didn't want to say his name. In case it made him less real, rather than more so.

'You didn't say.'

Shrug.

'OK, then. Promise to look after it?' Brigid flicked water over, a comical *doink*. And again.

Matty sat back. Slid a leg straighter, foot right between her thighs. 'Yeah.' Toe, digging softly in. Anything to stop her talking about being special, unique.

Brigid exhaled, a wide sound that echoed off the walls.

***

A cold, flinty day. North and west, the big roads became smaller, potholed ones. The wrist still hurt. Matty tried to minimise it, stay in fourth until the engine started sputtering, but the

256

discomfort was unavoidable. The map on the passenger seat slid off on one particularly fast bend.

It felt strange being so low down, after the height of Shifty's seats. But there was also a heady rush of independence, going further than just down to the lough or the shop. The big sky and new mountains up ahead.

'Are you coming back?' Brigid had said that morning in the kitchen. Half joking. Half not.

The breadth of the sky and the speed of the clouds brought optimism, focus. Back to Joe, and what would be said if he was found. *I'm the only one here. Who the fuck do you think you're talking to?* To some quaint village, and him, startled, in the centre of it all.

The first *Ros*-place was bleak, the road blue with recent rain. It consisted of a single-track road with sodden moorland and dry-stone walls on either side, before the sea suddenly appeared, rough and ferocious. There were only a couple of houses. Matty slowed, saw an old woman shuffle past the window in one, and a small school bus in the driveway of the other. It was a relief to get back onto a larger road again.

The next was an unromantic outpost, still not what you'd imagine from Maureen's description. Matty walked the length of the main street, and up into the side roads, feeling like a stalker. Bought some fruit in the shop, and asked. Asked in the garage, and the florist, and was first into the pub when it opened.

No one knew the name. It didn't feel right. If Joe lived in a little place like this, everyone would know him. The owner of the pub would definitely know him.

The third place was on a lumpy peninsula pushing out into the Atlantic. No shop, no pub, just a scattering of houses, each with its own long strip of rocky land descending to the sea. Matty drove slowly, tried to guess which house could be his, which car or van, looking for a Ronan's Interiors or something on the side of the trade vehicles, feeling hopeless.

Up ahead, there was a woman with two tiny dogs at her feet, taking in large plastic sacks from her car. Matty wound the window down, asked.

'Not that I know of,' she said. 'But I don't know everyone. Not been here that long.'

There was a long slab of sand the colour of bleached wood. Surfer's waves. The wind whipped away the cigarette smoke. Matty tried to imagine Joe here as a teenager – smoking too, lying down in the dunes, skidding around on a motorbike – or living here now, and couldn't. It was freezing. Joe hated the cold. Always turned the heat up, ignored Rosa's arguments above saving money.

He'd never been here and he didn't live here now. He was so far away, intangible. Not even a voice now, because of what had happened in the parking bay. The imaginary Joe too shocked to speak.

The road south. Matty went past the sign in the direction of Brigid's. Could keep driving, across the border, except that it might be a manned one, and they could do a check on the licence name, find there was no insurance. Drive to the nearest Irish airport. Passport looked at, an official sliding their eyes over to a list of names. Drive out into the empty, wide world, with no one who cared in it.

Brigid's kitchen smelt of roast vegetables, herbs and baking bread. She straightened from the oven, her hair in wisps around her face. 'There you are.'

'Hey.' Matty felt shattered. Broken apart and put back together wrongly.

'Did you see your friend?'

Dry throat. Dry heart. 'No.' Matty sat at the table, cradling the bad wrist, limp and inflamed. 'Wasn't in.'

Brigid was instinctive. She knew there was plenty not being said. 'Will I strap that up for you?'

She brought new bandages from the bathroom and Matty let her hoist the wrist up, strap it around a shoulder. 'Are you OK?' she said, quietly.

Every movement felt tiny, caustic. Head shaken. Lip bitten. A thumbnail digging into a finger pad.

She put a hand on Matty's knee. 'Was it an old flame you were after?'

'Something like that.'

The oven fan grumbled.

Brigid pushed a curl out of Matty's eyes. 'I was thinking. You'll stay for Christmas? It'll be nice.'

Where else was there to go? 'OK.'

That night, Matty lay in the single room, having slipped out from under Brigid's heavy arm. She spoke in her sleep, odd, otherworldly words, and had a slight snore, a tiny, comical sound on the inhale.

The wind did its high-flute whistle in the roof. A car, far off.

'Where are you?'

No answer.

'Where the fuck are you?'

He wasn't there. Not in Matty's head. Not in Donegal. He wasn't anywhere.

Chapter 11

Cormac was at the house again. He seemed to be round pretty frequently, but there was never any talk of the case anymore.

Brigid was standing at the kitchen counter in front of a huge pile of branches. The shine of holly and clusters of darker, blood-clot berries on thinner sprigs. Scattered leaves on the floor.

Cormac was leaning against the sink. 'Look at my atheist sister, getting all seasonal,' he said, partly to Matty. 'There's hope for her yet.'

She snipped the end off another thin branch. 'I'm not an atheist, as you well know.'

'Going to church, then, on Christmas? I'll come to the local one with you if you like.'

'Not a chance. I don't go in for all that patriarchal nonsense,' she said as she went into the living room to put her branch on a shelf.

'You never used to say anything like that.'

'I never used to be so enlightened.'

There was always a sense that they were performing for Matty, each subtly trying to outdo the other.

'And anyway, your man Buddha there was a fella,' he said as she came back in. 'Sid Arthur what's-his-name. A *human* fella, which is probably far worse.' Matty couldn't help a tiny grin, and he saw it, and grinned, too, at the floor. More than once, Brigid had talked encouragingly about the noble eightfold path and meditation instead of TV. She'd said she wasn't a Buddhist exactly, but she liked reading about it.

'I'm not being drawn into this,' Brigid said now. 'I'll be off down to Cork on Stephen's Day if you've time.'

Cormac's manner changed. Less pesky younger brother, more offhand. 'Probably working.'

'Well, are you or aren't you? So I can tell her?'

'Probably,' he said, sounding rattled. 'Not all criminals stop for Christmas. You off to family?' He was looking over at Matty, who'd remained standing by the wall.

'I asked Matty to stay here,' Brigid said.

He didn't seem to let out the long breath he took in. Nodded. 'Very good.'

***

The days piled on top of each other, moving towards Christmas. A heavy, thickening feeling. Matty's hips were losing their rak-ishness, abdominal muscles starting to become less defined. Press-ups and sit-ups had been unthinkable since the attack, the usual diet ignored. Had to get back to it.

Brigid caught Matty with a vest hoisted up on one side in front of the mirror in the hallway. She put a hand out, touched the skin below the ribs' eczema patch, which was a pearly, barely there glimmer now. 'Lovely.'

Not lovely.

'What's that you're listening to? Is it the radio?'

'No, it's one of mine.' Gang Starr, a horizontally lazy style, plenty of scratching and an insistent ringing bell. '*It's a long way to go when you don't know where you're going. You don't know where you're going when you're lost.*'

'Really? That doesn't seem like you.'

It's exactly like me, Matty thought.

The criticism started to come in other ways. Baths too long, even though Brigid liked to have the heat up high. How Matty smelt nicer before the first cigarette of the day. Too much TV.

'I liked it when you were reading everything in sight,' she said, with a hint of what was probably her teacher's voice. She'd always temper it with compliments, but they were never the ones that Matty wanted.

***

A cold evening. The pink-bellied clouds slid over the mountains, over the silver of the lough. That water-call – it practically hummed in Matty's blood. Three and a half weeks of no swimming. The last time it had been that long was aged eighteen, laid up with flu.

Their voices could be heard before the door opened. Matty turned the TV down a bit. *Trading Places* was on, the seasonal parts causing a pang of wistful sadness.

'Well, I need a drink after that,' Cormac was saying.

'You're so mean. It's the highlight of her year.'

'Then Miss Draper needs a lot more excitement in her life.'

It had been the village panto, an annual collaboration between the community hall and the school, Brigid stage-managing. Matty had declined, though would have been curious to see if Sheanna included the moves she'd demonstrated. But being spotted by those two little bullies might not have been such a good idea. Brigid had been told, and though she seemed a little surprised about Matty knowing Sheanna, had nodded, and said she'd deal with it.

'Well, just be glad I wasn't in charge,' said Brigid, putting her head into the living room. 'Hello, you.' She glanced at the TV.

Not turning it off. There were only fifteen minutes to go. 'Hey.'

'Matty, are you having a drink with us?' Cormac shouted from the kitchen.

'I'm good. Thanks.' Cutting down. More exercise, less booze.

Brigid had said he came to the panto every year. Tradition.

'Ah Jesus, you have got to be kidding me.' Cormac came in with a glass of wine. 'Are you telling me I just sat through *Annie*-meets-*Little Shop of Horrors* or whatever that was when I could have been watching this?' He sat down on the sofa next to Matty with a dramatic sigh. 'You've got to love Eddie Murphy. The man's a genius. *Beverly Hills Cop* and *Coming to America* are my all-time bloody favourite films.'

Matty grinned, a lightening of the soul not felt in weeks. 'Yeah?'

'Even *Beverly Hills Two* is bang on.'

Matty saw Cormac as Judge Reinhold, the earnest do-gooder, the bright eyes. 'Yeah, it's all right.'

'You seen it?'

'Course.'

'"My name is Johnny Wishbone, and I'm a psychic from the Isle of St Croy",' he said, in a very odd accent.

'"I'm a psychic extraordinaire".'

'"Phenomenon", isn't it?'

'He says both.'

Cormac looked pleased. 'Points to you, then.' He held his glass up and Matty picked up the water glass. *Clink.*

Brigid had come in and was standing by the sofa, watching them. 'You'll have to stay over,' she said.

They looked at her. Cormac glanced at Matty with a trace of guilt. 'It's fine, Bridge.'

'It's not and you know it.' She addressed Matty. 'He gets hammered after one.'

Cormac's cheeks reddened. 'Fine,' he said, his tone hard and mildly petulant, and drained his glass. 'I'll have another, then.'

'Hardly anyone knows.'

Matty was lying next to Brigid in bed. Cormac was in the single room – his old room, he'd said – so there was no chance of slipping out in the night. Brigid kept her voice low and Matty watched the candle's shadows on the wall, the sweet, peachy smell almost overpowering.

'He was just a boy. Got drunk with his pals and they all crammed into one of their cars. Took turns driving. He was at the wheel when they crashed. One of the boys didn't ever recover properly.' She put her hand in Matty's hair and there was a strong urge to shake her off. 'He wasn't yet eighteen, so he escaped charges. I think he became a guard to pay penance, partly. He didn't drink for ages, and now that he's back on it, it doesn't take much. He wouldn't normally have a drop before driving anywhere.'

'Wow.'

'He was just – I don't know – trying to impress you, I think.'

'Impress me?'

'You're an excitement to everyone, Matty.' She sounded amused.

'Thanks a lot.'

'No, I didn't mean – I just think he doesn't know quite what to make of you. Of us.'

Us. She said it with such confidence. Like it had roots.

Matty turned the light off.

Brigid left early, wanting to sort her classroom out before the last half-day of school. Cormac was standing in the kitchen, eating the last of his toast and taking his coat off the chair. A little pale, his hair unkempt.

'Good morning to you.' A little bravura in his words.

'That wine do you in?'

'No,' he said, suddenly defensive. 'Why, what did she say?'

'Nothing.'

The cat slunk past Matty's ankles and hissed violently.

That seemed to cheer him up again. 'You haven't charmed the cat, then.'

'She hates me.'

264

'She hates everyone. She hates *Brigid*. That thing has clawed the bejeezus out of me a couple of times for just walking by minding my own business. *Athena*.' He shook his head. 'Goddess of wisdom and war and taking great big lumps out of you.'

Matty couldn't help a quiet laugh. It was a relief to have someone take the piss out of Brigid.

Cormac glanced over. 'You look very different when you smile,' he said, before looking surprised at himself. He gazed at the door, holding his coat formally, turned back as if to say something else, and finally left.

***

On Christmas Eve, Brigid sent Matty out to the shop for some last-minute condiments. She'd had five recipe books out, scraps of paper with calculations pencilled on them. She didn't seem too worried about the cashier now. Safe in the knowledge that Matty was all hers, obviously.

The girl wasn't there, anyway. But Sheanna was, standing outside on her own singing to herself, purple earmuffs over her pink hat. She stopped when she saw Matty.

'All right?'

She nodded, her eyes wide.

'Those girls do anything else?'

She shook her head and kicked at the base of the plastic charity dog. 'Ms Kilduff talked to me and then I think she talked to them and then she did a talk in assembly about bullying and how bullies are cowards and the ones that get bullied usually go on to be actors and prime ministers and stuff.' Kick. 'I found out how fish make babies.'

'Did you?'

'The girl fish lay their eggs and the boy fishes go round and fertilise them. Some fish have boy bits and girl bits. I read it on the World Wide Web. And some fish start out as a girl and then

they become a boy and some of them can become girls again.'
She looked, keen-eyed, up at Matty. 'Is that what you're doing?'

'No.' A smile.

'What are you getting for Christmas? I'm going to get pony-riding lessons. Because my birthday is six days afterwards, I always get smaller things for Christmas and bigger things for my birthday. But I think pony riding lessons are quite big. So my birthday is going to be brilliant.'

A man came out with shopping bags. 'OK, Sheanna?' He sounded American. Gave Matty a cursory, though not unfriendly glance. 'Hi.'

'Merry Christmas,' Sheanna said.

'You too, mate.'

Matty heard her dad say, 'Making friends with everyone again, are you?' as they walked off and Sheanna saying, 'I can't help it. I'm really friendly.'

***

Christmas morning. Brigid gave Matty a book while they were still in bed – *Zen and the Art of Motorcycle Maintenance* – then flicked through it and talked about metaphysics. Matty had used the car earlier in the week to find something two villages south – a necklace that it was obvious Brigid didn't really like, though she did her best to pretend.

They were raised by the phone. It was Brigid's aunt, saying her mother had not been well. Brigid sighed heavily over a late breakfast before heading off to Cork.

Matty drifted through the house, listening to its taps and clicks, looking at all the cling-filmed dishes of food that Brigid had made yesterday. It was better to be here, alone. The first Christmas with no one.

A phone call to Heather.

'You were going to be our little Christmas gnome.'

'Yeah, well, you can probably pick another up off the street.'

A snort. 'Bloody heroin addicts and wasters round here, mate. Santa and me are passing them by. Who's this woman again?' Half-suspicious, her territory being strayed onto.

'Brigid. She's a teacher.'

'Well, tell her this from me: she's going to give you back at some point or I'm coming over there to have fisticuffs at dawn. Got new nails in for the season. Green and red.'

There was the sound of Val saying something in the background.

'Happy Christmas, mate.' Matty tried not to croak. Heather was the nearest thing to family in years.

'You too, nutcracker. Laters roast potaters.'

Matty felt an ache for Rosa, even though the last three Christmasses hadn't been spent with her, and though the ones before that had been laboured, sullen, hellish. There was a deeper, bruising ache for the Christmasses of long ago, when Joe would ceremoniously lay out a double measure of Jameson and a plate of malted milk biscuits, and be astonished the next morning, his mouth a perfect 'o', even after Matty was eight and knew perfectly well that it was all a charade. 'Now, what did my man bring for me this year?' he'd say, sitting down on the chair nearest the baubled tree. 'I've definitely been good enough.' Wink. 'Mostly.'

He was never going to be found. Matty had to face it. He left because he didn't ever want to be found.

In the early evening, there was the sound of the back door opening and closing.

'Hello?'

Cormac. A sense of relief that it wasn't Brigid, that somehow she'd decided not to stay in Cork overnight, their mum fine after all.

He stood at the entrance to the living room a few moments later, in his work clothes, holding his jacket in his hands. He took in Matty's bare legs up on the coffee table, the TV. 'Did she leave a while ago?'

'Yeah.'

'Been on your own?'

Matty held onto both elbows, shoulders drawing inwards. 'Just me and the cat.' A weak smile. 'Um, she said if you came over to say your food was in the fridge.'

'Right.' He disappeared.

The squeak of the fridge and the metal scrape of the oven door. There was a brief blast of the radio, a Christmas song played on tin whistles, before Cormac turned it off again.

He came back with two already-opened beers and sat down on the sofa next to Matty, passing one over. '*Sláinte*.'

'Cheers.'

EastEnders was on, diminishing the homesickness. Even though it was the wrong end of London, it was still nice to hear the accents. 'D'you want to watch something else?'

'You're grand. I'm braindead.'

Matty wasn't going to ask how his work day had been. Not today.

The episode ended, a bombshell about the pub being sold, and went into an Irish light-entertainment show, everything very loud and very bright.

'So, you avoiding the family thing as well?' He was looking over, his beer clutched in his lap. They'd never sat so close together before.

'I haven't got any.'

He looked back at the TV. 'Sorry.' After a while, he turned his head again. 'No one?'

'My grandparents in Italy. We fell out when my mum died.'

'Right. Sorry to hear that.' He had a policeman's frankness. 'Was that a long time ago?'

'Seven months.'

'Ah, Jesus. Was it a sudden thing?'

Flesh, rotting. The smell that hadn't quite been scrubbed from the house. Bloated belly. 'She killed herself.'

There was a sudden, perfectly timed shout of laughter from the TV. 'Right,' said Cormac. 'God. Sorry.' He faced the screen. 'Were you close, or ...?'

'No. Not close.'

The oven pinged. 'I'll just—' he pointed his thumb over his shoulder. 'Do you want another beer?'

'There is more,' Rosa had said on Boxing Day four years ago. 'All the leftovers from yesterday.' A pointed remark, Matty having made excuses for the day before. They had dinner in front of the TV, just like this.

'I'm full.'

'You don't eat enough.'

'I eat. I just work it off.'

'Yes, in your gym all the time, and your swimming. Look at those muscles.' She'd reached over, prodded at an upper arm, until Matty had shrugged her away. 'You want to go on World's Strongest Man?' A sour laugh.

'You're drunk.'

'Of course you do.' She leant down to the carpet for the wine bottle and sloppily poured more into her glass, shaking her head.

'You should stop.' Matty got up, went towards the kitchen. 'I'll make a cup of tea.'

'Who are you to tell me what to do, hmm? You are still young. Still growing.' She raised her voice as Matty put the kettle on in the kitchen. 'It will change. You will grow out of it. That is what I tell myself. So that I do not feel ashamed.' Her voice rose. 'You are my daughter. You hear me? My *daughter*.' Matty had slipped out, leaving the kettle boiling.

*

Neither of them talked as Cormac ate, the cutlery grating against the china, his jaw working. He seemed in lower spirits than on previous visits. Perhaps he always needed Brigid to spar with.

He scraped up the last piece of potato and put his plate on the table near Matty's feet. 'Well, it's better than the microwaved meal waiting for me at home.' He sat back again. 'You probably think I should be seeing my mother,' he said.

'None of my business.'

He spoke to the screen. 'The job wipes me out. I love it, but I haven't got the space in my head to do the visits as much as Bridge does. She doesn't even bloody recognise me. She thinks I'm her brother, or her first boyfriend, which is a lot worse. The stuff she's said to me. Mother of God.' He glanced over again. His eyes were that same arctic blue, but they seemed to be looking for reassurance. 'You think I should be there.'

'I don't think anything. My mum was mental. I mean, not like yours, but – shit, sorry. I didn't mean that.'

He just grinned, freckles gathering together on his cheek. 'Not a bother. She is mental. Here's to the pair of them.' He clinked the neck of his second beer with Matty's empty one on the table.

'Didn't see you as Italian.'

He was on his third beer now, and the box of chocolate liqueurs he'd foraged was nearly empty. Christmas cake devoured. Matty had relinquished control of the TV remote, and Cormac had been commenting drily on all the things he flicked between.

'Half-Italian. Half-Irish.'

Cormac almost spat out his beer. 'Seriously? Didn't see you as that, either.' Matty raised both eyebrows enough to make a question of it. 'You're a cockney sparrow, aren't you? *Cock-ney sparra*,' he said again, an appalling attempt at an accent. He sounded looser, the beer starting to work on him.

'Cockneys are East London. I'm North.'

'Ah, sorry. It's all the same to me,' he said, and grinned. Looked over. 'Catholic, then?' Not all the same to him.

'Once upon a time.'

He nodded at the TV. Maybe that was still a better answer than saying 'Protestant'. It was hard to tell. He talked about the border, drifting between decades. How his dad had helped swim cows across a river in the 1960s, how pigs were sedated with Guinness, the night a couple of people had drowned trying to get across when he was a kid. Matty pictured the map and its waterways – the rivers, loughs and hills that made their own boundaries, and how the border ploughed through them on its own, brutal path.

Cormac was talking about the roads either side of the lough, blown up and filled in and blown up again. 'All very *Mad Max*,' he said, a lightness to his tone that Matty knew was not the truth. He gave a sigh that suggested that was the end of it and put his feet up on the table next to Matty's. He'd taken his shoes off the last time he'd gone to the kitchen. His socks had cartoon reindeers on them.

'Nice.' A nod at them.

He uncrossed his feet and crossed them the other way round. 'Enough of that. I'll arrest you for antagonising a guard.'

They grinned at each other, both turned to the TV again at the same time. The edges of the smiles just shaved off. You'd arrest me if you knew, thought Matty.

'Do you really like her?' He spoke more quietly, and there was a rock-plunge feeling, chest to stomach. It wasn't because he'd mentioned Brigid again.

Matty swallowed, a dry noise in the back of the throat, looking past him to the scrunched napkins on the table. Couldn't lie, somehow.

Cormac blinked and shifted. 'Ah, I know how it is. She's got a way of making you feel guilty, has my sister.' He looked at the TV, and Matty knew he understood everything. Almost everything. 'It's just – she takes things seriously. You know, after all the shit she went through.'

A nod, uncertain.

'You know about her marriage, right?'

They were supposed to have a mutual friend. 'Not in detail. Just—' there was no trace of anyone else in the house. Brigid had only mentioned him once. 'That it stopped.'

'He got another woman up the duff. Not even a woman – a girl. Worked behind the counter at their local shop.'

'Shit.'

'It gets worse. She was fifteen. She'd been one of Bridge's first pupils, top year, a few years before. And one of her projects as well. She gets them sometimes, ones she can't quite' – the briefest of thoughtful glances to Matty – 'leave in the classroom, you know? Always the ones with the crap lives, the dads who beat their mammies up or what have you. She always takes them under her wing. And anyways, he had the gall to tell Bridge about it and then say he wasn't leaving her, that it had just been a mistake. That he wouldn't have anything to do with the young one or her baby, which just made the whole thing worse, you know? Because the girl was doing well at school, worked at the shop on weekends for extra spending money, planning for university, and he goes and does that.' He jammed an elbow on the arm of the sofa and scratched his head violently. 'Ah, God. Anyways. What a tool.'

'What did Brigid do?'

'Kicked him out, obviously. Went on a mad travelling spree and brought back the crap that's now all over the house.' He smiled. 'Don't tell her I told you all that. She'll roast me alive in one of her tagines. Extra cumin.'

A zipping-mouth-shut action. 'All right.'

He looked at Matty's lips. For too long.

*

272

Cormac had got up, mumbling something about the bathroom. When he came back, he tossed a small thin package, wrapped in the local newspaper, onto the sofa. 'Happy Christmas and all that.' He was standing with one hand behind his back.

Matty looked up, more pleased than was appropriate. It was obviously a CD. The wrapping came off. The airbrushed, near-alien heads of five beautiful boys on the front.

'Um. Thanks.'

'Well, I've got to school you. Especially seeing as now you're Irish and all that. These lads are the thing.' He nodded towards the TV, where the same group were all dressed in white, sitting on stools. 'Christmas Number One.'

'I didn't get you anything.' Because you're the copper who's looking for me.

He bent his head, a hand in his pocket, grinned at the floor. 'It's just a joke, really.' He brought out another square from behind his back, and sat down as he passed it over.

'Is this one Boyzone, then?'

'Maybe.'

It wasn't, though. It was Cypress Hill, the cover featuring a garish, helmeted skull and tattoo-style lettering.

'I tried to find the filthiest-looking one,' he said. 'You know, explicit content, skulls, weird Spanish titles. It's not long come out, so I thought that maybe you didn't have it.' He shifted. 'It is all right?'

'Yeah. It is. They really sell this, locally?'

'Jesus, no. I had to go to Dublin.'

'You went to Dublin for ...?' Me, Matty wanted to say. 'For this?'

He scratched his neck and seemed to blush. 'I had to go to Dublin for a few things.'

A subtle, welling warmth in Matty's chest. 'Thank you.'

'You're OK.'

There was a moment in which the air felt alive, atomised, before he reached for the remote. 'Right. Let's cut these boys off in their prime.'

Die Hard was on the other side, a third of the way through. 'Hallelujah,' he said, reaching for the box of chocolates. 'Class.'

It was. They both knew this one well, too, reacting before the quips or the next violent action came, Cormac quoting once or twice.

Matty had always both lusted after and wanted to be John McClane, grubby vest, glassed feet and all. 'Do you like war films?'

'I like all films,' he said. 'Except horror films. I'm not so good with the scary ones.' Cormac was halfway through his fourth beer, his elbow next to Matty's. He'd slipped down so that they mirrored each other's slouching position in the middle of the sofa, his head not quite touching the curls.

He didn't know. It was a relief to hang out with a guy again. He was pretty sweet, really, with the CD and everything. Giggly. Total lightweight. He didn't know.

Cormac was gazing at Matty's leg-hair. Matty sat up straighter and the movement startled him out of it. He blushed and faced the screen again.

There was something so different about him compared to his sister. None of the confidence Brigid had so quickly assumed about everything between them. Her almost parental sense of control.

It made Matty want to be honest, open, too. Partly. 'Can I ask you something?'

He looked back over, a suspended moment. Face far too close. The bird's egg freckles on his nose. 'Of course.' He swallowed. Didn't seem to be breathing.

Just say it. 'Can you find missing people?' The words were dry, bare as bone. 'I mean, people who aren't in the phone book?'

In an instant, his expression had righted itself. 'Depends. Who's missing?' A puzzled smile.

Each moment seemed to be slowing. The explosions on the TV becoming a muted blur. 'My dad.'

If he was surprised, he managed to conceal it. 'Right. How long's he been gone?'

'Fourteen years. He's – he might be only missing to me.'

'Fourteen years?'

Chin down. No tears. 'Yeah.'

'What's his name?'

'Joe. Ronan.'

'And he's here? In Ireland, I mean?'

'I don't know.' A tiny laugh that was only breath and a bitten lip. 'I don't know any more.'

'Have you a photo of him?'

Matty went to get it. From 1984, practically a watercolour through age and having lived in various wallets for so long. He was in a T-shirt that had a cowboy and cacti on it, holding barbecue tongs in one hand and laughing.

'Handsome fella.'

'Maybe.' There was a sense of floating, of unreality.

'I'll see what I can do. I'm off for a couple of days now, but – after that.' He gave a gentle, encouraging nod.

'Thanks.' Matty let out a long, shuddering breath.

They went back to watching TV. John reunited with his wife, hugs for the police officer. The bad men all killed.

'I'm sorry,' Cormac said as the credits rolled. 'You've had a shite time. And – losing your mother, and all.' He crossed his arms. 'Sorry you were on your own today.'

'It's cool. I'm used to it.' A glance. 'I'm glad you came over.'

This time, they didn't stop gazing at each other.

'Are your eyes blue or green?' he said, his voice small, faraway. 'I can't tell.'

Either. Neither. 'Bit of both.'

He blinked, lids heavy. 'I'm quite drunk.' Spoken like a child whispering a secret.

'Yeah, me too.'

Cormac made the slightest movement closer, and Matty knew what was coming, watched him hesitate, and put a hand on his cheek. The pull of each towards the other. A kiss. His lips stayed close and they kissed once more before he said, 'Ah God, sorry,' and sat forward, leaning on his elbows. He glanced back round. 'I'm not sorry.'

Something gave way. Matty took hold of his shirt and tugged him back. Cormac, with a surprised hum, had to put a hand out on the back of the sofa to stop from falling.

He tasted of chocolate and alcoholic orange. It wasn't like kissing Brigid. It felt like it meant something.

They stopped, looked at each other.

'This is bad, isn't it?' he said. 'Very bad.'

I know what bad is, Matty thought. This isn't it. This isn't close to it. 'Yeah.'

'So … you're really not a lesbian?'

Matty made the smallest sigh, head resting back.

'No. No, you're not. Sorry.' He was looking sheepishly at Matty's legs again. 'It's just because you – you're – there aren't really people like you up here.' He was babbling. 'I've always been attracted to girly … girls, you know? My last girlfriend – she was a nurse – she had her nails done every fortnight and when she got married they all wore sashes and terrorised Sligo with huge inflatable cocks. It was carnage.' A winning smile.

Matty couldn't help smiling back, despite all the girl mentions. He couldn't help it. A glance down at the obvious erection in his trousers. The need to touch him, to blot out fear. 'Nothing wrong with huge inflatable cocks.'

'Touché,' he said. His grin subsided. 'Would you like to go to bed?'

*

276

'Well, this is a first,' he said, standing in the centre of his boyhood room. A sweet, abashed look. 'Late starter and all that.'

Matty sat down on the side of the bed. Hands on knees.

Cormac turned the bedside lamp on and the main light off. Began to unbutton his shirt, stopped. 'Just a sec.' He disappeared.

The loudness of the clock, its limping hand. There was that floating sensation again, of being outside the body. The space in Matty's head where someone should have been saying, *You sure about this, crackerjack?*

He came back in and put a single condom packet on the bedside table.

'Did you have this all planned out or something?'

He looked impossibly virtuous. 'No. You should always be prepared, you know.' A small, self-conscious smile. 'It's been burning a hole in my wallet for six months.' He sat down.

He wasn't Dale. He wasn't like Dale.

Heart, high up. 'Will you be gentle?' Voice, high up.

He looked shocked. 'Of course.'

Matty lay back on the bed with him. Cormac was looking at the boy-pants in fascination, taking them off. T-shirt off. A kiss on the stomach. Higher. Matty pulled the vest down.

'Sorry,' he said.

The clock. The sounds of the TV still on down the corridor. He reached for the condom packet.

Bones and skin and muscle. That's all it would be.

'No hands.'

'No hands?'

'Not there.'

'OK.'

The van was a minor detail. He didn't know about the van. He never went into the garage. His arms were rakish, warm, and he smelt of fruit cake and beer.

The pain was immediate. 'Ow. Fuck.'

'What? What's wrong?' Cormac leant back a little and looked down. 'Jesus.' His hand came away with a daub of blood on it. 'Jesus.'

Up onto elbows. Matty pushed him away.

'Are you ... on your period?'

'Go away. Now.' A kick to his pale thigh, not gentle.

'I mean, 'cause that's fine, it's not a bother. You should have just—'

'Now.' This time, his knee crunched slightly.

Cormac still wasn't moving, kneeling between both legs, a look of realisation passing over his face. He started to say something. Didn't.

'Fuck off. Please.'

He moved off the bed, his palms outwards, unpractised hostage gestures. 'All right. I'm going.' He got up quickly, picking up his pile of clothes and shutting the door very carefully behind him.

The sound of the tap, gushing hard in the kitchen. A pause. Gushing again.

He shouldn't drive. He'd drunk too much.

The back door clicked shut, and his car started.

Matty's head went under the duvet.

Chapter 12

The phone was ringing. Eleven o'clock. It was Brigid, ringing to say Happy St. Stephen's Day, promising cakes when she returned later.

Matty attempted sit-ups, but they still weren't doable. Then a few one-handed press-ups, wincing. A handle fixed onto an extra-large, full bottle of water, though strengthening one hand and not the other was stupid. Some squats and cross-body punches, fisting out the mortification of the night before. The shame of not being able to do it. The shame at being tempted to.

The early afternoon was spent watching the washing machine, having already scrubbed at the coin of blood left on the sheet. The slop and slosh of the water mixing with the gale-force winds outside.

It was time to leave. Matty would have to think about what to do next. Stay in North London, and be constantly reminded of Rosa, or go somewhere else, far away from here. Get more work. Except that Cormac might put out a search for Joe. Be constantly reminded of Dale. Pretend it never happened. Except Cormac.

Matty was draping the sheet over the radiator when there was the sound of a car parking up. Not Brigid's. He hadn't crashed and died, then.

Cormac stood inside the back door, rain in his hair, keys in his hand. It was the first time Matty had seen him in anything other than his suit or the running gear. He was wearing jeans and a grey zip-up top that made his eyes look even more wintry, and there was stubble on his cheeks.

They sat down in the kitchen.

'I didn't know,' he said eventually, his sleeves rolled up, hands clasped on the table. 'Did you really never ...?'

'I never felt like it.' It had been a mistake. A drunk mistake.

Cormac nodded and stared at the dark hair on his knuckles. 'But – you felt like it with me?' There was the slightest trace of hope in his voice.

'Just wanted to get it over with.'

It was as if he had been readying himself to say something else. The breath he was taking stopped short and he almost looked like he was going to laugh, perhaps at himself. 'Right.' He unfolded his hands, one arm out straight next to Matty's. 'If I'd have known, I would have gone about it differently.' His voice sounded almost winsome.

Candles, wine, Westlife. Action movies. Foul-mouthed hip-hop. 'Would you?' The urge to tell him everything. To confess.

There was a growl to the wind outside.

Cormac's forefinger straightened, and he touched the raised bone of Matty's wrist. 'I'm sorry I messed it all up. You should have said.'

Matty saw Brigid's shadow at the door first, withdrawing the hand as she came in. The wind had blurred the noise of the engine. Cormac shifted suddenly back in his seat and stood up, the chair scraping.

She had a large canvas shopping bag, and glanced at them both before putting it down. 'I wasn't expecting you,' she said to her brother.

Cormac had his hands in his pockets. 'Happy Christmas, Bridge. Sorry not to catch you yesterday.'

She straightened, looking between them. 'Did you stay over?'

'No, no. Just – popped in for a bit.'

Brigid came and kissed Matty on the cheek. 'Hello.'

280

'Hey.'

The siblings spoke about their mother briefly, and Matty could feel Brigid's resentment that Cormac hadn't gone down there himself as she detailed the long night she'd had, the discussions with the aunt about respite care.

Cormac took a noisy breath. Coughed. 'I'd best get on.'

'I've only just come in,' Brigid said.

He picked up his car keys. 'Work. See you.' It was hard to tell which of them his farewell was aimed at.

***

The storms had returned in Brigid. Quieter, this time. More dangerous.

All afternoon she'd been tired, needy. Kept putting her hand out to touch Matty. Shoulder, thigh, cheek. It was hard not to shake her off. She'd sensed the diffidence anyway, had started to snap her replies.

'What were you and Cormac talking about?' she said, as they stood by the sink later, she washing the soup bowls, Matty drying.

'When?'

'When I came in.'

'Nothing. Nothing much.' Far too emphatic, and Brigid seemed to feel it, sending over another glance, the burn of it lingering after she'd turned back to the sink.

'You both seemed pretty serious.'

Intense dish-drying.

'Matty.'

A petulant look over.

'Did something happen? Did he say something? About the case?'

'No. He didn't.'

*

281

She let it lie for the rest of the evening, but it was obvious she was still thinking about it. In the morning, she asked again.

'Nothing. I can't remember.'

'You forget. I grew up with my brother. He's useless at hiding things.' She dug the knife into the loaf of bread with some violence. 'Something happened. Between you.'

'Like what?'

She sighed, tightly. There was a long pause. 'Did you sleep together?'

Matty went to lie. Closed lips again.

The crackles in Brigid seemed to feather away. Her shoulders sagged. 'You *slept* with him.'

'Not really.'

'Not really? What does that mean?'

A shrug.

'I thought you liked me.' That's how it had all started, with those words. How it could finish. 'My *brother*, Matty.'

'He asked. I – he's looking for me. Without knowing it. I didn't want to draw attention to myself.'

'*Attention* to yourself?' Brigid put the knife down and pushed her hair away from her face.

The long weeks in this warm house, the comfort of her, all dissolved. 'It's time for me to go.' Spoken frankly, as kindly as possible.

She sounded tearful, sour. 'Go where?'

'Away.' Away from you. 'I'm not going to stay here forever. I'm not your – I don't know what you expect me to be.'

'I didn't expect you to be anything. I can't believe you.' She looked up. Bitter green eyes. 'You used me.'

'I didn't use you. I didn't do anything. It was *your* idea to bring me back to— Why did you even help me?' She didn't answer, and Matty remembered what Cormac had said. She liked projects. 'You just want some bloody drama in your life.'

Her palms slammed down on the table. 'You think that's it? That I want drama in my life? You don't think I've had enough? You're unbelievable. If it wasn't for me—' She gave a sudden, tart laugh.

'If it wasn't for you, what?'

She laughed again, shaking her head. 'You're like a bloody teenage boy.'

'Is that why you like me?'

'Don't be a child.' She shook her head. 'I would have thought after everything I did for you ... I could have told him. At any time.'

'Go on, then. Phone him.' Part of Matty wanted Brigid to. To break everything open. For the guilt to have something new to grip onto.

'Fine,' she said. 'Leave.'

'I will.'

'Use a bag if you need one.' She was looking at the wall. 'I'm assuming you're not taking the van. Leaving that for me to deal with.' She took a breath in, exhaled vehemently. 'I thought we had something nice.' Eyes finally coming back over, wounded.

Matty didn't say anything.

'I'm going out,' Brigid said.

There was a sickly, yellow tinge to the deep grey of the sky. The low clouds looked as if they were full of rain but hadn't released any. Instead, the sun picked out the highest mountain peak like a beacon, the striations jaggedly visible.

Matty found a bag in Brigid's wardrobe. Packed up. Clothes stuffed in, toothbrush. Both of Cormac's CDs. Nicked a couple of slices of banana loaf from the breadbin. Felt lighter.

It would have to be a taxi. An expensive one, to somewhere with a long-distance bus route. It was a challenge finding a cab two days after Christmas – most of the numbers were home phones, the drivers sounding surprised. The fourth guy said he could be free in two hours.

Note paper. Matty wrote a cursory few words to Cormac, thought about leaving Heather's number, in case he found anything out, and decided it was too risky. Could always ring from a phone box sometime, just to check. He wasn't going to find anything out.

Matty wrote one for Brigid, too, shorter, with a cheque for one grand, to hopefully cover the van being taken, or resprayed and given a new number plate. Folded both notes, wrote their names on each, and placed them side by side on the kitchen table.

Shifty's metal was ice-cold, the door stiff. The closed air and the silence inside.

A few things from the glove compartment. The country music tapes.

'Ah, mate,' Matty said. Put a hand on the cold leather of the front seat, and looked at the long seat in the back.

There was a tiny shard of glass caught in the flooring and a dark blot of blood that might be mistaken for mud.

Matty left the garage door open, went back for a cloth and warm water.

The phone rang. Matty picked up, in case it was the cab driver.

It was Brigid's aunt in Cork. Matty took the message, found another bit of paper to write on. Ripped up the first note to Brigid and wrote a better one, more conciliatory. More grateful.

The rumble of a car engine. She'd returned already, maybe for another round. It would be fair enough.

Back outside.

Cormac was in front of the garage, looking in.

Matty went numb.

He glanced round, and back at the van. 'Is that – yours?'

Matty looked down at the tufts of grass leading into the garage. Looked back.

He held out the photo of Joe, his expression uncertain. 'I got it photocopied. So you can have it back.' He turned back to study Shifty again, his whole body still. 'So that's your van?' You could hear his mind ticking. 'What day did you come here again?'

'I can't remember.' Make it earlier. 'Twenty-fifth.' Too early, probably, for the injuries to be how they'd looked.

His eyes moved to Matty. Cheek. Ribs. 'Oh, sweet Jesus,' he said, his shoulders dropping.

The sudden awareness of the smell of the neighbours' peat fires, and the clouds moving fast.

He put his chin to his chest, a brief stillness, before he seemed to nod to himself. 'I need you to come in.' There was no shock in his voice, no disgust.

Matty swallowed, looked towards the back door.

He registered it. 'No,' he said. 'Come in. To the station.'

'No.'

'Why not?'

'I can't.'

'You don't have to say anything,' he said, and for a moment Matty thought it was all right. That he'd let it go. Pretend he hadn't seen it. He took a step closer. 'I am charging you with ...' his lips came together and he sighed. 'Attempted murder. You don't have to say anything. Unless you wish to do so.'

'Don't.'

'But whatever you may—' The words were bleached, characterless.

'Don't. Please. I can't.' Prison. A women's prison. 'Please.'

Cormac began to say something, stopped. He glanced towards his car and walked over to it, his eyes remaining fixed on Matty.

Drive away. Drive *me* away, Matty thought. Take me somewhere else.

He opened the driver's door, his back against the car, and reached towards the glove compartment. A glimpse of silver. 'May be taken down in writing and given in evidence.' He looked down at the handcuffs. 'You have to get in the car now.'

Head-shake.

'If you don't, I'll have to ...' He sounded defeated. 'Will you just get in the car?'

'No.'

'Don't make me have to do this.' He took two steps forward. 'I'm not going.'

His head came down. 'Ah, God.' Lots of breath in the words.

His eyes came up again, his expression becoming measured, careful, and it was clear when he was going to move and how he would. Matty got there first, pushing him, hooking a foot round his ankle and yanking, and shoved him in the shoulder.

Cormac staggered back, caught off-balance, and twisted as he fell back against the car, his skull catching the edge of the driver's open door. There was a dull, solid sound as he tumbled side-first into the grass next to the front wheel.

A moment of silence, broken only by a gull flying alarmingly low.

His eyes were shut. He groaned almost imperceptibly through his closed lips, and shifted. 'Fucking hell.' The words were muffled, as if he was speaking from under a pillow. His hands moved slowly towards the back of his head.

Matty grabbed the handcuffs and clipped the open one around his wrist, dragging his arm so that he was partly sitting upright and forcing the second cuff round the lowest spoke of the front wheel. He was mumbling something, his eyes still shut. 'Ah, bollocks.'

Into the car, climbing over to the passenger seat, and the glove compartment, fingers scrabbling until they touched something small and metal. Matty took the handcuffs key, backed out of the car and tossed it into the grass. Just in case.

*

A hand into each of Cormac's pockets, taking out the car keys from one and his mobile phone from the other. Matty locked the car, and threw them both into the grass too. 'I'm sorry.' Stood up, quickly. 'I'm really sorry.'

A small, distant sigh from him.

Go.

Matty took the bike and a single rucksack, leaving everything else, and pedalled as fast as possible down the hill. There was an uncontrollable sound on every outbreath, an unearthly whining. A blank headiness.

The quiet roads. Not the main roads. The lough road was best, at least to get out of the village.

The taxi would come in ninety minutes and the driver would find Cormac. It would take him a while longer to find the key.

Past the coaches. Wheeling past the dog, who hared out, more enraged than ever. Looping around the potholes.

The lough opened out, the quayside and the little car park. Tiny scudding waves and a seal head.

A seal head, and a hand.

An inland lough and a seal head and a hand.

Brake. The bike scuffed, skidded sideways. Matty circled and rode back to the gate of the car park. Throat scraped raw with the cold.

There was nothing there. The small, chipped-white waves, a mineral shine to the water. The island beyond.

But there was something at the end of the concrete jetty. A small pile of clothes. Matty wiped away mucus from each side of the mouth and squinted out, breath heaving and loud.

There. Again. A slick brown head, but a flash of paleness. Two hands, high up. Something pink.

Matty dropped the bike and rucksack and ran down the jetty, getting rid of the coat, tugging off boots and socks, and jumped in.

The all-embracing cold. In and over the head, gasping into the air again. The water immediately slowed Matty, pulled at everything, sleeves, jeans.

A quick, thrashing front crawl, the water much colder than it had been a few weeks ago. Biting arms, chest.

Matty stopped, whirled around. She'd been about here. Hadn't she? The water butted, shoved.

A bit further out, turning in a circle, more frantic.

There was a sudden glimpse of closed eyes and an open mouth before she dipped below the surface again. Matty propelled forward, dived under, hands out, desperate to touch something other than water, to touch something living.

Up. Another circle. Under again, fumbling, arms stretched as far as possible and sliding against something solid, skin, limp arms, something soft and mushy, and pulling, pulling her until they both broke free again.

Rolling over and clutching her close around her chest, Matty kicked them back to the jetty.

'Sheanna.'

The little girl was on her back with her eyes closed.

'Sheanna.' A gentle slap to one cheek, and then the other. 'Fuck.'

Drowning can occur in less than twenty seconds.

She was in a pink swimming costume and had one sodden white glove on. Purple socks.

Matty put the heel of one hand on her chest and gently pumped. One, two. Ten. Leaning into it, the full weight of the body. Fifteen. Thirty.

'Come on, Sheanna.'

Forehead, tilted back. Chin, tilted up. Her nose pinched between two fingers. Small, cold lips. One breath. Her chest rose. Two breaths.

Drowning victims can last up to an hour in the water.

Compressions again. One, two. Five. Imagining her breastbone snapping. Nine—

Sheanna suddenly convulsed, her eyes screwing up, and coughed, the sound guttering and wet. As she coughed again, Matty was turning her over, and she vomited, clear water and a gruel-like liquid.

'It's OK. It's OK.'

She blinked, and tried to lean up on an elbow, and vomited again, more of the same, onto Matty's hand.

A tiny, rodent-like whimper.

'You're OK, mate. You're out now, OK?' Matty scrambled for the coat, wrapped it around her. Pulled off the single glove and the heavy, wet socks. Sheanna's own clothes were in a neat pile on the concrete. 'What were you doing?'

Her skin was horribly pale.

'Sheanna, where's your house?'

She began to cry.

Matty got her to sit up. 'I'm going to carry you, OK?' An arm underneath her knees, the other manoeuvring around her back. 'Put your arm around me here.'

'Mermaid,' she said.

She was far heavier out of the water and was beginning to shiver violently.

'Sheanna, what number is it? Your house?' Sheanna was snivelling, a rivulet of bile trickling from one corner of her mouth. 'What's your house number? It's this road, yeah? Do you hear me?' Mouth, close to her ear. Rubbing her back, fast and hard.

Sheanna's words were indistinct.

'Thirty-seven?'

'Fifty-seven,' she said, in a distant, broken voice. A voice still threaded with water. 'Up there. I'm really dizzy.'

The gravel bit at Matty's bare feet, doubly hard with the weight. Twice they had to stop, Sheanna set down on the road, shaking. She wouldn't open her eyes.

Matty knelt down, blew on both palms and rubbed the girl's cheeks. 'We'll find your dad, and your mum.'

Sheanna shook her head, a tight hummed no.

'We're almost there. Sixty-one, look.' Matty hefted her up again, got her bottom under both hands, Sheanna's arms slung over both shoulders. She rested her head right in the well of Matty's neck. 'Just as well you don't live at five hundred and fifty-seven, isn't it?'

She didn't reply. Her cold nose against Matty's skin. Shivering like a rabbit.

The sloped driveway curved round to a large, newly built house and a porch in mismatched stone.

'Look. We're here.'

The door was unlocked. A porch, and another door, also open. The smell of a peat fire.

'Hello?'

'Hello?' A man's voice. 'Can I help you?' He appeared, a tea towel in his hands. 'Sheanna—' His voice immediately changed to one of direct concern, rushing over as Matty set her down on the carpet. Crouching. 'Jesus. What's happened?' He looked up.

'Daddy,' Sheanna said, exhausted and mouse-like, leaning against his legs.

Matty looked at him, and he looked back. A mirror-image, their two faces locking. Mouths opening.

A mirror-image.

Joe.

Chapter 13

Words were impossible.

He was a faded, expanded version of Joe, coming from the future and the past at once. Paler, greyer. A beard. Glasses. But it couldn't be anyone else.

They were both crouched over Sheanna, only inches apart. Staring at each other.

'Matty?' he said, the word slow, exploratory. As if he'd never said it before.

Matty stood quickly, went dizzy. Put a hand out against the wall and backed towards the door.

'It's ...' he said. His hand cradling Sheanna's head. 'Is it you?' A ghost-voice.

Head-shake. Over and over. Doorframe digging in.

'Scout,' said Sheanna, with a decisive, tired sweetness, as if reading herself the last words of a bedtime story.

Joe looked down at her. Back up. His lips hadn't shut once.

Drowning. *This* is what it felt like. Lungs filled with something other than air, an all-consuming crush of it. To swallow would be to make it worse. Light somewhere up there, very far away and dwindling. Matty's foot slid off the doorstep, an awkward jolt into the cold of the porch. There were coats, a child's mud-caked wellies.

'I – I don't know what's happening,' he said. 'But please don't go.' His voice, no longer just in the inner ear. Not just memories and imaginings. New words. Real words. 'Don't go, Matty.'

*

The hallway had slotted wooden tiling on the floor. Sheanna was shaking in a heap on the rug, her hair stuck to her cheek, Matty's coat still round her.

'Please,' Joe said, looking up. 'Tell me what's happened.' It sounded so formal. Almost as if it wasn't his native tongue. An arm around Sheanna, wiping at her mouth. 'What happened?'

'I was sick,' she said, and began to cry.

'She needs warmth,' Matty said. 'Hot drinks, hot food. Blankets. One thing at a time, slowly. Maybe a doctor. She fell in the lough.'

'Fell?'

'I wanted to swim under the water,' Sheanna said, with a shudder, her nose running. 'I'm cold. Cold, cold, cold.' She kept saying it, only the little percussive snap audible. Her feet and hands were a supernatural blue.

'OK,' he said, not seeming to understand.

'I had to—' A hand up to lips. Trembling. 'CPR.'

'Jesus Christ.' He looked aghast.

'I think she's OK.' Words felt thick, remote. 'She's talking. That's good.'

He looked up. 'Can you help me?'

Matty lifted Sheanna, holding her at the armpits and seeming to take most of the weight even though Joe had his arms under her waist. They carried her into another room, placing Sheanna on a sofa. He disappeared, stairs creaking, although he wasn't moving terribly fast.

Matty stood staring at Sheanna and dripping onto the carpet. Jeans glued to skin. Deep shivers beginning to come, and not from the cold.

The sound of the stairs again. Blankets and towels brought down. Kettle switched on.

He knelt down to Sheanna, beginning to undress her. 'I'm calling Dad, OK?'

Sheanna nodded. Her swimming costume was peeled off, patched arms held up. A glimpse of the same pale brown and white-mottled skin on her chest, her knees. Her teeth were still chattering, a pulsing in her limbs, as she was dried and put into underwear and flannel pyjamas with dolphins on them. Socks. Slippers. Wrapped in a blanket like a little Russian doll.

Matty's head was spinning. Dad. Daddy.

'Will you sit?' he said, rubbing Sheanna over the top of the blanket and glancing up, carefully. He looked so old.

'Don't rub.'

He stopped. 'OK.'

Matty sat on the edge of an armchair, clutching a towel.

'I don't – I'm trying to understand.' His eyebrows came together. 'Were you with Sheanna?'

'Not this time. I just saw her.'

'But you know her?'

It was too hard to explain. Nod, a small one. The bike was still out there. The bag.

'I wanted to be a mermaid like Scout,' Sheanna said. 'I wanted to learn how to be dangerous.' She hadn't seemed to grasp that it was odd for them to know each other.

'Like …' He seemed to try and digest the words. 'OK.' He shook his head. 'Sheanna, how many times have we said not to go past the gate?'

Bolt. Matty needed to bolt, quickly, because he was here, and it made no sense. 'I don't …' The words seemed very faraway. 'I don't get it. Who are you?'

They both looked up, thinking the question was for them. Maybe it was.

'You know who I am, dummy,' Sheanna said.

'You … you can't be.' Sadness, coming like a black tide. 'You can't.' She wasn't just a girl. She was his daughter.

Sheanna looked at Joe. 'Huh?'

293

'Matty.' Named again. He sounded more like the old Joe, just for a second. 'What—' He lowered his voice, as if he didn't want someone in a neighbouring room to hear. 'What are you doing here?'

Heart, still at crush-depth. 'Looking for you.' The words were pushed out, suddenly, breaths surging up, fast. An uncontrollable, quicksilver energy, racing outwards. Matty began to tremble.

'All right. Tea. We'll ... get you some tea, OK?' He didn't know how to speak. His words weren't the old ones. Not quite.

Matty curled up in a chair, knees to nose, soaking into the fabric. Hardly daring to look around. There were CDs in two slim bookcases. Big boxes of toys at the bottom of a shelf, one Barbie hanging out, half-stripped, matted hair over her face. Pictures on the walls with tinsel round them, a kid's collage of leaves in a frame. A Christmas tree, heavy with baubles, in the corner.

Hot chocolate for Sheanna, who was sitting up again. A purple plastic mug with a pink teaspoon in it. She'd been put in front of the fire.

'Will you change?' he said. Tea placed at the edge of the red-tiled fireplace – strong, reddish-brown, the way he used to make his own in London. 'You'll be freezing now.' He sounded hoarse. Voice as faded as the rest of him.

Matty started to shake again.

'Just a blanket, then.'

He came back with another blanket, placed carefully on one arm of the chair.

'Do you have any crisps?' The words were coming out crumbled, useless.

'Crisps?'

'Yeah.'

'I'll find you some crisps.'

But as he turned, a hollow, sulphurous feeling began to swell, squeezing itself upwards. 'I think I'm going to be sick.'

Vomit, lots of it, into the kitchen bin, the nearest place. Eggshells and vegetable peelings in there, making it worse. An empty box of Christmas biscuits. The tiles were white with black veins in them, and cold. He was hovering at the door. Red socks with navy blue toe, jeans, brown belt buckle. Hem of a blue T-shirt under a black jumper. Beard, much longer than stubble, brown and sandy and grey. The lines in his face. Thin-framed glasses.

A shuddering breath. It was unfathomable.

'Do you need a hand?' he said, very tentatively, as if talking a suicidal person off the edge of a roof.

'I've got to go.' The bike. Bag. Cormac.

'Go?'

There was the sound of the door. 'Hey. Joe? Sheanna?' A man's voice. Blunt, concerned.

Joe held a hand up, first at Matty, then to his forehead. He went out into the hall. Two of them, speaking, the words blurring. The living room, and Sheanna's voice mixed in with theirs.

Matty stood up again, mouth and throat acrid, as a second man came into the kitchen. It was the man who'd been with Sheanna outside the shop on Christmas Eve. Taller than Joe, more bulky and with greying reddish hair, small glasses.

Dad. Daddy.

Joe was there behind him. 'Matty, this is Franklin.'

No breath at all. It was there, in the pit of the stomach, not coming out. A void where thoughts should be.

The man stared. Looked back at Joe. 'This is—' His eyebrows came together, a stern, closed expression. 'I'm not quite clear what's going on.' He had an American accent.

'Nor am I exactly,' said Joe.

'OK,' Franklin said, taking a deep breath, both his hands out, big palms spread. 'Let's just take this one step at a time. Sheanna,' he said to Joe. 'Have you called the doctor?'

'No. Not yet.'

'Joe.' Admonishing.

'Sorry. It's been – quite a shock. For everyone. She's all right. She's talking, and that's a good sign.' A glance over, one that seemed to need to check that Matty was there at all. 'That's what you said?'

A small nod.

'Can you come and check?'

Sheanna was propped up on cushions, the blanket round her. A glow worm. She was still quivering.

Matty knelt next to her and put palms on her socked feet, felt her hands. Her fingers were pale, but not blue anymore. 'Warming up yet?' It seemed like someone else's voice, practical, nurse-like.

'Matty got her out,' Joe was saying, quietly, behind them.

Sheanna nodded, and jabbed several times at her feet. 'I'm still cold there.'

'Yeah. They'll be last.'

Sheanna nodded seriously, over-emphatically.

'She'll be all right,' Matty said, not looking up at them. 'You should get a doctor, though. To be safe.'

'You have to get out those clothes,' Joe said. 'Or you'll be the same.'

'I'm used to it.'

'Nonetheless,' he said, not understanding. 'You're soaked.'

'Scout rescued me,' Sheanna said. 'Like in *Baywatch*. I thought I could swim like normal and I kept trying to hold my breath and go under a bit but it was really, really, really cold.'

Up, swaying. Shivering. Still unable to look either of them in the eye. 'I've got to go now.'

'No,' said Joe, and he seemed to understand the fragility of the moment. 'Don't go anywhere.'

'I left the bike down there. My stuff.'

'Franklin will go and get it.'

'Sure,' Franklin said. 'OK.'

Upstairs, Joe opened some drawers, pulled out tracksuit bottoms, a T-shirt, a jumper. 'I'm not sure – I'll leave you to it here for a second, OK?' There was another towel already on the bed. He coughed, and it seemed to seize him for a moment before he straightened.

Matty couldn't look at him properly.

'OK,' he said, almost to himself, and shut the door.

A silence. The world reduced to this alien room, with its quilted double bed and bedside lamps, a pile of books on one side. A large, detailed map of North America on the wall above it, Canada in salmon pink. Two bottles of aftershave on a chest of drawers. No ashtray.

Matty's skin was still cold. Tolerance went fast if you didn't keep it up. Everything came off now, pants and sports bras included.

His clothes. A faded red T-shirt with a tiny hole at the shoulder. Navy-blue joggers. Thick woollen jumper. All of them new to Matty, and all of them him.

They smelt the same.

In the living room, Sheanna had a bowl of tomato soup on a tray. Joe and Franklin were sitting either side of her on the sofa. She'd pushed the blanket off.

'I still feel funny. Can I have another hot chocolate?' she was saying.

'After you've finished that,' said Franklin.

They both looked up as Matty appeared in the doorway. An extra T-shirt on underneath. The tracksuit bottoms overly bunched at the waist to keep them up. Everything else fit.

'Any better?' Joe said, standing up. He didn't seem to know what to do with his hands.

Nod.

'Will you have some soup?' There was a bowl of it already set on a small coffee table.

Head-shake.

The two men glanced at each other.

'So. You guys knew each other already?' Franklin said. A thread of suspicion in his voice. He was a large man, filled out. He had presence.

'Scout's a boy-mermaid,' said Sheanna, before slurping from her spoon.

There was subtle fascination in Joe's expression.

'OK,' said Franklin. 'You hung out or something, or ...?' He thought there was something untoward in it.

'At the car park,' she said.

'But you never said, sweetheart. You were talking to someone you didn't know and you didn't tell us about it?'

Sheanna held her spoon above the bowl. 'I wasn't sure if you were real,' she said, to Matty.

Stomach. A strange tug.

'Is Matty your real name?'

A nod wasn't quite possible.

'Sheanna.' Joe crouched down by her knee. 'Matty is ...' He dipped his head briefly, lifted it again. 'Matty is also mine. Like you are.' He touched her nose, a small, simple action. 'From quite a while ago.'

She put her spoon down. 'Yours and Dad's?'

He almost glanced over, didn't quite. 'No, just mine. Remember I used to live in London?'

She nodded, her finger in her mouth.

'Well, from then. Long before you.'

Told like it was a *Jackanory* story. Not a real one.

Sheanna turned her face to Matty's, her eyes wide and bright. Recovered enough.

*

298

There was a shallow pond in the back part of the garden, with a grassy island in the middle and a plank of wood leading to it. A picnic table. Bullrushes the height of Sheanna.

Matty had pulled on the boots that Franklin had retrieved from the lough – the bike was now leaning against the back wall of the house – and found the packet of cigarettes. Drew deeply on one now, wanting the tar to blacken everything inside.

All this time. All this time.

He'd never wanted to be found.

There was a light, stuttering sound. A goat, white and bearded, was in a small, partly fenced area, bleating again at Matty, a slack-jawed chewing motion. Dead eyes.

Joe came round the corner of the house and walked slowly up to stand by Matty. He had a cup of tea in his hands, and held it out.

'No, thanks.'

He faced the pond and then looked over, a surreptitious toe-to-head examination. 'I can't . . .' He shook his head. 'I can hardly take you in.' A voice full of wonder. 'You're so tall.'

'I'm not yours.'

He looked over properly.

'I'm not yours.'

He went to say something, and instead set the cup down, straightening again with an odd, cautious grace. 'I don't know how you're here. But you are. We've – there's a lot to talk about.'

'Who are they?' The question felt bleached, desolate.

'My—' There was a quiet, charged breath. He looked at the reeds as if for an answer. Another breath. 'My family. They've been my family.'

The bitter taste of the vomit was still there. 'Yeah, I think you can live without me.' Cigarette dropped, half-smoked. Stubbed out. Matty took a step away.

'Please. Please don't go. Not like this. Please wait.'

It had been ages. An hour, maybe, since leaving on the bike. More. They could be already looking, a search fanning out from Brigid's house. 'Is the doctor coming?'

'Yeah, someone's coming out. Perhaps she can check you out as well.'

'I don't need to be seen. I mustn't be seen. By anyone.'

Matty had forgotten the way one of Joe's eyebrows went much higher than the other when he frowned. 'Where are you staying?'

'I've been – not far away. But I was leaving.'

'On the bike?' Another uncomprehending frown.

'Yeah.' Police. A description put out. Maybe it would be safer to stay inside. 'When the doctor comes, I'm not here.'

'OK,' he said, carefully. 'Will you come back inside, for now? It's bloody brass monkeys out here.' He smiled, before a rasping cough took hold of him. 'For me, anyway.'

They sat in the living room. Chair, and sofa. The fire high. On Matty's advice, Franklin had taken Sheanna upstairs for a bath.

Joe was sitting at the front end of the sofa, his elbows on his thighs. Still doing the toe-to-head thing. 'I don't know where to start. Would you like to tell me … what's been going on with you, or—'

'Where have you been?' The words came out high, far too high, ridiculous-sounding. Fourteen years reduced to one question.

'Canada. And here.' He didn't even sound that guilty.

'What, that's it? That's all you've got to say?'

'No.' He looked perplexed. 'No, there's lots to say. I shouldn't have gone about it the way I did.'

A forced-out breath, a laugh that rashed like a nettle-sting. 'Are you fucking kidding me?' Hands becoming fists in Matty's lap. 'You just left.' The words hurt. 'With – what, with him?'

'With him, yes.' Quietly.

'Without telling me, without—' The sentence halted.

300

'It was badly done. It was a bad time.'

'What do you mean? How do you think it was for me?'

'I've no idea. I can't imagine.'

'I thought you were dead.'

His head tipped slightly to the side. A slight frown and the eyebrows again. 'Why would you have thought that?' He took a breath, and at the same time there was a crunch of gravel outside. He got up, looked at Matty. 'You don't want to be checked over?'

'No. Don't – I'm not here.'

'OK. Whatever you say.'

Matty was in a study, sitting very still, a female doctor's voice in the room next door. Joe's voice. It was older, like the rest of him seemed to be. Softened and creased.

There was a long desk, stacks of papers and box files, a computer. A tall filing cabinet. Photos. There was a photo of the two of them, a restaurant, Franklin's arm on the back of Joe's chair. A photo of a baby, unmistakeably Sheanna, her mouth wide and toothless, gleeful. Another photo of her, aged perhaps four, with chocolate ice cream all over her face. Matty picked it up and sat down with it again.

A one-two knock. Joe came in and shut the door behind him. Leant against it. 'The doctor's gone. Will you come downstairs? Sheanna's in her bed.'

'She's yours?' Matty already knew it to be true. The curl of her lip, the same grey-brown hair as Matty.

'She's ours, but – she is. We had a surrogate. In Canada.'

The words seemed to float and bump up against each other, still not quite making sense.

'We'll go downstairs. I can tell you everything. If you'd like.' He crouched down, better to try and catch Matty's eye. 'Would you like a proper drink?'

*

Irish single malt, the colour of honey. It burned, throat to stomach. Another gulp.

Franklin was standing in the doorway. 'Were you watching us?'

'What?'

'Joe said you'd been with Sheanna before. Were you watching the house?'

'No. I didn't know you were here. I've been looking, but ...' How could it be explained, Brigid's house, the van, coming past here on the bike. 'I didn't know – who she was.' The constant song of the water, the strange pull of Sheanna.

Franklin looked over at Joe as if not quite convinced. 'And so you weren't with Sheanna? At the time?'

'No,' said Joe. 'Sheanna – you'll have to talk to her. She had one of her mad schemes. It's that bloody book she keeps reading.' He faced Matty. 'If it wasn't for you seeing her ...' He shook his head. 'I can't imagine. We've only Matty to thank,' he said to Franklin.

'OK,' said Franklin, not seeming quite convinced. 'Thank you.'

'Have you really been looking for me?' said Joe.

'I've been looking all – I've been all over. Ros—' Matty couldn't finish.

Joe sat, unmoving. 'Well,' he said. 'You weren't far off.'

Franklin went to the kitchen to put some food on.

'How's your mamma?' said Joe.

'She's dead.'

He froze. A glazed look of horror, before his fingers tentatively came up to his temple.

'Killed herself. In June.'

'Ah, Jesus.'

The radio was turned on in the kitchen, and immediately turned down.

'God.' His breathing sounded laboured. He looked up. 'Matty.'

'I wasn't – I didn't cry. I never cried.'

He was touching his forehead as if checking it was there, and there was something almost satisfying about seeing his shock. 'Were you with her?'

'No.'

'I mean, living with her?'

A bitter exhalation. He really had no idea. About anything. 'I left home when I was sixteen.'

One of the peat logs suddenly collapsed, half of it breaking off.

His face was ashen. 'Is that why you decided to look for me?'

'No.' Matty drained the glass. 'She told me you were dead. I mean, I got it into my head that you were, and I couldn't get it out. It was the only explanation. And I asked Mamma, and she said that you were. Dead.'

He'd gone so still.

'I thought you'd drowned in the Pond. The Men's Pond. The police knew you'd gone there after work. I knew it didn't really make any sense, but – you never came back.'

There was the smell of something frying, onions and garlic, next door.

Joe closed his eyes. Opened them again. 'Matty. I don't understand. How you could have thought that. The letter.'

The word seemed alien, another language. Forming into something recognisable only slowly. 'Letter?' Matty said, lips dry. The whiskey smudging everything.

'Yes.'

The note, in Rosa's loft in Wood Green. *Give this to Matty.* 'You sent me a letter?'

'Yes. With the one to your mamma.' He gazed over. 'She never gave it to you.' It wasn't a question. He already understood. 'Did she give you any of them?'

It was as if someone had reached into Matty, was ripping open the breastbone, peeling it back. He'd written letters.

Franklin had cooked spaghetti, and neither of them could eat it. Instead, Franklin went back to the kitchen and ate there, the occasional sound of his fork, the music on the radio very low. He'd seemed concerned for Joe, a hand on his shoulder, an alarming ease of affection. Had brought him water and told him not to drink any more whiskey.

Joe ignored him, and topped them both up. He kept shaking his head. 'All this feckin' time,' he said, over and over.

'What did it say? The letter?'

'The first one just tried to explain I'd gone off for a few days, maybe a bit longer, and I'd write again really soon. We left pretty spur of the moment. Went up north. Lake District.' Guilt in his grey eyes. 'A few days later, I sent a forwarding address, once we knew we were going to go over to Canada. The phone number. Then I wrote every week.'

There was a cavity in Matty's chest. A bleak, simple space.

Joe was watching. 'She didn't give you any of them, did she?'

'No.'

'How long were you at the house for?'

''Til November.'

A small, aching sigh. 'God. And ... your grandmother?' He'd sent one to her, too. 'Matty, you can't think – I tried so many times to get in touch.'

Matty felt unutterably tired. Wanted to roll up in this chair and sleep forever, until only bones were left. 'What happened? Why did you go?' Dreading the answer.

'OK,' he said, sitting up straighter, one hand rubbing a knee. 'You've no idea how many times I've rehearsed this in my head.'

A painful twang of recognition.

'She hit me. Rosa. More than once. I tried to hide it from you. No one wants a dad who's getting beaten up by a woman.'

'I knew.'

'Did you?'

'Only later. After you'd gone.' A deep, slow breath. 'How long did it go on for?'

'A couple of years. Three, maybe. Mostly arms, chest. She got my face a couple of times. I'd had to tell you, and the lads at work, that I'd walked into a lamppost, or a door. Clumsy eedjit and all that. I was never going to be the type of man to hit her back.'

'Was it because she found out you were . . .?' It still didn't seem fathomable.

'I wasn't. Not then, anyway. What I mean is, I didn't know any more than she did, not really.' He sighed and put his hand round to cradle the back of his head. 'No. It was just her and this – anger, a crazy sort, coming from nowhere. She'd always had the temper, but – one day it went that bit further.' His eyes drifted to the side of him, as if visiting the memory. 'She'd use whatever was nearest. Book. Ashtray. You'd be surprised how much of a mark a hairdryer leaves.' He glanced up at Matty, and there was shame there. 'It wasn't just the being hit. It was the stuff she said. Really vicious. If not that, then the silent treatment. She just stripped me bare, after a while.'

Matty should have known, at the time. Should have seen.

He gave a noisy sigh. 'Anyway, so it was going from bad to worse, and I did my damnedest to keep you in the dark over it, and I ended up going swimming. At the Ponds, there. It just became a bit of a refuge. No women.' A weak smile. 'I got talking to this guy one time, and I'd see him there on and off. He was just someone good to talk to, you know? I ended up telling him everything, because I couldn't tell anyone who knew me. And that guy turned out to be the one I'm still living with.' He glanced over towards the kitchen. 'He said he'd take me away for a while.

305

I thought that sounded nice.' The huge, weighted irony of understatement.

'Did you tell her about him? Mamma?'

'Not in so many words, no. It was bad enough as it was, between us.' He put his fingers absent-mindedly to his mouth. 'I would have told her, if she'd ever let me speak to her.' He looked more animated. 'I never thought she'd have gone so far, Matty. Said that to you. Or hidden the letters. Or everything – taken you away, moved, left no bloody trace.'

'You left me with her.'

'I didn't think it would be forever. I know it wasn't right, Matty. I'm sorry. I just – I couldn't take it anymore. I just needed to get away for a bit. I knew she'd never hurt you. She was only hell-bent on knocking the crap out of me.'

'I thought she might hit me, once.'

He looked up, startled.

'I said I'd hit her back. So she didn't.'

Joe bit his lip, amused. 'Ah, well, I always knew you would. A man can't do that. I wouldn't have done that.'

'You don't get it, though. What it was like with her. She hated me.'

'She didn't hate you. Of course she didn't.'

'She – wanted me to be – not me.' He would have understood, if he'd stayed. He was understanding now, maybe, just about. He'd been studying the shaved sides of the head and the shoulders and the low voice as if Matty was something miraculous, unearthed.

'I wanted to find you,' he said. 'I promise to God. It broke my heart to be so far away from you. As soon as I was in Canada it felt like a mistake. I've never forgiven myself, Matty. I won't, not as long as I live. Longer.' He sat back and stared at the fire. He looked drained. Deep hollows under his eyes. 'I can't believe she's gone. How did it …' He took a long breath. 'How did she do it?'

'Pills.'

He didn't say anything. Nodded, numbly.

Matty felt exhausted. Scraped bare, just like he'd said Rosa had done to him. 'I've got to go.'

'Can we take you? Where are you staying?'

'No. I've just got to leave.'

'Where are you going?'

'Away.' Matty sat forward, head in hands. 'I just – I've really got to go now.'

'You're not going anywhere. No bleedin' chance. You're staying. At least tonight.'

New injuries. Lungs, stomach, heart. Internal bruising.

Matty lay on the sofa bed in the study and listened to the sounds of the two of them moving around, checking on Sheanna. The small piping of her voice. Bathroom door and taps and them murmuring together in the bedroom, for a long time. Joe's cough, and maybe the sound of him crying.

It was too much to absorb. The whole world had suddenly expanded, at the time when it needed to be small, focused. A sea, not a rill.

Matty had hit Cormac and left him. The taxi driver would have found him, or Brigid before that. Cormac knew everything, and knew that it had been concealed, which made it all worse. Matty was going to prison. And all of that seemed far away, another country, because he was here.

Joe was here, and alive.

Chapter 14

Matty woke up to find Sheanna standing by the bed in her pyjamas, holding a fluffy killer whale.

'Hello,' she said.

It was too early. It was still too much to take in. She was more than real. She was the same skin and bone.

The toy was pushed close. 'This is Orla. The orca.'

A slow nod. 'OK.'

She put the orca on top of the duvet and drew her finger along one of the raised cotton ridges made by Matty's body. 'You're my sister.'

'No, I'm not.'

Her face coloured with alarm. 'Brother?'

'No.' Matty moved the orca off. 'I'm not.'

Sheanna kept tracing lines on the duvet, before slowly turning and walking out of the room.

Rain on the window. A tiny, persistent tapping. The tapping of the radiator, in sympathy. Matty scratched a rib, and another, and realised that the eczema was back in force again.

She came running back in after a couple of minutes. '*Sibling.*' She looked triumphant. 'I didn't know I had one, and now I do and it's like magic. Why didn't you tell me?'

The slightest softening. 'Because I didn't know.'

'You didn't know, either?'

It was hard to look at her. 'No.'

'I'm to tell you that there's breakfast downstairs. I'm having eggy bread with maple syrup.' She did a little skipping hop out of the room.

Matty had always been alone. One. It wasn't possible.

The three of them were sitting at the breakfast bar in the kitchen by the time Matty came down, all talking at once. A teapot and a cafetière and toast and eggs. Happy families.

Joe slowly got off his stool. He was in pyjama bottoms and a jumper. 'Been keeping it warm for you.' A hesitant smile. There were the same bruised shadows under his eyes. 'Did you sleep OK? Do you want coffee, or tea, or …?'

'Let Matty just sit down, Joe,' said Franklin, who had his big forearms over the counter, a paper open, as if everything was perfectly normal.

'I'm doing it. I'm being mother,' Sheanna said, with deliberate enunciation, kneeling on her stool and leaning over to reach the handle of the teapot. 'Because I am the only girl in the house,' she said, in an only slightly quieter stage whisper.

There was an amused, awkward silence. A deep awareness of Joe's gaze, tentatively curious.

Franklin watched Sheanna pour the tea, holding her elbow to help. 'Careful, sugarpop.'

'I can do it,' she said, sounding affronted as she shrugged him off, biting her lip in concentration and setting the teapot down again. 'You went in.' She looked at Matty.

The two men looked between them both, not comprehending.

A tiny nod, and a tinier answer. 'Yeah.'

'Matty's a mad swimmer. She – he – Matty goes in freezing cold ice water, like a polar bear, just for fun. Like a mermaid. A modern mermaid.'

Joe was looking at Matty. 'Do you, now.'

Everyone was staring. Franklin seemed to sense the discomfort, and demonstratively turned the page of his paper to show Sheanna a picture of a robin shaking its feathers out.

There were Christmas cards on the windowsill. Boxes of cereal, kids' and adult types. A bird feeder hanging outside. Everything was so – homely. Joe couldn't seem to be still, washing crockery, putting more toast on, casting discreet looks over. His ears seemed bigger. Longer. There were creases in his neck. It was alarming, still, to see how small he was, and to remember that it was only because Matty had grown.

They were all talking again, Sheanna with a raft of bird facts, Joe asking her for more detail, Franklin gently correcting her.

'Where did you go in Canada?' Matty said.

They all looked over. Franklin glanced at Joe, as if perhaps he and Sheanna should leave them to it again.

Joe shook his head. 'It's fine,' he said to him.

Franklin wasn't American, but Canadian, and a house-builder. Not an architect, he'd said, but he organised everything. Project manager. He'd lived in London for a while and had wanted to head home to Nova Scotia and build his own set of houses. Expand. He made it sound like it had almost just been business, Joe ending up doing the interiors, a partnership.

'And this one came along,' Franklin said, putting two knuckles lightly over Sheanna's nose. She wriggled out of his grip and cocked her head to listen again, adult-like. 'And a few years ago, we started noticing that over here was coming up in the world.'

'This so-called Celtic Tiger and all that,' said Joe. He looked discomfited, itchy.

'There's a *tiger?*' said Sheanna.

'Not that kind,' said Franklin. 'The money kind.' He closed the paper. 'So we thought we'd try and make a go of it over here. Build houses both sides of the border, eventually. It's been good, hasn't it?' He and Joe exchanged a quiet, untranslatable look, proud but strangely melancholy.

'It has,' said Joe.

Simple as that. Except for the things that Franklin had left out. That Joe had run away with him. Abandoned his child. That two men had had another child by surrogacy. That two gay men were living together in Ireland, full stop. That *we* sounded very much like Franklin, rather than the both of them.

Matty couldn't say anything.

'So I did what I thought I'd never do,' Joe said, over-brightly, glancing out of the window at the rain. 'Came back to all this miserable shite.'

Sheanna slid off her stool. 'That's twenty pee, Daddy.'

It went through Matty like an arrow. Daddy.

'Ah, bollocks.'

'*Daddy.*'

Joe leant down to a coat that hung over the back of a kitchen chair, before holding out his cupped hand with a few coins. Sheanna walked round and gazed at them very seriously, before picking one out. 'I'll make you rich yet,' he said to her, and winked.

'Then I can put you in a home for people who swear all the time,' Sheanna said, disappearing into the hallway.

Their easy rapport. The way they moved together, and how their words slotted in. The way they used to between Joe and Matty.

Franklin said that he'd take Sheanna out, a drive to the beach and that yes, there could be hot chocolate and that no, Matty didn't want to come.

The kitchen was much quieter without them. The air exposed.

'I didn't sleep much,' Joe said, a small wryness that was so familiar. 'Did you?'

'You didn't tell her about me.'

He looked taken aback. Blinked. 'I wanted to. But with you gone, I didn't know how much good it would do. Telling her, and not being able to introduce you. I was waiting for her to be a bit older.' It sounded like he was lying.

There was a raw, corroded feeling. 'You got yourself a real one.' The pink and purple, the ribbons, the Barbies.

'What? No. No, that's not it at all.' He put a hand out on the counter, quite close to Matty's hand. 'That was never it. It just happened. One thing after the other. Everything just happened.'

Matty moved back, away from him. 'You left me.'

'It wasn't supposed to be like that. It was never supposed to be like that. Just a short time away. Rosa took you, Matty. She took you away from me.'

'You should have tried to find me.'

'You think I didn't?'

'Not just letters.' The word framed with a quiet disdain.

'Like I said.' There was a little more bite to Joe's words. 'You think I didn't?'

A chill swept over Matty, a sleet storm.

'You know I phoned, don't you? More than once. It was like having a bloody heavy breather on the other end the first few times, and then she'd just put it down, as soon as she knew it was me. It was never you. At least I don't think it was.'

A slow shake of the head.

'When I didn't hear from you, after I sent the number, I figured that Rosa might have said some bollocks to put you off me. Not that I was bloody *dead*. I thought I'd give you a bit of space, at least. A cooling-off period, let you settle down. Stay over in Canada. Just to get my head straight, have a breather.' He exhaled heavily. 'Worst mistake I ever made. I tried to find you, Matty. I did.' His eyes looked very tired. Lines like dry stream-beds in his forehead. 'First I knew you'd moved was finally having the phone answered again and some Greek man answering, and a baby crying the background.'

He'd phoned the electricity company, gas, but they wouldn't pass on the details. Phoned Italy, where Nonna had refused to say anything. 'And I tried your new school. Two or three times. I reckon your mamma put out a few horror stories about me. I don't know what, but the secretary was as helpful as the bloody secret service. Shut me down. Just as bad in the flesh, as I recall.'

'You were there?'

'I was.' He talked of coming to London, months later – after Rosa and Matty had moved from Golders Green. No forwarding addresses. Flying out to Italy, before they had gone out to live down the coast from Nonna and Nonno.

It was a new story. Not the one that Matty had carried for fourteen years, nor the one since finding the note in Rosa's loft. An entirely new one.

'I went to the hotel, but Johanna's folks said they didn't know where you'd gone to. I tried to talk to the secretary at St George's, like I said, and was told they'd call the police. Hung around instead outside the gates, feeling like a bloody flasher-in-waiting. But I didn't see you.'

'I went to a different school once we moved.'

Joe put his head down. A long, quiet sigh.

There was an unspeakable emptiness in Matty's stomach. The lengths that Rosa had gone to to hide them. It had been calculated.

'I should have done more,' Joe said, to the kitchen counter. 'I know I should have. I should have held your grandparents hostage until they spilled it. I just – I never wanted to hurt anyone. I thought about a private detective, even, but that seemed ridiculous. And Rosa – I did get her on the phone once, early on. I don't know if you were there, but she said you weren't. She said ...' He glanced up only briefly. 'She said you didn't want to see me ever again.' He shook his head. 'I'd half a mind for it not to be true, but—' He stopped and gazed out of the window at the rain.

It seemed as if he might leave it there, not say another word. But he seemed to galvanise himself. 'Matty, I hated myself. Hated myself for what Rosa was doing to me, for not managing it. For finding that I liked – that I was attracted to a man, to men, for leaving. After a while, I tried to face up to it. That you hated me.'

'Why would you have thought that? How could you believe I wouldn't want to see you?'

'Because I was ashamed. Of what I was. What I am.'

'You should have told me.' Their cups of coffee were both cold, and Joe had got up, moving gingerly as if he had an injury, to put the kettle on again.

'Which part? About being – about falling in love with a man?'

'I'd have understood.'

'If I'd told you …' He looked over Matty's head, as if caught in a memory. 'If I'd talked to you, I would have stayed. You'd have talked me out of it. Or those eyes would have.' His slow, sad smile faded. 'I'm not saying it was right. I've always regretted it.'

'No, you haven't.' Spoken more blankly. 'You've got the perfect life right here.'

'Well now, I wouldn't call it perfect.'

Typical Joe. Just as he'd always been. Optimistic when it suited him, and then stirring in the pathos.

'I saw Maureen.'

They'd moved to the living room, Joe saying the hard stools were no good for him for too long. He was starting the fire and looked round with near-alarm, a match in his hand. 'My sister Maureen?'

'Yeah.'

'How did you find her?'

'She's in a house. They all are, there together.'

He looked shaken.

'Why didn't you ever go and see her? Find her? If I managed it, then you could have.'

He struck the match, watching the firelighter spurt into flame, before turning and sitting to the side. It was a shock, somehow, to see him on the carpet, as if he was the child and Matty the parent.

'She's a religious woman, my sister,' he said. 'Well, the whole family. Not, you know, God loves all of you, rain or shine, but the sort that thinks men who – gay men should be basted on the devil's Saturday afternoon barbecue. Most of Ireland was like that, and my lot more than most. We didn't come over until it was all legal, and even then, it's felt pretty ...' He gave a heavy sigh. 'Close to the bone. Not really in anything that anyone has said, we've been lucky, and we're bloody discreet, but it hangs over you. This country might have changed, but not everyone in it has. That'll take time.' He stretched one leg out. 'When I was a teenager, I had the odd ...' He sent over a wry look. 'You know, stirring. Nothing more than that. I felt like I was evil to my marrow.' He seemed resolute. 'I know I came back here but it wasn't for my family. Not the old one, anyway.'

That hurt. Matty looked out of the window.

'I didn't mean that. Matty. You know that's not what I meant.'

'I've worked in Canada.'

'Have you?' Joe's face lifted. 'What were you doing there?'

'Kids' camps. Adventure-type stuff.'

'What do you know. Is that what you do?'

Matty shrugged. 'Sometimes.'

'That's grand.'

He wasn't allowed to do that. Be proud.

'Listen, you haven't told me anything,' he said. 'About you, and about ... your life.' The word spoken so lightly.

And that's all it was. 'Not much of a life.'

315

'I'm sure that's not true.'

'It is.'

Matty could see how Joe seemed to assimilate the weight of that, of how much of it might have been attributed to his leaving. Wanted him to feel that.

He didn't say anything for a while. 'How long have you been in Ireland? What made you come looking here? I mean, *I* didn't even know I'd end up here again.'

Deep breath. Joe remembered Clive – 'pretty hard to knock that fella out of your memory', he said – before Matty listed the places stopped at, the swimming, which he couldn't quite get over. How Maureen had talked about a place beginning with *Ros* in Donegal.

'Is that what she said?' He looked puzzled.

'Yeah. On the west coast. A small place.'

His face cleared. 'Rossnowlagh,' he said. 'It's a beach a few miles away. Not quite in Donegal. Went there with a mate a couple of times to skid around on motorbikes. He had a cousin who was a surfer up there and I had a go. I was shite.' He smiled. 'It's where Franklin and Sheanna have gone. I had a soft spot for it, so when we saw that land was for sale here, it seemed right.'

Rossnowlagh. Just a few miles from here, and from Brigid. Matty felt the three syllables settle, and watched the fire. 'You're not in the phone book.'

'No. Ex-directory. It's easier. We don't get much bother, but – just in case.'

'Made it a lot harder to fucking find you.'

'I realise that. Now. If I'd have known you were looking.' A weary, understated smile. 'I always thought you wanted shot of me.'

'I thought about you every day,' Matty said, the words lean, and saw something in Joe fold, quietly shatter. He put his head down, and when he looked up again, his eyes were glistening. It was an effort to keep Matty's own tears away. 'You were in my head.' Accusatory. Finger, jabbing temple.

They sat, both caged in their own grief, as the rain came down, harder.

'I have to tell you something,' Joe said.

There was hardly anything left of Matty to absorb anything new. 'OK.'

'I've been thinking about how to find you again. Recently, I mean. A lot. Driving Franklin round the bend.' There was the sound of a car on the road, and he listened to it for a moment. 'Putting an advert in all the British papers, thinking somebody that knew you would see it, even if you didn't. Or finding you through the internet somehow. I put a message on a website. You'd be amazed at how much time I've been trying to look up North London Ronans.' His look was almost chiding. 'You're not in the phone book either, I might add.'

'I haven't really had a proper address.' All this time, and Matty had been untraceable. Not just Joe.

He had stopped talking. He'd seemed to be leading somewhere and now all he was doing was waiting for Matty to look up again.

'Franklin said I should tell you,' he said, eventually. 'Sooner rather than later. Just so you were – in the picture.'

Matty didn't look away. Was held in his warm, tired eyes.

'I've not got long,' he said, and there was an elegance in the way he said it.

'Not got long before what?'

An almost-smile. 'I've not got long.' A little more weight on each word.

Matty's blood stilled. His paleness. The slight looseness of the skin on his forearms. His cough. Not just age. Not just normal illness.

The white noise of rain against the window.

317

Everything tightened, as if an astonishing pressure was being placed around Matty's body. He was watching. Waiting.

Not got long.

Lips making a dry click. 'Is it – AIDS?' There'd been tubs of pills in the bathroom cabinet with cryptic names.

'What?' A flash of surprise, as if he'd been insulted. 'No, it's not.' His voice became softer. 'No. I was—' He cleared his throat. 'Very careful on that score. If I wasn't scared enough already with what I was getting into, there was all that kicking off, putting the fear of God into me.' He coughed again, shifted, his hands placed on his knees. 'No. Lung cancer. One of the unlucky fuckers who got it early.' The muted irony in his words. 'All those years on thirty a day. That'll teach me, eh?'

Lungs.

An awareness only of heartbeat, and breath, and the rain.

Joe sat motionless.

Matty gazed out of the window. The mist obscured the view of the lough. Nothing of it. 'But you don't – seem that ill.'

'All the excitement has pepped me up a bit,' he said. There was a small, distant light in his eyes. 'I'll sleep later.'

'But ...' He seemed so unruffled. It couldn't be real. Matty tried to start a sentence, several times. 'How – how long?'

'Six months. At a push.'

Matty stared at the floor. At his feet and how the thick carpet rose up around them. Finally looked up, back at him, his grey eyes.

He'd known for a while. Had gotten used to the idea. 'I'm glad you found me, Matty.'

Franklin and Sheanna returned. Sheanna's cheeks were rosy, her fringe wet. She'd brought back a razor clam shell and a broken piece of cuttlefish bone, one for Joe and one for Matty, and stood in front of each of them, explaining loudly where they'd been found.

Franklin stood in the doorway, and exchanged a look with Joe. One that meant, *You've said?* And Joe's in return, that meant *yes.*

Matty was curled up again in the chair, unable to respond. Joe had said that Sheanna knew he was ill, how serious it was, but not that it was terminal. They'd been working up to it. He'd described going to the hospital a year earlier for an X-ray and coming out with a diagnosis for Stage 4 lung cancer. The chemotherapy and how he'd decided to give it up, seeing as it wasn't making any difference. He'd wanted to be at home as much as possible, not travelling to hospital and returning spent. He was well versed, used medical language. Pointed to his torso, his hand circling, fingers expanding. It had spread to his lymph nodes. Could spread further.

As Sheanna gave a lecture on the rock pools she'd just been poking around in, Matty watched Joe, properly. The fragile effort with which he moved, even on the sofa, a dialogue with the pain he was bearing. Of how most of him was utterly engaged with Sheanna, but one small part occupied elsewhere, as if there was a blurring at his edges.

A hologram. Something here now, but gone soon.

The two of them talked. With Joe's encouragement, Matty told him about the work over the years, how it had started at the climbing wall. Working with kids in Yorkshire, North Wales, Cumbria. The swimming. All the time thinking, *He's going to die he's going to die he's going to die.*

'That's absolutely cracking. The lot of it. I bet they're lucky to have you, all those kids.'

'Maybe.'

''Course they are.' He gave Matty a measured, up-down look. 'You're – you look bloody fit. Strong as an ox.'

A tiny bloom of pride, blinked away. 'Not as much as usual.'

'No?'

'No.'

'Why so?' He looked eager, expectant.

There was a small moment, a feeling of being in the middle of a rope bridge. Two ways to go. Matty could leave, now, and he could remain oblivious – until there was something about it in the paper, him finding out another way. Something unfastened. It couldn't be hidden forever. 'I got hurt.'

He looked sympathetic. 'Some kid drag you off a cliff-face?'

'No.' Matty got up, shut the living door and sat down again.

The smile disappeared, and he inclined his head a little. A questioning frown.

'I'm in trouble.'

Joe blinked. Bounced back. 'Tell me what it is, and I'll get you out of it.'

'It's not that simple.'

'We'll see.'

'I was ...' There was still time to retreat. Go back to the middle of the bridge. It could make him more ill. 'Attacked.'

That curve of his eyebrow. He hadn't been expecting that. He sat forward. 'Someone hurt you?'

'Yeah.' Matty was starting to feel light-headed. A burning in the chest. 'Quite a lot.'

One side of Joe's face tautened. 'Where are they now?' He thought he could do something.

'Dead.'

The bravado in his expression caught halfway.

'I did it.' There was a release, a sudden flurry of small breaths, one after the other. 'I was defending myself. He was going to – he was – I thought I was going to die.' It was becoming harder to breathe, chest and throat restricting. 'I didn't mean to.'

'Matty. Try and breathe.'

'I just wanted to get him off me. He was going to r—' Say it. Just say it. The room began spinning. 'R– rape me.'

'It's OK. Just breathe for me.'

'I – can't.' The smash against the van, face in the water, fingers against neck.

'I'm right here. Just keep breathing.' Joe's hand, on an arm. On Matty's back. He seemed very far away. 'You're all right.'

Matty was panting, exhaling wordless sounds. Chest, rising and falling. Spikes of light on every blink.

'You're all right now,' Joe was saying again.

'I'm sorry.' Nose and eyes running.

'It's OK. You're OK.'

I'm not. 'I'm sorry.'

He was shaking his head. There seemed a year-long moment as breaths began to smooth, the room slowly coming back into focus. The fireplace, the carpet, the stray hairs on his shoulder.

Matty drew up a sweatshirt cuff, wiped both cheeks. Nose.

'OK,' said Joe. He put his lips together, a long, intense outbreath through his nose. 'Right. Where did this happen? In London?'

'No, here. Just up the road.' A shuddering inbreath, almost a laugh. 'He crashed his car. Think he died from that, but . . .'

'Christ. That one? I saw that on the news, I think. Youngish lad? Your age or so?'

'Yeah.'

'OK.' He was nodding a lot. It was too much for him, of course it was. He was weak.

Matty explained how Brigid had been there, had provided harbour, respite. That Cormac was her brother, and a detective. That he'd seen the van. Realised. The sleeping with them part was omitted. 'And I – it was left badly.'

'You scarpered. On the bike.'

'I handcuffed him to his car first. I hurt him. Accidentally.'

'OK,' said Joe, manfully. 'Right.'

'I'm sorry.' Throat, scratchy. 'I didn't mean for any of it.'

'Of course you didn't.' A self-motivating nod. 'OK. We'll work it out.'

'How?'

'I'm not sure yet. Let me talk to Franklin.'

'Don't tell him.'

He hummed, a short, darkly sceptical sound. 'Let me think about this.'

'I should just go. I really need to go.'

'No,' said Joe, suddenly vehement. 'That's not happening. You're not going anywhere. Not now.'

He scoured over all the details, wanted it told from the beginning, properly. It hurt to talk of it. To talk of the pub, being seen as a gay man, as a woman. To talk of the roadside, the van. Matty was shivering, mouth dry, teeth chattering. Hypothermic. The body becoming smaller and coiled, knees drawn to chest. Dale wasn't named.

It had got to the part about Brigid coming along the road again when Franklin came in with some food, and they both sat back. Joe didn't say anything to him, watching Matty, distracted when Franklin tried to talk.

Matty stood up, looked at the two columns of CDs, an uncontrollable trembling in one leg, shifting to try and still it. Stacks of music, artists he used to listen to on tape. Country music compilations. Some rock albums. Queen.

'I hope I'm going to pass the test,' Joe said. He sounded almost natural, as if nothing had been said. 'They're mostly mine.'

'Yeah,' said Matty, trying to seem normal too.

It was easier with Sheanna there. She seemed quite happy that Matty was suddenly part of the equation, and probably hadn't entirely taken it in, though who knew how much Franklin had explained while they were out. She sat between them with a book on marine life to point out the illustration of the living cuttlefish, before moving on to submersibles and megamouth sharks.

Joe fell asleep. 'He does that sometimes,' Sheanna said in a whisper. Franklin put a blanket over him, up to his shoulders, and took her out again. Matty sat in the opposite corner of the sofa, head against a pillow, watching his chest rise and fall. His mouth was open, ungracefully. There was a textural quality to his breath.

Matty fell asleep, too.

The rapid thud of feet coming down the stairs. 'There's a man outside.' Sheanna skidded along the polished wood of the hallway and poked her head round the door. 'Someone's outside. He's in the garden.'

Matty sat up, went to the front window. Saw the dark blue car with its dents and looked at Joe, who was stirring. 'It's him.' A desperate flare of panic.

'It's who?' said Franklin, leaning towards the window.

Joe rubbed one eye, stood up. 'OK.'

Cormac was walking round from the back of the house towards the front. He had his hands in his pockets, and was craning to look up at the second floor.

'The bike,' said Matty. It was still leaning on the wall around the back.

Sheanna had already opened the door and was shouting a greeting.

'Sheanna, shut that door,' Joe said. He turned to Franklin. 'Will you take her upstairs?'

Franklin was looking between them. 'What's going on?'

'I'll explain later.'

'Joe.'

'Just take her up. Now.'

Franklin put his lips together. Left the room, calling to Sheanna.

'I don't know what to do,' said Matty, consumed with fear that was almost hallucinatory. Cormac was here. He must have found Joe's address. Just like that.

'You stay right there,' Joe said, oddly calm.

Matty stood against the wall in the living room, gut leaden. Listening to the new shape of Cormac's voice, its downbeat gravity. Matty had pushed him and he'd fallen and hit his head and been cuffed to his car and he was here.

'Joseph Ronan?'

'That's the one.'

'I've reason to believe that you're harbouring someone wanted in connection with a very serious crime. And a smaller one.'

'All right.'

A small pause. 'Are you going to let me in?'

'Do you have a warrant?'

'I'm a detective.'

'And I'm an interiors fitter, so that's all out in the open. Do you have a warrant?'

There was a pause. 'Will you just let me in?'

'Let the man in, Joe,' Franklin said, from the top of the stairs. 'He's a guard.'

Cormac stood in the living room, casting a quick eye at the Christmas tree, the two men. There was a blueish, oblong lump on his right temple. He looked at Matty. 'I'm arresting you on suspicion of manslaughter. And assaulting a garda.' His eyes wintry, resolute.

Manslaughter. He'd talked to Brigid.

'Nonsense,' Joe said. 'Come back with a warrant.'

'I don't need one.'

'Why have you not got anyone else with you? Where's the cavalry?'

'Because it doesn't have to be done like that.' He looked towards Matty for affirmation.

'Well, you can come back with proper troops.'

'I don't need them. Do I, Matty.' It wasn't quite a question. As if he already knew the answer.

Eyes down to the floor.

'Look,' said Franklin. 'I'm sure this can all be cleared up if we just do as the detective says.'

'Not without proper procedure,' said Joe.

'What is this all about, exactly?' said Franklin.

'Matty's a suspect in the death of a man,' said Cormac. 'In self-defence, probably, possibly, but nonetheless. And guilty of assaulting a garda, like I said.'

An intake of breath from Franklin.

'The garda being you,' Joe said. He gestured to his own temple. 'You've got a bit of a shiner there.'

'The garda being me,' Cormac said.

Matty could hardly breathe.

'Are you going to come with me?' There was almost something beseeching in Cormac's voice.

'I did it,' said Joe.

Everybody looked at him.

'Did what now?' Cormac said.

'I attacked the lad. The lad you found.'

'Joe.' Franklin sounded aghast.

Cormac put his hands on his hips, and removed them. 'I'd like to hear how.' He gazed at Matty, and back at Joe. 'When?'

The slightest pause. 'November twenty-seventh.'

'But that's not what happened.'

'It might have been.'

'But it didn't. There's no evidence.'

'Apart from my confession, you mean? Is that not enough these days?'

Cormac gave a baffled shake of his head, and shifted the weight to his other foot. 'There were injuries.' He gestured to Matty's torso with a finger. 'All over.'

'That'll be right. I was defending my child. I'm not saying Matty wasn't attacked. We were together that night. Family reunion. We hadn't seen each other in quite a while.'

'That's not true.'

'It's perfectly true. Since 1985, in fact.'

'No, I know that, but—' He straightened, as if resetting himself. 'Look, I know that it's just not bloody true.'

Joe folded his arms. 'How do you know about the injuries? All over, you just said.'

'That's not your concern.'

'Isn't it?' Joe looked at Matty. 'How did he know about your injuries?'

Cormac looked at the carpet and glanced up again, as if willing Matty not to say anything.

It was the only way. 'We sort of slept together.' Started to. Failed at.

'Did you now,' Joe said, only to Cormac. 'I think that's you off the case, pal. Sleeping with suspects.'

'It's ... that's really not your concern,' Cormac said.

'I'm not sure that'll go down so well in court,' said Joe.

'This is madness. Look, I know you've only just met, or I think you have, but – this isn't how it works. I can come back with more people if that's what you want.'

'That's not what we want,' said Franklin. 'Is it, Joe?'

'It's fine by me,' he said. He seemed charged, alive.

'I'm going outside,' said Cormac, mostly to Matty. 'I'm not leaving. I'll give you a minute to collect yourself.'

Joe sat down.

'What the hell are you doing?' Franklin said.

'Protecting my child. What difference does it make? I'm on the way out anyway.'

'Well, that's just typical. You've got to be the hero. The martyr.'

'Not heroic. Just doing what should have been done a long time ago.'

'Going to jail for something you didn't do? You think it's not enough already, what we have to cope with? If Matty has done this, then—' He glanced over. 'I'm sorry – but it's Matty who needs to take the rap. You're being ridiculous. No one's going to believe you've done that. I'm probably your damned alibi. And you heard what he said. Matty assaulted him. A guard.'

'I'll go and talk to him,' said Matty, and stood up.

'Don't go anywhere,' said Joe. 'We need to get a lawyer.'

'No. I'm going out there. Just to talk.'

Cormac was standing by the pond, his hands in his pockets.

Matty stood next to him, hood up, boots unlaced. Took another careful glance at the injury on his forehead. 'How did you find me?'

He continued looking at the pond. 'Looked your dad up.'

'As simple as that?'

'Phone records.'

The rain made bubble-wrap pops on the water. Circle after circle appearing, disappearing.

'*Brigid*,' he said, turning slightly. 'You got Brigid to lie for you.'

'I didn't. She did all that. She covered for me. I didn't ask her to.'

'I've got to take her in. My own bloody sister.'

'You don't have to take her in. You don't have to do anything. Please.'

'Why did you do it?'

'Didn't Brigid say?'

'I want to hear it from you.'

'You saw what he did to me. He attacked me, he shoved my head in the lough – I thought he was going to drown me – he beat me up. He was going to rape me.' It wasn't any easier to repeat that word, having already said it once. 'I thought he was going to kill me.'

Behind them, the goat made a stuttering call.

'If you tell the truth in court, it'll be easier on you,' he said.

'You're the only other witness to my injuries.'

His shoulders slumped. He'd have to be a witness, and it would look like he'd covered it up.

Gaps in the rain as it slowed. 'I was doing well, you know,' he said. 'Up for an award and everything.'

'Please. My dad's dying. I've only just found him.' Gravel, stuck in the throat. 'It's been fourteen years and now he's fucking dying.' The tears came, suddenly and violently.

Cormac stood, watching. 'No more of your lies, now,' he said, sounding uncertain.

'I'm not lying.' The words were broken. 'Lung cancer.' Another uncontrollable rush of tears.

He sighed. 'Jesus,' he said, and stepped forward, putting his arms around Matty.

Weeping, onto his shirt. His jacket.

'How long?'

'Not long.'

'Years?'

'Months.'

Matty clung on to him for another moment before he stepped back. A noisy sigh. 'I'm going to go now. I need to have a think.' And he walked down the slope to the driveway and his car.

Chapter 15

They waited.

Joe said they'd get Matty on a plane. Matty said no. There was no point in running again. Searching and hiding and running. It would never stop. They would just wait for Cormac to come back. If Matty had to go, then it would be so.

Franklin was told everything, and it was obvious what he thought, even with it being self-defence. That Matty was dangerous – more than dangerous. Untrustworthy. He was always in the room when Sheanna was there, a bodyguard, an obtuse presence. Yet he yielded to Joe. They had an odd dynamic, Joe often the more docile, submissive, but he could stand up for himself when he wanted to. And standing up for Matty was something he now insisted upon. He asked Franklin what he would have done, if someone had been laying into him as this man had.

It *had* given him energy, this extra excitement. There was an unnatural brightness in his eyes, more than the first day. He kept looking to the driveway as if he was readying himself for a Wild West shootout. Instead, with Sheanna occasionally buzzing around them, they talked. There was no chronology. It was a patchwork, an arbitrary visiting of the fourteen years they'd spent apart.

'Did you never love Mamma?'

'Ah no, I did. Course I did. She was a stunner, your mother. We had something for a while.' He looked up. 'When did you last see her?

'Three months before she – I was going to say before she died, but – three months before she was found.'

'What's the difference?'

'She wasn't discovered for almost three weeks.'

It was as if he was hearing about her death for the first time again. Worse. His eyes seemed to lose their colour, a hand moving over his mouth with a slight tremor. It was surprising, almost, how upset he looked. 'Oh, God.'

'She didn't have any friends. Not really. There were men that came and went but ... I wasn't very good in the end, at seeing her.'

'It's not your fault.'

'I don't know.'

'Matty. It's not your fault. You hear me?'

The morning passed. Cormac didn't come.

'You've got a goat.' There was an allotment too, up on the highest ground, two long lines of cabbages and hard green shoots under webbing.

'I know.' He looked almost embarrassed, but not quite. 'Believe me, I know.'

'You didn't like Ireland. You always wanted to leave.'

'I was glad to see the back of it when I was younger, honest to God. I miss London. I always did. But things have changed. I'd never have dreamt that this country would drag itself up the way it has. It's got the bloody internet, for God's sake. In the *towns*. I didn't ever imagine living practically on the border like this, but ...' He shrugged. 'Well, it looks like it's heading in the right direction. Touch wood and all that.' He stepped forward and tapped the edge of the plank bridge. 'And Franklin – well, he saw some opportunities. He's a canny one.' A guilty smile, one that couldn't help still being warm.

'He's been good for you?'

Joe seemed suddenly faintly imbalanced, as if small parts of him had been unfastened. He looked down at his feet. 'He has.'

'Did you really sleep with the copper?'

It was lunchtime, and Cormac had not come.

'Not really. Not exactly. Slept with his sister.'

'Right.' The look he gave Matty was the one he used to have. Faintly amused, quietly supportive. The opposite of Rosa's brewing rancour.

'How did you meet Franklin?' They seemed different, on the surface at least. Franklin was neater, sharper, a little bossy. A trim haircut and a gold watch.

'We just started up a conversation one day at the Ponds, and I'd see him on and off. Seemed to start going at the same time as each other. He was – you know, it was getting so bad with Rosa. I could talk to him about it. It's a terrible thing, Matty, being hit by a woman. It's a hard thing to admit to. He was the only one who knew. He said I should leave, and he was right. I didn't do it the right way, I know that.'

They watched the clouds scud over the mountains.

'I shouldn't have left. Not the way I did. I needed to get out of there, but – I should have sat you down, first. I should have taken you with me.' There was fortitude in his look, as if to have done so was as good as jumping over a ravine.

'Yeah. You should have.'

His half-smile faded. 'I'm sorry, Matty.'

There was no saying, 'It's OK.' It wasn't OK.

They ate. Joe had insisted on making pancakes, grew tired, and supervised Matty instead. Chocolate spread and peanut butter. He watched Matty eat, hardly touching his own plate.

'What's the coldest you've swum?'

'Zero point five degrees.'

'Sweet Jesus. How are you still breathing?'

'Practice.'

'The furthest you've swum?'

'Twelve K.'

'Christ. Fair play to you. Nicest?'

'I dunno. South of France once, maybe. After a job. The Ponds.'

'Really?'

'Yeah. Got to know it a bit, after you left.'

'The ... Mixed Pond, you mean?'

'All of them.'

'And Sheanna's – mum?'

'Canadian. A friend of Franklin's. Incredible woman, really.'

'Does Sheanna know?'

'Well, she knows she has a mother, if that's what you mean. You can't imagine her not having worked out basic human reproduction by now. We send her a photo every year and Sheanna writes a letter. It's weird, but – she's got kids of her own. Four of them. It works, somehow. Always a bit scared that she's going to change her mind, try and come over and get her. But there were contracts written, that sort of thing.'

'Did you ever have any trouble?'

'With what? With us? Once or twice. We don't shout about it. There's not many people that know, if we can help it. The school does, obviously, but they're surprisingly good about it. Only one of us ever goes to assemblies and parents' evenings, mind.' He looked knackered. He'd gone to the bathroom earlier, and there'd been the sound of him coughing violently, spitting. 'Has it been hard for you? I mean, before what happened here?'

'Yeah.'

'And your mamma?'

'What do you think?'

*

It began to get dark.

'How did you do in school?'

'Not great. Got an A in PE.'

'Well, that's the one that matters.'

'I want to know more. About anything, really. I don't feel very clever.'

'There's plenty of time for all that.'

A swelling silence, knowing that it was only true for one of them.

'And you are. Clever.'

They watched *Good Morning, Vietnam,* late into the night.

No cars came.

***

'What's that one again?' Joe said to Sheanna the next day, pointing to a page in her book of the seas and oceans.

'Don't be horrible.'

'I'm not. I just want you to tell Matty what it is.'

'You're being mean.'

'I'm not. Go on.'

Sheanna gave a frustrated sigh. 'Aneno – am – amenomone.'

Joe gave a quiet snigger.

'You *are* mean. I hate you.'

'No, you don't.'

She put her hands on his shoulders. 'No, I don't.'

He looked over. Matty didn't say anything.

'Please can I show Matty what I got for Christmas?'

'You're asking the wrong person,' Joe said.

Sheanna walked over with a little reluctance to the side of the chair. She knew that Matty had withdrawn, grown detached. She put her hands behind her back. 'Please can I show you my Christmas presents?'

Impossible to say no. Not while she was looking like that, her mouth and nose screwed up, as if she was trying to answer a hard maths question. And not while Joe was there. 'Yeah.'

She was back in no time, kneeling down and displaying her presents as if selling them at a market. 'This is a book on whales, because I've already got one on dolphins, and it's the next one. It's got quite a lot on humpback whales, I think. It's got lots of illustrations. Look.'

There was the prickling awareness of Joe watching them, pretending he wasn't. The weight of careful expectation, wanting a connection. Matty refused to make it that simple. The kid was eight – nine in a couple of days. She was a sparkling, brainy, mad little girl and she had taken Matty's place.

She was continuing to showcase the finest features of everything in front of her. A massive-eyed, beaked furry thing. Two animated films on video, both starring insects. Pony riding lessons. 'And socks.' She shrugged.

'Nothing wrong with socks,' Joe said, leaning back into the sofa, his legs crossed.

'I know there isn't, I just don't know what to say about them. They're just socks.' Sheanna piled everything on top of each other and looked at Matty. Looked to the carpet as if trying to think of something to say. 'What did you get for Christmas?'

A step nearer to jail. 'A book and a couple of CDs.' The latter from the man who would be putting Matty behind bars.

'What did you want for Christmas?' said Joe.

What I've wanted every Christmas, Matty wanted to say, hating how much it hurt.

In the afternoon, Joe slept on the sofa. His beard was the colour of wet sand at his cheeks, and grey at his chin and towards his throat. Matty watched him, looked at the folds at the base of his neck, the looseness of the skin there. Saw that he was still handsome, really. Imagined his lungs blooming not with water but cells, flowering with them, speckling him like the end of an old video game.

A cigarette on the front step that night, waiting for Cormac to lead a line of Gardaí vehicles up the road. Handcuffs at the ready. Head being pushed down to get into the back seat. Court, testimonies. Brigid. Being seen as one thing. Labelled.

Joe came out and sat down, gingerly. 'Sheanna's in bed. She wants to know if you'd read with her. I said I'd ask.'

Matty took another drag.

'Just so you know, she doesn't ask either of us to anymore. She reads just fine on her own.'

'I'm all right, thanks.'

'OK.' He looked out towards the lough's blackness, indistinguishable from the sky, the trees.

'I can't just – you can't just expect this all to be easy.'

'I know. I don't. Just . . . I can't apologise for her. I can apologise for everything else until the cows come home, and I will, until my last bloody—' He stopped. 'I can't apologise for her existence. I won't.'

Franklin finally changed his expression after two days when Sheanna told them about the bullying girls, and how Matty had warned them off. He knelt in front of her, his hands on her feet. 'But honey, why didn't you say anything?'

'Because you were busy with everything with Daddy.' Sheanna looked at her hands.

'No,' said Joe. 'I'm not important. We're never too busy to see off two spiteful little gobshites who should know better. Though it sounds like someone else took care of it.' He looked over at Matty. 'Thank you.'

Sheanna had slipped away.

'Her teacher knows,' Matty said. 'Probably worth keeping an eye on.'

'Thank you,' said Franklin. 'We appreciate it.' He put his fingers to his forehead. 'I can't believe she didn't want to tell us.'

Sheanna had tiptoed back in, with her swear jar.

Later, Franklin brought Matty a cup of tea. 'I made some sandwiches, if you'd like one?'

'No. Thanks.'

He nodded, hesitated. There was something more humble in his stance. 'OK. Well, they're there, if you want them. Just ...' He began to turn away.

'You took him away from me.'

He stopped as if caught, a torchlight flashed in his face. 'I'm sorry,' he said. 'It wasn't supposed to be like this. Not forever. How was Joe to know what your mother would do, hiding you away so he couldn't find you?'

'Don't blame it on her,' Matty said, and looked squarely him. 'This is on you. And now he's dying.'

He looked choked. Nodded again, a shine to his eyes behind his glasses. 'I know,' he said. 'I know.'

They watched the news. Garda annual leave had been cancelled and hospitals had extra staff in the event of automation failures. Everyone would be watching Australia and New Zealand carefully.

It went on to a piece about the Millennium Dome in Greenwich, with aerial camera shots.

'It looks like an alien spaceship,' said Sheanna.

'It looks like a feckin' disaster is what it looks like,' said Joe. 'An alien spaceship would be more useful. Take us off this planet before the Millennium Bug sends us all into meltdown.'

Matty went swimming, in a T-shirt and shorts. Joe had said he didn't believe that Matty *liked* swimming in the cold. The three of them had stood on the jetty and watched as Matty swam halfway out to the island and back, though in truth it was hard and there'd been an hour-long bath afterwards. Joe had taken a photo.

***

New Year's Eve. It had been three days, and Cormac had still not come. Sheanna was up even earlier than usual, and ripped open her presents, of which there were many, in the living room.

Matty had gone to get a drink and stopped in the doorway, retreated. Joe was weeping quietly in the kitchen, and Franklin holding him.

In the afternoon, eight of Sheanna's classmates came round for a party. Franklin had said they should cancel, and Joe said that no way were a raft of guards going to come and ruin Sheanna's afternoon, and that they'd all be on Millennium Bug duty now anyway. There'd been a fierceness in his voice.

A cake had been delivered. Pink, with a stereotypical mermaid, tail curled up, on the top. The kids had run around on a sugar-high after that, with the two parents that had stayed to help trying to shush them all. Joe had sat in the kitchen, watching the madness with an exhausted, valiant look on his face.

'Do you want some mermaid?' Sheanna said, almost colliding with Matty and holding up a deformed figure. 'I saved you the tail.'

To the pond to smoke. It was hard to be confronted with it, to imagine all the birthdays she'd had. The attention lavished on her while Matty drifted, fatherless.

The evening was coming in.

Joe opened the back door and walked slowly out. 'You should give those up.'

'All right.' One last draw, and the half-finished cigarette was dropped, swiped under a toe.

He glanced over, eyebrows raised in slight surprise. A nod. He put his hands into his armpits.

'You should go inside.'

'No.' He sounded feverish, almost confrontational. 'I wanted to say. You're both mine. You're both part of me. You always have been. You've never been gone. Do you hear me?' He turned his head.

Matty didn't turn. But nodded.

Later, the two of them watched the night from the front garden, the gravelly crunch of fireworks across the west of the valley.

The year didn't just change, a quick click of digits, the world cracking apart. It was a slow bleeding. One thing into another.

Joe looked at his watch. 'Well, we're all still here,' he said.

PART THREE

2000

The pondwater was pale. The twilight sky leached. One coot floated out into the centre with a scraping, matter-of-fact call.

Grief took the colour from everything.

***

Joe had lasted seven months. After New Year, after waiting for the gardaí who never came, Matty had gone back to London, to Heather's sofa above The Haggerston, to the halal meat and kebab shops, the Hindu centre and the techno club. It had felt better to be out of Ireland, away from Cormac, away from Brigid. But knowing he was there – it was impossible. *He* was impossible. He would send text messages to the mobile phone he'd given as a present. Postcards, addressed to the pub. 'Another one from The Father,' Heather would say. 'Fuck's sake, Matts, get the prodigal son thing over with.'

We miss you. Over and out.

Come and see us, Matty. It's stopped raining.

So Matty had returned. It had been shocking to see how the weight had fallen from him in only six weeks. The greyness in his skin as well as his beard. Franklin had cleared his work from the study to make more room, and didn't glare as he had the first time round.

*

One day, Matty had got a lift to the village that had a bus to Sligo, and waited outside the Garda station for an hour, hands in pockets on the pavement opposite. Eventually Cormac had come out and stopped dead before crossing the road.

'You've got some balls,' he said. They'd watched the school traffic edge past. 'You know I could still arrest you.'

'I know.'

'What are you doing here?'

'I wanted to say sorry.'

'For which part?'

'Hurting you.'

'Which part?' he said, a little more quietly.

Matty looked down at the concrete.

'You know I had to tell them that Brigid had clouted me.' A quick glance over. 'They believed me and all.' In different circumstances, they would have smiled. 'Have you seen her?'

'Thought I'd see you first.'

He said that Brigid had got herself on some Irish matchmaking organisation's books and had already notched up two weeks of frenzied dating with artists, vets and tree surgeons. 'She's giving me all the gory details. Far more than I ever need to hear. I think it's punishment. They're all fellas, by the way.' He'd folded his arms, shifted. 'How's your dad?'

'Yeah. Hanging in there.'

He was nodding, looking out the same way. 'I'm sorry. That's such shite.' Turned. Something vulnerable in his eyes.

'You can, you know. Arrest me.'

He'd unfolded his arms, let them hang by his sides. 'I'm not going to arrest you.' Sighed. 'Don't tempt me.'

***

They looked at photos. Every one of them stung, but they were necessary. Toronto, sightseeing. The restaurant at the top of the

CN Tower with a tiny Sheanna on Joe's lap. Franklin in front of a half-built house in Halifax. The land that this house had been built on, a little Canadian flag jammed into the soil.

Matty had brought some, too. The things that had been important. Michelle and Martin and Matty, two with black-ringed eyes and three with sour expressions. A longer fringe. Swearing one-fingered at the camera in Camden. One with a bunch of kids in hard hats and high-vis jackets. The best lakes, the shocking colour of them. Heather, with an old girlfriend in their neon clubbing gear. Joe had looked at them all and wept.

One morning, Franklin had sat down next to Matty in the kitchen. 'I wanted to tell you,' he said. 'Properly. How sorry I am. For all this. For you having not seen him. I whisked him away too quickly. He wanted to, but – I didn't have a kid, then. I didn't quite know. Not really.' He produced a small box file full of paper. 'He wrote to you all the time. Ones he never sent. I didn't know for ages. He's said to give them to you afterwards, but …' He sighed, looked over, tearful. 'I figured sooner rather than later.'

After a couple of phone calls, they went to see Maureen, Matty driving the car. It was just her at home, none of the others, waiting there on the doorstep in her slippers with her arms folded. 'You daft fucking eedjit,' she said to Joe, opposite her on the sofa, after fifteen minutes. Neither of them mentioned Franklin, or Sheanna.

***

Once, Joe was sitting on the front wall, staring out across at the lough, his walking stick next to him.

Matty joined him, putting a blanket over his shoulders. 'You shouldn't be out here. You'll get cold.'

'It'll be a lot colder where I'm going.' A slanted smile, the flash of old fox in the tiredness, as a blanket came round his shoulders.

343

They'd sat watching the sky steal the silver from the lough. 'I'm sorry, Matty. For everything.'

He'd said it, over and over. It was never quite enough. 'I had to do it all on my own.'

'I know.' A gull came across, a loutish call. 'Will you forgive me?'

A moment that might have been a pose for a painting. The younger, looking out at the water for a long time. The older, turned towards his child, watching.

'Yeah,' said Matty.

***

He'd insisted on being at home. Had said that he didn't care how terrible he looked or sounded, that he would clean up his own mess until the mess stopped. It wasn't quite true. Franklin had done most of it, but Matty had been there more than once, turning him over, a wad of tissues in a fist, or watching the yellowish liquid drain from his lungs through the tube in his chest, holding the bottle. They'd had trips to hospital, but he'd always demanded his own bed, no matter how dizzy he was, no matter that he couldn't sit up any more.

July. The doctor had come, and said in a low voice that it wouldn't be too much longer. A day or two. Sheanna was taken round to a friend's house, clutching her orca toy.

Death had been slow, meandering. One thing into another.

In the final days, his sentences shortened, theatrical weight between them. 'I used to imagine. What you'd be like,' he said, immobile on his back. 'How tall. What your hair. Would be like. And it's funny. Because it might have gone different ways. But. You're exactly what I imagined.' A long space between his in-breath, and his exhale. 'I'm proud of you, Matty. Of what you've. Become.'

'I haven't become anything. I've not done anything.'

344

His head moved from side to side on the pillow, a great effort. 'You've become. Yourself. You're better. In your skin. Than I have been.'

'I'm not.' Only in water.

'You are. You are.'

On one of the last evenings, he fumbled for Matty's hand. His skin was near-translucent, blue blotches like water under the surface. 'Sheanna. She's besotted. Please,' he said, and didn't need to say more.

Matty couldn't say yes, and couldn't say no.

'You bastard,' he said, into the darkness.

Matty sat up. 'Me?'

'He is. She is.' He nodded, and his eyes looked luminous. 'This Death character.' His ribs rose, the words pushed out on hard-earned air. 'What a miserly cunt. Loads of old fuckers here. Still knocking around. Aged. A hundred and five.'

Matty's laugh was a painful rush of breath, nothing more.

'You're beautiful, tiger,' he said. 'Not a bastard.'

A whole night of it, taking turns with Franklin. The gaps between his breaths growing longer, as if he was extending the arm-pull and the kick, not needing to turn his head.

'I wasn't,' he said, his words slurred, and Matty blinked, tried to be awake. 'I wasn't there,' he said, and his breath smelt of old potatoes. He fumbled for a hand. 'I wasn't there.' His throat was clogged with liquid.

'You were. I told you.' Matty tapped a temple. 'Always bugging me. *Feckin' this* and *feckin' that* all the time.'

A smile, struggling to get to the surface. 'Ah, God.' He stared upwards and Matty imagined his lungs, filling. The ceiling with a sway, the bright world refracted above it.

They held hands.

'Dad,' Matty had said.

And he had gone, riverwater into seawater.

***

'Is he in heaven?' Sheanna was curled up like a shell on her bed, her toys around her.

Matty had been sleeping on the floor beside her. Looked up at the ceiling. Stars stuck on there, as there had been in Golders Green. 'Yeah.'

'Does it take long to get there?' Her voice was shrunken, exhausted.

'He's just introducing himself to everyone.' One part of Matty was here, present and practical, answering these questions, making Franklin eat, and the other was a numb knot of grief.

Sheanna had thrown a tantrum at her friend's house and been brought back before Joe was taken away. She'd gone into their room, kissed him on the cheek and touched him there, a small, testing prod with one finger.

'Does he have angel-wings?'

'Yep.'

'He'll get into trouble if he swears.' Impossibly forlorn.

'No, he won't. You can do what you like there.'

Sheanna sat up, her hair matted on the side of her face. Peered over. 'But – is heaven real?'

Matty sat up, too. Elbows on knees. 'Do you think mermaids are real?'

'I'm not sure.'

'Do you remember in your book? About the manatees? How sailors thought they were mermaids?'

She nodded. 'They sang and everything.'

'Well, maybe it's real but not in the way that we think. Maybe it's not up there.'

She lay down again. 'It's down in the ground? Or under the water?'

'Yeah.' Matty lay down on the carpet again, too. 'It's under the water.'

The funeral was in a small church two villages away. Lots of people there, from the village and work. Maureen looking stoic. Sheanna the quietest she'd ever been.

At the crematorium, they had played Kris Kristofferson and Matty had got up, stumbled out. Breathed in the damp air.

***

Matty stood motionless among the trees as the dark came in, fingering the letter in one pocket. Handwritten, on paper with stocky teddy bears in the corner, posted to Heather's. Sheanna thought it the coolest thing ever to sometimes live in a pub.

Dear Matty,
Dad is a bit angry about the ashes but I think its OK. I am sad that you have gone away though. But I hope that soon you will come and visit us again and maybe live with us even though I know Daddy is not here anymore. But maybe you can bring him back with you. Because it is really nice to have a grown-up sibling and I really like your muscles and your card-games. Thank you for rescuing me from the lough that time. I am going to have swimming lessons so soon I can be a mermaid for real, I am just joking. I got this address from the fridge.

Love from XXSheannaXX

PS I did'nt ask before but am I ever allowed to call you Matilda sometimes like in the Rohl Darl book or am I not. It is OK if I am not. Also the detective guard came looking for you but he did'nt say what he wanted.

There was someone else here now, at the Not Allowed Pond. A tall silhouette, arms hanging down by their sides, facing the water. Fingers drumming thighs.

'It's you,' Matty said, just loudly enough.

The figure turned around. Unstartled. 'Do I know you?'

'We used to come here together. One summer.'

'I don't remember.' The voice was smoother, golden.

'It was a long time ago.'

'Hmm.' A short, what-do-you-know sort of sound, high in his throat. He looked out at the water again. He was less jerky, as though he'd grown into his skin. A little paler than Matty remembered, though perhaps that was just the moonlight. He turned, suddenly. 'Wanna go for a swim?'

'Yeah.'

'Come on, then.'

'I haven't got my stuff.'

'You don't need any stuff.' The merest sliver of a grin, maybe. He was more subtle than all those years ago.

'OK.'

He moved smoothly, as if he was already in the pond, standing and stretching once before walking in. The languid sound of water, shifting.

Matty took everything off, hairs raised up by a tiny breeze. Looked at the urn. Lifted the lid for the first time, shone the torch in.

There. All of him, held in the crook of an arm, grains of different sizes. A gleam of dull white, a little larger.

At the edge of the water, Matty crouched down, wetted two fingers, and dipped them into the urn. Wiped the grains on both cheekbones. Forehead, lips, chest, left shoulder, right shoulder. A long line across the stomach. The patch of eczema was larger than ever, itching.

Nicks was watching from the water.

348

Mud gathered around the soles of both feet as Matty walked into the skin of the pond. Knees, hips, waist. The silk of it. Shoulders. Clutching the urn close, Matty trod water, chin up. Unable to let it go just yet.

Joe.

'Maybe I do remember you,' Nicks said, his face suddenly close. A sway of the water from where his legs moved underneath him. 'Did something happen?'

'I kissed you and then you went away.' Matty's voice was as small as a pebble.

That tiny sound in his throat again. Totally unbothered. 'Well, I'm back now. Come on.' He let himself curl back round onto his front, before slinking into the shadow-water. A supple sound, swallowed by the night.

A few moments more. The stars, their soft fire. The dark fingers of the trees.

Matty let the urn drop, watched it roll, fill with water, and begin to sink.

Followed it under.

Author's Note

Various water myths and folklore swim in and out of this novel, and are drawn on, hinted at, twisted and thwarted. Several only rose up to the surface after the writing had been done.

The *nix, nixie, neck* or *nokken* is a shape-shifting water spirit in Germanic mythology, with variations in Scandinavian tales. They try and lure people into the water and are portrayed as malevolent in some stories, and kind and harmless in others. In one Scandinavian version, the Fossegrim agrees to live with the human who has fallen in love with him.

There are several tales with poisoned or enchanted kisses; in the English folk song 'George Collins', the protagonist is the lover of a water-sprite, but then leaves her; she rewards him with a fatally poisonous kiss.

Traditional murder ballads where a man attacks and kills his lover by water include 'The Oxford Girl', 'The Wexford Girl' and the Appalachian song, 'Down in the Willow Garden'.

Selkies are beings in Scottish folklore that change from seal form to human form on land, shedding their seal-skin. Their stories are especially found on Orkney and Shetland, where they may be referred to simply as merfolk. The Irish merrow is sometimes referred to as a half-seal, half-person.

The classic selkie story features a fisherman who finds a naked woman on the shore, falls in love with her and so steals her sealskin and marries her. She often bears children with him, but never loses her yearning for the sea and her true self. Usually she eventually finds her skin and returns, either leaving her children or taking them with her. It has possible origins in, or at least parallels with, the swan maiden myth. There are similar stories found in mermaid and merrow folklore.

Male selkies are also described as very attractive, and tend to seek out those dissatisfied with their lives and marriages.

Melusine is a woman of European folklore who is serpent or fish from the waist down. She marries a nobleman on the proviso that he never looks at her in the bath, and she leaves him when he does.

Sheanna's story of an evil lough-dog is based on the legend of the Dobhar-chú ('water-hound') at Glenade, County Leitrim.

The traditional ballad 'The Two Sisters', which has countless variations all over the world, includes a jealous older sister pushing a younger sister in the water to kill her.

I deliberately didn't choose a traditional Irish traveller surname, to avoid any inference. The name Ronan means 'little seal' in Irish.

***

I wrote and arranged some of the songs on my You Are Wolf album, *Keld*, at the same time as writing part of this novel. It's an album exploring freshwater folklore. The original track 'Breathe in Breathe Out' is inspired in part by Nicks and Matty. The album also features versions of 'George Collins' and 'Down in the Willow Garden'.

Acknowledgements

To Ana Fletcher, for such patience, kindness and awesome editing; to Robin Robertson, especially for suggesting the swimming heartlands of central Ireland very early on, and to Daisy Watt; to Justine Taylor; and to Jessica Woollard, my agent at David Higham Associates.

To the Society of Authors, whose kind grant enabled me to write the second half of this novel.

To Nicholas Purchase, for 1980s Highgate Men's Pond scene-painting, and to Chris Smith from the Highgate Men's Pond Association. To CN Lester, author of the brilliant *Trans Like Me*, for some early advice. To Halimah Manan for an invaluable sensitivity reading. To Alia Nardini for help with the Italian. To Jim Collins for the clarification of garda/guard/gardaí terminology. To Kevin Lynch for knowledge of the border area around Leitrim and Fermanagh, as well as the lovely AirBnB cottage at Garrison. Further AirBnB shout-outs to Eagles Rock Cottage, Glenade and the Architect's Thatched Cottage, Co. Donegal. To Mum, for the companionship and better driving skills on initial trips to Ireland.

To all my friends and acquaintances for enthusiastically piling in on Facebook threads about video players in the 1980s and mobile phone use in the 1990s. To Dan Faircloth for the hand-held computer games knowledge.

To Dr Sandra Cass-Courtney, and to Scarborough's Crisis team. To the Mindful Movement, Lisa A Romano and the Amrit Yoga Institute on YouTube. To Mum, again, and to Ian.

To the Brockwell Lido fam, and all other outdoor swimming friends over the years, for their company and inspiration. In fond memory of Neil, late publican of The Haggerston.

To Andy, my number one outdoor swimming partner and my Men's Pond spy, who introduced me to Roger Deakin's *Waterlog* and the world of water, a world in which I always know myself.